Maria Louise Pool

In the First Person

A novel

Maria Louise Pool

In the First Person
A novel

ISBN/EAN: 9783337036751

Printed in Europe, USA, Canada, Australia, Japan

Cover: Foto ©Andreas Hilbeck / pixelio.de

More available books at **www.hansebooks.com**

IN THE FIRST PERSON

A Novel

BY

MARIA LOUISE POOL

AUTHOR OF "MRS. GERALD" "DALLY"
"ROWENY IN BOSTON" ETC.

NEW YORK
HARPER & BROTHERS PUBLISHERS
1896

CONTENTS

IN THE FIRST PERSON

A GRAY COLT

"I SHOULD think by the looks out there in the west that there was a dretful tempest comin' up."

Aunt Lowizy was hurrying into the kitchen with a hot flat-iron in her hand. This iron she had taken from a kerosene stove that stood lighted on a table in the "unfinished part," where we did most of our housework in the summer. It saved labor, and gave us an opportunity to stay in the back of the house, and keep the front rooms more than usually shut up and darkened.

My mother heard Aunt Lowizy's words, and went with floury hands and an anxious face to the porch, where she gazed at the blue-black mass of cloud which was heaping itself up, and on whose bosom the lightning was darting in dazzling crinkles, followed after a moment by a rolling sound of thunder.

It was so hot that, as father said, "jest to stand still and think made a feller sweat." The leaves on the maples in our yard did not move, but the poplars showed the white under-side of their foliage even without any wind: and that was a sign of rain.

I had read a little poem about the poplar's leaves, and I felt like quoting it, but I held my tongue.

The tree-toads were making their bubbling noise; there was one on the side of our chopping-block under the brakes. He was near enough for me to see his little gray shape as I stood behind mother on the porch.

"I shouldn't wonder if we did ketch some of it any-way," said mother, in her subdued voice, "though most-ly, you know, Lowizy, they foller the river. But we do need rain amazingly. I'm glad the house ain't all het up. I can't bear to have the house het up when there's a tem-pest."

Mother hurried back to the buttery. She was kneading dough for the second rising for bread, and we intended to have "riz biscuit" for supper. We held that riz biscuit were in every way better than the same thing made with baking-powder.

She called to me through the open door of the pantry:

"Sis, I wish you'd go out 'n' look 'n' see if your father's in sight. I shouldn't wonder a grain if he got caught. It's jest like him to get caught. He'll stay down to the store talkin' 'bout his colt till all is blue 'n' green."

I sauntered down the long yard to the road. The grass was already ankle-high in this yard, and the dandelions had gone to seed and blown away; but some of their tall stems were standing. I pulled one of these stems, split it down the length of it, and put it in my mouth to make a curl of. Do you know the bitter taste of the cool stem? Does the taste recall days of hot sky and long, long hours when you felt as if life were made for you to drink of, as I used to think the gods drank nectar on Olympus?

It wasn't a great while since I had learned that there had been gods, and where they lived when, as we say, they were at home. Being new acquaintances, I thought much of them, and I would refer to them occasionally, arousing the great interest and admiration of mother and Aunt Lowizy. For I had had "advantages."

That's the phrase which was used in speaking of any girl who had been sent away to school.

The neighbors wondered why Lemuel Armstrong had taken it into his head to give his daughter "advantages."

"What's your notion, Lem, anyway?" they asked him.

He used to look at them and wink, and answer that he believed "in training colts, 'n' why shouldn't he have his gal trained? And if they didn't know up to Mount Holyoke how to file down and polish up a gal, he guessed they didn't know anywhere. He said he called his Billy halter-broke, 'n' now he guessed experience would have to make her run in harness. Experience 'd make the very Old Harry run in harness, single or double."

Then he would burst into one of his laughs that sounded so whole-hearted and honest.

I am Billy. Father began calling me that as early as I can remember, and mother and Aunt Lowizy fell into the habit, though they occasionally tried to say "Miny."

I suppose it is rather a dreadful thing for a girl over twenty years old to think of herself always as Billy.

Our minister and his wife invariably say "Wilhelmina," and I suppose it is that which makes me feel so respectable when I am with them. But somehow I don't exactly enjoy feeling respectable. It's something like wearing a pair of tight corsets. You feel a great deal better when you have taken them off. And there's the Venus de' Medici—our physiology teacher used to tell us about the Venus and that she was a beautiful example of the uncorseted female form. But the physiology teacher was the tightest-laced woman in the whole seminary—it wasn't a college then. So we didn't swallow much that she said, unless we felt good enough to die—which wasn't often.

We didn't mean to be so good that we should have to die young.

Father came up when I graduated. I felt kind of queer when he talked with some of my chums, and called me "Billy." I was Wilhelmina up there. Only my dearest friend, who meant to go to Germany, and was giving a good deal of time to German, she would insist upon saying "Vilhelm" always; and I sign my letters to her invariably "Vilhelm."

Though I wished father could use a little grammar when he talked, and that he didn't wink so often, I was bound not to show that I wished it. I took him everywhere; and I had a chance to introduce him to the principal. He shook hands with her, and swung her hand round so hard that she grew red in the face, trying not to have vertigo, I suppose. But she would keep on smiling; I just loved her for that, and for being so sweet and unsurprised when pa said:

"Now, don't you think my Billy is as promisin' a little filly 's you ever snapped a whip at?"

"But we don't snap whips here, Mr. Armstrong," she replied, with one of her best little laughs, as if father were an ex-governor who had just made a joke.

Then father winked, and burst into an enormous laugh which made everybody in the room turn and look our way.

But I held my head up, though my face was on fire; and I took pa's arm and walked him out as soon as I could.

When I had him by myself I thought for a moment I would ask if he would, as a great favor to me, stop doing that perfectly awful wink. But when I examined his face it all came over me as it had never done before that his was precisely the kind of a face that had got to wink. It wouldn't do any good to try to prevent him, for the wink was in his soul. So was his great laugh.

I heard somebody in our village say once that he supposed " Lem Armstrong's laugh had sold more horses than you could shake a stick at. A feller jest wanted to buy a horse when he heard that laugh."

I was mad—indignant, I mean—when I heard that. But I thought it over, and somehow it seemed to me there was truth in those words, though I didn't understand.

I told mother, and I shall never forget how disturbed she looked. What she said was :

" We all have our peculiarities."

It was a year ago since I graduated—I had been at home all that time. People seemed to think I ought to get a school to teach somewhere, but I told father, to begin with, when he began to talk of sending me to South Hadley, that I wasn't going to be a school-teacher. I would rather work in some factory. He said he guessed there wasn't any hurry about my earning anything. So I was at home, and helped mother and Aunt Lowizy ; but I didn't work very hard. I liked to sit out of doors as soon as it became mild. I liked to sit and let the sun shine on me—just loaf. Aunt Lowizy said I was the biggest loafer she ever saw.

Sometimes I would repent and set to work hard, and make blisters on my hands.

To-day I hadn't done much. I had taken the scythe and mowed down the grass between the two maples, and put a barrel-stave hammock there. I had made the hammock the day before. This afternoon I had spent lying there, under the maples, until an hour ago.

Now I looked down the long white road which led past

the house.   I looked in the direction of the village, which lay two miles away.

The birds were flying about swiftly, uttering short calls as they do when a tempest is coming up.

" We shall catch it," I said, aloud.

In front of me was the west, and there the clouds were bluer and blacker than ever, except the very tops of them, which were a soft but brilliant white.

There was a distant roar somewhere, and I knew it was the wind rushing through the gorge between the high hills a few miles to the north of us.

The breeze would be here presently, but now it was so quiet that one wanted to gasp.

How excited it does make one feel to look right at a coming tempest!   It was as if something alive were on the way, and would presently snatch you up and toss you somewhere.

My heart began to beat.   Somebody says it's the electrical state of the air that is so exciting.   I used to read about it up at Holyoke.   But it didn't take the mystery away, this explaining.

I stepped out into the road and began to run down it, for I saw, far along at the curve, a carriage coming.   The horse was trotting fast, stepping high, and making a cloud of dust.   I was sure it was the gray colt that father had just trained, and that was for sale.

As I ran I saw that there were two people on the seat of the light buggy, and then I almost thought I had been mistaken in thinking it was father coming.

But no—there was no other horse with such a dash and stride as that.

And now I saw that it was a woman with father—somebody he had taken up on the way, of course.

The roar of the wind grew louder and nearer.   The gale

bent over the trees; it swept up a blinding cloud of dust and dashed it at me, so that I turned and scudded back to the house, my skirts flying out before me and I feeling as if some great hands were pushing me forward.

At the same moment some big drops splashed slanting along; then floods and floods sluiced across the hot earth, and boiled, and roared, and hissed.

Through the falling water I saw the big gray spank on by me, and whirl the buggy in at the open gate of the road that led to the barn.

I heard my father shout: "Hullo, Billy! Scud into the house this minute! Scud!"

The woman with him had her head bent, and she was holding her hat down with both hands.

That's all I seemed to see; yet as I did scud, as pa had said, I thought "She isn't a neighbor."

A flash of lightning came full across my eyes as I stepped into the entry. Mother caught my hand and drew me in, slamming the door after me.

The thunder cracked and split, and appeared to be tearing the world apart. I clapped my hands over my ears.

"You're wet as sop," I heard mother say. "Go right upstairs and change your clo'es."

But I didn't go directly. I stood in the middle of the large comfortable kitchen and looked out at the tempest. Though it was broad day, how dark it was! The rain itself was thick enough to shut out the light of heaven, even without the clouds.

Aunt Lowizy came in from the other part of the house. She had been shutting a north window which had been overlooked, and the front of her gown was drenched.

"The wind's goin' to change," she said. "There's a strip of clear sky below the cloud a'ready. 'Twon't rain more'n

five minutes more. 'N' we sh'll have a rainbow, I guess.
I always do love to see a rainbow. It makes me think of
God's promise."

" Did somebody come with your father, Sis?" asked
mother. " I thought he wa'n't alone when I had a glimpse
of him."

" 'There's a woman with him," I answered.

" I s'pose it's Eunice Small, ain't it? I knew she'd gone
up to the village this morning."

" No ; it isn't Eunice. It's a stranger."

" I'm sure I d' know who it can be," was the response.
" I guess she'll go on when it slacks up. Of course they'll
stay in the barn while it comes down like this."

We three women drew our chairs into the centre of the
kitchen, after we had shut all the doors so that there should
not be a draught anywhere, for we thought that lightning
was liable to follow a current of air. We always talked in
low tones during a tempest. Mother said it wasn't "seemly"
to be making a noise at such times. She said that to her it
was as if the Lord was speaking in His holy temple.

Mother was a Second Adventist. She didn't say much
about her belief, and she went every Sunday to the " Ortho-
dox Church " at the village. But once in a while, when I
was alone with her, she would speak of the coming of the
Lord, and her face would flush and her eyes begin to shine,
while her voice wasn't quite steady.

At such times I used to look at her in wonder and feel in
my soul some curious and answering cry of mysticism. But
I didn't believe in the second coming of Christ, though I
used to try to believe it, thinking that such a belief might
perhaps make me as good a woman as mother was.

Now, as we all sat in the kitchen and waited for the
tempest to abate, I couldn't help noticing the kind of glo-

rified look there was on mother's face. She watched the blinding flashes, her eyes growing brighter and brighter.

Once Aunt Lowizy reached forward and put her hand on mother's arm.

"Serissy," she said, "now don't go and get excited."

"No, no," was the answer, "but I can't help thinkin' it's awful grand. What if He should come in His might, ridin' on the cloud?"

I heard this, though I did not appear to hear it. I wondered what father thought of this kind of talk, and then I knew intuitively that she would never speak in that way before him.

Presently there came longer spaces of time between the flash and the thunder, and then the rain grew less heavy.

The sun came out. I ran to the door and opened it; there was the rainbow, growing brighter every minute. A great rush of damp, sweet smells came in. The birds began to sing again, now in that triumphant way they have after a rain.

Two figures came hurrying in from the barn. They were father holding an umbrella over the woman. They stepped into the porch, and mother went forward to meet them.

"Who in the world is she?" exclaimed Aunt Lowizy; "I'm sure I don't know her from Adam."

"Wall, Serissy," said father, "you see, I did git caught this time. But I guess I've sold the gray colt. Though, of course, there ain't anybody goin' to give me all he's worth. I declare, I ain't got the cheek to ask all the critter's worth, and that's a fact."

Mother made no answer to this remark. She was looking at the woman who had come in with father, and who was standing behind him, glancing from one to the other

of the group in front of her.   There was a slight smile on
her face, and an extremely amused look in her eyes.   No
one would for an instant have taken her for one of the
townspeople.   She was as different as a person could well
be.   She was dressed in a dark gown with absolutely no
frill, or fold, or ruffle, and we country folks were greatly
given to frills and ruffles on our frocks.   Having had "advantages," I knew that this woman's gown fitted in what I
thought a marvellous way; but I had also a dim idea that
it was, after all, more her carriage—her pose, perhaps, I
mean—than her dressmaker's art that gave her that dis-
tinguished air.

She appeared old to me.   I was young enough to have
thirty-five seem an age when one might just as well die,
for life could have nothing more for a person who had
lived out such a number of years.   She was light; she had
an immense quantity of chestnut hair, streaked somewhat
with gray; she was tall; she had broad, well-knit shoulders, and she carried her head high.

When she spoke there was a precision in her enunciation and a sonority in her voice.   Altogether she was so
different from any one I had ever seen that she gave me a
bewildering sensation, as if I were somewhere else, or
somebody else, myself.

"There are my folks," said father, taking off his wet
coat; "it's my wife, and my wife's sister, and the young
one is Billy.   I hope you'll make yourself to home, Miss—
Miss—I can't seem to git the hang of your name, somehow."

"Runciman," in a tone so clear that the word seemed to
be presented bodily to us.

"Wall, Miss Runciman, you'll stop to supper with us.   I
s'pose we're goin' to have a picked-up meal, but you'll
make allowances for that."

Mother stepped up nearer and held out her hand.

"Yes," she said, "you'll have dinner. It'll be ready in a little while now. Ain't you wet?"

"Thank you, no; I'm not wet—only my hair a little. I shall be so glad to stay a while. You see I had driven over to this town because some one told me that Mr. Armstrong had a horse for sale. I was looking for one to make out my team, and it happened that your husband was at the village. He wanted me to drive with him and see how the colt went. So I did. We were caught in the shower, and he said we were nearer his home than anywhere else, so we came here."

Having made this explanation to mother, Miss Runciman, in answer to an invitation to go into the other room, asked leave to sit down in the kitchen. She said she hoped they wouldn't make company of her, and that every moment she spent in a farmhouse like this was like—she hesitated, smiled, and continued—

"I was going to say like wine to me, but I don't mean that. I mean like one of my childhood's days come back again."

So she sat down by the window and looked out, or looked at us, and sometimes spoke a few words, saying them with a wonderful, new kind of gentleness, and in some mysterious way putting a great deal of meaning into them.

I helped about getting the meal. We had fried ham and eggs, and Miss Runciman, when I came with the basket of eggs, rose and said she wished I would let her attend to them; that it was a thousand years since she had broken eggs into a spider with hot fat in it, and had to jump back for fear the fat would spatter on her face.

So I brought her the little flat spade that we use to turn the eggs and take them out. She took the instrument, but

she remarked that she had never been used to luxuries like
that, and didn't know as she could adjust herself to it.
Then she laughed and we all laughed; and I, for one, had
a sense of pleasurable interest that lacked very little of
being excitement. I began to think of how I would describe this woman in a letter to my friend, who called
me Vilhelm; and I finally decided that I couldn't describe her at all, because the very thing that seemed so
interesting was a thing, whatever it was, that hadn't a
name.

We were usually very silent at our meals, but to-day we
grew gay and full of talk. Even mother told a little story,
and told it with a zest that was charming; and Aunt
Lowizy remembered something that had happened when
she was a girl, and took such delight in telling it that we
all shared her pleasure.

As for father, he beamed and shone. I didn't know what
ailed us. The stranger did not talk much. Her eyes, brilliant, laughing, stimulating, glanced from one to the other,
as she said a word or two.

And it was good to have a guest so hungry. Miss Runciman ate with a relish. I furtively watched her large,
white, strong-looking hands. They gave me an idea that
she could do anything. These hands had the unmistak-
able appearance of not working; the nails were pink and
polished.

Very likely it is silly in me to try to tell so much about
this woman's appearance, when, as I have hinted, the vital
thing can't be told.

After supper we all went to the barn to see the colt again.
He was led out into the middle of the great floor and Miss
Runciman walked round him, looking at his legs and lifting
up his feet to see his hoofs.

" I never would allow a frog to be cut off so much as that," she said, emphatically, holding one of the forefeet in her hand and putting the tip of a finger on the frog.

Father burst into asseverations that the horse had never walked a lame step; that he had the best shoer in the county; that the hoof was sound as a dollar, and would have gone on if the lady had not interrupted him.

"I know the hoof is sound," she said, " but it's a cruel thing to cut a horse's foot to fit a shoe, instead of fitting the shoe to the foot. Do you think this fellow will let me mount him?"

For the first time my father failed in his glibness of speech. He hesitated.

" I didn't know you wanted a saddle-hoss," he said.

"Let's try him," she responded, cheerfully.

In a few moments my old side-saddle was on the gray's back, and he was tossing up his head and his eyes were distending.

" I vow, I'd ruther you wouldn't!" exclaimed father.

Miss Runciman did not reply. She was standing in front of the horse, looking at him, and stroking his nose. He stopped throwing up his head, and in a moment the head drooped slightly toward her, as if the animal were asking for another caress.

" Just give me a hand, Mr. Armstrong," said Miss Runciman.

" I tell you I don't like it!" cried my father.

The lady smiled and said again :

" Please help me up."

Father extended his hand and our guest sprang into the saddle.

The gray snorted and made a dash out of the barn.

" Darn fool !" cried father, in a low, furious voice ; " this'll spoil the sale! And I was goin' to git five hundred for that colt! What's she want to ride him for?"

"Lemuel!" said mother, reprovingly.

But father only swore under his breath.

We ran out of the barn to see where the colt had gone.

There he was, galloping down the road, going at a great, swinging pace, the wet sand flying up from his feet, his long gray tail straight out behind.

"What kind of a woman is that, anyway?"

It was Aunt Lowizy who asked this.

"I d'know," said father, "but she's a woman who's got to buy the colt, anyway."

"I hope you ain't misrepresented anything to her, Lemuel," said my mother.

"Misrepresented! Don't you go 'n' be a fool, Serissy. That woman knows a hoss 's well 's I do. Them frogs was pared down too much; 'n' I give the blacksmith a good cussin' for it, too. Thunder! There they go into the cross-road! I do hope the colt won't smash her all to flinders. I ain't settin' up the gray for a saddle-hoss. She said she wanted a hoss to go with another in some kind of a private travellin' coach. One of her animals had broken his leg."

Father spoke with what seemed profane emphasis.

As soon as he had finished he ran down the road until he could see along the cross-road, and I followed him.

There was a hill in this road, and evidently the colt and its rider had gone up the hill and down the other side, out of sight. Anyway, we could not see them when we reached the corner.

I knew how alarmed father was by the whiteness of his face.

He kept running on, and I kept beside him.

"I wish I'd stopped her!" he panted. "I wish I'd stopped her by main force!"

We mounted the hill, and could now see the long line of wet road with its bushes and trees glistening on each side.

There, farther ahead than seemed possible, was the gray horse and his rider.

"Thank the Lord, she ain't got throwed yet!" cried father. "I guess 'tain't no use to try to foller any further."

I did not say anything. My eyes were fixed on the woman who rode the big horse, sat him with an easy sway to his stride that made me directly put away all apprehension.

"She's all right, pa." I said, after a little.

"By George! I do believe she is," was the response. "But I'll tell you, Billy, though you needn't let on to your ma, that the only two times I ever tried to get on the gray's back he kicked and cut up so that I went off like a shot, and I gave it up. I thought if I trained him to harness 'twas good enough. There! She's turned round."

We sat down on a stone by the roadside and watched the gray as he came along flinging his feet up and carrying himself in that proud way which so stirs one to witness.

Miss Runciman pulled him up in front of us.

"Wall?" said father.

He was still white; and when he went to the horse and put his hand on the glossy neck his hand trembled a little.

"I suppose it isn't policy to say anything in praise of the horse until he is mine," responded the rider.

Father looked relieved. He stood there twisting the gray's forelock round and round in his fingers.

"You c'n say what you're a mind to," he answered: "there's the hoss, 'n' if you c'n pick flaws in him you're welcome to do it. I don't pretend he's a trotter, you know,

But he's young 'n' sound, 'n' he c'n road his twelve miles in an hour without a whip. All you've got to do is jest to suck in your teeth to that hoss, 'n' he'll start, I c'n tell ye."

Miss Runciman laughed gayly. Her face showed exhilaration and delight.

"Now I ought to beat you down on your price," she said.

At this father looked injured. He thrust his hands into his pockets and rattled the loose silver.

"I ain't askin' you what the animal's really worth," he said, solemnly. "You bein' a woman, I ain't goin' to try to git the better of you 's I would if you was a man. I calkilate a man knows how to look out for himself. But I tell you I don't never take advantage of a woman when I'm dealing with her."

Miss Runciman laughed again. I wished father wouldn't talk just like that. But he was very serious.

"Now if I were a man," said Miss Runciman, "how much would you ask for this horse?"

"Five hundred and fifty," was the prompt reply.

"And now?"

"Five hundred."

"And you take off fifty just because I'm a woman?"

"Eggsactly," with the utmost solemnity.

"Oh, this is gallantry indeed!"

My father's face did not change. He nodded gravely.

"I d'now whether it's gallantry or not," he said, "but you can't make me take advantage of no woman. I never did 'n' I never will."

Miss Runciman's face showed such keen amusement that I felt the blood rush hotter than ever to my cheeks.

She glanced at me and then seemed to try to subdue her mirth.

" I'll take him at five hundred," she said.

" All right."

Father's countenance looked almost dejected ; but I knew he was full of triumph.   Still one would have said that he had just made a very poor bargain.

" I'll send you a check to-morrow, and will write you where to bring him."

Then she shook the bridle, and the gray galloped round into his own yard.

I followed lagging.   I walked so slowly that when I reached the house the buggy, with the colt again hitched to it, and father and the stranger on the seat, was just turning into the road.

Miss Runciman made a movement, and father drew in the horse.   I went up to the side of the carriage where the woman sat, and she leaned out and extended her hand to me.

" Good-by, Billy," she said.   " I must call you Billy because that's the name by which your father introduced you."

" Good-by," I answered.

She was holding my hand closely and looking down at me.   It seemed to me that she had not looked at me before.

" How old are you ?" she asked, suddenly.

" Twenty-three."

" Have you ever earned any money ?"

" No."

" Should you like to earn money ?"

" Yes, but I don't want to teach school."

She smiled.   I thought she was going to say something more, but she only repeated her good-by.   Then the gray colt sprang forward, and I was left standing in the road staring after her.

2

"That's curious," I said to myself. "I don't know why she asked if I wanted to earn money."

When I went into the house I found mother and Aunt Lowizy talking about the woman. Mother was saying—

"I don't know what to make of her, I'm sure. I can't tell whether I like her or not."

"I can tell," said Aunt Lowizy. "I don't want nothing to do with her. What's she going round buying horses for? And who is she, I should like to know? I hope Lemuel won't let her take the colt away 'fore he sees her money."

Lemuel saw her money the next day, as she had said. The check came, and father took it to the bank in the town and got the cash.

"How does she know but I'm goin' to keep hoss 'n' money both?" he chuckled.

There was something in the note which accompanied the check which made my blood start with wonder. It was this:

"Please bring the horse to the Ottawa Hotel in Chilton on the 17th, and please also let Billy come with you. When I see a child with a face like hers I have a wish to see her again. Don't fail to bring her."

Father read this note slowly to us when he came home with it. He looked at me.

"What does she mean by 'a face like hers?'" he asked. "What's the matter with Billy's face, anyway?"

Mother turned and gazed at me, and her own face grew troubled.

"I don't know, I'm sure," she answered. "I never thought Mina was pretty."

"I'm not pretty; I know all about that," I said, decisively. "I haven't an idea what Miss Runciman means, but she doesn't mean that, and I want to go with pa. It's

thirty miles to Chilton, isn't it? Yes, I must go with you,
pa." And, of course, I went.

The 17th came two days later. We started early in the
morning in the light buggy, the gray colt in the shafts and
another horse hitched to the back of the wagon, that he
might take us home again.

The long drive stands out in my memory as distinctly
as if it had been taken yesterday. It was early summer
and we drove through a country of great farms and wide
pastures, where cows and sheep were feeding. The sky
was blue and the sun hot, but the wind was fresh from the
west and filled with the odors of grass and lush brakes and
wild roses. Do you know what such an air is?

Over the plains of heaven does any sweeter air blow?

Father was in great spirits. He talked, and whistled,
and sang snatches of song in a rough bass voice, and I
joined him in the song when I could.

We drove at a good pace and were entering the city
of Chilton in less than four hours from the time we had
started. Father always said that eight miles was enough
to drive in an hour when you were on a long journey.

The Ottawa Hotel was a big building with fluted white
pillars in front, standing on the main street.

My heart was beating very fast when I sat in the ladies'
parlor, waiting for Miss Runciman to come down. Father
sent me in while he had the horses put up. He said he
would be round and call for me in an hour or two.

I had told the servant to inform Miss Runciman that
Miss Armstrong had come.

The man disappeared, having gone out of sight in the
elevator which was sliding up and down directly opposite
the open door of the parlor.

There was no one in the room when I first entered it,

and I gazed about at the big, soft chairs, the marble tables, the stiff palms in green pots in the bay window.

Very soon a man and two women came in. The two women sat down, but the man strolled about, holding his hat and cane, and diffusing an odor of cigar smoke. He looked at everything, including me; looked with large, authoritative eyes that did not linger, but that apparently comprehended.

Another servant appeared and took their cards from these people, and then he also was swallowed up in the elevator.

One of the women, slowly wielding a fan, spoke. She said :

"It's so difficult to catch Miss Runciman. Ronald, are you sure she was to be at the Ottawa?"

"I'm sure the paper made such a statement."

"But you can't tell anything by the papers."

"I know they lie like troopers," he responded.

"But you can try to see Miss Runciman. You'll never see her if you don't try."

"I do wonder how she looks when you meet her in a room like this," said the other woman. As she spoke, she rose and moved uneasily to a window.

II

"WHAT'S AN UNDERSTUDY?"

I sat very still, far back in my big chair at the end of the long parlor. I wondered what Miss Runciman was, anyway, and why it was "so hard to catch her." Evidently these people did not know her, but then why did they want to see her?

The woman with the fan, whom her companion called "Cornelia," sauntered slowly down my way, apparently saw me for the first time, looked irresolutely at me for an instant, then paused in front of my chair. She was dressed too richly, I thought, and the perfume of "frangipanni" was really quite stifling as she waved her fan back and forth; the breeze thus created moved the short, dark hair on her forehead, and I was afraid the rice powder, visibly deposited on her cheeks and chin, would be wafted abroad in the room.

"Perhaps you're acquainted with her?" she said to me, with a little air of condescension.

As she spoke the man drew near and stood staring at a lurid painting of the "Plains of Heaven" which filled the space on the wall behind me, between the top of my head and the ceiling.

"I don't know," I answered, somewhat confused, for I had not supposed she was going to speak to me.

The man brought his eyes down from the painting and,

tucking his cane under his arm, began to smooth his silk
hat round and round with the palm of his hand. A diamond
on that hand flung a spark into my vision. It seemed a
very large diamond, indeed.

"Miss Runciman, I mean," went on Cornelia. "Perhaps you've met her."

"Yes," I answered, and I felt quite proud. I flushed
up with still more pride as I added, "I came by appointment."

"Oh!" lifting up heavy, white eyelids with a more animated stare. "Ronald," turning to the man, "this—per—
I mean this young lady, knows Miss Runciman. She came
by appointment."

The gentleman—I had a dim idea that he was a gentleman, notwithstanding the size of his diamond—glanced at
me and then turned away, saying :

"Well, Cornelia, she is more fortunate than we are, then.
Perhaps we might better go, and come some other time."

He made a movement as if to put on his hat, recollected,
and did not put it on.

He commenced to walk round the room again, and I
thought he began to hum a tune, but stopped immediately.

The elevator opposite the wide door of this public parlor
had not omitted arriving and departing, and people had
not ceased from stepping out of it and into it. Two or
three times some one had come to the door, glanced in, and
then gone away. Two women had entered, rustled about,
and gone. A black servant came in with a salver in his
hand, but he apparently did not find the person he wanted.

Every time any figure approached the door my heart
gave a jump. There was the elevator stopping again ; this
time a tall woman stepped from it and walked forward with

that decision of motion which showed that she came in with a purpose.

She had a parasol in one hand and gloves in the other, and a large hat on her head; I thought I had not known a hat could be quite so picturesque, though my friend who calls me Vilhelm knows how to wear a large hat.

Of course this was Miss Runciman. I did not move, for I felt as if this gentleman and these two ladies would have the first chance of an interview.

Cornelia, the woman with the fan and the frangipanni, did indeed step forward instantly, exclaiming:

"Oh, do forgive us, Miss Runciman! But when we knew you were here at the Ottawa, we—"

Miss Runciman, as she walked forward, glanced over the speaker, but her face did not change into the very slightest smile as she responded:

" Pardon me."

That was all she said as she came towards me. I rose. She held out her hand and asked:

" How do you do, Billy?"

" I'm very well, I thank you," I answered.

" And how's the gray colt?"

" He's all right. Came in at the end of his thirty miles as fine as when he started from home."

" Ah! That's the kind of a colt to have."

She began to draw on one of her gloves, looking at me as she did so. I grew red and white, but she did not withdraw her eyes; she would have gazed at something inanimate in just that way, I was sure.

" I'm glad you came," she said, at length; "I thought, perhaps, your mother would forbid it. I'm going out just now. I want you to wait until I come back"—she walked a little way from me and touched a button on the wall.

A black man came gently forward from somewhere. "Take this lady to my room," she commanded. I followed the servant, who said I was "to please to take the elevator." I did so, and found myself going up and instantly stopping. The black man wasn't with me and I stood in a wide hall, a sense of confusion upon me, which was mitigated, however, by the immediate appearance of the servant, who knocked on a door near.

Somebody said "Come in," in a muffled voice, and I opened the door, finding myself in a large parlor where a young woman was arranging the folds of a velvet skirt over a "form." It was a red velvet skirt, and the train of it, lined with white silk, was laid out several yards over the floor.

The girl was kneeling down as I entered and closed the door softly behind me. She had her mouth full of pins and couldn't speak very clearly. She looked back over her shoulder at me as I stood just within the room. I will confess that I was awed somewhat by the great grandeur of the gilt and plush chairs, the gilt mirrors, and the general sense of glitter from the heavy, embossed paper on the walls. I wasn't used to hotels, and didn't know that there is usually a great deal of plush and gilt in them.

"Miss Runciman's gone out," said the girl, thickly, one pin dropping from her mouth as she spoke.

"I know it," I said.

She held her hand under her lips and ejected all the pins into it; but she continued kneeling.

"Miss Runciman's gone out," she said again, as if I had not heard.

"I know it," I answered for the second time.

I was irritated by the way the girl looked at me, and so I would not volunteer any explanation of my appearance.

"Have you seen her?" she asked, now sitting back on her heels that she might the better gaze at me.

"Yes," I answered.

I apparently irritated her, for she exclaimed :

"Can't you speak more 'n that?"

"Yes, I can. Miss Runciman told me to come here and wait for her," I replied.

"All right, then. Sit down somewhere, and make yourself to home."

I advanced into the room upon this. I went to a table upon which lay a heap of cabinet photographs. The first one was a picture of Miss Runciman in street dress ; she was looking right at me with that same expression of gentle imperiousness I had seen in her face. The next one was a picture of Miss Runciman in ermine and velvet robes, with her head flung up, her hand out, the whole attitude one of queenlike command. I felt my eyes begin to distend as I went on with the photographs—they were all of Miss Runciman, though in some the features and expression were so different, not to mention the dress.

I dropped the last card on the table and turned to my companion, who was still on the floor, by the skirt.

"What!" I exclaimed, "is she an actress?"

There was that in my manner that made the girl, who had again filled her mouth with pins, once more very hastily drop them into the palm of her hand.

She gazed up at me.

"Gracious !" she cried, as if I had betrayed an ignorance beyond her understanding.

I was very uncomfortable, but I persisted, as, perhaps, was my way.

"Why don't you tell me?" I inquired. "I suppose it isn't a secret."

"Well, I should say 'twasn't a secret," she burst out. "I declare I didn't know there was a person in the civilized world who didn't know what Miss Runciman is."

I was aware that I had a strong desire to go up to this girl and slap her; but I suppose it is vulgar to slap people. I stood still and glared. I was suffering from curiosity, but I would ask no more questions. I said stiffly that I lived in the country, and that there were some things that country people knew, but there were other things that they did not know.

Having said this, I walked over to the window and gazed into the street, with my back to the person on her knees. I heard her laughing to herself, and I had a feeling of great virtue because I did not, even now, go forward and "give her a hit," as we do when we are children and a playmate becomes too exasperating.

Presently the girl rose to her feet and went to the other side of the room contemplating the skirt on the form, with her head on one side. She was still laughing somewhat.

"I'm sorry I'm so very funny," I said, severely.

"The idea," she cried, "of asking who Miss Runciman is!"

"She may be a very great person, indeed," I retorted, "but you see every one does not know it."

"So it seems," was the response.

The girl came towards me. She threw herself down in a chair near me, and stretched her arms over her head as if she were weary.

"Yes," she said, "she's a actress, and she's more'n that; she's a opera singer. She's a primy donna—A number one every time."

"Is she?"

I suppose my face must have shown the awe I felt. I

had never been to an opera in my life. But we seminary girls had acted in an operetta once, and I had taken one of the leading parts, and had wrung my hands and sung at the very top of my voice. The local papers afterwards said that "Miss Wilhelmina Armstrong had performed her difficult rôle with surprising facility and effect." I bought twenty copies of that paper and sent them to as many different people with deep, black strokes around the above remark.

After having received this information, I asked no more questions. I gazed out into the street, but I saw nothing more than a confused jumble of men and women. There was a sort of fearsome glow over me that would every now and then give place to a delightful chill. It was a very curious and wonderful thing that a "primy donna" should have come to our house and have bought a horse of father.

I don't know how long it was that I sat there looking from the window upon the streets of the city. I saw my father come along with his hands thrust into the pockets of his duster. His hat was on the back of his head and he was whistling. He turned in between the fluted pillars of the hotel entrance. After a while I became aware that I was watching for Miss Runciman, watching with all the curiosity and eagerness of a woman who has not yet ceased to be a child. I wondered what she had said to Cornelia.

Some one touched me on the shoulder. It was the girl who had received me. I started.

"She's come," she said. "You're to go in there."

There, as she pointed, I noticed a door opened into another room. I walked towards it. Miss Runciman was lying back in a long chair with a fan in her hand. Her hat and gloves were thrown on the bed near.

"You're a good child to wait," she said. "Sit down there where I can see you."

I obeyed. She looked at me up and down, and down and up.

"I believe you told me how old you were—twenty-three?"

"Yes."

"And I'm thirty-five," she laughed, and then she sighed. "At thirty-five a woman begins to remember when she was young, and to be surprised that she doesn't feel old. And people, in speaking of her, begin to say 'she was,' instead of 'she is.'"

I was silent. She swung her fan languidly, her half-shut eyes fixed on my face.

"The critics haven't dared to say 'she was' about me yet —but they are waiting." Then, suddenly, "Haven't you a singing voice, Billy?"

I blushed and hesitated. Finally I answered :

"I believe I can carry a tune."

"Of course you can. You have what I call a violin face. Sing me something."

As I was silent, she said : "Anything, you know."

Frightened almost out of my senses, I piped forth feebly one verse of the first thing I could think of, and that happened to be "Come, ye disconsolate," which I had sung at the funeral of old Deacon Marle the week before, at the request of "the relatives."

My listener could not help smiling somewhat as I went on. When I had finished she exclaimed :

"What a dismal little thrush it is!   Now I'll sing it."

She sat up erect and began. By the time she had finished the line, "Where'er ye languish," I was ready to throw myself at her feet and become hysterical in my admiration.   But I did no such thing.   I sat perfectly still, my eyes cast down, my hands clasped tightly in my lap.   And

I said nothing when she ceased singing at the end of the verse.

"You have a good natural voice," she remarked, "but I don't know why you sing coldly."

I had nothing to say to that, either, so I kept still.

"I understand that you are frightened," she went on, more kindly. "But we won't talk about singing any more now. I must tell you that I am a woman of whims; I suppose every one who amounts to anything has whims. When I saw you at the farm-house the other day I took a fancy to have you along on our trip this summer. It's my vacation. Another whim of mine is to go on a long carriage trip—live in the carriage, you know—stop here and there—get acquainted with nature. And I want to make sure and not have any one about who will jar. I hate to have a person near me who doesn't know that a woman may have moods. Such people ought to be shot. And when you are going on forty, and haven't become reconciled to the fact, it does seem as if you are justified in killing people who jar. Don't you think so, Billy?"

She spoke in the most genial tone, and she held out her hand to me as she asked the last question. I rose and went to her side. She placed her hand on my arm.

"I do hope you haven't a lover," she remarked, and I said "No."

"Then I don't see but that you can go in a house carriage this summer. And I can try your voice. Do you sing in your village?"

"Yes; I sit in the seats," I answered.

"The seats?"

"The choir; the singers' seats, I mean."

She laughed, seemed to recover, and then laughed again.

"Forgive me, but you don't know what a picture your

words recall to me. Now you may go home and get a wool frock made. We are not going to be stylish. Be ready in a week. I'll send you word."

I was a bit nettled at the way I was dismissed. I walked to the open door of the room, and there I paused to say:

"I don't think my mother 'll be willing for me to go."

"What!" in surprise.

I repeated my words. Miss Runciman frowned slightly; then she said, "I'll write to her."

I understood that I was to leave. I walked through the large adjoining apartment and did not notice the girl there. I was so confused that I could hardly find my way to the public parlor. I entered that room rather blindly, and was thankful to hear a hearty, familiar voice saying:

"Well, Billy, how are things? Have you seen her?"

I went up to father and took his hand.

"Yes, I've seen her. But I don't know how things are," I answered.

He drew me closer to the window and looked sharply at me. "What's the matter, anyway?" he inquired. "Your cheeks are jest as red as fire, and your eyes are startin' out of your head."

"I guess I'm kind of excited," was my reply. "Can't we go home right away, father?"

"I guess you be excited," he responded. "I s'pose you know she's a great opery singer?"

"Yes, I know it now. And she made me sing to her. Father, let's go home right away."

He laughed; he seemed to be laughing at what I said. He put more questions, and when I told him that Miss Runciman wanted me to go with her in her house-carriage he stared and exclaimed:

"What for, I sh'd like to know?"

"Because," I answered, "she is a woman of whims."

When I made this answer I wished again that father wouldn't laugh so much. It seemed to me that this was serious enough for him to seem concerned.

He put his big, rough finger under my chin and lifted my face up. Then he said:

"Well, Billy, I guess you're in luck this time. They say she makes lots of money. Of course you'll go. Mebby she's taken a notion to you 'n' will leave you her prop'ty."

After this remark I had no inclination to talk any more on the subject. I drew back and walked mechanically to the marble-topped table that stood in the room. A fan was lying there, and I detected the odor of frangipanni. I took the fan and unfurled it, not thinking what I was doing. At that moment a man entered from the main hall and came forward, hat in hand, his somewhat bold eyes— very bright, and, as I had thought before, full of authority —on me as he advanced.

"I beg your pardon, I'm sure," he said, " but my sister sent me back for her fan; she was quite positive she had left it here. Oh, thank you!"

I awkwardly held out the fan, provoked with myself that I had been found with it in my hand.

He thrust the article into an inner pocket of his coat. He glanced at my father, who still stood at the window. Then, without any hesitation, he walked across the room and said:

"You'll excuse me, I'm sure, for speaking to you, but that's a mighty fine colt you've brought into town. I saw it at the stable just now. I'm looking after a good animal myself."

How animated and pleased father grew on the instant!

"If you want a good hoss 's ever was sold in this State,"

he said, in his loud, hearty way, "why, I'm the man to come
to, and that's a fact every time."

I was not looking at father, but I'm sure he winked as he
made this assertion.

"How lucky for me!" was the response. "Where do
you live? A man that knew how to raise that gray is the
man to pick out my horse for me."

The gentleman pulled a little note-book from his pocket
and held his pencil poised over a page as he glanced interrogatively at my father, who answered that anybody out
our way could tell where "Lem" Armstrong lived—"out
Worthing way, you know; cars leave you within five mile;
lem me know when you're coming 'n' I'll be to the deepo with as good a piece of horse-flesh 's you ever seen."

"Thanks"—the man wrote in his book—"I'll set the
time now," he said, as his pencil moved; "we'll say on
Wednesday, the morning train. Will that do?"

"First rate."

The stranger put up his note-book and drew out a card-
case from which he extracted a bit of pasteboard, his diamond making a great glitter meanwhile.

Father took the card, the man made a fine bow and
walked out of the room.

"Great swell, ain't he?" father exclaimed, searching for
his glasses. "I tell you what 'tis, Billy : if I sell another hoss
I'll make you a stunnin' present; di'mond, or something."

I advanced and looked at the card. "Mr. Ronald Maverick" was what I read; and father read it aloud after me ,
as if he were spelling the words.

"Wall, all I've got to say is, if Mr. Ronald Maverick
c'n 'ford to wear a ring like that, he c'n 'ford to pay a good
stiff price for his hoss. Now le's go to a restaurant, Billy,
'n' have a howlin' good dinner."

So we went, and father ate, and talked, and laughed; and he winked at the waiter, and was in extremely good spirits.

As we were on our way home, while the sun gradually went lower and lower down the clear blue sky, father questioned me more about Miss Runciman, and seemed to have no doubt as to my going with her.

" You'll be a reg'lar fool if you don't go," he said, in his good-natured way. He was almost always good-natured.

Mother was in the yard when we drove down the road. The bright red light of the setting sun was on her, and I felt a sudden, strange pang as I saw how delicately lovely her face was, with its large, mysterious-looking eyes, which seemed to be able to see strange things.

For the first time in my life this question came to me: " How did she come to marry this man ?"

Immediately the query seemed to me so disrespectful and disloyal to them both that I hastened to put it from me. But it had come once, and I had a curious feeling that it would come again and again.

It is a significant time in the life of a daughter when she begins to judge her parents, not as her parents merely, but as human individuals like herself.

" Hullo, mother !" called out father. " I've brought Billy back this time ; but mebby next time I sha'n't be so lucky."

He pulled in the horse and I sprang out of the carriage. Mother extended her hand quickly and took hold of mine. She smiled rather a wistful smile, and she kissed me, which she very rarely did.

" I can't be thankful enough you've come," she said, softly. " I don't know why 'tis, but it seems 's if I'd got you back from something dreadful."

The horse and carriage had gone on into the barn. We

could hear father whistling as he unharnessed. Mother led me on into the orchard, which was at the other side of the yard.

"Lowizy's bakin' the biscuits," she said. "Ive been so nervous 'bout you, Wilhelmina, that it was all I could do to hold myself together. What 'd that woman want?"

I hesitated. I held mother's hard, thin hand fast.

"I thought you liked her when she was here the other day," I responded.

"So I did; so I did," she answered, quickly. "Somehow she made me feel so kind of satisfied with myself, 'n' 's if I was real bright 'n' smart. What is she, anyway?"

"She's a great opera singer, what they call a prima donna."

I spoke proudly. Mother looked at me fearfully.

"Oh!" she exclaimed, in a whisper. "One of them opera singers? Did she make you sing, Sis? You've got a beautiful voice, I think."

"Well, you're mistaken about my voice," I answered. "She did not care for it. And she says it is cold. She wants me to go with her this summer in a house carriage. She says she has whims. She's got a whim to have me."

Mother hurried me along down the slope of the orchard until we were under the old chestnut-tree and out of sight of any one. There she stopped. She laid a hand on each of my shoulders. A glow of beautiful, solemn light came from her eyes.

"My daughter," she said, impressively, "you mustn't go with that woman. She won't do you any good. No—no. I see a picture of your life. I see—"

"Oh, mother—don't! Don't!" I cried.

Some great wave of mystery seemed to be rising higher and higher in my soul. I couldn't bear to have her go on.

I flung my arms about her neck and leaned my head down on her shoulder. I was a tall girl, and she seemed very frail to me then.

"We'll pray about it," she said, in a few moments, during which she stroked my hair softly, for my hat had fallen off.

"You know it may help us to pray, and something has got to help us. I've passed a sorrowful day. All the time I've seen my little girl drifting away from me, going into bad places that glittered and looked like good places. Yes, we'll pray right here. Wilhelmina, kneel down close to me."

Mother knelt down on the grass, and I placed myself beside her. She put her arm close about me and drew me to her. Her eyes were wide open and fixed on the bright western sky where the sun was slowly going down. The brilliance of the sky dazzled me, but it did not seem to dazzle her.

"The Lord is coming," she said, at last, in a solemn voice.

I started in uncontrollable terror. I tried to look straight into the glory of the heavens. But I could not, and again I hid my face on her shoulder. Why did she think the Lord was coming? I was afraid of the Lord; I did not want Him to come.

"On pillars of white fire," she said, in a half-whisper, "and He will take us, or He will leave us forever. For years I've looked for Him—"

"Mother," I said, with my lips close to her cheek, "you said you were going to pray."

"Yes, so I did—so I did."

She held me closer yet, but she did not pray aloud. I remained motionless, my heart filled with awe and a kind of delightful fear of I knew not what. I could feel mother's heart beat, pressed as I was against her, and that it grew to a calmer movement, as the moments passed.

The sun had just dropped below the pine ridge when we rose from our knees. Mother was clasping my hand tightly, and she dropped it and held my face a moment between her palms, smiling at me with a sort of beatified smile. I didn't know why this smile should make me cry out: "Mother, don't you worry. I won't go with that woman. At least"—here something tugged at my consciousness—"I—"

"Stop! Stop!" she said. "Don't make any rash promises. You'll be in God's hands wherever you are."

I did not understand why I should be aware of a feeling of rebellion against being in God's hands, and a conviction that I could take care of myself quite well. I had a sense of being a prisoner. My wings were grown; I wanted to try them. I knew I was wicked — my consciousness of wickedness made me indignant.

"Serissy! Serissy! Where are you?"

It was Aunt Lowizy's voice coming stridently across the still orchard spaces.

"Yes, yes—here I am," was the answer; and the expression of gratified resignation faded from mother's face, leaving it old and tired.

"Come in to supper right away," returned the voice. "Lemuel's ready, 'n' the biscuit are out 'n' gittin' cold."

We hurried back to the house. Though the doors were open, the kitchen felt hot and close, and there was a strong smell of boiling tea. We always boiled our tea, for father said there wa'n't any taste to it unless it had had a good bile on; 'n' if bilin' brought out the pizon, why, he'd resk it. He'd drunk biled tea for more'n forty years, so he guessed 'twas mighty slow pizon, anyway.

This was a remark he usually made when we had company to a meal, and the almost black decoction was poured into the cups.

"Billy says they don't have such lookin' stuff up to Hadley," he would say; "but then we folks that 'ain't had 'advantages' can drink this. Mother, I wish you'd turn me another cup, will ye?"

I thought that every one who heard father must for the moment think they liked this beverage better than anything else. I remember once overhearing two women who had been spending the afternoon with us. They were putting on their things, which I had just brought from the spare bedroom. I had gone back into the bedroom to find a missing veil.

"What a dretful pleasant man Mr. Armstrong is!" said one of them.

"Yes, indeed," was the response, "and my husband says he'd ruther be cheated by 'Lem' Armstrong than git the best of a bargain with anybody else. 'N' I don't wonder. I don't think his wife 'preciates how good he is in his fam'ly. I tell you I don't much care what a man is out round, if he's only good in his fam'ly."

What further conversation there might have been on the subject of their hosts I nipped in the bud by entering the room with the veil, which I carefully tied around the head where it belonged, sternly putting away the desire to draw the article chokingly tight.

Yes, father was a very pleasant man; but of course he didn't cheat.

After supper that night he bade me to come out to the barn and hold the lantern for him. But when I asked him, after we had reached the stable, where I should take the lantern, he sat down on the meal-chest, picked up a straw

from the top of it, and began to chew it, as he said: "Stan'
right where you be with it. What's your mother been sayin' to ye down in the orchard?"

As I hesitated he went on: "You needn't hold back
nothin'. Your mother'n I are one, you know, and," wink-
ing, "I'm the one."

The light of the lantern was directly on his face, and I
had a strange fancy that I had never seen his wink quite so
plainly.

"Speak up, Billy, that's a good girl," he said.

"She didn't say much of anything," I replied.

"She don't want you to go with that woman, does she?"

"No; I don't think she does." He leaned forward and
took hold of my arm.

"Now look here, Billy," he said, in a low voice. "You
needn't mind bothering 'bout what she says in a case like
this. She's one of the best women in the world, but she's
got mighty queer notions—I call 'em Advent notions. You
go with the opera singer. 'Tain't best to throw away
chances. You go with her, if she sticks to the idea. But
she may forgit all about it. That's what I'm afraid of, that
she'll forgit. Lord! didn't she ride that colt good? You
go with her. Here, give me the lantern. Run in now, 'n'
you needn't say I've said anything."

I obeyed. When I entered the kitchen where mother
was washing dishes she looked at me anxiously, but she did
not speak.

The next few days were full of a feverish interest to me.
Every day I watched father when he came from his drive to
the post-office. But I tried not to care whether Miss Runciman wrote.

It was on the fifth day that he tossed a letter into mother's lap. She turned pale and clutched at it. I held myself

perfectly still where I sat by the window. I would not even look at the group in the room, but gazed persistently out at the horse and buggy, which were standing in the yard.

But I heard the sound of the tearing open of the envelope and the unfolding of the paper.

"No, no!" exclaimed mother sharply, after a moment.

"Now, Serissy," said father, in a low voice, "I shall be dretful sorry to have you act foolish. Lem me read it."

He had got his glasses on. He read aloud, in sort of half-voice, but he read so slowly that I understood.

"To Billy's Mother:

"MY DEAR MADAM,—Your daughter thinks you may not allow her to spend a month or two with me in driving about the country. Let me explain to you that when I saw her I immediately had a fancy that I might be able to train her to be my understudy—if she had a voice, and I was nearly positive, from hearing her speak, that she did have a voice. But it's cold, and of course it isn't trained, though she sits 'in the seats.' I used to sit in the seats a thousand years ago. The matter resolves itself into this simply. Let the child come with me for my summer vacation; I shall make up my mind as to her capabilities, and if by fall I don't think she has the required gifts, she will have had a pleasant summer, I hope, and can go back home. I needn't tell you that I am very sanguine that she will, in time, be what I want. I think, now that you understand the matter, there can be no objections to her joining me some time next week. I will send you more definite word shortly.	Very sincerely yours,

"LEONORA RUNCIMAN."

As soon as father had read the name he lifted his eyes, saw me, and exclaimed :

"Hullo! There's Billy herself. Billy, what's an understudy?"

"I don't know."

I rose and came forward. I saw that father was in great spirits. I looked fearfully at mother, and she met my gaze

with such beseeching eyes that I ran to her and dropped
down on my knees beside her, leaning my arms across her
lap.   .

"You don't want me to go?" I whispered.

Before she could answer father said: "Now, Serissy!"

Mother seemed to shudder, and father said: "I'm 'fraid
you're gettin' nervous, Serissy.   Don't you go 'n' begin to
worry now."

She drew herself together as she met father's gaze.

III

I DID not feel as if I ought to stay in the room. There
was that sense of something in the air which I cannot describe, and which surprised and excited me; and, more than
that, I had a curious and confused sense of disillusion-
ment. I gazed at father, who did not glance at me. He
was looking at mother; his eyes had a peculiar, contracted
appearance, and I had never noticed before that they were
so near together.

I walked towards the door, but just as my hand was on
the latch father said, quickly:

"You needn't go, Billy. Mother 'n' I ain't goin' to talk
any secrets from you. Se' down."

I obeyed, but I longed to get away. Mother was now
sitting with her hands folded in her lap, her eyes cast down.
I thought as I looked at her that I had never seen her face
so cold and expressionless; and I had a sudden terror at
her remoteness. I wanted to hurry to her side, but I knew
father would think I was very silly; so I kept quiet.

He had the letter still in his hand, and he was flapping
it gently against his trousers-leg as he talked.

"When you really come to think it all over, Serissy," he
said, "you ain't goin' to stan' in the child's way; are you,
now?"

Mother's face quivered slightly. I thought she was

going to speak, but she did not; and she did not raise
her eyes.

"You see, Serissy, it's jest about here, I call it: We've
always be'n real proud 'cause Billy could sing, but we never
felt we knew exactly how to have her voice eddicated; 'n'
so we ain't done nothin' about it. But here's Providence
steppin' right in 'n' openin' the way. Do you feel like
stan'in' in the way of Providence?"

"Not if 'tis Providence."

Mother did not raise her eyes as she answered, though
I was watching eagerly to meet her glance.

That sense of remoteness from her still continued, and
it made my heart sink lower and lower.

"I guess we sha'n't quarrel about that," returned father,
in his jovial way. "Now, if you'd jest let Billy know that
you was all right on the question of her goin', why, then,
we'll call the thing settled; sha'n't we, Serissy?"

Mother did not speak for a moment; then she turned
towards me, but still without raising her eyes.

"It's all settled, Miny," she said; "you're to go with
Miss Runciman."

"That's the talk, mother!" exclaimed father; "now
you're sensible!" He went to her, and gave her a loud
kiss on the forehead. Then he turned to me, and said:
"You never 'll be so pretty as your mother, child; you
needn't never expect it, either. Now you c'n run away."

As I turned to go I saw him stoop and take mother's
hand, and her fingers closed around his.

I went up to my room, a sense of elation taking the place
of every other feeling. I began to look over my very
modest wardrobe, my heart beating delightfully as I did so.

Miss Runciman had mentioned a wool frock as something necessary. How curious it would be to drive about

and stop where one pleased, and to—but I could not go on coherently. My imagination ran wild. And how that woman had sung "Come, ye disconsolate," after my poor little piping! What could an "understudy" be? And where should we go?

I left my gowns on the bed and sat down by the window. I extinguished my light first, so that I might see into the beautiful night; but I remember that I did not think much of the beautiful night. My thoughts were galloping hither and thither into the future, and the color of rose was over everything.

At last I left the window and put my frocks back into the closet. It was already late for our household. The June days were long, and it had been dark now more than two hours. There was nothing for me to do down-stairs, so I undressed and crept into bed. But, of course, I did not go to sleep. I lay staring at the grayish patch in the wall, which was the window.

My eyes were thus when the door moved softly. I instantly dropped my eyelids, and did not stir as steps drew near. Some one—I did not need to look to know it was my mother—stooped over the bed. I heard a long-drawn breath. I was longing to let her know that I was not asleep, but something made me keep very still. Was it that I was afraid, if I spoke to her, I should suddenly tell her that I would not go? And I wanted to go—yes, I longed to go. Something brilliant and dazzling was beckoning to me and smiling. Mother had consented, and father had more than consented. I would keep still.

Presently mother sighed again. I thought she whispered, "God bless the child," and then she noislessly left the room. I turned and began to sob into my pillow.

The days went quickly enough after that, and with every

day I fancied mother's spirits seemed to rise, for every day made greater the probability that Miss Runciman, being a woman of whims, had forgotten her last whim. And all the time I wondered, among other things, what an understudy might be.

It was ten days later. June was getting well on, and I had now nearly given up the hope of going anywhere in a house-wagon with that great opera singer.

Miss Rachel Cobb, who lived on the river road, was spending the day at our house. Miss Cobb was fat, and she had eyes as small and bright as a pig's eyes; and a little mouth, with protruding teeth that made a kind of snout of the lower part of her face. When she talked, which was nearly all the time, her jaws clacked and snapped as if they were going by a sort of machinery that had been wound up, and that was not at all near to running down. Father, in the privacy of his own home, called her "piggie-wiggie," and said that it was a great mistake that she hadn't some front legs and a little tail with a curl in it.

Miss Cobb often referred to the fact that she had never married; and always said that if Timothy Hopkins had lived she was sure he would have married her, and that they would have been the happiest couple in the world.

"Not," she explained, "that Tim had ever paid her no attention, but that he was so homely there wouldn't no girl under the canopy but her have him."

Here she would chuckle, and her jaws would click, and her eye-glasses fall off.

When she told this at our house father would roar out his laugh, and say that Hopkins was the unluckiest man in creation because he was dead.

Here was Miss Cobb sitting near the open end window making some new sleeves to put into her brown flannelette "body." She always spoke of a dress waist as a "body," and the word never failed to affect me uncomfortably.

It was known throughout the neighborhood that Rachel Cobb's rule was to spend three days of every week visiting. It will be perceived that such a rule, closely adhered to as it was in this case in a country town, will bring a person with frequency to every house. But she did not stop at every house. She openly acknowledged that she couldn't bear to visit where "the victuals wasn't torrable good; for her stomach wasn't that kind that could bear everything tossed into it as if a person was nothin' more'n a hog. She'd got a digestion now, 'n' she meant to keep it," and so on—clack, clack, snap, snap.

"There's b'en a lot happenin' this week," said Rachel, as she ran her "shears" through her silesia lining. "I d' know 's you have heard nothin', have you, Serissy? You're one of them kind that don't ever seem to know no kind of news, even if you live right in the midst of it."

Aunt Lowizy, who was washing dishes in the kitchen, and continually running to the sitting-room door with a dish and a towel in her hand, now appeared, passing her towel around and around a blue-edged pie-plate.

"That's jes' so, Rachel," she remarked. "Serissy don't bring home no news, even when she goes to the ladies' aid, up to the vestry. News rolls off her as if 'twas water, 'n' she was a leather shoe all tallered up for winter."

At this the two women laughed, and mother smiled. She was slicing potatoes for the "shin stew" for our dinner. Her hands did not pause in their work, but Miss Cobb laid down her shears and contemplated her hostess. After a moment she said:

"There was Lyddy Lowndes, over t'other side the gris'-mill. She was a Adventist, 'n' she was jes' so. Some Adventists ain't more'n half on this earth, anyway; they're so taken up listening for Gabriel's trump they can't hear much else. I don't mean no offence, Serissy," resuming her shears. "I'm sure if I was expectin' the trump to sound, I shouldn't one grain mind who was married or dead. But I've noticed that when you're lookin' for Gabriel he don't never come."

The shears slashed through an extent of flannelette.

"But you 'ain't told your news, Rachel."

It was Aunt Lowizy who spoke; she had darted back to the sink, put down her dried plate, taken an undried one, and darted back again to the door.

"That's a fact, so I 'ain't "—click, clack, with jaws and shears. "Wall, 'twas las' night. I'd eat some hull corn for my supper over to Lorin Waite's; 'n' either there wa'n't sody enough put in it, or else 'twa'n't cooked enough; anyway, it didn't set well, 'n' I was up with my stomach pretty much all the time from ten o'clock till daylight broke. 'Tain't a pleasant thing to be up with your stomach when you ought to be gittin' your rest.

"'Bout 'leven I was sippin' some pain - killer, when I heard the sound of wheels, 'n' laughin', 'n' talkin'. Somehow the laughin' 'n' talkin' didn't seem jes' like folks' round here. I wropped a shawl tight over my shoulders, 'n' went to the front door. There was a great big carriage comin' awful slow 'long the river road, jest about by the falls. You know the scenery there is first-rate, 'n' folks come from quite a ways off to see the falls, 'n' the gorge, 'n' the mountains back there. I think myself it does look well, 'specially when the sun or the moon is risin' and shinin' on the falls. It was the moon that was shinin' on the water now; 'n' it glittered; the mountain was black where 'twa'n't in the light, 'n' everything was kind of strikin'.

" My house is near enough so I c'n watch the excursionists that come from off. 'n' see how odd they look when they're starin' at the scenery. Scenery does affect some folks queer enough sometimes, I tell you.

" This was a wagon different from what I'd ever seen; it had two great horses to it, 'n' when it stopped a tall woman got out and walked slow towards the edge of the river. Somebody in the wagon seemed to want to come, too, but the woman flung her hand at them—not like any one else flinging her hand—and she said : ' Come not, at your peril ! I would be alone !' That's exactly what she said, and then she laughed, and somebody inside the wagon laughed, too.

" I guess I kinder forgot 'bout my stomach, for I walked along in the black shadder of them hackmatack trees till I was considerable near. The wagon was something like a photygraph car, you know, only han'somer. There was a funnel runnin' out of the roof at one end. The harness on the horses glittered like anything, 'n' when they shook their heads some little bells jingled.

" I stood in the deepest shadder, 'n' watched. That woman had gone down to the river's edge, 'n' jes' then the moon had got to the top of the mountain, 'n' struck on her, 'n' on the falls. I could see her good 'n' plain—tall, with a red cloak fallin' from her shoulders, 'n' nothin' on her head. I s'pose she's a play-actor, or something of the kind. Jest as the moonlight reached her, she put up her clasped hands and began to sing. I will own up that I shivered up 'n' down my backbone, 'n' gooseflesh crept all over me. I tried to hear what she said. It sounded like ' Caster deever—caster deever.' I couldn't make out nothin' more. Some foreign language, I guess.

" She only sung two or three lines. Then somebody on

the back steps of the wagon, where I couldn't see, clapped
hands, 'n' hollered ' Brarver!' though there ain't no sense to
a word like that ; but what c'n you expect of folks that'll
travel 'round in a cart with horses with bells on 'em ?

"The woman kep' stan'in' there s' long that I began to
be shivery. So I went back real ca'ful to my house. I
took some more pain-killer to keep the cold from strikin' in.
I was jest thinkin' I'd run out agin, jest to see what they
was up to, when steps come to the front door 'n' then a
knock. I've lived too long all by myself to git frightened
very easy. So I marched right to the door 'n' opened it a
teenty crack. There was the woman who'd been singin'
'Caster deever.' You ain't 'fraid of nothin' but a man,
anyway, so I flung open the door and told her to walk in.
She stepped inside, and said she seen a light, so she ventured to come. I said yes, I'd been up with my stomach,
'n' had to take something. She gave me the curiousest look,
'n' said for her part she ' didn't know which of her internal
orgins she'd ruther be up with.' "

Having reached this point in her narrative, Rachel Cobb
paused as if she were leaving the chapter to be continued
at some indefinite future time. She lifted the old flannelette waist and contemplated it absorbedly. Aunt Lowizy
had come in and sat down with her towel and plate in her
hands. Mother had stopped paring potatoes, and her pale
face was turned steadily towards her guest.

"I declare!" cried Aunt Lowizy. "That's the same
woman, I do believe, Serissy!"

Rachel glanced shrewdly from one to the other. As for
me, I did not move, and I didn't take my eyes from Miss
Cobb.

"Well ?" said mother.

"Oh, there ain't so very much more to tell," responded

Rachel. "The woman had come in, 'n' I didn't make no reply to that remark of her'n. I was sorter nettled. I felt as if she was laughin' at me, though she was solemn as an owl.

"'I thought,' said she, the next thing, 'that p'raps I could get some milk here, or cream, for our coffee, 'n' mebby a fresh egg or two. We're jes' goin' to have supper.'

"'Supper!' I cried out, 'at this time er night?'

"'Oh, yes,' as easy 's you please; 'you know tastes vary!'

"'I sh'd think they did,' I says.

"'Can you let me have any milk?' she asked.

"Now, you know I 'ain't kep' no cow sence more'n two year ago, 'n' I told her I hadn't; 'n' how I come to sell it, 'n' not git another. That's quite a long story, you know. Serissy; 'n' I thought she oughter know that cow was gargety; 'n' how I felt sure she got the garget 'cause I fed her too much meal that last winter I kep' her.

"When I got through the woman said she thanked me warmly for the tale of the gargety cow—I'm giving her very words—'n' she hoped the cow wasn't havin' as much meal at the present time.

"'No,' I said, 'I guess she wa'n't, for she'd been put in the beef barrel 'n' et up long ago.'

"Then I ast her to se' down. She said she'd ruther stand; 'n' had I any milk I could let her have? She had been the solemnest-lookin' bein' you ever seen, but I felt eggsackly 's if she was laughin' at me the wust kind of a way; and it made me mad.

"I ripped out that I didn't use nothin' but condensed milk sence I sold my cow. I'd got 'bout a table-spoonful of that if she wanted it. No basket of chips was ever pleasanter 'n' she was. She explained that she was already the owner of several cans of condensed milk, but, bein' in the country, and so forth—and then she ast if my hens had become gargety and been sold, or did I have some eggs?

" I got her half a dozen eggs, 'n' I charged her twenty-five cents, though they ain't but thirty cents a dozen down to the store, I b'lieve. I don't care if they ain't.

" She took the eggs off in a corner of her cloak. When she got to the carriage, you should hev heard the laughin'. I put on my shawl agin', 'n' I crep' round in the shade till I was near enough to hear, 'n' I heard that woman goin' on an' sayin' jest what I'd be'n sayin' to her, 'n' I had to pinch myself to see if 'twas me talkin' or not. I was mad, but somehow I couldn't help laughin', too, to save my life.

" I heard another woman's voice, 'n' a man's voice; 'n' a half-grown boy was takin' the horses outer the sharves an' rubbin' 'em down. I stayed till I begun to shiver agin'; then I went back, 'n' I took more pain-killer, but I didn't hev a very restful night.

" I shouldn't wonder one mite if my body wouldn't fit my sleeves, nor my sleeves my body."

The transition from her night adventures to her present dressmaking was so abrupt that it was confusing.

Aunt Lowizy rose, and having forgotten the plate in her lap, it fell with a crash to the floor. She stooped and picked up the fragments mechanically, gazing at mother meanwhile.

" I do declare, Serissy!" she cried. " How curious things happen!"

Miss Cobb glanced sharply at the speaker, but she said nothing. She had not spent so much of her life in visiting without having learned a good deal about refraining from asking questions. She would interrogate an unsuspicious child if it were away from its guardians, but she was very wise in her refraining at other times.

Mother gave her sister a quick look, which Miss Cobb did not fail to see, and Aunt Lowizy retreated into the kitchen.

"I guess likely, from what you say, Rachel," said mother, with an air of being willing to tell everything. "that that woman you saw must be the one that bought Lemuel's gray colt."

"I want to know!" was the response. "Now, ain't that odd? I heard over by the Great Medders that she was a play-actress, 'n' he got a tremendous price. But he's one that always doos git good prices."

"It's a remarkably good colt," returned mother, with some severity, and Miss Cobb hastened to asseverate she knew it; oh yes, everybody from Great Medders clear down the river knew that gray Armstrong colt was real tiptop.

I remained sitting quietly in my chair until it seemed absolutely beyond my power to keep still longer. Perhaps Miss Runciman had not, after all, forgotten me; perhaps she would soon call; perhaps—here I rose abruptly. I felt mother's eyes on me, but I would not appear to notice them.

I caught up my big straw hat from the grind-stone in the shed where I had last flung it. I hastened with it in my hand out through the yard and along the low path that wound towards the river. This path was used by many people, for it cut off more than half a mile if one wished to go from our vicinity to the falls. It was along this path that Rachel Cobb had come in the morning with her reticule holding her silesia and her "body."

I had not gone many rods when something made me look back. There was mother standing at the shed door. I hesitated, a throb of rebellion in my heart. She was looking at me, but she made no sign to recall me. So I hurried on ; but there was still a faint pain which I resented. I said to myself that mother really must have strange notions; and she had told me I might go to Miss Runciman. Not that I was going to her now—by no means. I only meant to stroll along until I came near Miss Cobb's little house. There was no reason why I should not go to Miss Cobb's house ; it stood in the most picturesque spot in the town. I had often been there, and sat and gazed at the falls, and the gorge, and the far background of mountains.

There was Bidwell Blake just jumping over the fence into the path. Of course he saw me ; he always saw everything. He had a pitchfork over his shoulder, and a pail swung on the pitchfork.

" Hullo !" he cried. " Goin' down to see the circus ?"

I shook my head. The tall young fellow's face was positively animated. I was indignant, to begin with, for I knew what he had called a circus.

" Oh, you'd better by half go," he returned, standing leisurely in front of me. " Red 'n' yeller wagon, full of plate-glass winders; elephant goin' round; monkey dancin' on the grass; band playin'; flags a-flutterin' to the breeze; all free gratis, for nothin', 'n' nobody goin' to pass round the hat. Walk right up, ladies 'n' gentlemen. Tootle—too—tootle—too—tum !"

He put one hand to his mouth as if he were blowing a trumpet. His eyes laughed at me over his brown fist.

" You ought to get a place as clown somewhere, Bidwell," I said, with emphasis.

. " Oh, I've got a place now," he answered; " clown for Worthing, the Great Medders, 'n' the falls. Seen the circus wagon, Billy ? I ain't jokin'."

" Where is it ?"

I suppose there was something unusual in my face, for Bidwell suddenly gave me a keen, searching look, which I pretended not to see. He wheeled about and pointed down the valley.

"There, the other side of the birches. You can see smoke comin' out of that funnel."

"What is it?" I asked. I put the question as if I didn't much care whether he answered me or not.

"It's folks that don't know whether they tread on ye or not," with a quick ferocity in his tone — "folks that look at ye 's if you was dirt, 'n' they was goin' to rub their shoes in ye if they was a mind to. There he is now!"

The figure of a young man emerged from among the birches where the carriage stood. This figure lounged forward into the full sunlight. It was not very near, but my eyes were strong, and I saw that this stranger wore a short coat of gray, that his gray trousers ended at the knees, and were met by rough stockings. He had on no hat; his hands were thrust into his pockets. He appeared to be whistling, for the higher strains reached us.

"Who is he?" I asked, repeating my question with a change of pronoun.

"How do I know? There's a curious gang down there. That feller was over to our house this mornin'. He said he wanted to buy some chickens; 'n' he wanted a little pig to roast whole. Father was goin' to sell him something, but I come along jest then, 'n' when I seen the cut of that feller's jib I jest said up loud that we hadn't got nothin' to sell, not a darn thing."

"What did he say?"

"Oh, he looked me over 's if I was pu'sley, and he drawled, 'Nothin' but cheek, eh!' Then he whirled round 'n' walked away, he 'n' his brindle dorg behind him. I wanted to fire a stone at the dorg, but I didn't."

I was always quite frank with Bid Blake, and I was frank now, for I immediately informed him that he seemed to have acted like a fool. He swung his hayfork from his shoulder and leaned on it.

"Think so? Wall, I differ; that's all. Do you think I'm goin' to have a feller from a red 'n' yaller wagon, with short britches on his legs, come 'n' look me over? No, I ain't. How's your mar to-day, Billy?"

Bidwell made this inquiry with a rapid change to good-humor. I replied that mother was quite well. All the time I was looking at the figure further down the river, and this figure appeared entirely absorbed in contemplating the falls. But I was not really thinking intently of the strange young man. I was really wondering where Miss Runciman was.

"I'm awful sorry you've had 'advantages,' Billy," exclaimed my companion.

"Why?" I spoke vaguely.

"'Cause a girl like you 's good enough 'thout 'em. 'N' then, 'advantages' make ye kind of—wall, kind of far away, somehow."

"Oh, pshaw! They don't either."

"Yes, they do, too. I wish—"

I hardly heard him. Another person, a woman, had appeared from the direction of the wagon, and she was advancing towards the young man, who had not noticed her.

"Oh!" I exclaimed; "I wonder if that is she?"

Bidwell flung himself around. "What she you talkin' 'bout?" he asked, sharply.

"Oh, no; it isn't," I said, not paying any heed to him;

"it isn't her carriage; she isn't tall enough, and she isn't old enough. It's—it's somebody else."

A keen apprehension came to me. What if Miss Runciman had had another whim in regard to some one else, and taken that some one else, and. forgotten me? A black certainty that she had done so seized me.

"What's the matter?" asked Bidwell, apprehensively.

"Nothing. I'm going home."

I turned and began to retrace my steps hurriedly. The young man kept beside me until I was nearly frantic in my longing to be left by myself. I paused.

"I wish you'd go on!" I said, impatiently. After all, I had no chance of going with Miss Runciman. It was terrible. I was shut in the dark, away from full and glowing life. Not until this moment did I know how eager I had been. Why, I could not bear it.

"Won't you go?" I repeated, sharply.

"Yes, if you say so. But what in the world has happened?"—solicitously. "Do lem me help you, Billy!"

"I do say so!"

I couldn't even try to answer his other words.

Bidwell looked at me an instant; then he turned and hurried away in the direction from which he had come. When he had left me I stopped walking. I stood still until Bidwell had gone so far that there was no likelihood of his returning. And even then I hesitated.

At last, however, feeling tolerably certain that no one down there by the falls would see me, I slowly retraced my steps, watching those two who stood there gazing up the gorge. Yes, that was a young girl. Miss Runciman had changed her mind. I must give up all hope of going with her. My spirits sank and sank. Not being one who easily sheds tears, I did not shed them now. But I had a very

romantic, and, I thought, terrible conviction that my heart
was weeping. I had read of heroines whose hearts wept
while they themselves wore what was technically· termed
"gay masks."

I was certainly very unhappy. And I must really think
of some way of earning money. Of course father could sup-
port me, but even a girl has now and then a wish for an independent individual existence.

I had chosen to sit down under a small, thick, growing
pine. It did not seem to me that I should be observed. I
leaned my elbow on my knee and my chin in my hand and
gazed downward. Ah! some one else came from the neighborhood of the carriage now. Yes, that was Miss Runciman herself. She came slowly up to the group; they
seemed to talk; the elder lady gestured in that large, free
way of hers. Then she turned and looked about her; she
walked up and down the river-bank with her hands behind
her. I heard the high notes of something she was singing.
With her face in my direction, she suddenly paused. She
turned and appeared to speak to the young man who joined
her and gave her something from his pocket. The next
moment I was aware that an opera-glass was levelled at me.
My cheeks began to burn. Miss Runciman lowered the glass,
spoke again to the young man, who now left her, was lost a
moment to my sight, then appeared on the nearer side of the
thicket of birches. He was rapidly and unmistakably coming towards me. I rose in confusion. I wavered between a
desire to run away and a wish to remain. Of course I remained.

I watched the stranger's approach. He was bareheaded,
and I saw how white his forehead was, then how noticeably
luxuriant his hair was; his beardless face, square jaw, with
a decided cleft down the middle of the chin; and yet, in

spite of that chin, his long, dark eyes gave a sort of dreamy, foreign look to his face. There was no dreamy look in it now, however, as he came up the slope towards me; and my after-fancies concerning his countenance are here prematurely put down. This was the man to whom Bidwell Blake wouldn't sell chickens because he, Bidwell, was made to feel like dirt!

I sat perfectly still and grew more and more excited. It does not require much to excite a girl who lives in a place like Worthing. There was the brindle dog, nosing leisurely along at some distance behind his master.

This young man came up to within a few yards of me, paused, and bowed.

"I beg your pardon," he said, "but are you Billy?"

"Yes."

"Then I am to ask you to go down there," waving his hand in the direction from which he had come. "Miss Runciman sent me for you. Miss Runciman is my aunt. If she wants a thing, she has to have it. She wants you."

I rose, but I didn't feel quite like going with him, now that I had lost my chance. That is the way I looked at it. Miss Runciman had some one else, and I had lost my chance. I stood in evident indecision.

"Come," said the young man.

"But I don't know that I want to go," I responded. My glance slid away from his somewhat mocking eyes. In point of fact, I was afraid that if I met Miss Runciman she would discover how disappointed I was. And I was angry with her for playing with me.

The brindle dog came up to me now and sniffed at my skirts, then licked my hand.

"No," I said, suddenly, "I think you may ask Miss Runciman to excuse me."

And as I spoke I was afraid I should choke in the intensity of my anger and disappointment. It was mean of her—yes, mean of her.

The young man did not look at me now. He stood glancing down the valley, with his hand on the top of his dog's head. But I had a conviction that there was a hint of amusement in the corner of his mouth. As this conviction came to me I was glad that the Blakes hadn't sold him a little pig or any chickens. I stood up quite stiffly.

"Please ask Miss Runciman to excuse me," I repeated, in a tone to match my attitude.

He turned away without speaking, and began to run down the path. Was he laughing? I was almost certain he was laughing. Now, in the light of a great deal of wisdom acquired since that day, I know that I ought at this stage to have made a dignified retreat. But I did not. I sat down again under the pine-tree, and I watched Miss Runciman's messenger until he joined her and related his adventures. I saw them all turn and look up to where I was sitting. I suppose they were all laughing.

In a moment Miss Runciman left her companions and began walking up towards me. Then I began to be ashamed of my childishness. How could they know that it was because of my disappointment that I was behaving in this fashion? Miss Runciman came on easily and lightly. She wore a loose blouse waist, abbreviated skirt, and heavy shoes. She walked directly to me, where I waited in a foolish agony. She came and put her hand on my shoulder.

"What's the matter?" she asked, authoritatively.

IV

" NOTHING," I answered.

Into what an idiotic position I had put myself! Miss Runciman's eyes dwelt upon me as she stood there silently. Then she asked:

"Are you sulking?" I tried to put on an air of dignity.

" Sulking?" I repeated, not too politely. "Why should I do that?"

" Indeed, I don't know; but you seem amazingly like a sulking child who ought to be whipped."

Having made this very humiliating remark, the lady sat down not far from me and occupied herself with gazing at the scenery. If I had done just what I longed to do at that moment I should have screamed savagely. My present attitude was all my own fault, and for that reason I was furiously indignant with what I called fate. It's such a fine thing to be indignant with fate.

The moments went by, and still my companion contemplated the prospect. My furtive glance at her showed me a serene face turned towards the mountain. I looked down the river-bank; the two figures were gone.

Now, when I had thought I had successfully overcome all symptoms of "going to pieces," I suddenly began to cry. I was bitterly ashamed of myself, but I couldn't stop, try as I would. I know that Miss Runciman turned and looked at me in a puzzled way, in which there was some impatience. I heard her exclaim:

"What queer things women are!" and then, in a voice below her breath, "I didn't think this one was of the crying kind."

I was stung. I flung up my head.

"No more I ain't!" I cried out fiercely, my tears burning on my cheeks.

"Oh!"

"I'm not," I repeated; "I don't cry once in a hundred years—mother 'll tell you that. But I've been suffering. Yes, and you made me, and I've hoped, and hoped; and then you didn't come—nor send—and I tried to give it all up, and the more I tried the more it hurt. And it's too bad, too awfully bad, of you to be a woman of whims! There, now, I've said it!"

My tears were effectually dried now, you may be sure. I didn't care what I said. The accumulated hope and uncertainty of the past fortnight were pushing the words out of my lips. I sprang to my feet. I blush now as I remember my impertinence. I was rushing away when I heard the words:

"My dear child!" The tone of them was like a hand laid on my arm, and I stood still. What storms youth does invoke!

"Sit down here by me," were the next words. I hesitated, but I obeyed the next moment.

After a silence Miss Runciman asked:

"Have you had a quarrel with your lover?"

This question seemed contemptible to me. That she had asked it injured my ideal of her.

"I told you I had no lover," I replied.

"So you did: I remember. But you know it is a tradition

of the world to ascribe any real suffering of the grown femi-
nine to some masculine."

I made no answer. I was still quivering with my recent
emotion. And now she was disappointing me by talking
thus! Had I not just told her? Was she stupid, after all,
this great prima donna?

"Is it the simple truth you've been telling me?" she inquired after a time.

"Yes."

She turned towards me smiling.

"Though I've been a young girl myself," she said, "I still
think a young girl is the most mysterious thing God has
ever created."

Of course I had no reply to make to this. And I didn't
know what she meant, either. That was a very foolish way
people had of talking about girls.

"You didn't seem very eager to come with me when I saw
you in Chilton," she said.

"But I was eager," I answered, in a low voice. Then I
hurriedly continued: "Mother didn't want me to go—mother
thought that—that it was something glittering but not good,
that—that— But, oh, dear! I didn't mean to tell—I—
What must you think of me?"

I looked at the face near me. It was smiling, but there
was a bright gleam in the eyes that I could not understand.
She did not speak, and I went on:

"But, now you've got some one else, it's all over. And
mother will be glad—yes, mother will be very glad." I
tried hard to get comfort from this fact.

"I haven't got any one else," said Miss Runciman.

I turned towards her, but I did not speak. She gazed at
me for an instant, then she exclaimed:

"Oh, youth! youth!"

What did she mean by that? She laughed gently.

"I certainly was not mistaken. You have the violin face. But when am I mistaken in such matters? Oh, I know some things about the divine, human countenance!"

Here she fell silent again, gazing at me. As for me, I didn't think much of what she had just said. Perhaps that was the way great opera singers liked to talk. I was fast growing happy. I had been mistaken. She had no one else. I had rashly jumped to a conclusion, and she had not let us hear from her for so long. But nothing mattered now. I had not lost my chance. My soul was growing radiant again. She still watched me. At last she said that she didn't know why I should think she had some one else.

"Because—because there's that girl down there. Of course I thought you were going to make her into an understudy. And you said you were a woman of whims."

I was surprised at my boldness. Miss Runciman's laugh rang clearly. She seemed much amused. She suddenly bade me walk about a little on the level ground in front. I rose and walked about, forgetting in my newly come good spirits to be self-conscious.

"Now stand where you are and sing me a bit of something," she commanded.

It was a curious thing that I could think of nothing this time also but "Come, ye disconsolate," and I was ashamed to try that again.

"Come!" imperatively.

My mind was one sheet of white paper with "Come, ye disconsolate" written on it. The blood rose to my face and threatened to burst from it.

"I can't," I said, feebly.

"Good heavens! You're not a stick, are you?" she exclaimed.

Then I dashed wildly into—

> " I'll chase the antelope over the plain,
>   The tiger's cub I'll bind with a chain ;
>   The wild gazelle with its silvery feet
>   I'll give thee for a playmate sweet."

That was what Aunt Lowizy sang sometimes from morning till night as she worked about the house. On such days father used to say, "Lowizy's got onto her wild gazelle." Miss Runciman rose as I finished.

"You've been crying, and your voice shows it," she remarked. "Now, let's go down to the carriage, and then you can go home and tell your mother you've seen me."

I followed her as she walked on along the path. Often she stopped to look about her, but presently we were at the river's edge, and then I saw two figures sitting on a black bearskin which was spread beneath a hackmatack by the bank. These two rose and came forward. One of them was the young man whom Miss Runciman had sent for me. The other was a girl about my own age, I judged. She was dressed in a short flannel suit, and altogether had apparently as much freedom of movement as the young man. This freedom, though it seemed desirable to me, yet also had a quite indescribable flavor of something not respectable. I wished to gaze unrestrainedly at her, but I had no opportunity, particularly as she was staring at me with undisguised persistence. She stood leaning on a rough stick she had evidently just cut from a clump of chestnuts near her ; and she had an open pocket-knife in her hand. The young man, who had called himself Miss Runciman's nephew, was behind her, looking over her head. I could not but have a feeling that they considered me a country creature who could be examined quite at their leisure. I stood straight, and shut my mouth to keep it from quivering.

"You've heard me speak of Miss Armstrong, children?" said the elder lady.

The girl nodded and resumed the trimming of her walking-stick. She glanced up to say: "You called her Billy."

"So I did. I hope she forgives me. Vane, come out here—don't hide behind your sister."

The young man stepped forth.

"Miss Armstrong, let me present my nephew, Vane Hildreth. He has a pretty tenor voice. He can already do a lover on the stage very well."

"Not so well as I can, Miss Armstrong," said the girl, quickly. "Young men don't know how to make love until we've taught them. I did Romeo once; you ought to have heard and seen me. Romeo had a contralto voice; he couldn't have sung a tenor note to save his life. And a girl fell in love with me and sent me a bouquet with a three-cornered note in it. Oh, Jupiter! I wish girls were not always fools."

"So do I," I responded, fervently, whereat we both laughed.

"So don't I," exclaimed Mr. Hildreth, "for if girls were not sometimes fools, who would smile upon us?"

No one paid any attention to this remark. The girl now said that she had not been introduced, and she thought that she was worth knowing.

"So you are, Bathsheba," responded Miss Runciman, "and you never will fail because you hang in the background. She's my niece, Miss Hildreth," continued the speaker, glancing at me.

"Commonly known as Bashy," amended the girl. "We'll make a fine team, Bashy and Billy."

Here she laughed shrilly and showed a great many very white, sharp-looking teeth. She had a look as if she might, if she were angry, defend herself by biting. I did not know why I should begin to feel homesick. I tried to think of something to say that should be an opening for me to go away, but I could think of nothing. I stood silent and awkward. Finally I summoned courage to announce that I must go home.

"Let us sing something first," cried the girl.

"Oh, no, no! I can't!"

I shrank. Somehow my independent spirit deserted me before Bathsheba Hildreth.

"But everything here hangs upon whether one can sing," responded Bashy. "We don't ask if you're good, or beautiful, or anything, but can you sing?"

"Pshaw!" exclaimed Miss Runciman, impatiently.

"But isn't it true, what I say, Aunt Nora?" lifting unblenching eyes to the elder woman.

"It's of no consequence, anyway," was the response.

"Miss Armstrong," said the girl, "don't you believe her. It's just like this: If you were suspected of murder, and forgery, and a few other trifles, and you came to my aunt, she wouldn't ask if you were guilty; she would want to know if you had a natural voice, and how many octaves. Oh, we are an awful lot! We don't care much about the Ten Commandments. Thou shalt not sharp — above all things, thou shalt not flat; and thou shalt learn the Rubini method. Aunt Nora, you know I'm telling the truth."

" I think it's time for me to go home," I said again to my hostess.

"You see you have frightened the child, Bashy," said Miss Runciman, with some severity.

5

"No; I'm not frightened, and I'm not a child," I responded, with dignity.

The girl laughed as she whittled at her stick. The young man, her brother, as I understood, had walked away. I saw him lying on the bearskin, reading.

"Good-bye!"

I looked at Miss Runciman as I spoke.

"You won't mind Bashy after a little," she remarked.

"Oh, no," I answered; "I sha'n't mind her."

I looked over at the girl as I spoke. My fingers were tingling with anger. I could hardly tell why I was so angry. And a wild, silly hope that I might be able to sing better than she came to me. I knew it was wild and silly, but I could not put it from me. I wanted to sing better, far better, than that girl who was laughing and whittling, and who was despising me. Wasn't she despising me? Our eyes met for an instant. She had small eyes, but they were well set, sparkling, and expressive.

"Good-bye," I said once more to Miss Runciman.

"Very well, if you must go," more indifferently than I had expected her to speak. "I think we shall remain here for a few days. It's really delightful, and then we are near Miss Rachel Cobb," with a laugh. "Do you know Miss Rachel Cobb?"

"Yes; she is at our house this moment," I answered.

Then I nodded at Bathsheba Hildreth and walked away. I was choking. Everything was ruined by that horrid girl. I doubled my hands into fists as I hurried up the path. But I wanted to hear her sing. I must really hear her. I had as little technical knowledge as one may have, but I could trust to my natural taste to tell me something of her powers. Oh, yes, I would hear that girl sing before another twenty-four hours had passed. I went faster and faster; the pace I was going was the only expression I could give to my excitement.

In the kitchen of my home I found Aunt Lowizy and Miss Cobb. The latter informed me directly that her body wouldn't fit nothin', and there wouldn't nothin' fit her body; so she'd given up tryin', after having spoiled two yards of flannelette and a yard and a half of silesia. She was sitting with her hands resting on her lap. She looked at me with exceeding sharpness. She asked me if I felt as well as usual, and had I seen Bid Blake?

To both of these questions I answered yes. She then remarked that Bid had jest been there, and that she for one thought there was something heavy on his mind. She had made inquiries and he had told her that he had never felt quite so well in his life; but she knew better. There was something on Bid's mind, or else set her down for a hen with her head cut off. Having said so much, she suddenly asked:

"You seen um, I'll bet?"

I looked at her in momentary indecision. Then I answered that I had.

"Did they want to buy something?"

"No."

"Wall, they will. 'N' you'll feel 's if—oh, land, p'raps you won't, either! Mebby you're one of them kind yourself. Jew see um all?"

"I guess so."

"How many was they?"

I told her.

"That ain't all. There's a boy that tends to the hosses. I'm bound to see every one of um. They can't put me down—no, sir, they can't do it."

Mother came into the room at this moment. Yielding

to a strong impulse, I went to her quickly. I was about to throw my arms about her when I caught Miss Cobb's eyes on me.

"You look kinder hystrikey," she remarked.

"I am," I responded; "and if I am, I have a right to be."

Then I flung out of the room and ran to the barn. I climbed into the hay mow and sat down on the hay. I hoped mother would come here to find me. But the moments passed and no one came. I had plenty of time to decide that I had no reason to expect mother. I leaned back on the hay. The new crop was still to be put in, the most of it; but I was lying upon a pile of fresh-cured grass that had been tossed up into the mow but the day before. Its fragrance filled the place. I looked up into the roof. From rafter to rafter were the same dusty, voluminous cobwebs that had been there ever since I could remember. They were swaying now in the warm wind that swept through the open windows, and in at these windows the barn swallows were flying and sweeping about in the peak of the roof. I looked at them until their movements grew dimly rhythmic, then more vague. I was asleep in that blessed way that allows you to know you are asleep.

Very soon, or I thought it was very soon, I heard steps on the floor below, then on the stairs. Mother was coming at last. I did not take the trouble to open my eyes. I lay there half-awake in that delicious state which sometimes comes between sleeping and walking, thinking absolutely nothing, conscious of life as a happy baby ought to be conscious of it.

Yes, the steps had ascended the stairs. I lazily opened my eyes and saw a man standing hat in hand not far from me, gazing at me. I sat up quickly, feeling the blood surge up into my face.

"Mr. Ronald Maverick!" I exclaimed.

The man bowed. "I suppose you're Mr. Armstrong's daughter?" he said.

"Yes."

I had a confused wonder as to whether he knew how fine he looked. He was dressed in white duck, even to his shoes, and the hat in his hand was white also. To my surprise I noticed now that he was somewhat bald. My eye unconsciously sought the diamond on his finger; yes, there it was, sparkling in the gloom of the hay mow.

"If I only knew you a little more, I'd ask you to let me sit down on this hay," he now said.

I made no reply to this remark. I didn't wish to have him sit here. I rose.

"Father expected you more than a week ago," I informed him.

"Yes; I meant to come then, but I was detained, and as it was so uncertain when I could come, I didn't write. I hope he can get me a horse?" questioningly.

"Oh, father can always get a horse if anybody wants one," I answered. Then Mr. Maverick said, "So glad, I'm sure," and laughed a little, showing beneath his carefully trained mustache a great deal of gold in his teeth.

I wanted to ask after Cornelia, but I knew I mustn't do that, so I stood silent until I could think what to say.

"Won't you come in the house and wait for father? He's only gone to the village to get his mowing-machine mended."

"Thank you; I'll stay out-of-doors. I don't want to be in a house if I can help it."

He stood aside deferentially for me to move towards the stairs. Then he followed. When we were in the barn-yard he asked if I would tell him which way was the pleas-

antest for a stroll.   I hesitated.   Then I answered that I
liked all the ways, but strangers usually went down the path
to the falls.   He looked at me as if he were going to ask
me to accompany him; but he said nothing.   He only made
one of his impressive bows that somehow gave me the feeling that I was a very attractive sort of a person.   Then he
started on down the river-path and I went into the house,
giving the information that a "man wanted father."   This
I felt to be extremely meagre and insufficient in regard to a
being like Mr. Ronald Maverick.

Rachel Cobb was just putting her scissors and thimble
and "body" and silesia into a much rubbed leather bag
which had always accompanied her in her years of visiting.
She was telling mother that "she thought she'd better go
home early, for somehow she kinder felt 's if she ought to
be round 's long 's that set of folks in the long wagon was
down by the falls."

As she tied the strings of her sunbonnet she looked at me
and informed me that she was hopin' I'd come, for she
wanted me to go back with her, 'n' she'd send some of the
seedlin' strawberries by me in time for our supper.   The
seedlin's was jest in their prime now.   I did not manifest
any eagerness to accept this invitation.   I was not particularly happy in Miss Cobb's society, but Aunt Lowizy now
said she did hope I'd go.   So I found my hat and walked
out with Miss Cobb.

There was a bicycle leaning against a fence.   I had not
seen this before.   My companion called it "one of them
critters," and guessed that the feller in white down there
ahead of us must have come on it.   So I guessed, though
he was not in cycling suit.   We had not gone far along the
path before Rachel turned her sunbonnet towards me and
from its depths said, in a mysterious voice:

"I've jest found out her name. It's Runciman. That's why I wanted you to come with me. That's why I thought of the seedlin's; though I guess there is some left that you can take with ye."

I immediately felt the sting of a vital interest. But what did she mean? I asked her. Her jaws snapped and clacked with great vivacity as she answered:

"Why, I mean that woman that b'longs in the wagon. I didn't know her name. Your mother says it's Runciman. Now I jest want you to see something 'bout her. I knew I reck'lected the minute your mother spoke the word. 'Tain't a common name, somehow. I'll show ye. I saved the paper; but I always save papers, for kindlin', you know. This is a Philadelphy paper; come 'round some cotton flannel that Miss Rill sent me; Miss Rill's brother 'Gustus 's in Philadelphy—works there. That's how 'Melia Rill come to have it, you see. I guess I know jest where to lay my hand on it; I guess it's the third paper from the bottom in the old pile. It's quite a spell ago. But I remember jest as plain. Land! I guess I do! I tell ye what 'tis, Wilhelminy Armstrong, when you see a woman kinder dif'rent 'n' kinder takin', somehow, 'n' kinder not takin', either, you may jest be sure 't there's be'n somethin' or other in their lives that won't bear too much light."

Here the clicking stopped for a moment, and Miss Cobb turned the opening in her sunbonnet to me again, gazing intently at me, her gaze seeming intensified by the concentration, if I may call it thus, of her glance in the bottom of her bonnet.

"I've been awful 'fraid, sometimes," she said, "when I've be'n thinkin' of you, Wilhelminy, that you was one of them kind yourself. I hope not; I do hope not, for your poor mother's sake!"

" What kind ?" I asked, sharply.   " That I'd done something to be ashamed of ?"

" No—not that, eggsackly.   I can't tell jest what I do
mean.   I s'pose now you're mad 's you can be, ain't you?"

" I am—some mad," I acknowledged.

Then I asked myself why I should care what this woman
said ; and why her words should produce a kind of excitement as well as indignation.   I tried to laugh.

" I always did say you hadn't ought to have be'n sent
to that boardin'-school.   You ought to have be'n kep' to
home."

I stopped in my walk and I caught hold of Miss Cobb's
arm.   "What do you mean ?" I asked.   "What's the matter
with me ?"

" Nothin'," with a sharp click, " 'n' I'm jest a fool, that's
all.   Here we be 'most to the bars."

At the bars she paused long to enough say :

" I s'pose 'twas your face 's you come in to-day after
you'd seen them folks that made me say such foolish
things.   But you always was kind of a favoright of mine.
Yes, here we be to the bars.   That top one 'most always
sticks.   How strong you be !" as the rail clattered down
beneath my hands.   " Come right in 't the back door.   Can
you see any of them folks stirrin' ?   No, there ain't nobody
in sight.   Likely 's not they're gone to bed.   Folks that
stay up all night 'n' have suppers of hearty victuals at
eleven o'clock must go to bed some time."

Miss Cobb began to fit the key in the door, but her eyes
were so drawn down to the locality where one could dimly
distinguish the glossy, bright side of the wagon among the
trees that her key went here and there, but not into its proper
place.   I stood as patiently as I could.   I was thinking of
the third paper from the bottom in the old pile.

At last Miss Cobb's key went in quite accidentally and was turned; the door opened, and I followed my companion into the little "entry" that was not large enough to hold us without a great deal of crowding. How hot it was at the west side of that bit of a house! It stood sheltered from the wind, and the sun had been shining on it all the afternoon. There was a close smell, as of heated flannel, diffused in the rooms.

"It doos git close here," remarked the owner. "You se' down."

I sat down, gasping. There was one plate, one cup and saucer, and one spoon, with a knife and fork, set rigidly on a table drawn against the wall. The cover was large blue and white squares, over which a few flies walked investigatingly. Rachel said she liked to have her table set; it seemed more social like. To me it appeared one of the most desolate, unsocial sights I had ever seen.

Miss Cobb hung her bag on one of a row of nails that ran along against the wall. She hung her sunbonnet on another, patted her hair a little, then went straight to a closet, the door of which she flung open. She brought a chair and climbed into it. I saw piles of newspapers. I rose and also walked to the closet. I eagerly held out my hand, and I knew that my hand trembled. She had been right. She knew just where to find what she sought.

"There!" she dropped the paper towards me. "You jest see what you make of it. There's several places where she's mentioned."

I walked out of doors, notwithstanding her request that I read where I was. There was a chopping-block standing by a pile of "trash wood." I sat down on this block. The first thing my eye caught was a paragraph beginning:

"Perhaps Miss Runciman is not Miss Runciman at

all." I read rapidly. "This famous—or shall we say noto-
rious?—woman declined to state, when questioned, whether
her name is really the name by which she has become so
well known. She said that was her affair, which is very
true. She has displayed a good deal of shrewdness and
sagacity. Probably she is a genius. At any rate she is as
good, or as bad, as a genius. And now, more than ever,
people are flocking to hear her sing. And she sings better than ever, with an indescribable fervor, passion, *abandon*, which sweep her audience along. Still, she never
oversteps; there is always that subtle restraint which, after
all, is the hall-mark of genius. Leonora Runciman's vogue
was never greater than now."

I read this paragraph through twice, each time as if with
one sweep of my eye. Then I turned the sheet; I turned
it about and about. Presently I saw another paragraph :

"The crowd at the opera went wild over Miss Runciman's Lucia last night. It was really magnificent. It is
a curious fact that the women stand her friends as they
do. They say she is the most maligned person in the
world just now. But women, when they do take up another woman, are as unreasonable as a flock of sheep.
It is likely to be all feeling with them. There is one
woman, however, who will not, probably, profess any love
or admiration for the prima donna, and that is Mrs. Drew
Hollander."

What did these insinuations mean? Of course I did
not know; but the keen bitterness, the sneer, I did recognize.

My heart was sinking like lead. What if mother knew
this? I was not aware that sometimes too much weight
need not be given to the innuendo of a newspaper; I was
ignorant that some papers print a paragraph one day that

they may deny it the next. Anything in a public print was of mighty consequence to me.

I hurriedly scanned every bit of the paper. But I could find nothing more, save the advertisement of the appearance of Miss Runciman in *Ernani*. Of course Rachel Cobb had found this. She found everything. I wished to do some bodily injury to her. Why was she nosing about among 'Melia Rill's old things? I flung the paper from me with an exclamation. I saw Rachel's face at the window over the sink. She was looking out at me. The breeze carried the paper away, and I heard it rustle as if a hand had caught it. A hand had caught it. Miss Runciman herself was coming along the path that led to the door. She was carrying a small basket. She was probably coming for more eggs. This was my frivolous thought as I first saw her.

"Well," she said, "what has the poor newspaper done? And do you think Miss Cobb's hens have laid any eggs to-day?"

I did not notice her words; I only heard them mechanically. I jumped down from the chopping-block and walked towards the lady. I was foolishly excited. If I had had time to think I should not have said what I did.

"Miss Runciman," I asked, quickly, "why was it that the women stood your friends?"

She seemed to stiffen slightly as she stood; but I did not notice that her face changed; I was not, however, very well acquainted with her face, yet—

"What?" she said.

"TO YOU, MY LOVE, TO YOU"

"WHY did the women stand your friends?" I repeated as steadily as I could; but I was now beginning to be frightened at my own audacity in putting the question at all.

Miss Runciman began to smile. Her eyes sparkled. She glanced down at the paper crushed in her grasp. And I, following her glance, had a curious notion that that strong hand might crush a great many things. But before she made any reply she put her basket on the ground and examined the paper.

"Ah!" she said, "ten years ago! Newspaper rot ten years old! Who has been giving you this stuff?" (Her eyes travelled over the columns as she spoke.)

"Miss Rachel Cobb," I replied, concisely.

"Oh! And she is doubtless watching us now from somewhere. Yes, there she is!"

Certainly, Rachel was still looking through the window over the sink.

Miss Runciman nodded at the face as seen through the glass. "Good-morning, Miss Cobb!" she called out.

Miss Cobb left her place of observation and came to the open door. She looked confused.

"It was 'Melia Rill's paper," she said. "Her brother 'Gustus has worked in Philadelphy for a good many years."

She actually had the air of apologizing.

"I'm sure you ought to be grateful to 'Melia Rill," responded Miss Runciman. "You are, aren't you?"

"Yes," answered Rachel; and then, hastily, "I mean no, I ain't grateful; I don't care nothin' about it; it ain't nothin' to me."

"But you saved the paper, my dear Miss Cobb. You had a feeling that you'd need it some time, eh?"

The speaker's eyes, with metallic brightness, looked over the old maid's figure in a relentless way.

Rachel rallied. She stood more firmly, and she grasped the side of the door with one hand. Her little pig-like face grew braver.

"I d' know," she said, "'s you need to look at me like that, Miss Runciman, if you be Miss Runciman, or whoever you be, anyway. I guess I've got a right to save 'Melia Rill's old papers if I want to. Yes," gathering courage, "'n' I guess I've got a right to show um, too."

"Bravo!" cried Miss Runciman, and there was such a sneer in her face and voice that I quite shrank for Rachel's sake.

"I d' know what you mean by your outlandish words," said the woman in the doorway.

She turned away and sat down. I could see her sitting there looking white and tired.

Miss Runciman saw her, too, and the next moment her aspect changed. The glitter left her eyes. She advanced to the doorway. How cordial her voice was as she said:

"We are not going to quarrel, though, are we, Miss Cobb? If you knew as much about public life and newspapers as I do you wouldn't have saved this thing," dropping the paper on the floor. She had now evidently cast the whole matter behind her. She went on, still with that air of good-fellowship: "I do hope your hens have laid some more eggs, Miss Cobb. I want every one you can spare."

Rachel drew a long breath. She gazed wonderingly at the woman before her. I don't know why there seemed something pitiable in her appearance to me at that moment. Her face changed from its expression of anger and suspicion to something I had never before seen on her countenance. But then I had never taken much notice of Rachel Cobb's face, save to be glad mine was not like it, not that mine was anything to boast of, Heaven knows. She rose; she extended her hand for the basket.

"I guess I c'n spare you a few," she said. "You'd better come in while I git um."

As Miss Runciman stepped over the threshold I walked away. But I purposely kept in the path that she would naturally take when she returned to her carriage.

Presently I sat down under a tree and waited. It was very hot; the tree branches hardly protected me from the afternoon sun that kept searching me out more and more warmly. But I was not hot; I was cold: I seemed to be cold with suspicious questioning. Who was Mrs. Drew Hollander, and why wouldn't she stand by the prima donna? And perhaps, if father knew about those paragraphs, even he would withdraw his consent to my going with that woman. And I kept thinking of what mother had said about something that was glittering, but was not good. More and more I was convinced that I must find out for myself whether it was good or not.

The sun was certainly very bright. I turned; I stretched myself out on the grass, with my head so that my gaze could take in the space down below there at the foot of the falls. The lovely mist rose up from the falling water; I heard the soft monotone of the falls. Yes, and in a moment I heard something else—a female voice, not far from me, beginning to sing. I held myself rigidly still, for I did not wish to lose a note. I was sure it was Bathsheba Hildreth singing. At first she seemed to be playing with a few notes, tossing them about and catching them again. I had always envied the possessor of a contralto voice, and now I began to envy this girl.

I couldn't make out at all what she was singing, for at last she did sing some song—or, rather, a sort of recitative, which changed into a song, mellow and sweet and persuasive, but surely lacking somehow. I was wicked, for I was distinctly glad that this voice was lacking. I knew I was mean-spirited. Gradually I sat up, that I might listen the better. I had no more than gained an upright, sitting position than the singing stopped, and at the same moment I was saying to myself: "She flats; it is horrible to flat." I began to go over in my mind, on a higher key, what I had just heard.

Almost immediately a man's voice, farther away—Vane Hildreth's voice—took up the tune lightly, but dropped it directly to say, with brotherly frankness :

"I don't see that you get over your flatting in the least."

"I didn't ask you whether I did or not," was the retort.

There was a slight rustling, then a hand put aside a branch close to me, and Miss Hildreth's face appeared among the green leaves. "You've been listening!" she exclaimed.

I nodded.

"Well, then, do you think I flat?" she asked.

I hesitated, then I nodded again.

"Oh, the devil you do!" said this young lady. Then: "You mustn't mind my saying 'the devil.' It's enough to make any one say it, and worse to be told that you flat. But I don't believe it, all the same. I kept to the key. Just listen!"

She burst tumultuously into something that I knew afterwards was a song of Azucena's. I thought she sang gloriously, and told her so.

"But did I flat?"

"Ye-es," I answered, hesitatingly.

"Are you sure?"

"Yes."

Then, to my utter surprise, Bathsheba Hildreth threw herself forward on the grass and began to cry with fury and considerable noise. I did not quite dare to beg of her to stop. She paused in her sobs long enough to articulate indistinctly: "You must know that the woman who flats is as bad as the one who hesitates."

Then she sobbed again.

"But I don't know what becomes of her," I said.

She raised her swollen face. "Oh, the d— I mean oh, good gracious! Don't you? Oh, that is good!"

"Is it?" I asked, irritably.

"Yes, indeed!"

She sat up. "Why," she said, "she is lost."

"Oh!"

I was deeply chagrined. I thought some one might have told me before this about that woman.

This ignorance of mine seemed to compensate Miss Hildreth in some way for my having told her she flatted. She drew a handkerchief from the pocket of her blouse and dried her face.

Somebody else now came from the other side of the tree. It was Miss Hildreth's brother, and he inquired:

"Was that you blubbering, Bashy?"

"No; it was Miss Armstrong," was the prompt reply. "She was crying because she can never hope to sing as well as I do."

The young man looked at me and took off his cap with great gravity.

" Be sure you are right technically," he said, as if he were giving a lesson. " First be as mechanically correct as a machine, then put all the feeling you choose into your voice, but be a machine first."

" Oh, bosh !" from the sister.

"That's one reason why Bashy fails," he went on; "she has omitted the machine stage, and another reason is, she hasn't the voice. Two serious defects, Miss Armstrong."

I could not help gazing curiously at these two people. But they did not appear to notice me much. I wondered if they knew anything about Mrs. Drew Hollander. But that had been " newspaper rot ten years ago," and ten years ago these two, like myself, had been far more childish than we were at present.

Vane Hildreth looked at me now.

" Perhaps, as the Dominie says in *Guy Mannering*, you will kindly cantata with us — just for fun, you know, Miss Armstrong."

"Oh no ! No !"

His eyes dwelt on my face.

" I think you can sing," he said. " I suppose not at present, but some time."

I rose. I said something about being obliged to go. I hurried away and almost ran into Miss Runciman, but, fortunately, I did not break the eggs she was carrying in the basket. She paused in her walk.

"What have they been doing to you ?" she asked.

" Nothing."

I had glanced at the woman's face. It was cold and hard, and the metallic glitter was in her eyes. She did not

6

linger.   If I had ever thought she was interested in me I did not think so now.   She walked on without saying another word, and I hurried back home, feeling snubbed and discarded, and wondering how I could ever, even in view of her own words, have had any belief in Leonora Runciman's apparent interest in me.

I found the family just sitting down to the supper-table. Father was in excessively good spirits.   He had just sold a horse to Mr. Maverick, who was coming the next day for the animal.

" I tell you," said father, " I made him pay for wearin' a ring like that.   I ast him exactly fifty dollars more on account of that di'mond."   Here the speaker gave a laugh and reached forward for more griddle-cakes.

" But, Lemuel," began mother, in her gentle voice, " do you think that was quite fair ?"

" Pooh !" good-naturedly; " you jest tend to your religion, Serissy, 'n' I'll run the other kind of things.   I know more about a hoss trade in a minute than you'd know in a year. I'm goin' to git you 'n' Billy some kind of a present with that extra fifty dollars."   He looked at me.   " How's the opery business, Billy ?"

I said, gloomily, that I didn't know.   Mother glanced at me anxiously, but father went on with his griddle-cakes, smacking and gurgling over them.   I felt sick and tired of everything.   Life seemed one great confusion, and I felt myself very old.

I washed the dishes and hurried off to walk somewhere until bedtime.   I did not want to even see mother.   I was continually thinking of Miss Runciman's cold, hard face.   I don't think I cared very much for what I had read in the newspaper Rachel Cobb had shown me.   Those paragraphs made the prima donna more mysterious and interesting.

But nothing mattered. I should have to stay at home and be just nothing. It was too bad—oh yes, it was too bad. There was no doubt at all about Miss Runciman being a woman of whims.

"I just about hate her!" I said, aloud.

I was leaning on the top rail of a fence that divided our "mowing" from the pasture-land. Twilight was deepening. The whippoorwills were calling down below there. The sky was clear, and the summer air sweet and soft. But something had taken the charm away. I could hear the sound of the falls in the valley, and the sound brought still more plainly to my mind the encampment there. I had never seen such people before. But then I had never seen much of the world, though when I had come home from Hadley I thought myself quite worldly-wise. That was two years ago; I hadn't been wise at all at the time ; I knew that now.

I began to hum the gypsy song I had heard that girl sing. I remembered every note of it. I pitched it higher, however. I had a high voice in singing.

For the second time I began, and was part through it when I became aware that some one was whistling an accompaniment. I staggered on with the inarticulate song for a moment; then I stopped and looked about.

A brindle dog advanced from the gloom of a huckleberry-thicket and came to me, slowly wagging his tail. He was immediately followed by his master, Vane Hildreth, who took off his cap, saying as he did so :

"Stage set for sylvan scene. Heroine leaning on fence, singing. Enter hero in corduroys with his faithful dog. He advances up right front to heroine, takes her hand, kisses it respectfully, and asks her how she does."

Mr. Hildreth took my hand and kissed it, and as I was not at all used to such salutes, I felt my face growing hot and uncomfortable. There was a certain air about him, too, which I did not understand. I pulled away my hand and said I was very well, and just thinking about going home.

He made no response to this information, but asked me, with a great appearance of interest, if I remembered that Azucena song just from hearing Bashy sing it.

"Yes, I had never heard it before," I said.

"Some people can remember like that," he remarked; "it's a gift. But you're soprano," in apparent surprise, and as if he were saying, "You're English, when I supposed you were Hottentot."

"Of course I'm soprano," I answered.

He still held his cap in his hand, and he leaned on the rail at a respectful distance, and contemplated me steadily, much as though he were looking for the reason for my having that kind of a voice.

I gave him a quick look, which made me think his face very foreign indeed, as I had first thought it—quite outlandish, in fact. His long eyes were now well opened, and did not have a languid appearance. I had had a fancy, such as I imagine many young girls have, that I could make up my mind immediately concerning a person, could guess correctly as to what his or her leading tendencies were, and I knew at one glimpse as to whether the person was going to find favor in my eyes.

But I didn't know whether I liked this young man or not. At one moment I was sure I should like him extremely; at the next I thought quite the opposite. I recalled that his aunt had said of him that he had a pretty tenor and made rather a good operatic lover. I had a sudden, deeply rooted feeling that I despised any man who "made a good operatic lover."

"It's really astonishing that you are soprano," he now said.

" Why ?"

" Because you overturn all my theories."

" I'm so sorry to do that," I answered.

" Well, you ought to be sorry," he responded, " for it's a dreadful thing to do—to crash right into one's theories. You'll have to make it up to me in some way."

" No," I said, " I'm not called upon to do that. Good-night, Mr. Hildreth."

" Don't go, please," as I turned. " It seems so kind of romantic to meet you here. If you'll stay a bit longer I'll sing to you. It's something I'm getting up for an encore next season. You see, we poor singers have to be pegging at something even when we are doing nothing. Our vacations are poisoned by the fact that we have to see that our voices don't get rusty. My aunt would kill us ruthlessly if we should permit a rusty note. Don't you want me to sing to you, Miss Armstrong ?"

I certainly did wish very earnestly to hear him sing. I turned back and leaned on the fence again. The brindled dog sat down on his haunches with a resigned appearance, glancing at his master and then at me.

" I warn you," said Hildreth, " that it's real sentimental, and I'm going to sing right at you."

" Very well ; I'll try to bear it," I replied.

" So good of you," was the response. The young man cleared his voice and flung up his head, his eyes fixed on me. I was a bit excited, but I took a nonchalant attitude and compelled myself to look at him, though I fixed my gaze judiciously on the tip of his nose. So he began. This is what he sang :

" To you, my love, to you,
    I drink this crimson wine ;
To you, my love, to you,
    I bring this heart of mine."

Before he had finished the second line I knew very well what Miss Runciman had meant by calling her nephew a tenor lover. He had not a remarkably powerful voice, but the tones were heart-breakingly sweet, and he sang in what seemed a wickedly impassioned way. The tears gathered in my eyes; my heart beat heavily. I stopped gazing at the young man's nose; my eyelids drooped until I saw nothing.

He sang two verses of that commonplace stuff; but I had no idea it was commonplace, his singing was so delicious. Still, I was afraid of it. And he sang at me so that I could easily have thought it was really for me; and this notion made me just enough indignant to tone me up a little. But I couldn't, to save my life, prevent the tears from coming.

In the beginning of the last line the dog suddenly rose to his feet, the hair along his backbone stood up stiffly, and he growled. Mr. Hildreth finished his line, however, but he had no more than done so when in the deepened dusk a figure stepped from the same clump of huckleberries, strode up to the singer, and put a hand rudely on his shoulder.

Mr. Hildreth flung himself about. The dog leaped forward at the intruder, and I did not scream, though I choked in the suppression of a cry.

It was Bidwell Blake who had thus reprehensibly appeared, and who now caught the leaping dog and threw him over the fence.

Bidwell was in his overalls and jumper, and he immediately stepped back and said, in his cool drawl:

"I guess you'll have to excuse me, Mr. Singer. I didn't mean to tip you over, but I s'pose it's kinder hard to keep your balance 'n' sing like that at the same time. Mebby you'd better call your dog off. If I should git hold of him agin I might throw him further."

Mr. Hildreth straightened himself and seemed to swallow something. Then he spoke to his dog, who did not come, but who stood a few yards away growling and grinning.

Bidwell contemplated the other young man in a way that could not have been soothing.

"I wonder," he said, "now 'bout how much would they pay ye for singin' like that to um, eh?" He puckered his mouth and whistled the strain, "To you, my love, to you." Then he asked again, "Good pay, eh?"

"Excellent," was the reply. The singer put on his cap, took it off again, bowed to me, and then walked away, followed, growling, by his dog.

Bidwell pushed back his big straw hat as if the better to watch the retreating figure. Then he began to laugh, silently, but with great apparent enjoyment. And I laughed too, though the strains of the song were still ringing in my ears.

Finally I said : " You're a regular brute, Bid."

" I know it," he said, "but that feller ain't; that feller's sweet as honey in the comb; but I ain't the kind of dirt he's goin' to walk on—not by a long chalk. Let me see you home, Billy. If you stay here he may come 'n' sing to ye some more; in which case I'd knock his little damn head off. If you'll kindly overlook my language, Billy, I sh'll be thankful."

I was tried with Bidwell, but he was usually so good-natured that you couldn't hold out in a bad temper against him.

I turned away and began to walk towards home. Bidwell jumped over the fence and walked beside me. He talked a good deal, but I could not follow him, and at last gave up trying to do so. After a while he grew silent. When we reached the house he would not come in.

Father was smoking near the back door. " Hullo !" he called out; "that you, Billy? Who've you got with you?"

I told him it was Bid Blake. Bid looked at me in the dusk. I sat down on the bench with father, who puffed serenely at his pipe. Bid lingered a moment; then he said good-night, and his long figure slouched away in the dusk.

When we were alone together father said : " Billy, something's happened."

VI

"THERE'S MY NEPHEW, VANE"

I DREW nearer to father as he said that.

"Oh, what?" I exclaimed. Then, as I saw how peacefully he blew the smoke from his lips, I thought that nothing very serious could have occurred.

"Your mother's gone." I rose quickly, as if I would immediately go in search of her, and my heart sank.

"Yes," said father; "just after you went off this afternoon Nick Freeman brought a telegram over from the depot. 'Twas from your gran'mother. She's sick. There was exactly time for her to git ready 'n' ride back with Nick to ketch the train for Kyle, so she went; 'n' we can't know anything more about it till we c'n git a letter."

I stood silent for a few moments. Kyle was a four hours' ride away in the steam-cars. An unreasonable dejection took possession of me.

"Didn't she leave any word for me?" I asked.

"She left her love. She was in an awful hurry, you know. I s'pose she didn't take half the things she'll want. We'll have to send 'em to her, I guess."

"And she left no word for me?" I repeated.

"Her love, I tell ye. She hadn't any time, you know."

Father took his pipe from his mouth and looked at me in the dusk. "You ain't goin' to be silly, are you?" he asked. "I sh'd think her love was about all she could

leave ye, anyway.   Did I hear somebody singin' in the
paster ?"

"Yes."

"Who was it ?"

"Mr. Vane Hildreth."

"Oh, the feller in the fancy cart at the falls."

"Yes."

"Ain't you goin' with 'em, Billy ?"

I moved uneasily.   How good-naturedly father spoke!
As if he hadn't much interest in the matter, anyway.   And
yet I moved again.

"Eh ?" said he.

"Miss Runciman was coming over to see mother to-
morrow," I answered.

"What for?   I thought 'twas all settled."

"Yes; I think 'tis.   But she wanted to see mother.
Good-night, father."

I hurried into the house.   It was desolate.   Aunt Lowizy
was sprinkling the clothes for to-morrow's ironing.

"Her goin' was dretful sudden ; I can't get used to it,"
she remarked, as I came to the table where she was at
work.   Her words sounded as if mother were dead.

"Don't !" I cried.   I ran up to my own room.

Mother was never away from home.   Once a year grandmother usually came from Kyle and made us a long visit.
I sat down by my open window for an hour.   I could hear
the soft sound of the falls.   The scent of father's tobacco
came to me.   When I lighted a lamp and went to turn
down the bedclothes I found a bit of paper pinned to my
pillow.   I knew who had put the paper there, and the very
sight of it made me sob.

Mother had written in pencil : "It's hard to go without
seeing you.   Am I weak and foolish to wish you would

feel like deciding not to go with that singer-woman? God bless and keep you, my precious child!" Below, in faint marks, were the words: "I guess I wouldn't tell your father. I gave my permission, and I don't take it back."

I sat down on the side of the bed, with the scrap of paper in one hand and the lamp in the other. I read the words over and over. Every time I read them I wished that I could make up my mind to decide as mother wished me to decide. I felt, somehow, sure that she was right, though I did not know why. But I couldn't make up my mind—no, I could not do it. When I fell asleep I but went over and over, in the confusion of dreams, the same matter. And through the confusion I heard a velvet tenor voice singing "To you, my love, to you."

Miss Runciman came the next day. She came walking up the path with her nephew's dog at her heels. She did not seem in a mood for much talking, and she said very little to father, who kept at home, I was sure, that he might see her.

"I want you to bring over your things," she said to me. "We may stay here a few days longer, and we may go in an hour." There was a set look about her mouth, and a faded aspect to her eyes that rather startled me. "Come with me now," she said, looking towards me. "I want to try your voice. Vane and Bashy have gone for the day; there'll be no one to hear us. Come."

Of course, I obeyed. Father suggested that I come back and put my things together, and he would take them over. I walked away, following Miss Runciman as she went down the path. Once I looked back at the house. There came a stricture across my chest that made it difficult for me to breathe. I thought I saw my mother standing at the open shed door and beckoning me to return.

"Miss Runciman," I said, suddenly. She turned and waited for me to go on. " I—I—" but the words would not come. My companion came to me and took my hands. Her face softened with a marvellous quickness.

"What is it?" she asked. "Do you hesitate?"

I clung to her hands that held mine strongly. I tried to stand erect.

"No," I answered, after a moment; "I don't hesitate."

She did not say anything more, but resumed her walk, and I followed her.

People often come to a parting of the ways, but rarely, I think, are they conscious of that moment. But I knew; I knew that I was stepping out of my old life. Perhaps it was some mysterious inheritance from my mother, some freak of imagination that made, at the instant I stepped again after Miss Runciman, a picture appear to unroll before me of all my past, even to that time, which I could but just remember, when I could not go to sleep unless mother sat on my bed and held my hand. The picture of the future was blank.

It was curious that I always believed that if mother had been at home that day I should not have gone with Miss Runciman. I believed this, notwithstanding that my character contradicts this belief. But how little youth knows of itself! Wait until years have pointed out to you the furrows that this habit and that inclination have made—too late to smooth them out, too late to etch the picture differently. Why is it that we poor human beings must pay such a price for our knowledge?

Recalling the moment when I walked down the river path that morning, I am weak enough to moralize, and to be as weak as that is to be very weak, indeed. But you may be sure that I did not moralize as I went on in this sunshine.

And it was not ten minutes before all my morbid imaginings had left me, and I was treading joyously forward. As we came near Rachel Cobb's house, that person was visible behind the screen door. It was one of her days at home. She stepped outside and came forward, shading her eyes with her hand, blinking at us and looking more like a pig than usual.

"I was watchin' for ye," she said, without any preliminary greeting. "The young feller, your nephew," nodding at Miss Runciman, "came back to tell me to tell you that they might stay all night, after all. Billy, where you goin'?"

I answered briefly. I had not much patience with Rachel Cobb this morning. She looked at me intently, so intently that I thought, perhaps, her errand was really to me. When we started, she followed on behind me. After a moment she touched my arm, and as I looked around she made a gesture towards the woman in front, and shook her head with such violence that her eye-glasses fell off. She stooped to pick up the glasses, and I did not linger. She called after us that she "guessed her hens would lay more eggs by to-morrer."

For the first time I entered the house-carriage which stood among the birches and hackmatacks close by the falls. I was trying not to be excited. I wished to look about me calmly. It was a little room, and things were as compact in it as in a ship's cabin. Matting was on the floor, bamboo folding-chairs that could be leaned against the wall, a table that folded up and was also now close to the wall; no pictures, no bric-à-brac—a suggestion of nomadic life, as if the place were a kind of tent that could, like the other articles, be folded.

Miss Runciman spread out one of the chairs and placed

herself in it.　She told me to sit down and rest.　She did not speak again for a full half-hour.　I sat still and looked about me.　There was a pile of music on the floor in one corner.　On the wall hung a guitar and a banjo.　The dog had come in and was lying stretched out on his side near me on the matting.　The windows, which were large, were open and protected by screens.　Through them came the sounds of the country and of the falls.　A catbird sat on a birch close by and sang his lovely notes.

"Well!" at last said Miss Runciman.

When I turned towards her I knew that she had been watching me, and I blushed painfully.

"Yes," I said.

"Now I'm going to put you through the scale."

I braced myself.

"Stand up."

I did so.　She continued looking at me.

"I once knew," she said, "a woman who could sing the scale in a way to draw your soul out of your body.　Begin."

I began; how I went on and finished I didn't know. But the high notes always were a sort of inspiration and challenge to me.　I liked to seize them as if I were their conqueror.　I stood there with my hands clasped behind me, singing.

"Again," said Miss Runciman.

I did better the second time.　When I had finished she sat upright in her chair.　There was a slight flush on her cheeks.

"I was right," she remarked.　"You have the same kind of a voice that I have.　That's why I wanted you. In you I may renew my own youth, my triumphs.　But they will be your own triumphs, just the same.　Still, it all depends upon you—all.　You may have the voice of an angel, but it will not avail if you haven't work in you. Can you work—work like mad—work day and night, harder than any man ever toiled in the fields? Can you? For that's what it means to be a good singer. Tell me; can you do it? Do you want to do it?"

I was on fire. Her questions were like a stimulating draught to me. But I could not find any words in which to tell her. I was trembling pitiably. My companion was looking at me with probing eyes, eyes that had no compassion, I fancied, and that were searching me as they would have searched into some musical mechanism of which their owner would avail herself.

"Answer me; do you want to do it?" she repeated.

I took a step forward. "Yes, yes!" I cried out. "I want to do it." My face and eyes were burning; furious pulses beat all through me.

"Ah!" she said, in a half-voice; then she laughed softly, as if at some thought which I had suggested. "Come nearer." I went to the side of her chair. "Do I look like a wicked woman?" she inquired.

The question was so unexpected that I could not speak. She did not wait for my answer.

"I wonder if people expect that a person can sing out of a blank past. It can't be done. Of course, musical sounds can be made on any musical instrument. To be able to sing you must be able to live. The fulness of life! Do you think that means a sheet of paper with nothing written on it? Bah! Some folks make me sick! Those were pretty paragraphs in the paper that woman showed you—that little pig woman, I mean." From flaming heat I began to go down towards icy coldness. "The thought of them makes you shrink away from me?"

"No," I said.

"Better go back to your home now. You have the chance now. Give up the hope of singing."

"No," I said, again.

She contemplated me through half-shut eyes, as she had done once before. At last she asked :

"Have you ever heard the phrase 'a woman with a past'?"

"I don't think I have. What does it mean?"

"Oh, it always means something bad—always."

She offered no explanation of the remark, and I did not dare to ask for an explanation.

"People like to say things, you know," she went on. "For instance, a writer has just put this fine thing into his book : 'The basis of the musical temperament is sensuality and egotism.' What do you think of that?"

"It—it frightens me," I answered, in a low tone.

"Oh," carelessly, "his assertion doesn't make it a fact. Though he may be right, after all—only why didn't he make it a still more sweeping thing by saying the artistic temperament? That, now, would have covered a wide ground."

She rose and went to the pile of music. She selected a sheet and turned towards me with it in her hand.

"What are you thinking?" she inquired, quickly.

And as quickly, without reflection, I answered :

"Of Mrs. Drew Hollander."

A deep red rose over the woman's face. She waited an instant before she put her second question.

"What do you know about her?"

"Nothing. She was mentioned in that paper Rachel Cobb showed me. It said that probably Mrs. Drew Hollander was one of the women who would not stand by you. Oh," I burst out with, "I wish I hadn't said her name ! I don't know what made me do it !"

Miss Runciman was now pale.

"Your instinctive truthfulness made you do it," was the response. "But let's drop the subject. I'm going to sing; I want you to take notice how I do it. And have I told you," looking at me with a keen, searching expression, "your voice isn't cold to-day. I thought it was unaccountable that it should be, with your face. But I fancy it is liable to moods. Well, you'll learn to summon any mood. Now, listen to me."

She stood turning the leaves of her music for a moment. Then she laid down the sheets. How strangely, how wonderfully her face softened! Even before she had opened her lips I was conscious of the coming of a delightful excitement.

It was something I had never heard that she sang—but, then, I had heard nothing.

> "By the first rose thou hap'st to meet,
> Send fondest greetings to my sweet."

I stood silent and agitated. This, I knew, was what was meant by the phrase "perfection of technical culture," which I had once read applied to Jenny Lind's singing. And this was something that Jenny Lind had sung at Leipzig. I was trying to remember what I had read, for by thus exerting my memory it seemed to me I could divert my mind so that I might be able to bear this voice which pierced my soul as if it were a knife that could divide the very spirit.

"In the soul that vibrated in her tones, and in the charm of a peculiar *voix voilée*, an inimitably tender organ, her piano was a breath such as angel lips might breathe."

I kept up my endeavor to recall these words, for I was afraid—of what? It must have been for fear of the loss of that self-control which the sane person grips hard.

7

As Miss Runciman stopped singing I sat down suddenly
in the nearest chair and covered my face with my hands.
This was what I had dreamed about, and longed for as
something impossible. It was possible, after all; God had
given something very precious to some of His children.
Was it possible that He had given this precious thing to
me? What would my mother think if she had heard this
singing? It was from her that I had inherited my voice,
though mine was stronger and better in every way. Why
had mother so often said that she thought a "musical gift
was a dangerous gift"? But father used to assert, with
his laugh, that "Serissy hadn't much hard sense, anyway.
Serissy was as full of dreams 'n' notions as an egg was full
of meat."

Miss Runciman opened the door and stood leaning
against the casing. She was standing thus when I took
my hands from my face and timidly looked at her. I was
timid because she seemed superhuman to me just at that
moment. Without turning her head, she asked:

"Did you like it?"

"Like it?" I repeated, as soon as I could speak. "Is
that the way you sing in public?"

"Sometimes; but sometimes I'm just a wooden machine."

"You can't be wooden."

"Can't I? How do you know?"

She turned now quickly towards me with that manner
which had been hers when she had stopped at my home,
the manner that put you at ease and somehow gave a stim-
ulus to your mind. My spirits began to be released and
to flow towards her. Instead of answering her question, I
said:

"I shall never sing like that."

"Not like that—better," she responded. She smiled at me, but her face was very sad in spite of her smile. "Yes, better. You will have all my high notes, and you will have a more powerful lower register; notwithstanding the furore they make about a soprano voice, it is the lower tones that move one most. That floridness, that profusion, is decoration, and decoration in any kind of art never stirs the depths."

"But you move the soul." I could not speak clearly.

"Oh yes; I know it. And it's my life-blood that does it, and every time you offer such a libation as that you are just so much impoverished."

I did not understand her, but I would not ask what she meant. I had a feeling, however, that one might be willing to pay a high price to be able to move the multitude. How could I know then how much of the glamour of youth was over my eyes?

I began that very day—yes, that very hour—to study. Miss Runciman said she was sorry I was so old, that she wished she had found me years before. "Say at sixteen; but then the time was not ripe; I shouldn't have been ready to take you then; I was thinking of other things. Did you ever notice, Billy, that, strive as we may, nothing happens until the time is ripe?"

She began to turn over the music sheets in the corner of the room. She was on her knees.

"I confidently expect that you will master the first studies rapidly," she was saying. "You must, because you've lost so many years. Let me tell you one of the great things now. Are you listening?"

She caught hold of my skirt, and I stood looking down at her.

"Speak clearly — enunciate — enunciate — enunciate —

make as much of the words as if you were an actor. Consider your words first. Will you remember?"

I nodded my head, but I thought she was telling me a
strange thing.

"Even if you sing in a tongue your listeners do not
understand, you must understand, you must suck the meaning from every word, and the meaning will flow into your
tones. Who cares, save superficially, for warbling like a
bird? That isn't what you desire. Sing like a human being—like a woman who hopes and despairs, who loves and
hates, who lives. Billy, know, to begin with, that you are
to be a dramatic soprano; that's the promise of your voice;
don't do anything to vitiate that promise. If you go and
fall in love and marry, I shall be disgusted with you—disgusted. Fall in love if you please; girls are constantly
doing that. Emotional experience enriches the vocal powers.
But keep your love in hand, and tell your lover he may
only adore from afar. It will be good discipline for him,
and what lovers chiefly need is discipline; they don't get
half enough of it."

Here Miss Runciman paused to laugh slightly. She released my skirt from her grasp.

"When you practise, accustom yourself to singing in all
sorts of positions. Now, this is hard—to cry out at the
top of your voice, melodiously"— still on her knees, she
wheeled about and extended her hands, clasped, forward
and above her head—"Edgardo! Edgardo!"

The tone swept into the warm air outside and along
the summer stillness of the country, pleading, beseeching.

"You see," she went on, rising to her feet, "the mere
effort almost makes you lose your balance and fall over
backward. And you must do it spontaneously, and as if

you meant it; otherwise you are ridiculous. Every time you are sentimental or romantic you are so perilously near the ridiculous. That old saying about its being but a step, you know, is the truest thing in the world.

"I'm giving you quite a lecture. But I'm not going to do that very often. Billy, don't disappoint me, please."

She glanced at me.

"I shall do my best," I answered, with enthusiasm.

She did not reply. She was walking about the little room. She stopped in front of me.

"I'm rather in a singing mood," she remarked, "and then I want you to get an idea as to how the thing is done."

She began:

> "Stay, Corydon, thou swain,
>   Talk not so soon of dying;
> What tho' thy heart be slain,
>   What tho' thy love be flying:
> She threatens thee, but dares not strike;
> Thy nymph is light and shadowlike;
> For if thou follow her she'll fly from thee,
> But if thou fly from her, she'll follow thee."

She sang, it seemed to me, as no one else ever sang, and as no one ever would sing. I stammered out something to that effect, and she laughed.

"That's very sweet of you," she answered, "but have you ever heard any one else?"

I was obliged to confess that I had not. She made no reply to this response of mine.

"Now, there's something I want to warn you against," she said, suddenly.

I waited, looking at her. She seemed displeased by her thoughts.

"It's very annoying, but it's my nephew, Vane. He'll be making love to you, of course."

I drew myself up. I was angry. "I don't think we need to worry about that," I responded, in a very high manner.

"Don't you?" she laughed, but there was a fold between her eyes.

"Indeed, no."

"Oh, you don't know Vane. He's a born lover. Perhaps I ought not to blame him. He'd make eyes at a wax doll if there were nothing alive near. Why, I shouldn't be surprised if, without speaking a word, he had somehow made that little pig woman—what's her name?—Cobb— think he had a tenderness for her which a cruel fate obliged him to nip in the bud. Oh, Vane Hildreth must make love to some one. If he were only a little younger, I would cut a switch from one of these birches and use it across his shoulders. He will try to make love to you, as sure as you are standing before me. Now, will you please tell me what course you are going to take? Will you snub him?"

She looked at me quizzically, but still earnestly. I was indignant to the very tips of my fingers.

"I think I can snub him," I answered. I was wishing I might see that switch applied to the young man's shoulders, and I was aware that this was a grossly unladylike wish.

"But you may overdo the thing, in which case he will suspect. He is a very quick-witted boy. It is really phenomenal how the women like him."

"Do they?"

"Yes; you see, he is what you'd call lovable."

"Is he?"

"Certainly. He sang to you the other night, didn't he?"

Miss Runciman's eyes suddenly made a dive into mine.

I stiffened myself and stared back at her. I wished I was brazen as brass.

"It was last night," I said, boldly.

"I thought I heard him from a distance. He's learning a new encore. He must have somebody to try it on. It's quite a lovesick little thing. Did you like it, Billy?"

"He has a sweet voice," I answered.

"Yes, like the scent of a jasmine flower. I do hope you didn't let him stare at you. He has great faith in the power of his eyes."

I turned away. I thought we had had quite enough talk about Vane Hildreth. I didn't dare to say much, but I did remark that if I had been on the verge of falling in love with Mr. Hildreth, I was now sufficiently forewarned. I ought to be perfectly safe. Miss Runciman smiled.

"That's right. Now let us get up some kind of a lunch. I find I'm hungry at the oddest times. By-the-way, I'm going to give you a lesson every forenoon, and you must practise all the rest of the day. You'll have to go into the great out-of-doors to do it. I'm sure that, at this stage, your voice will strengthen out-of-doors; usually we ought to fence in our tones, you know. Go as far afield as you please, only peg away—you're to make up for lost time."

We had a lunch of sardines and biscuit, and some wine, which I did not drink. I had never seen a woman with a wineglass in her hand before, and the sight of it and the smell of it made me shrink as from a tangible evil. There seemed to be something low-lived in the drinking of wine. I had heard that some women did such a thing, but in my mind the act smirched them. Do not forget that there are many hamlets in New England where the people still feel as I felt then.

Miss Runciman filled a beautiful little glass and pushed it

towards me across the table. The odor filled the room. I was conscious of a sense of repulsion such as I had not thought I could know towards this woman.

"It is only Tokay," she said. I shook my head. I had signed the pledge when I had belonged to our minister's Bible class. I had hardly thought of the pledge from that day to this. It had meant very little to me at the time, and this was the first opportunity I had had to break my promise. I was not in the least tempted. That delicate glass with its fragrant contents to me was literally of the devil. I think only the New England country girl can understand me, but she will understand. Vague pictures of bad men and bad women rose up before me. I did not know that my hostess was observing my face until she suddenly said :

"You look as if you were disappointed in me." I made no reply. "Is it the wine?" she asked.

"I don't think it's nice to drink. It seems wicked, and—and—"

"What ?"

"Low."

I flung out the words desperately. Miss Runciman contemplated me in silence. Then she set down her glass of wine, which she had not tasted; but she did not seem aware that she had not tasted. She drew a long breath. She took up a lemon and put a few drops of its juice on the sardine which lay on her plate. Then she pushed her plate from her.

"I know what you mean," she said. "I know, because I used to feel just like that. But I had forgotten all about it; I'm glad I had forgotten. I don't want to remember. Besides, you are wrong. This glass of Tokay would do no harm. You'll soon drink a little wine now and then with no more thought than if it were tea. We don't keep our youthful notions. We should be idiots if we did. Idiots !"

To my inexpressible surprise, Miss Runciman laid her arms down on the table and her head upon them, and began to sob.

VII

BROKEN BONES

I SAT motionless. If Miss Runciman had suddenly become a maniac I could not have been more amazed. I longed to go to her and put my arms about her, but I did not dare to move. Suddenly upon the stillness of the place there came the sound of a voice singing hastily, the sound coming nearer and nearer. I recognized the voice, as did Miss Runciman. She raised her head, but she put one hand over her eyes. I saw the tremor of her mouth as she smiled.

"She flats on F," she said; "and how I have drilled her!" The speaker took her hand from her eyes and raised her head.

The next moment Bathsheba Hildreth sprang up the outer steps that led into the room. She had on her blouse and her short skirt and her knickerbockers. She wore a polo cap on the back of her head. She had a stick in her hand. She landed close to her aunt's chair, as if she had just vaulted over something and the jump had brought her to that spot. She gave a quick glance at Miss Runciman and then asked: "What's the row?"

She leaned forward and took the flask of wine. She sniffed at it and exclaimed: "That baby stuff! I want a nip of whiskey. Where is the whiskey-bottle?"

She did not wait for a reply, but hurried into the next

room. She came back with another bottle and a bit of a folding silver drinking-cup. She put some whiskey in this cup and tossed down the liquid.

"Billy, you are shocked," she said, looking at me. Then she turned to the elder woman and continued: "Now I'll tell you what's happened. But then it might better happen now than later. He'll manage to be out in time for our first night, I reckon."

"What are you talking about?" sharply from Miss Runciman.

"Vane, of course. I don't know how many bones he's broken." Bashy took a sardine in her fingers and pulled a morsel from it. "I've run until I'm one mass of palpitating flesh. These sardines are not as good as the last ones. Billy, will you pour me out a few spoonfuls of that Tokay?"

I gave her the flask. For some reason I did not wish to pour the wine.

"Is Vane hurt?" still more sharply from Miss Runciman.

"If it hurts to break a leg and a few ribs and a clavicle or two, he's hurt."

The girl's aunt crossed the short space between them and took hold of her niece's arm as one takes the arm of a refractory child. She shook Bashy, and I was glad to see her do it.

"Now tell me what you mean!" she commanded.

"Just what I say. It was over on that long road that leads to — well, to Gehenna, I fancy. It's five miles away if it's a rod. It follows the river, you know, and there's another gorge there. You remember we thought of outspanning in that place instead of here. Vane never has common-sense about steep places. He wanted to go down into that ravine after we had looked into it. He said there

was a flower growing there that made him think of our new
soprano"—here the girl gave me a glance. "And he said
that it was the proper thing to go down in ravines after
flowers. So he did it, and he lost his balance. He went
crashing on until I thought I should die watching him.
Please remember, ladies, that I've had my fright, and you've
just got yours. So I'm not so hard-hearted as you appear
to think. I scrambled after him, though I knew I couldn't
lug him out. He lay still there, white and groaning. He said
he hadn't a whole bone in his body. I scrambled back up
the bank and stood in the road a minute thinking. It was
four or five miles to anywhere. People didn't come along
this road very often. I decided to start in the direction
that would lead me to Four Corners. Perhaps I should
meet some one there, and not have to go the whole distance. And I did meet some one in a farm-cart—that
fellow who scorns us, and who won't sell us chickens nor
pigs. You know him, Billy. What's his name?"

"Bidwell Blake," I explained, in surprise.

"Yes. Mr. Bidwell Blake couldn't refuse to go to the
ravine at my request. I got into his cart and he whipped
his horse. But, oh, it was an awful job to get Vane up!
Bidwell Blake knew how to do it, though. He told Vane
he should half kill him, but he'd got to be half killed, or
stay where he was. He asked me if I had any kind of fac-
ulty for lifting, and I said I guessed I had; and he told me
now was the time to raise up my muscle and see what I
could do. So I took hold of Vane's feet and Bidwell Blake
took his shoulders, and we went along till we came to a
better place to climb up, Vane swearing like Beelzebub, and
Bidwell Blake not speaking a word. When we did come
to the place Bidwell Blake said he'd got to take Vane in
his arms, and he was sorry he'd been swearing so, for now

he'd need more swearing by a great sight than he had before. Then Vane shut his lips as he does when he's stuffy,
and Bidwell Blake took him and went up the steep side.
And when he was up and put Vane on the ground, Vane
was limp and white. He had gone into a dead faint. But
we brought him to life again and got him into the wagon,
and I sat down beside him, and Bidwell Blake walked his
horse, and when we got near here I said this cart was no
place for a man to be who had a job of knitting bones on
hand, besides injury to his insides. And where do you
think Bidwell Blake has taken him?" Bashy drank some
more Tokay. "Why, to the little pig woman's, close by.
Yes, he's on Rachel Cobb's best bed, and Bidwell Blake has
taken his horse from his wagon, got on the horse's back
and galloped after a doctor, and I've come over here to
tell my tale."

Here the speaker poured more Tokay into her cup and
drank it. Miss Runciman stood as if she had hardly
taken in the story to which she had listened.

"But what did Miss Cobb say?" I asked.

"Oh, she hasn't said anything," was the reply, sipping at
the wine.

"That's odd; she generally says things," I responded.

"Well, you see, she hasn't had a chance to say anything
yet. She doesn't know it."

"Not know it?"

"Oh no; she wasn't at home. Visiting somewhere, I
s'pose. But I'd seen her put her key on the window-ledge
behind the lilac. So I looked for it, and there it was.
Bidwell Blake said he wouldn't be responsible; he said it
was burglary; but I didn't care what it was. Vane had got
to go somewhere, and this was the place. So I unlocked
the door and led the way into the bedroom that leads out

of the sitting-room. The sun was beating down, and it was like an oven. You never saw a bed stand up so high as that one did, and there was a quilt on it made of large yellow birds, with red wings, cut out and sewed on. I couldn't help seeing and noticing the birds. I should have noticed them if Vane and I had both been dying. I flung back this cover, and Bidwell Blake put Vane down on the bed. He had come to by this time, you know. He told me to take that cursed thing with the birds on it out of his sight; he told me he'd kill me if I didn't keep it out of his sight; he said it was a damned discord. I threw it on the ground back of the house. The hens there are afraid of it, and they are protecting the cockerel from it."

Miss Runciman had gone into the other room of the wagon. She now came back with a rubber pillow and a few things for her nephew's comfort. She was very pale, and she did not notice us as she passed on by us and left the carriage. I saw her from the window hurrying away in the direction of Miss Cobb's cottage.

My companion sat down quickly. "I'd go with her," she said, "but the truth is I'm played out. You wouldn't think it perhaps, but I am." She leaned back in her chair. I noticed now that she looked exhausted. "I wouldn't sit here if there were one thing I could do," she went on. "But just now there isn't, and Aunt Nora 'll stay with him. The doctor can't be here under an hour and a half at the shortest. I've got to rest while I can. We shall have a pull with Vane now, I tell you. We shall need all the strength we can get. Oh, I am sorry!"

Here the girl's voice trembled. I was afraid she was going to cry, and I was somehow out of sympathy with her, though I was deeply sorry for her. She did not cry, however. She sat quite still for some moments, and all the

time I was trying to think what to say to her. I felt as if
I seemed quite hard-hearted.

Suddenly she exclaimed, "I wish you'd give me some more
wine. I feel as weak as a mouse after all this." I rose
and carried the bottle and a glass to her. "Pour it out
for me, please." I hesitated. I knew as well as any one
how inconsistent my hesitation was.

"What's the matter?" in surprise.

"I don't know. I hate to pour wine," I answered, growing red.

"Well, you are a curious one!" She seized the flask and
glass.

After she had drunk she said:

"There's one thing I wish you'd do."

"What is it? I want to help you."

"See that Miss Cobb, and tell her what's been done with
her house."

"But I don't know where she is."

"Watch out for her. You ought to know her habits. I
haven't the patience. I should give her something tough, I
know I should."

Bashy rose and left me; I sat there by myself a few moments. I was trying to recall Rachel Cobb's routine of
visits. As nearly as I could remember she ought to have
gone over to the "Great Medders" about this time. The
Great Medders settlement was three miles away. She
would get a "lift" over there with the butcher, and a lift
home with the baker. But she wouldn't be home until
afternoon; she would come early enough to feed her hens
before they went to roost. I wished to catch her at some
distance from her home; I wanted to have time to explain
matters and to let the truth sink into her mind. But there
were several hours to pass through before I could expect

her. Miss Runciman and Bashy would be with Vane Hildreth. I should be by myself.

Presently I left the carriage. I purposely wandered off
towards the road that led to the village. Here this road
was very solitary. I kept in the high pastures, but within
sight of the highway. I began to try my voice; I ran up
and down the scale over and over again, noting critically
the volume of sound and its quality. I was not afraid that
any one would hear me, so I let lungs and throat have full
play. As soon as possible I knew that Miss Runciman
would give me a few hints as to these exercises.

I was standing up to my full height, head back, and
"holding on" to high C, when a rustle in the sumacs
close to me made me drop my note suddenly. But it
was only a brindled dog that came out of the bushes
towards me. He came slowly and inquiringly, but when
he had reached my side he licked my hands eagerly, and
with a pathetic sort of questioning. He sat down on his
haunches and looked at me. I put my hand on his head.
Of course, I recognized the animal as Mr. Hildreth's dog,
whom he called "Lotus." His owner had explained that
he had given the dog this name on account of its striking
inappropriateness.

"Why are you not with your master?" I inquired.

Lotus wagged his tail furiously and whined. He was
explaining, but I could not understand. Having risen to
go through with this explanation, he sat down again with
the air of one who begs not to be driven away. At this
stage of our interview I heard a shout of "Hullo!" down
in the road. I looked and saw a man on horseback galloping. He was swinging his hat towards me. Immediately
he dismounted, tied his horse to a birch-tree, and came up
the hill. I had directly recognized Bidwell Blake.

" I s'pose you've heard ?" he said, as he came near. I nodded. " Pretty kettle of fish !" he exclaimed. " I've seen the doctor. He's on behind with splints 'n' bottles 'n' bandages, 'n' he'll need um all. I can't stop but a minute. He said he might want me to help—he couldn't tell ; 'n' it wouldn't do to count on the feller's womenkind. Didn't he swear, though ! Yes, he did. But I vow I couldn't blame him. Whose dorg's that ?"

" Mr. Hildreth's. He's just come to me." Bidwell glanced at me frowningly. " Why don't the dorg stay where he b'longs?" he asked. " I thought dorgs was the only faithful things in the universe. Why ain't he with his master ?"

I said I didn't know. Bidwell continued to frown as he gazed at me. Then he remarked that if he was in the habit of kicking dogs he should kick this one.

" The cheek of the critter to come to you in that way," he exclaimed; " jest 's if he had a right to ! Why don't you drive him off ?"

" No," I answered, " I shall not drive him off."

Bidwell whistled, but the expression of his face was still a scowling expression. " Wall, I must be goin'. The doctor 'll be along, 'n' I must be on hand." The young man turned and walked a few paces ; then he came back. He gazed at me a moment before he spoke. " I s'pose you're goin' with them folks, Billy ?" he said. Yes, I was going with them. Bidwell gazed at me intently. Something in his gaze made me uncomfortable and indignant. I thought he intended to speak again, but he did not. He suddenly swung about and hurried down the slope. I watched him ; he mounted his horse and rode away without looking in my direction again. Lotus was sitting at my feet. He glanced up at me deprecatingly, drooping his clipped ears.

It was a strange day. I remained out in the pastures all the time, wandering here and there, singing, breathing great draughts of the delicious air. If mother had been there I should have gone home for a while. About noon I went down to the carriage. I found no one. I discovered some bread and cold meat, and Lotus and I had a lunch. The horses belonging to the wagon were kept in the nearest stable, which was half a mile away. I had a sudden wish to go to that stable and see the gray colt; but I controlled that wish. I must watch for Rachel Cobb.

When I went out again I went to Miss Cobb's house, Lotus going with me. The doctor's sorrel mare and gig were still at the fence. An air of strange stillness was about the place. It was always still, but this was something different. Bathsheba was sitting at the open door, on the threshold. She had her elbows on her knees and her hands supporting her face. On the ground not far away I saw in a heap the bedquilt with the yellow, red-winged birds on it. I gathered up this quilt, shook it, and with it in my arms I advanced to Bashy.

"How is he?" I asked.

"Bad," without looking up. I wanted to ask if he would die, but I could not. I stood there hesitatingly. Then the girl said:

"Doctor says there's a chance for him; but perhaps the doctor doesn't know anything. They mostly don't."

I went softly in and put the bedquilt on a chair. The dog came treading behind me. He sniffed at the open door of the bedroom. There was the sickening odor of anæsthetics in the air. I went out as softly and quickly. I had had a glimpse of the figures of Miss Runciman and the doctor. The whole house seemed entirely changed, and yet it looked the same. I saw Rachel Cobb's plate and

cup and saucer on the checked table-cloth of the table
that set up against the wall.

I did not speak again to Bashy as I hurried out. I was
several rods away when I heard a low whistle from the direction of the house. I looked back; there was Lotus following me at a gentle trot. He also looked back in response to Bashy's whistle, but he did not obey. He glanced
at me pleadingly. I was surprised. I had not thought of
his following me now; and I was touched at the same time
that I decided that he must be a fickle dog. And were
dogs fickle? I didn't know much about them. I tried to
motion Lotus away. He crouched down, slowly and interrogatively moving the tip of his tail.

Then I went on again. I heard Bashy whistle once more.
I plunged in among the birches and huckleberry-bushes in
the direction of "Great Medders." When I came to an
opening I glanced back. There was Lotus, stepping softly
along. He stopped the instant I looked at him. I smiled
and held out my hand. He dashed forward, stump of a tail
up, ears cocked. How eagerly he licked my fingers! How
joyfully he whined! I knelt down and took his head between my hands. I gazed intently at this new companion
of mine. He had bright, light hazel eyes, a snub nose,
protruding lower jaw, a scar on the right side of his grizzled
face.

"You don't look inconstant," I said, "but you must be
so." I rose. "Well, come on;" and he trotted cheerfully
at my heels all the long afternoon, or he sat down gravely
by me when I sat down.

It was altogether, as I said, a strange day to me, and it
seemed a week long before it was time to expect the Farwell
baker to be on his way from Great Medders. But I was
sitting on a big rock under a pine-tree on the Great Med-

ders road at so early an hour that I knew that the baker would not escape me.   If Rachel Cobb should not be with him, I should be greatly surprised.

At last I heard the tinkle of bells.   There he was, and there was a woman on the seat beside him.   Very soon I saw the leather bag in her lap.   That bag held her "body." I walked out to the roadside.   Presently the wagon was sufficiently near for me to see that Rachel's jaws were clicking up and down.   The baker wore a drowsy aspect. Poor man !   He had heard that clicking for nearly an hour. He roused.   He evidently expected a demand for cookies.

Rachel leaned forward and stared at Lotus.   "Why!" she exclaimed, "that's them singers' dorg, ain't it ?"

"Yes," I said.   "I wish you'd get out, Miss Cobb, and walk home with me from here."

"Gracious!" was the response.   "Of course I will. What's happened?   Have the hens be'n stole ?"

When I assured her of the safety of the fowls she said there'd be'n a "terrible time to Great Medders with hen thieves."   While she spoke she was climbing down from her seat, and the baker, looking much relieved, was saying, "Whoa!   Sh!   Stand still, I tell ye !" to his horse, though the steed was drooping forward with an air of not being able to move again.

Rachel landed safely on the ground, and the baker then handed to her a paper bag which its owner explained contained "dried high-tops " from the Mosely farm.   These high-tops were early sweet apples, and Rachel would stew them in sugar and water, and eventually eat them in milk in conjunction with bread.   I volunteered to carry the apples, and we started forward " across" towards my companion's home.

"You said 'twasn't the hens," she remarked, as soon as

we were well on the way, and she had cried "scat!" two or three times to the dog, as if he were a cat. He had manifested a wish to smell of the leather bag, and she was equally determined that he should not smell of it.

"Nor fire?" she asked, before I could speak. "You've got kind of a look 's if 'twas fire."

"No—no," I answered. I felt very much embarrassed. It was an indefensible thing that had been done. I plunged at once into my story.

She stopped in her walk to listen. I held the bag of apples well up in front of me and spoke as fast as I could. Twice she exclaimed: "The old cat!" and when I was through she said, "Goodness gracious me! I do declare!"

Then she sat down on a convenient stone, and announced that she could not noways take it in, and she didn't know as she should ever be able to take it in, and she hadn't, so to speak, got no home to go to, she that set so much store by a home, too.

She talked thus for some time, and I did not interrupt. Indeed, I had nothing to say. I thought Bathsheba Hildreth had done an unwarrantable thing. Her brother should have taken his chances in the big wagon. I would not, in my own mind, admit of the possibility of Bashy's being right in what she had just effected. At last I was aware that my companion was asking a question.

"Can't you speak?" she inquired, fretfully. "I've been askin' you over 'n' over what in the world I was goin' to do."

"You might visit," I suggested, timidly.

"Visit!" she repeated. "What do you mean by saying anything like that? I know," in a milder tone, "I s'pose I might go visitin' some day times, but I've got to be here nights 'n' mornin's, for there's my hens, 'n' my cat must be seen to. You say that feller's all smashed to a jell?"

There was a certain satisfaction in her tones : a satisfaction, I suppose, in the distinction lent to her house by the fact that a man so smashed was at present its occupant.

"No." I answered, irritably. " I didn't say so."

"Wall, I d' know 's it makes much dif'runce. whether he's partly jell. or all jell." She rose and took up her bag. "We might's well go 'long. I guess," she remarked.

I offered to accompany her and carry the dried apples. She walked on ahead along the field path. and she talked all the time. but, owing to my not listening and to her face being turned away from me. I only heard a word now and then.

When we came to the door we found that it still stood open. but Dashy was not there.   I extended the apples to Miss Cobb. but she said " I'd got to come in 'n' introduce her. 'n' kind of see how things were."   I shrank from doing this. but I could hardly refuse.   I tried to have no feeling about the matter.   I followed her into the solemn, hot little house.   The sickening scent of ether was still in the air.   Miss Cobb paused in the entry. and snuffed audibly.

Perhaps Miss Runciman heard this snuffing.   Anyway, she came forward from the bedroom and paused by Rachel : she glanced at her. then laid her hand on her arm and pushed her gently outside again.   I. being behind Rachel. stepped out quickly.   Miss Runciman looked very pale and very gentle.   I saw that the owner of the house tried to resent being pushed out of her dwelling, even though the ejecting were kindly done.

"I s'pose I've got a right here." she began, but in a hushed voice.

" Don't let's waken him . I think he's asleep," says Miss Runciman.

We all stood just without the door now. and Miss Cobb

performed a kind of snort, her eye-glasses dropping off in the process.

"Yes," said Miss Runciman, in her kindest way, "and that's what troubles me. It'll be so kind of you to let us stay – though you can put us out, of course. But we shall be so glad to pay you almost any sum—and if you would only remain and aid us by your advice and—"

I turned and walked away at this; and I smiled to myself. I heard Miss Runciman's voice indistinctly for a few moments, then a sharp call from within.

"Aunt Nora!"

Miss Runciman hurried into the house. She came back almost directly. "He wasn't asleep, after all," I heard her say. Then she came to me. "Billy, Vane thinks he wants to see you. Will you go in?" Of course I had to say yes. "Come, then."

She seemed to be going, then she stopped. "You know it's only a whim," she said. "I haven't an idea why he should ask for you. Is Lotus coming?"

Yes, evidently Lotus was coming. He walked behind me, and I walked behind Miss Runciman.

"Here's Miss Armstrong, Vane," said his aunt, as this little procession filed into the small room where the young man lay on top of the enormous Cobb feather-bed.

"We've telegraphed to Clinton for a mattress and springs," said Miss Runciman, as if this feather-bed were very prominent in her mind, as well as before her eyes.

Mr. Hildreth, I thought, looked as if he would like to say: "Damn the feather-bed!" But he did not say anything for a brief space of time. Then he turned his eyes to me and tried to smile.

"I was a great idiot," he said. "Bashy told you how I went down the ravine?"

"Yes," I answered.

"There were some flowers there," he went on. "They made me think of you—ridiculous—when you're not like a flower. I think"—a hesitation and a smile that seemed mocking—"I think they must be dramatic soprano flowers; anyway, I did not get them—that's the main point."

"Vane, aren't you talking too much?" asked Miss Runciman.

"No," crossly. "Perhaps by to-morrow I can't talk at all. Where's Lotus?"

"He's been with me," I said.

"Will you allow him to stop with you? Bashy told me—"

"I'll let him stay," was my reply.

"Now you may go," was the response from the bed. I was walking out of the room when the irritable voice exclaimed: "Are you going like that?"

"In what other way can I go?" I stopped in the doorway as I asked this.

"Why, it's barbarous not to shake hands, I call it!"

I went to the bed and held out my hand. His own hand, as it clasped about mine, was hot and pitiable, somehow.

"I don't know when I shall sing the little song for the encore again," he said; and then, not waiting for any reply: "Well, good-bye! If I'm not dead, I wish you'd let me hear you practise when you know how to do it. Well, good-bye, I say!"

I was now permitted to go, after I had said good-bye. I was so sorry for him that my voice was not perfectly steady. The dog lingered a moment by the bedside, and licked his master's hand. Then he followed me.

"What on earth 's he be'n sayin' of?" eagerly inquired Rachel, who had remained in the next room, but who ap-

parently had not been successful in her attempt at listening. She looked at me in a kind of gloating way.

" Nothing," I answered, shortly.

"Oh, land ! Wilhelminy, I hope you ain't goin' to be interested in him !" she exclaimed.

To this I made no answer. What could I say to such a
remark as that? To assert or deny would be equally useless. I was silent.

" Of course," she went on, "you needn't tell if you 'ain't
a mind to. But if you go 'n' set your mind on that singin'
feller you'll be master sorry; 'n' what do you s'pose your
mother 'd say ?"

"Wait till I do set my mind on him," I snapped. " I
went in there because Miss Runciman asked me."

I walked out of the house. I hurried down the river
path. I did not pause until I had entered the big carriage.
I don't know why I should be surprised and annoyed to
find Bashy there. She was sitting in one of the long chairs,
with her hands clasped over her head. Her face was red
and swollen.

"Very likely he'll be a cripple," she said, as I entered.

" Did the doctor say so ?"

" No; but you can't very well break every bone in your
body without being some kind of a cripple. And he's so
interested in his singing. And he doesn't flat, as I do.
We shall have to get a new tenor, and that's an awful
nuisance. Aunt Nora 'll hate that." She looked at the
brindled dog who had followed me. " That's confounded
odd about Lotus," she said.

VIII

YES, it was certainly a very strange summer, and it passed as if it were but a day; and, though it seemed as if I were doing one thing all the time, it was not monotonous. It was strange, also, for me to be living so near my home and yet not there. In my heart I felt far off. But I used to go there once or twice a week—Lotus and I. Mother was still in Ryle. She wrote to me at intervals, but she was not one who was at home with her pen, so I felt curiously forsaken, though I knew I was not forsaken. Grandmother was very feeble, and begged mother from week to week to stay with her. Aunt Lowizy kept house for father, so he was comfortable, and I was with Miss Runciman.

"It seems as if my duty lay here," mother wrote.

As for me, I did one thing; I studied to sing. I did not know I could study so. Instead of urging me on, my teacher was obliged to restrain me. She said I must keep in robust health, or my voice would suffer; I must not practise too much, or my voice would suffer; I must not practise too little, or my voice would suffer. Above all, accustom throat and chest, by cold bathing, exercise, gradual exposure to cool air, to changes, so that I should not contract that detestable habit of taking cold. A singer who was always taking cold was of no account.

Miss Runciman said that many things would have to be omitted in my training, because I had begun so late, or, as she phrased it, because "she had not found me earlier." "But you have intelligence," she added, looking at me keenly; "you will be constantly picking up things."

The summer had turned out so differently from what I had expected. We did not travel about; the carriage remained there by the falls; it seemed as stationary as Rachel Cobb's little house itself. And Vane Hildreth was shut up in that house. A nurse had been brought from Chilton, a middle-aged woman, who was very patient, who did not resent it even when her charge snatched up her own hymn-book from the stand by the bed and threw it at her. Fortunately the hymn-book missed fire, but it landed squarely against Miss Cobb's mirror, which was hung upon the wall opposite the bed. The glass splintered symmetrically from the centre outward, and at almost the same moment the owner of it, who was in the kitchen stewing currants, rushed into the room and said she thought she heard a crash.

Bashy, who was visiting her brother at just this time, and who gave me the account of what occurred, said that if Vane had had a pistol within reach she supposed he would then and there have shot the three women congregated in the room, and afterwards turned the weapon upon himself. He was sitting bolstered up in the bed. The nurse had just entered, singing "Hark, from the tomb." Not only was she singing this, but she was snuffling, as if the nasal passages were obstructed. Bashy informed me that she did not in the least blame her brother, whose temper was becoming "something perfectly awful."

"What would you be, Billy," the girl interrupted herself

to ask, "if you had been shut up in Rachel Cobb's bedroom for more than four weeks?"

I felt myself unable to guess what I should be.

"Well," went on Bashy, who was sitting on the bearskin which was spread on the river bank, " Miss Cobb came in as if she had been thrown from a mortar by somebody who had aimed her as near Vane's bed as she could alight and not be actually on it. She had a handful of currants in one hand, and the red juice dropped on to Vane's face. She looked around the room. 'Didn't I hear a crash?' she asked. Then she saw the mirror and flung up her hands, the currants dropping into Vane's neck. Of course he swore ; he doesn't do much else now, poor fellow, and you can't blame him much. 'My lookin'-glass!' cried Miss Cobb. Then her eye-glasses fell off. 'It's the one my great-grandmother had when she married her second husband— and it's a dretful bad sign ; it's a wuss sign 'n hearin' the death watch or seein' three white hosses one after the other. Somebody in this house 'll die 'fore the year's out. I never knew a broken lookin'-glass to fail—never !'

"Having told us this cheerful bit, Miss Cobb proceeded to gather up the fragments and carry them out. The nurse followed. She said she didn't suppose her presence was necessary while Mr. Hildreth had his sister with him. What do you suppose Vane did then ? Well, he cried ; he actually sobbed like a girl, and I cried with him. He said if the looking-glass knew what 'twas about he'd be the one to die, and a good thing, too ; he never 'd be able to sing another note, and wouldn't I ask Miss Armstrong if she wouldn't please come in and sing to him ; he wanted to know how she was getting along. Now, will you go ?"

This request had come so very unexpectedly that I hesitated involuntarily. I had not seen Mr. Hildreth since that day when he had been brought to Miss Cobb's. Seeing my hesitation, Bashy flushed and said, quickly:

"I hope you're not a prude as well as—"

"As what?" I asked, quickly.

"Oh, as well as having notions about wine and cards, and being a little Puritan generally."

This made me angry. If there was anything I did not feel like, that thing was a Puritan. I rose.

"I'll go now and see your brother," I said.

I walked away; I walked slowly because I wanted to run. I felt my cheeks burning. I heard Bashy's contralto voice singing in a very irritating way. This is what she was singing, apparently improvising the music on the spur of the moment:

> "Did you ever see the devil,
>   With his little spade and shovel,
>   Digging praties in the garden,
>   With his tail cocked up?"

These words did not seem appropriate to me or to the situation, but the girl was singing them with great air, as if they were remarkably fitting. I would not turn my head. I heard her laugh. Then I asked myself if she had told me the truth—had her brother really made that request.

However, I had said I would go, and so I kept on. Lotus had come from somewhere, and was sedately following me. I walked slower and slower as I came near Miss Cobb's house. That lady was in her kitchen. There was the smell of boiling sugar in the air, and a dish of currants was standing on the table. Miss Cobb was flushed as if from some recent excitement. On my appearance she instantly told me, in a high voice, that she hoped I'd never let a young man into my house, no matter if he had broken every bone in his body. And then her eye-glasses fell off and narrowly escaped going into the syrup on the stove.

I passed on to the bedroom. Mr. Hildreth's face was towards me; it changed greatly when he saw me, and I thought he must be very grateful to any one who would come to see him. He tried to raise himself higher.

When I entered I saw that the nurse was sitting in a large rocker by the one window. She rose and said she would go and see about "his broth." Bathsheba had told me that the nurse never spoke of her patient by his name, but always "he" and "him," just as if, said Bashy, "she'd been his wife."

"Shut the door," said the man on the bed. "I don't want those creatures to look at me."

I didn't like to obey him. It seemed so ridiculous to do as he ordered. I swung the door a little.

"Now come here!" I advanced to the bed and put my hand in his extended palm. "You see I can't be polite," he exclaimed. "Oh, how good it is of you to come! I lie here day after day with nothing to do but look at those two women and think how I might be out-of-doors—perhaps with you—and I'm afraid I shall swear my soul into hell. Oh, do forgive me! Sometimes I try to think a few good thoughts, but I can't do it—I'm like that man who would rather curse than bless any time, because it 'seemed more fittin'!'"

The speaker's face, now that it had grown thin and pallid, brought out his noteworthy eyes still more; and what I have called his foreign look was emphasized.

"Sit down in that chair," said he; "you look now as if you were going directly." I sat down in the chair. I was uneasy, and I had a very strong feeling that Miss Cobb might be listening behind that half-shut door. I suppose

I glanced that way, for my companion immediately asked, "Do you think that pig-woman is listening?" I observed that she might do such a thing. "Might! She would—I know she would. Well, since you won't shut the door, I'll see if I can talk so that she can't possibly hear me. It's so good of you to come! You're a regular missionary, aren't you? And I always hated missionaries."

"Thank you."

"Never mind thanking me, since I don't hate you. Are you happy?"

I didn't quite like to answer this question, but I did say "yes."

"My aunt is good to you?"

"Oh yes, yes!"

"Ah! Then I know your voice is coming on all right. Won't you move your chair up a little nearer this cursed bed—no, no, I mean this—well, this blessed bed?" I obeyed him. "Now, please, let me hold your hand. It is as if, when you touch me, a stream of health came into my poor veins. Thank you. You are a missionary, surely. Sometimes I hear you a good ways off practising. Sing the scale to me."

I sang the scale. I don't know how I sang it, for Vane was looking steadily at me. In my heart I called him Vane, for I heard his sister continually speaking of him by that name. He groaned.

"And to think I sha'n't be the tenor this fall!" he exclaimed.

I would not respond that I should not be the soprano. I only made the remark that he was so much better that he might sing before the season was out.

"What, come in on crutches and hobble about the stage? Besides, my voice is as lame as I am. Just hear it!"

In a half-voice he sang, "To you, my love, to you." I
felt myself blushing, and then blushing yet more hotly with
rage that I had done so. Certainly this man's eyes were
more effective in his white, hollow face than they had been
when he was well. At this moment the door was pushed
slowly open, and Miss Cobb asked, "Did you call?"

"No," snarled Vane.

I saw Rachel's eyes dart to our clasped hands, but I sat
quiet, without starting in the least, though my impulse was
to spring away. I wondered where would be the next
visiting-place of our hostess, for there would she tell a tale
about me and this sick man. The door was drawn back
to precisely the position in which I had placed it, and
Rachel retired.

"You are ever so much better," I repeated, hardly knowing what I said.

"Am I? Yes, I know that I am. But—" he paused,
gazing at me. His look was so wistful, so piteous, that
something seemed to melt within me. It was as if his dog
had looked at me thus.

"You are sorry for me," he whispered ; and I whispered
back, "Yes, I am sorry."

I did not understand why this whisper interchanged
should have such an effect of intimacy, even more than
our mutual handclasp had produced.

"Well," he said, drawing a deep breath, "it's something
to have you sorry for me. Please don't go yet," as I withdrew my hand. I sat still. "I've almost made up my mind
to tell you something," he said, still in a half-whisper. "If
I were sure that woman wouldn't come in, I'd try to tell
you. You would let me?" eagerly.

"Certainly," I replied, promptly. And then it almost
seemed as if my promptness annoyed him. He turned

his head restlessly on his pillow. He looked at the door.

"I suppose you don't want to shut that door and latch it?" he said.

"No; there's no reason why I should do that."

"But those damn women—I mean those dear women—may come in at any moment."

"No matter."

"What!" He raised himself on his elbow, and his face grew red. "Supposing you were a man who had seen a girl who was—whom you—who wasn't like any other girl you'd ever met—whom you thought of every minute—whom you couldn't see because you had broken all your bones—and—and you heard her voice sometimes—and you ate your heart out lying and thinking of her—and now she was sitting beside you—and though you hadn't really known her, it was just as if you had known her a long time, what should you— Oh, the devil!"

He sank back on his pillow as this exclamation left his lips. The nurse was just entering with a tray on which was a cup of steaming broth.

"It's quite time he had his nourishment," she said, looking at me. I rose.

"Are you going?" he asked. This inquiry was made with such a desperate air that I sank back in my seat.

"Take that broth away!" Vane commanded.

"But the doctor's orders are to keep up your strength," responded the nurse, standing in the middle of the room.

"Take that broth away!" repeated the young man.

I rose again. I felt that I would not remain another minute. I walked to the door. There I turned to say "Good-bye."

"Miss Armstrong," cried Vane, with a still greater ap-

9

pearance of desperation. "If you won't stay until this lady with the hot broth will go, why, then, I must tell you before her—"

"Mr. Hildreth!" I exclaimed, my heart jumping with still greater excitement. But he would not be stopped. His eyes were flashing fire.

"That I love you, Miss Armstrong! Yes. I haven't known you long, but I began to love you the first time I saw you, and have gone right on loving you more and more. Now," glancing furiously at the nurse, "hand me that broth!"

I hurried from the room, coming plump upon Rachel close to the door. She caught at my sleeve as I was trying to go by her. Her jaws snapped and her glasses dropped off.

"Good land, Wilhelmina Armstrong!" she cried. "Did you hear that?" She had fast hold of me, and I could not go on without taking her with me. "Of course he must be raving crazy, or he wouldn't think of such a thing."

This complimentary remark I swallowed in silence, hardly noticing it at the moment. But I recalled it later with no exhilarating effect on my self-esteem. I made another attempt to go, but Rachel was not ready to release me. She was staring at me and listening at the same time for sounds in the next room.

"Yes," she said, "them broken bones have gone to his head. The doctor said they might." She now manifested a willingness to walk along with me. I hurried out of the house. As soon as we were in the yard Rachel seized me again. "He's certainly crazy," she repeated. "I d' know, I'm sure, what I should do if any man should tell me, 'fore folks, that he loved me. I do s'pose I should go right into hysterics."

She spoke as if hysterics were something made and provided as a retreat for women before unexpected declarations of love. I began to laugh excitedly. Then I bethought me that, if Mr. Hildreth heard me, he might think
I was mocking at him. I stopped as suddenly as I had
begun. My one longing at this instant was to get away
from Rachel Cobb. And Rachel plainly intended that I
should not get away just yet. She had more to say. The
incident was too full of interest; it was something to roll
under the tongue now and for many a visit yet to come.

I hurried down the narrow path towards the road, Rachel
close by my side. She had given up listening to what
might pass between the nurse and Mr. Hildreth, deciding
that she would rather, in view of the circumstances, be with
me for the next few moments. I saw that I could not shake
her off. Instead of trying any more to do so, I suddenly
stopped at the turnstile in the fence and leaned upon it,
putting on an air of leisure. Rachel did not lean; she
stood upright close to me. I was quivering with excitement, but I called up all my self-control, that I might hide
that fact from my companion.

"I never did!" she exclaimed, after a silence, during
which she had stared closely at me. I made no reply to
this. "What you goin' to do 'bout it?" she asked.

"Do? Nothing."

"Nothin'? Sha'n't you soo him?"

"No: I don't think I shall sue him."

"Wall; you'll have to do something. You can't let such
a thing pass 'thout doin' nothin'. 'Twouldn't be right. I
guess your father 'll see 'bout it. Why, it's equal to breach
of promise, or divorce—or—or—" Imagination failed Miss
Cobb at this juncture. I remained motionless, leaning on
the turnstile. "He ought to be took up," clicked Rachel.

"I don't believe but what the s'lectmen can take him up. If you want me to, I'll speak to 'em 'bout it. I s'pose you'll feel kind of delikit 'bout doin' it yourself."

"You needn't speak to them on my account."

"Needn't? Wall, jes' 's you say. But I hope you ain't goin' to take any stock in what that feller's jest said." I made no reply. I was asking myself in a startled way if I did "take any stock" in his words. "Be ye?" insisted Miss Cobb.

"I don't know," I answered.

"All I c'n say is, you'll git dretfully took in if you do. Why, he's makin' fun of ye. Anybody c'n see that with half an eye. I call it shameful! He ought to be took up."

Here my companion turned and went back into the house. Thus released, I hurried along the river path. But I was not going where I should be likely to see any one. I went on past the falls. Bathsheba, under the hackmatacks, called to me to come and practise with her, but I shook my head. I was sure I could not sing now. I heard Miss Runciman's clear high notes from somewhere beyond the carriage. We never know when there will be an apparently causeless revulsion in us. I wanted to put my hands over my ears as the delicious notes reached me. I ran on. Be sure I had not forgotten anything that Miss Runciman had told me about her nephew. I was thinking of what she had said all the time I was listening to him.

Yes, of course, he was amusing himself. There could not be the slightest doubt about that. And I resented the fact deeply and seriously. Still—well, this was the first time any man had ever told me he loved me, and naturally the words had a different effect from what they might have had upon another listener—Miss Rachel Cobb, for instance. Certainly Mr. Hildreth was trying to kill time; he couldn't occupy himself entirely by swearing. He needed some other recreation. Still, I could not help recalling his eyes, and the peculiar vibration in his voice. At the same time, I knew that his eyes and his voice could ably take part in a scene of love-making. Taking everything into consideration, it seemed very fortunate that I understood Vane Hildreth—this phase of him—so well; very fortunate, indeed. Otherwise I might, having had no experience in love affairs, have taken him rather seriously; yes, I might even have gone so far as to "soo" him. Here I began to laugh, and I was still laughing when some one spoke just behind me.

It was Miss Runciman, and she said she was glad to find me so happy. She came forward, pausing close to me. She looked at me; then she looked again. "What have you been doing?" she asked.

I made up my mind on the instant. Rachel would tell the whole affair to a great many people before twenty-four hours were over. I would tell it, too. It was not like other tender declarations. "I have been hearing a man tell me he loves me," I answered, promptly.

She glanced still more sharply at me. "Remember," she said, with emphasis, "that you are to be a singer. A singer gives herself to her art wholly. She mustn't play at love, save on the stage."

"I know it," I responded, eagerly. Before I could speak again, she said:

"I hope you made young Blake understand. Of course, he, however, could not tempt you."

"It wasn't young Blake." How very odd that she had thought of Bidwell!

"Not Blake?" She put her hand on my arm, and turned me more fully towards her. I looked in her eyes; I suc-

ceeded in keeping my gaze in hers during the next question
and reply.   "Who, then?"

"Mr. Hildreth."

"Oh!"   Here her gaze wandered, and she visibly relaxed
in her attitude.   If I had been cherishing anything sentimental in regard to Vane Hildreth, I should have received
another blow now.   Miss Runciman gave a little laugh.
"Oh!" again.   "So Vane has been taking up his time in
that way?   Poor fellow!   I hope you'll overlook his weakness.   Still, he ought to know better.   How did you find
him this morning?"   I replied that he seemed very impatient, but that he was gaining.   "Yes; he will be out of bed
within a few weeks, the doctor says.   But the whole affair
will be very tedious.   Do you feel that those lower notes
are strengthening any, Billy?   Try them—but try not to
appear as if you were uncertain, you know.   Attack them
with confidence.   I wish I could give you an example, but
my lower register—bah!   I'm growing old."

I did as she requested, and I felt myself excelling all my
other efforts.   I sang so that my soul seemed to catch fire
from my voice.   And all the time I watched Miss Runciman's face as if that were the source of my inspiration.
And I saw it change and glow with greater and greater
triumph—and what was that?   How could it be suspicion?
Suspicion in regard to what?   When this question entered
my mind it seemed to have an instant effect on my voice.
I stopped singing.   Miss Runciman suddenly and impulsively took me in her arms, pushing my hat off and thrust-
ing the hair from my forehead.

 "Magnificent!   Magnificent!" she cried.   "Oh, I wasn't
wrong in this whim!   But—"   Here she paused.   I could
not ask a question.   "I suspect you—yes, I suspect you.
But no, that is impossible!"

I had not the slightest idea as to what she meant. I stood there in silence while her eyes continued to dwell upon me as if they were trying to probe my soul. After a little she released me, saying, as she did so, "What a clear lake your consciousness is! Well, that's a good thing. But the trouble with good things is, they don't last. Billy, in five years, nay, in two years from now, I wonder if your soul will be as transparent?"

Again I did not answer. I did not know that I was transparent in any way. It occurred to me, fleetingly, at this moment, that I had hitherto been very little self-conscious. I had never analyzed a thought, a feeling, or a motive. Did people analyze themselves? That must be a strange thing to do.

When Miss Runciman spoke again, she said, lightly: "It's quite a relief to me to know that you have not imagined that you had an entanglement with that young Blake. Such affairs sometimes make more or less unpleasantness. But as for Vane—" here she paused and laughed. She did not finish the sentence. It was really not worth while to contemplate Vane's love-making to me.

The next morning Miss Runciman had the gray colt saddled, and rode off to the post-office. She occasionally did this, and every time I saw the colt gallop away carrying her upon his back I was seized with a harrowing fear that he would throw her off. I confided this fear to my father one day when we met the gray tearing home from the village with Miss Runciman in the saddle. The gravel flew up from the horse's hoofs as he dashed by.

"He'll throw her some day!" I exclaimed.

Father took the pipe from his mouth and winked and laughed. "Don't you fret, Bill. That's a woman that can take care of herself. Besides, she's paid for the colt.

I sha'n't lose a cent if she does git throwed — not a cent."

I turned and looked at father. I remember that this was the first time that I really suspected that he wasn't joking when he said such things—that he really meant them. Something cold seemed to touch my heart. I made involuntarily a slight shrinking movement. I saw that he noticed that movement. A curious glint came to his eyes; but he laughed again as he said: "You ain't goin' to set up to be like your mother, be you, Billy? But," with unction, "there ain't many such good women 's your mother, now, I tell ye."

It was the very next day after that—it was the last day of August—that I hurriedly entered the kitchen when Aunt Lowizy was picking over huckleberries.

"I've come to say good-bye," I announced. "Miss Runciman has decided to move on. We start.this afternoon."

"I want to know!" Aunt Lowizy looked up from her berries. I glanced about the old-fashioned room, and then, without the least warning, I began to cry.

"Oh, I wish mother was here!" I exclaimed.

Aunt Lowizy said: "There, now, so do I. But she'll be here when you come back, sure."

When I came back! To my exaggerated sense it was as if years might pass before then—and I had a wild, intense feeling that I couldn't—no, I could not—go without seeing mother. I tried immediately, however, to control my emotion.

There was father coming in from the barn. I struggled with myself to such good purpose that, though my face was red, I was yet able to tell father when he entered, in a matter-of-fact way, that the big wagon would start that afternoon—that I had only an hour. He walked out with

me, keeping with me along the river path. He asked if Bid
Blake knew; and I said no, the decision had been reached
since Miss Runciman heard from the post-office. And I
asked him to say good-bye to Bidwell for me.

Father kissed me when we reached the curve in the path,
and he told me that if I had a mind to play my cards right,
Miss Runciman would probably do first-rate by me. Then
he kissed me loudly again, and turned, while I went on
towards the carriage. I stopped and looked back at him,
a strange, confused feeling having possession of me.

As I stood there gazing at him, Bathsheba from below
called: "Billy, come down here! Don't stand sentimen-
talizing. Help me pack these eggs. It is as if we were
going into an eggless country."

At almost the same time Rachel Cobb appeared outside
her door. "Wilhelmina," she called, distinctly, "Mr. Hildreth wants you to come here."

I hesitated between Mr. Hildreth and the eggs. I had
not seen this gentleman since the interview I have narrat-
ed—the interview when he had, before witnesses, informed
me that he loved me. Miss Cobb had apparently recov-
ered from the excitement caused by that declaration, and
she had not, to my knowledge, communicated with the
Selectmen concerning it. But she had, as father had told
me, "peddled it all over the neighborhood."

As he gave this information he had looked sharply in my
face. I replied that it was perfectly ridiculous, and that I
supposed it had happened because, as Rachel had suggested,
the young man's bones had gone to his head. Whereupon
father had given his great laugh and had said nothing more.

As I stood undecided, Miss Cobb called again, and this
time Bashy also heard her and immediately advised me to
obey what she said was the higher call. So I went.

Mr. Hildreth was sitting in the shade of the house in a large chair. Two crutches were resting against this chair. He leaned forward as I approached. Lotus was lying on the ground near him. The dog now often visited his master. I naturally felt some embarrassment as I drew near, and this feeling was not lessened by the knowledge that Rachel was standing in the doorway carefully examining me.

"I'm so glad you are better," I exclaimed. I held out my hand, which was taken and retained.

"Thanks—so much," returned Vane.

Then he glanced at the woman watching us. With extreme politeness he begged for a glass of water. Rachel moved reluctantly away. The instant her back was turned Vane kissed my hand; and he said in a low voice: "You've been atrociously cruel to me. Don't you know I meant what I said?"

I smiled, and I'm afraid I blushed also. But I was able to say, lightly: "I suppose I haven't given the matter much consideration."

It was Vane who grew red now. But before he could say anything Rachel came hurrying out with the water. I said we were all so thankful that Mr. Hildreth would be able to get away so soon, and that Miss Runciman now felt confident that he would be able to sing before the season really closed, and—Good-bye, Mr. Hildreth!"

The young man had drawn himself up in his chair quite rigidly, and he was very white. "Good-bye, Miss Armstrong!" he returned.

And I went away, with Miss Cobb looking at us both. Presently I heard a soft footfall behind me. There was the brindled dog following. At almost the same instant his master called him sharply, fiercely. Lotus paused; I glanced back to see him hesitate. He whined a little under his breath. His master called again. The dog went slowly back. I hurried on. I did not go to the carriage immediately. I sat down in a retired spot and listened to the sound of the falls. I hoped that Bashy would not happen to find me just yet. Very probably she had seen me returning from Miss Cobb's. I was grieved that Vane had called Lotus back in that way. And Lotus had wished to come with me. Yes, I was sore about that. He might have let the dog follow. What harm would his coming have done?

IX

BY THE UNQUENCHABLE SEA.

In the middle of that September there was a great southerly gale. It was to be our last week in the carriage. Miss Runciman had kept near the coast. Sometimes we travelled fifteen miles in a day, and some days not at all. We always stopped not far from a settlement, but never in the village itself. The young man, or rather big boy, who was driver and hostler would then unhitch the horses and take them to a stable, finding some place for his own stay; Bashy or I would sally forth to get whatever provision we needed, and Miss Runciman and the girl who remained with her would prepare the meal. We had very good times at those meals. Miss Runciman possessed great skill with a chafing-dish, and many were the curious concoctions she made. Some of them Lotus ate when he had been with us, but the most of them we devoured. I should have been ashamed of my appetite if the others had not been equally hungry. And they drank wine with luncheon and dinner. Our most elaborate meal was at night. For a time the having dinner at night was, as Rachel Cobb would have said, "most upsetting" to me. Occasionally we all went to the hotel nearest us, and Miss Runciman, who was what seemed to me ridiculously fastidious, would make the waiters there rather unhappy.

But it was the custom of drinking wine to which I could

not become reconciled.   It was some light wine at luncheon, and often a bottle of champagne at dinner, or supper, as I always thought of the meal.   And there were many delicate, beautiful glasses from which to drink, and two or three curious silver cups which our hostess had picked up in her travels.

I recall that I wished to drink from those vessels—there was a charm in connection with them ; wine in such receptacles was a draught of romance.   At the same time I shrank, and had the feeling that it was low to do such a thing.   These feelings were contradictory, but then emotions are frequently contradictory.

And I was horribly shocked when I perceived sometimes that Bathsheba's spirits were a little higher after her champagne than before it.   I suppose she saw this in my face one evening as she was leaning back in her chair after dinner.   She had been trolling out a drinking-song.   In the midst of the chorus she suddenly stopped, gazing at me.

"Dear little Puritan maiden Priscilla !" she exclaimed. "Look at her, Aunt Nora !   Is it my champagne or my song that brings that expression of horror ?"

Miss Runciman was sitting twirling her delicate-stemmed glass absently around and around between her thumb and finger.   There was a slight flush on her face.   She smiled at her niece as she responded : " Bashy, you flatted at F in the last line."   She rose and suddenly flung up her hand with her glass in it.   There was the fine freedom of a Bacchante in her gesture and attitude.   I leaned forward eagerly, my heart beating fast.

Standing thus, Miss Runciman burst out singing, or, more accurately, chanting :

" Go, let others praise the Chian!
This is soft as Muses' string,

> This is tawny as Rhea's lion,
>   This is rapid as his spring.
> Bright as Paphia's eyes e'er met us,
>   Light as ever trod her feet !
> And the brown bees of Hymettus
>   Make their honey not so sweet."

I cannot describe the enchanting swing and rush of the words as enunciated by this woman. By the time the last line had left the singer's lips I had sprung up from my chair. I did not know what I was thinking of doing. Bashy laughed. How could she laugh? My eyes were burning as they rested on the woman's face. Bathsheba poured some champagne into a tall-stemmed glass. She rose and held out the glass to me. I was hardly conscious that I extended my hand for it. I had already grasped it when a curious change came to Miss Runciman.

"Bathsheba!" she cried, sharply. She reached forward and suddenly gave a sharp, though slight, blow to my hand. The glass fell, breaking on the table; the wine spread on the cloth.

"Well, Aunt Nora!" exclaimed Bashy, "you are a queer woman. What do you mean by that?"

Miss Runciman was cool and calm on the moment. She placed her own glass by her plate and sat down deliberately. " I mean just this," she observed, "that if Billy has any individual notions about wine—or—or—brown bread, why, let her have them."

Here the speaker laughed. She glanced at me. My face was hot. I was grateful to her for knocking that glass from my hand. And I was thinking of mother; and I was trying to keep the tears back.

"Thank you," I said, in a whisper.

"No," said Miss Runciman, seriously, "you needn't

thank me. If there be any blame in the matter it belongs to me more than to Bathsheba."

And when I came to think the matter over by myself I agreed with her. I determined to write all about it to mother, but the days kept going by and I did not find time, and I think I became a trifle bewildered concerning the subject. Once I asked myself if I was making the drinking of an occasional glass of wine stand for too much. When I saw my mother I would have a long talk with her. But, then, in the bottom of my heart I knew that mother did not approve of my being with Miss Runciman and learning to sing of her.

I hardly know how I came to tell of this little incident when I began this chapter by speaking of the great storm in that September. Our big wagon was standing on the shingles close to a cove that was called Peggotty's Cove. We had arrived the night before, and had sat on the beach until almost midnight. Not a person had come near us. Off to our left was the stretch of rocks running out to protect the entrance to a small harbor. On this point of rocks burned the Bug Light like a little candle, throwing its beams upon a naughty world. There were small cottages over there, and we could see the lights in them. It was breathlessly still that evening. The water rustled placidly on the pebbles.

We three women talked very little, but we sang a good deal. I had been learning some of *Il Trovatore*. Miss Runciman said she had a fancy to see what I would do with it. I went over several of the soprano solos at her request now. I sang the English version of the libretto, for she wished me to understand my words. She laid great stress from the first on my knowing the meaning of what I sang, word for word.

"It's a good time for that first solo of Leonora's," Miss Runciman remarked. "Try it." I did try it. Let me say that to me Verdi's opera, that everybody has heard so many times, was all fresh and new. It appealed to me keenly. I was carried along on its tide of emotion.

I began, "The night, calmly and peacefully," and I went on until I had reached "A wand'ring minstrel sung," then I stopped suddenly.

"Well, continue," commanded my teacher.

I hesitated. I had not a single secret to keep; I was in love with no one. Yet I had a kind of dread in regard to singing. The next moment, however, obeying her request, I finished the solo.

> "To heart, and eyes, with rapture filled,
>   The earth like heav'n appeared."

Miss Runciman had been noiselessly picking up pebbles. Now she dropped the stones and turned deliberately towards me. But the dusk prevented any clear sight. Still, her gaze was fixed for a moment or two; then she reached forward and laid her hand on mine.

"Of course, your hands are cold," she said; and that was all the remark she made then. I was disappointed. I wished to know what she thought of my voice; but I could not ask her. After a little Bashy exclaimed, glancing at her aunt: "I say, Auntie, sha'n't you some time be jealous of your understudy?" I had begun to tremble with the reaction.

Miss Runciman laughed. "No, my dear Bashy. I triumph with her."

The elder woman's face, when we went back to the carriage, where the lamp was, seemed very white, the eyes shining steadily.

At the door we all delayed to look at the bank of black cloud which lay along the southern horizon. A fisherman came slouching along as we stood there, his great rubber boots flapping about his legs as he walked. "Better reef all your sails, you folks!" he called out, as he rolled by. A strong scent of whiskey came from him; and we heard him swearing to himself as he went on. In the night, or rather in the early morning, I was wakened by the roaring of the wind across the harbor. The carriage rocked and clattered. The gale had begun, and a southerly gale on the Massachusetts coast is something to be remembered. I could not think of sleeping again, and just as the light grew more clear I rose and dressed. The wind always excited me. I was afraid of it, and yet I longed to be out in it. As I crept along noiselessly by the hammock where Miss Runciman lay, she caught me by the sleeve.

"Where are you going?" she whispered.

"To see how it looks," I replied, in the same tone.

She still held my sleeve.

"Have you slept?" she asked.

"A little."

"I have not—not a wink," she said.

"I'm so sorry."

"Yes; I'm sure you are. What do you suppose I've been saying over and over to myself?"

"What is it?"

"Why, this: The king is dead; long live the king! Now go. Perhaps I will have a nap."

I went on, asking myself what Miss Runciman could mean. But I forgot to wonder when I was trying to walk across the shingles towards the village, which was more than a mile distant by land; but across the harbor water, from this bit of a peninsula, it was not half that distance.

The clouds raced over the sky, and the stars shone fitfully. The rocks and the black hollows looked blacker than ever. The wind drove from the land, flattening every wave that tried to rear a crest out there beyond the low-tide line. The Bug Light shone. I had a wild idea that the world was whirling off somewhere, and that, if I watched, I could see it going. I would go on. I had never been on the coast until I came this journey with Miss Runciman ; when I was by myself I had a kind of feeling as if I were bewitched.

My skirts and long cloak wound about me so that I could only move slowly. My hat had blown off as I had stepped from the carriage; it had instantly whirled away into space, and I knew I could not reclaim it. I pulled up the hood of the cloak and drew it far over my face.

I moved on towards the village, thus facing the gale, and conscious of a delight in it. The gray of the morning was fast becoming luminous. Suddenly the east became flushed ; the sun came up and went into a cloud.

" It's going to rain," I said. I had reached the corner where the road left the coast somewhere and curved towards the bit of a hamlet where fishermen and farmers lived. Perhaps some of them would be up and I could get some new milk to carry back with me. I knew how early country people rose. I walked on, with head bent, not seeing anything but the ground I stepped on, and not knowing that I had passed a corner of a highway that led inland. The wind was roaring in the tops of some elms by the roadside ; the sumacs by the path were laid over half their height, their great maroon-colored tufts draggling in the road.

I had hardly had a vague thought that there was a sound of rushing steps somewhere, I did not know where, when something hit me and I fell. My principal sensation was of the palms of my hands smarting from rubbing on the gravel. Before I could gather myself together, some one was lifting me up. I had a glimpse of brown gauntlet gloves which were unfamiliar to me.

"Do tell me you're not hurt!" exclaimed a man's voice.

I withdrew myself from the detaining arms and answered promptly:

"I'm not hurt at all. But what knocked me over?"

I looked up, staggering by reason of the wind as I did so.

"What!" said the man's voice. "It's you, is it?"

"Yes; but who—"

I had managed by this time to see the person who was talking to me thus. A tall man, with bright, strong eyes. Where had I seen those eyes? Oh, yes—

"Why, is it Mr. Maverick?" I asked. I was surprised that I recalled his name, but it came pat enough the instant I saw his eyes.

"Yes; it's Mr. Maverick." He took off his close cap as he spoke. "And it's Miss Armstrong. How curious! But tell me again you're not hurt."

"Not a bit."

I was preparing to resume my walk. There seemed no reason why I should stop and try to talk in this gale with a man whom I knew so very little.

"It was horribly careless of me," he went on. "But I never dreamed any one would be on the road as early as this. And this wind makes my horse wild. He has come five miles like a crazy thing. He dashed around that corner as if he were possessed."

"Are you staying here?"

Mr. Maverick had put on his cap with a firm gesture; he

had turned and taken his horse by the bridle as if he would accompany me.

"I'm staying a short distance from here," I answered, "for a day or two."

"You really must let me walk with you for a little," he now said, "until I've satisfied myself that you're not injured. By good rights, you ought to have a broken bone or a sprain."

"But I haven't."

"Nevertheless, I won't be sent away just yet."

We walked on side by side, he leading the horse, which I recognized as the one father had sold him. The wind shrieked and roared around us. It was not a good opportunity for conversation if we had wished to talk.

"No broken bone develops itself," he shouted, after he had watched me walk by his side for a few moments.

"No," I shouted back.

And now I supposed he would go. He seemed to be looking here and there. Presently he said: "They told me a few miles back that that travelling house carriage was somewhere down here."

"Are you trying to find that?" I asked, rather startled.

"Yes," at the top of his voice. "I was going to put up my horse, and then explore until I found it. I want to see the lady who 'runs it,' as they said when I inquired. Of course, you can't tell me. You haven't seen it."

"Yes, I've seen it," I replied. I turned and pointed in the direction from which I had come. "When you get around that corner you'll see the carriage—on the beach."

"Oh, thank you!"

He paused and asked again if I were sure I was all right; and again I told him.

He stepped near his horse, put his hand on the animal's withers and sprang into the saddle.

The horse plunged; its rider snatched off his cap once more, then the horse dashed into a swift gallop. Even above the wind I could hear the smiting of its hoofs on the ground. I resumed my walk. Suddenly it occurred to my mind to wonder why I was out walking in such a gale. Was it merely to be in a gale? I hurried up to the lee side of a barn and sat down on a piece of timber lying there. I was looking towards the north, where the sky was still clear, as if the wind had swept it. I could feel the old barn reel as I leaned my back against it. Presently I heard the sound of feet on the floor within. A horse "nickered"; a man's hoarse voice spoke. Then came the sharp, well-defined noise of milk falling in small streams into a tin pail.

After a few moments I rose and was about to go around to the entrance of the barn and ask to buy some milk. As I reached the corner of the building the gale gave me such a buffet full in the face that I shrank back again. There was a dash of rain in the wind, too. I saw, coming through the slanting rain, the "depot wagon" from the first train.

I did not think anything about this fact, however, and I stood in the shelter, idly thinking that it could not rain long with such a clear sky to the north.

Somebody in the barn said: "Hullo, Bill, that you? Ain't ye 'bout blowed? Got any passengers?"

"One. He's goin' to git out here. Ain't this the nearest to that cart with them women in it?"

"Yes, I guess 'tis."

Something more was said, but the wind began a still more violent shriek and wail.

"What, still another visitor?" I was saying to myself.

The next moment a man spoke. He must have been

close to the other side of the boards of the barn wall. He asked: "'Bout how fur is it to that wagon where the women stay?" When I heard the question I jumped. It was my father who had made the inquiry. I stood still for an instant to take in this fact. Then I ran around to the entrance, pushing against the wind as against a solid wall. I ran up to father and caught hold of his arm. The question in my mind was so dreadful I could hardly speak it.

"Father," I cried out, "is there anything the matter with mother?"

Father had his big rubber coat on and his cap tied over his ears.

"If there ain't Billy herself!" he cried, and he kissed me resoundingly. The milk ceased going into the pail, and I knew the man on the milking-stool had stopped work to listen to us.

"How is mother?" I asked again.

"Oh, I guess she's all right," was the answer. "She ain't got home yet."

I grew weak with the relief I felt. I had not heard from mother for nearly three weeks. I stood staring at father. He didn't return my gaze. He moved towards the horse stall, slapped the animal on the hip, then walked in beside it, opened its mouth, and looked at its teeth. I began to feel an ill-defined but decided resentment stirring within me. Then I reproved myself for that resentment.

Father came from the stall and stood beside me. He took a pipe from an inner pocket and carefully examined the contents of the bowl; then he tapped the bowl against the timber at the end of the stall. He seemed entirely occupied with what he was doing, and yet I suddenly imagined that I detected a slight embarrassment in his manner. As for me, I resolved that I would stand there and choke with my rising curiosity before I would ask why he had come.

I could not understand why there was a current of rebellion or indignation in my mind, a rebellion growing stronger every moment.

"Terrible hard wind, ain't it?" asked father.

"Yes," I answered.

He put his pipe back in his waistcoat pocket. He spat on the floor. Then he asked:

"Ain't there no place where you 'n' I c'n talk a minute?"

I reflected. With a stranger already at the carriage there seemed no room there. And the wind blew so—then I thought of a place.

"We can be sheltered on the north side of that cliff," pointing.

"All right: come on, then."

Father started, and I followed. The rain had ceased. The wind blew us on. In ten minutes we were standing safely under the big sand cliff. Father pulled out his pipe again. This time he filled and lighted it.

"I hope nothing has happened," I said.

He looked at me and laughed.

"Oh, yes, something's happened," he answered. "It's something that happens to most girls some time or other," and now he winked. What in the world did he mean? I decided that he would tell in good time. I waited in silence. "I s'pose you've kinder understood young Blake all this time, ain't ye?" he asked.

"Understood him?"

"Yes. You ain't no fool, ye know. Of course, you knew he wanted to marry you."

"No; I didn't know it."

Father chuckled as if this were a girlish denial. I felt

the blood rising to my head. And in my mind was the per-
plexing question as to why I seemed to feel differently to
father from the way I used to feel. There was some re-
morse in this question.

"Course, you want to say that; that's all right, you know,"
was the response. "Wall, Bid's been comin' over a good
deal, 'n' smokin' with me on the back stoop there; 'n' so
finally he told me how 'twas with him. He said he never
got screwed up to speakin' to you. He was in a great state,
now, I can tell you; 'n' you goin' off 's you be, 'n' so on.
You c'n imagine all that. The long 'n' short is, he thought
I'd better come 'n' see you 'fore you went still further away.
So here I be."

"Bidwell needn't have sent you, father," I said, with
rather a high air.

"Why not?"

Father's tone was short.

"Because I sha'n't marry him."

"Sha'n't you?"

This question was followed by a slight laugh, different
from father's ordinary laugh.

"No."

Father leaned back against the cliff, with his hands in
his pockets. He was looking at me with narrow eyes.

"I d' know how much of your mother you've got in you,"
he said, after a momentary silence, "but I guess we'll have
one good, square talk. Then we'll know how we stand, 'n'
what kind of a trade we c'n make—'ain't that so?"

I nodded my head.

"You know the Blakes have got the biggest 'n' best farm
in the county, 'n' Bid's the only child. Now I look at it in
this way: there's nothin' more uncertain under the canopy
than whether you'll make a go of this singin' business. The

chances are you won't. There can't be only 'bout so many big singers, 'n' we can't expect you to be one of 'em. If you should turn out one, why, of course, you couldn't hardly be expected to marry Bid. Now, I should say 'twould be a capital plan to give Bid your promise—you see that'll be security, so to speak. You c'n fall back on Bid if you don't make a go, and if you do make a ten strike, why, how could a feller expect a first-class opery singer to marry him 'n' settle down on a farm? I can't live forever, 'n' I ain't so well off 's some folks think I am."

Father's pipe had gone out. He lighted three matches before he could kindle it again. I watched each tiny flame start and grow, as if I were thinking of nothing else. My heart was like lead. How expressive that old phrase is— a heart like lead !

"Wall, what do you say, Billy?" when he could puff out the smoke once more.

"No," I answered again. I wanted to tell father that I understood the proposition he had made, but my tongue just then could only utter monosyllables.

"What?"

"No."

Several puffs of smoke, and then father remarked in a very mild voice :

"P'raps you've be'n 'n' got a notion for that singin' feller —the one that was laid up at Rachel Cobb's, 'n' that made love to you 'fore 'em all."

No answer to this.

"Have you?" he insisted, still in the mildest possible way. "Gals 'll do awful queer things sometimes. I don't expect you to be more nor less than a gal, nohow, Billy. Have you?"

"No."

Father's eyes, still narrowed, were on me. I did not blush in the least as I answered.

"All right. I did hope you wouldn't be such a thunderin' fool 's that. That feller didn't mean nothin'. I guess he was rehearsing."

"Yes," I responded promptly, "he was rehearsing."

"You knew it, then?" exclaimed father, gazing still more keenly at me.

"Oh, yes; I knew it."

"Oh, by gum! That's a good joke on Rachel Cobb, ain't it? She's be'n peddlin' the story all over creation."

I winced inwardly, but I made no reply to this remark.

"I guess we c'n come to an understandin' all right now, Billy," father went on with his most comfortable manner. "You jest git engaged to Bid. You'll be allfired glad of it when you find you can't be a first-class singer. He's a real good feller. Of course he 'ain't had advantages; I s'pose he don't talk no better grammar 'n' I do. But he'll make a prime husband. Now you say yes, 'n' I'll go back 'n' tell him, 'n' he'll come right down to see you himself."

"Will he?"

But what did I care for the fact that he had let father come on such an errand?

"You bet he will. Wall, it's all settled, ain't it?"

"Yes."

Father seemed to have the power to wellnigh take away my speech just now.

"That's a good Billy. I knew she was father's own girl."

Here he kissed my cheek. "Now I guess I better take the next train back." He looked at his watch. As he raised his eyes from the timepiece I suppose something in my face made his gaze remain on me. I made an exertion.

"It's all settled," I repeated, "but not in the way you wish."

"Eh?"

"Not in the way you wish," raising my voice even more than was necessary. "I'm not going to engage myself to Bid Blake, thinking I'll keep my word if I fail in my profession, and that I won't keep it if I succeed."

"What?"

I went over my sentence again, word for word.

"That's the way you look at it?"

"Yes."

"You needn't git up any high-minded tantrums about that," responded father, still in his most calm way. Then, as if to himself, "I always did kind of suspect she had something of her mother in her, though she 'ain't shown it much." He turned and looked at the water as if he saw it for the first time. With his face thus averted, he went on:

"You jest engage yourself to Bid, 'n' then you 'n' he can manage as you please. I didn't know 's you was going to take my little plan so solemn like. I didn't mean nothin' out of the way."

"No," I answered, "I won't engage myself to him."

"Don't you like him?"

"Very much indeed."

"Then what you kickin' against?" I could not reply to this.

Father was gazing at me now, and I thought there was contempt in his expression. There was a strange feeling rising in my heart.

"It's that singer feller, after all!"

And then father swore emphatically, and I stood silent and drooping until there was a chance for me to say:

" I told you no."

" What if you did ? But I guess we won't talk any more. I must try to ketch my train so 's to git back in time for the chores to-night. Good-bye, Billy !"

He kissed me on both cheeks, and started to walk up to the road. I watched him, his big boot-tops flapping, his burly frame bent over to meet the wind. Suddenly, without knowing that I was going to do so, I called:

" Father ! Father !"

He did not turn. I suppose the noise of the wind drowned my voice. I started to run after him. But I only ran a few yards before I stopped. I returned slowly to the shelter of the cliff.

I said, aloud, " I feel horribly about father."

In a few moments I left the shelter ; I wanted to be out in the wind ; it was good to feel it striking me hard blows. Stoutly I climbed up on the grassy side of the cliff, feeling like a pygmy twisted about by a giant.

Youth is a strange phase—nay, a strange thing—for sometimes it seems something tangible. I was not thinking now of father or Bidwell, or even of singing, but only of that poem of Elizabeth Stoddard's which Miss Runciman had read to us two girls after we came to this place.

Inexplicably at this moment the lines seemed to have some definite mission in my life.

Was it this very headland upon which the poet stood ?

> " What is my recompense upon this soil,
>   For other paths are mine if I go hence,
>   Still must I make this mystery my quest ?
>   For here or there, I think, one sways my will.

*   *   *   *   *   *

Here, but the wiry grass and sorrel beds,
The gaping edges of the sand ravines,
Whose shifting sides are tufted with dull herbs,
Drooping above a brook, that sluggish creeps
Down to the whispering rushes in the marsh.
And this is all, until I reach the cliff,
And on the headland's verge I stand, enthralled
Before the gulf of the unquenchable sea—
The sea, inexorable in its might,
Circling the pebbly beach with limpid tides,
Storming in bays whose margins fade in mist."

I said aloud, " The unquenchable sea !" and then something pulled my cloak from behind — something that was
not the wind.

There was Bathsheba.

" Well, I must say," she exclaimed, breathlessly, " that I
didn't think you were quite such a donkey as to come out
on this cliff and quote poetry in a gale like this ! And
where's the milk for breakfast ?"

" Breakfast !" I cried, irritably, " who supposed we should
have breakfast for two hours yet ?"

" You never can tell," responded Bashy, putting a hand
on each side of her mouth and shouting. " Aunt Nora sent
me to find you—great call for Billy Armstrong—audience
won't leave—Billy ! Billy Armstrong ! Bouquets thrown on
the stage. And — listen ! There's a man come ! Man
with a diamond ring—and eyes !"

Having shouted this the girl turned and ran, or rather
was blown, down the cliff. And I followed.

X

THE man with the diamond ring — and the eyes — was sitting with Miss Runciman when we entered the house carriage. The lady was at the table stirring something in the chafing-dish which was over its lamp.

It was a very small room, and this new-comer appeared to fill it.

"Here she is!" said Miss Runciman, glancing at me.

Mr. Maverick rose.

"What, you?" he exclaimed. Our hostess looked again at me, this time keenly, but she said nothing.

Mr. Maverick immediately and deferentially explained how we had met before. Bathsheba stood by me listening; then she poked her elbow at me. When the gentleman had finished, which he did in a very few words, Bashy gave him this information:

"She doesn't flat, Mr. Maverick; but I do, at present; though I'm expecting to stop it."

Mr. Maverick smiled and stroked his mustache. He did not seem at all like a man who underestimated himself. Bathsheba that day gave him the name of Ahasuerus, and generally called him thus thereafter. As he stroked his mustache his diamond glittered. It sent a ray of light straight into my eyes.

"I flat myself sometimes," he said, much as if he had

affirmed that he was human, though we might have thought him more than human.

"You sing, then?" I asked.

He smiled and Miss Runciman smiled. I felt annoyed.

"Yes," he answered, "sometimes."

"He is to be our new tenor," said Miss Runciman; and Bashy giggled. But how was I to know he was a tenor?

"Yes," said the new-comer again, and still looking at me with a slight smile, he continued: "Miss Runciman has done me the honor to send for me. I've been a singer ever since I was born, it seems to me."

"Oh!"

This was all I could think of to say, and I had an awkward consciousness that I seemed stupid, and also a still keener feeling that I did not wish to seem so.

There was very little more holiday for us. In a week the house carriage was put up in a barn, one of the horses was sold, but the gray was kept for its owner to ride when she wished. We went to a town within a few miles of New York city, and then began harder work for me than I had ever imagined.

When we broke up I asked Miss Runciman if I might go and see my mother. She was at home, and had taken grandmother there for the winter. I had heard this the day before.

Miss Runciman was sitting with a guitar on her lap, singing in a half-voice from a sheet of music before her. She glanced up. There was a marked coldness in her eyes.

"No," she answered shortly. She had never spoken like this before, and I had a sensation as of having been struck. I turned away. She put her guitar down and called:

"Billy!"

She was smiling now, but there' was a glitter in her smile.

"I don't wish you to see your mother at present," she went on. "I want your heart and soul, and all you are. You are to work like a horse, an ox, a slave, all winter. Do you shrink?"

"Not from work."

"From what, then?"

"I don't know—from hardening, I think."

The woman laughed.

"You need not shrink from that process—welcome it."

We were in a quiet house, and if any one came to see Miss Runciman she declined the interview. We sang, and sang, and sang, or rather I did, and the rest more desultorily. I sang in my dreams as well as in my waking hours. I grew thin and excited, but I was well. I could not write home to mother, save little non-committal notes that must have been very unsatisfactory. But mother tried to write me all the news. I knew how she must labor over those epistles. She wrote that Bidwell Blake came very often and smoked with father. She said she thought father wasn't as well as usual; anyway, his spirits were lower: but she supposed he missed his Billy. He never sent me any word.

Mr. Maverick, the new tenor, was not with us. Bathsheba informed me that he did not need to study and practise, because he knew everything already. In the first weeks in December, after much sending and receiving of letters, Miss Runciman and Bashy went away. They went South to begin their "season." I was left with a housekeeper and a great many directions, and twice a week a teacher was coming from New York to instruct me.

"You'll find out what stuff you're made of now," Miss Runciman remarked to me as she informed me of her plan.

I used to wonder in the days following of what stuff I was made. Left to myself, I returned to my country-bred customs and rose early. I sat at the piano and sang for an hour; then I breakfasted; after breakfast I went to walk, and then I took my exercises in breathing.

Though the place was but an hour from New York, it was solitary, and seemed remote, as it was not on the way to any large town. Nearly all the people I saw were market gardeners or their families. These carts, loaded with winter vegetables, sometimes went slowly along over the narrow, yellow roads, which were muddy if it were mild, or frozen in deep ruts and "hubbles" if it were cold.

It was not interesting to walk anywhere, but I persisted; I walked in the forenoon and in the afternoon, and generally I went to the post-office, which was in the railroad station one mile away. I was always looking for a letter from mother, and I usually received one on Tuesday afternoon. So, if I missed going any day to the post-office, it would not be on a Tuesday.

I used to have curious fancies in those days; the strangest among them was the fancy that I was somebody else; not at all the Billy Armstrong who went to Mt. Holyoke Seminary and who later made barrel-stave hammocks on the home farm and dreamed hours away in them.

Though I knew I was not that girl, I had not in the least decided who I was. And I studied and sang and sang and studied, and solfeggio and arpeggio and high quick notes and low slow notes were in my mind dreaming or waking. It was not an unhappy time. But some days would be colorless, days when my work was drudgery, though I loved my work with enthusiasm. I would have hours of grieving because father sent me no word. I wondered if he were really angry with me. I began to think

that I had not known much about him.   I recall with what
childish delight I used to measure my chest and find how
my singing and breathing had increased its size.   My routine
was like the routine of machinery, but I had a very un-
machine-like enthusiasm.

Miss Runciman did not write to me save once, and then
it was merely to tell me to learn the opera of *Trovatore*
as best I could, and to consult my teacher when I was uncertain.   When I did first consult him he looked at me
queerly, and permitted himself to say that Miss Runciman
had curious notions.   He never praised me in the least;
and he always listened as if he could bear it because he
was resolved to bear it.   Two or three times after I had
sung to him he remarked: "Well, Miss Armstrong, that was
not as execrable as it might have been."   But he took no
end of pains with me.

Do you ask what had become of Vane Hildreth in these
months?   I did not know.   I used to wonder, when I had
time, where he was, and how he was.   Bathsheba, from
New Orleans or Mobile, or some other city, would sometimes send me a square envelope with a square card within, on which would be scrawled a few lines:

"Jolly time here—house packed—Aunt Nora in splendid feather—
and even poor I had an enormous bouquet. Guess I didn't flat much.
Mr. Maverick is perfectly magnificent to sing with—he just carries one
right along. Hope you are gay. Ta-ta.   BASHY."

But Bashy never wrote of her brother.   It was as if she
had forgotten him.   Still, she wrote me such scraps of notes
that it was not strange that she did not mention him.

It was one bitter cold day in January that I was hurrying
along the lonesome road to the post-office.   The snow
creaked beneath my feet.   But I was warm.   The sky was

gray — one smooth gray, out of which more snow would surely come.

"Be sure and get back before it storms," Mrs. Ridge, the housekeeper, had called after me.

With rubber boots, a thick jacket, and a fur cap one cares little whether it storms or not. I had just reached the railroad when the mail-train from New York came sliding almost noiselessly along the track. I paused for it to stop at the bit of a station and go on. It barely paused, then started off. I ran across the track and into the building to wait until the mail was assorted; it would not be many minutes, for very few letters came here. I noticed one passenger—only one. He was a tall man with a slight stoop in his shoulders, closely cropped gray hair, and a closely shaven face. Perhaps I noticed him more particularly because, though the air was so biting cold, he wore no overcoat. Having seen this, I further saw that his clothes, brown in color, looked quaint and somewhat old-fashioned, as if they were a suit that had been long laid aside and now taken out and donned.

All this as I passed by him into the station. Then I forgot him in watching the postmaster take out the letters. There was nothing for me; no, absolutely nothing, though this was a Tuesday, and I had expected to hear from mother. When I went out the tall man was standing by the red-hot cylinder stove, his hands spread over it.

I hastened on up the slight acclivity from the track, the sharp wind in my face and cutting like a knife. The mile I was to traverse looked rather long to me now. I turned up my jacket collar and bent my head. I wished mother had written. Surely, if she were ill, Aunt Lowizy would send me word.

I hurried; I thought of the warm room that awaited me.

Half of the distance was traversed when I felt an imperative wish to look behind me. Not that I heard anything.
The wind carried all sound from behind farther away. I
turned, and was startled to see, a few rods in the rear, the
man who had just alighted from the mail-train. His tall,
emaciated figure looked taller and longer against the snow.
His shoulders were drawn together in a pitiable manner,
his narrow velvet coat collar was pulled as high as possible.

I did not linger to gaze. It was an absolutely solitary
road for the most part—acres of market-gardens lined the
way, but there were few houses, and those were set in back
some distance. I was not easily alarmed; I had never
dreamed of anything to alarm me in my walks, though Mrs.
Ridge sometimes said that she did not like to be so near
New York and yet in the country; she prophesied that
some dreadful creatures would eventually stray out our way.

Perhaps this was one of them. I glanced back again.
Indeed, I was now bewitched to look back. The man was
always coming on in just that manner. He did not appear
to see me, although of course he did see me. And I soon
began to fancy that he was gaining on me. Yes, he was
gaining. I hurried faster than before. I glanced behind;
he was hurrying faster, too, and still he did not appear to
see me. At this I slackened my pace. I felt that it would
be better to let him overtake me than to go on like this.
And I was rather ashamed at my lack of courage. Why
should I be afraid? This man looked forlorn, but not
wicked. That is, his forlornness was certainly his most
visible attribute just now.

I will confess that my heart was beating up in my throat
as I heard the snow creak nearer and nearer. In another
moment the stranger had ranged up alongside and was
fingering his hat brim with his blue, bare fingers.

"I hope you'll pardon me, miss," he said, huskily, as if the cold took away his voice, "but the man down at the station told me that if I followed you I should find the place I'm after."

Having fingered his hat brim by way of respect, he hurriedly thrust his hand back into his trousers pocket.

"Where are you going?" I asked. He really did not look like a person to be afraid of. He was walking by me now, save that he kept, respectfully, somewhat behind.

"I'm looking for the old Holloway farm-house," he answered.

"The Holloway house!" I exclaimed.

"Yes."

He came up alongside again and gazed at me out of red-rimmed, faded eyes of a green gray color. They did not seem to be bad eyes, though there was something a little peculiar about them, almost as if they were veiled in some way.

He dropped back, saying as he did so:

"I've been there before; but this railway wasn't here then, so I was kind of turned round in my mind. I didn't come to it from here. It was all woods here. I was a young man, then, yes—a young man."

We went on in silence for some time. The place where I was living was called the old Holloway house, from the name of the family who had put up the building. I immediately thought that the man was on his way to see Mrs. Ridge. He must be going to see her, since it was certain he was not my visitor.

As we approached I thought he grew agitated. Though I could not see him I was sure he was agitated.

Suddenly I felt a light touch on my arm. The tips of his fingers rested on my coat sleeve. I looked around at the man. His blue lips were trembling.

"You see I'm weak, and—and hungry," he said, hurriedly. "I hate to have her see me this way.   I hate it!"

He spoke the last words with a kind of feeble violence.

"I want to be strong, and well, and prosperous when I see her.   Prosperous!"

He glanced down at his shabby figure, and repeated the word "prosperous!" in an indescribably bitter tone.

"But I had to come, anyway."

I had nothing to say.   I began to walk on again.   I was getting very nervous, having this person just behind me in this way.   I had never suspected the slightest mystery in connection with Mrs. Ridge, who was a middle-aged, prosaic woman.

When we had approached still nearer to the house the man came closer again.   I saw that his eyes were wandering eagerly, and yet fearfully, over the front of the building.

"I suppose," he said, quaveringly, "that I should have a little more courage if I were not so weak from hunger." He looked at me appealingly.   "You see, I haven't had a bit to eat since my last meal—there.   I only had money enough to pay my fare here—or only a dime over.   I didn't know just what the fare was, and I was so afraid I shouldn't have enough.   I couldn't have borne that—no, I don't think I could, anyways, have borne that.   If I hadn't been weak I could have walked all the way.   But I didn't dare to risk it."

He was evidently impelled to talk, and all the time he was speaking his eyes were wandering over the house.   He had been eager in his walk, but now he slackened his pace as if he dreaded something.   He turned weakly and appealingly to me.   From the time he had begun to talk I had forgotten all thought of fear.

"No," with puerile repetition, "I didn't dare to risk that."

He stopped and leaned against a post of the fence. The icy wind now blew a few flakes of snow that swirled and swirled about without seeming to fall anywhere. Two snowbirds came down into the yard and pecked at the ground.

"We cannot stay here," I said; and as I spoke I resolved to ask him into the house. I was hoping that Mrs. Ridge would see us, recognize him, and come to the door. She did see us, and the door opened. She had a broom in her hand, and her manner was as if this article were a weapon of defence.

"Miss Armstrong," she called out, "come right in this minute. You needn't stay out in this cold talking to tramps."

I took a step forward.

"What!" I exclaimed, "don't you know him?"

"Know him? No; I guess I don't. You'll ruin your voice if you keep standing there."

I took another step.

"I'm going to ask him in, I announced boldly.

Mrs. Ridge raised her broom a little.

"Is he a friend of yours?" she inquired.

"No; but I'm going to ask him in," I repeated.

I said this so resolutely that Mrs. Ridge lowered her weapon. But she remarked:

"I s'pose he's a burglar. You've got to be responsible."

While this conversation was going on I noticed that the stranger paid little heed to it; his eyes were still darting from window to window, fearfully and hopefully. I now informed the man that he must come into the house. He bent his head and humbly followed me up the path. When we were inside the door he whispered quickly:

"Do give me a morsel to eat before I see her! and a cup of coffee—for God's sake, a cup of coffee!"

I led him into the kitchen. By this time I had almost decided that he was not quite sane, and I was trying to think what we two women must do. I was annoyed that Mrs. Ridge had made me responsible. What if he were a burglar come to spy out the land? But it was a poor place for thieves if they expected much booty.

I moved a chair to the kitchen table and he sat down in it. Mrs. Ridge resumed her seat by the window and pretended to go on with the paring of some apples. I brought out cold meat and bread and put them before him. He began to eat hurriedly, ravenously; but at the same time it was evident that he was trying in some measure to control the savage manifestation of the beast of hunger within him.

I was sure that he wanted to claw and tear and devour. His face flushed as he made the attempt to eat like a gentleman. I brewed some coffee as quickly as possible. I grew more and more sorry for him. As I passed near Mrs. Ridge she caught hold of my skirt.

"For mercy's sake!" she whispered, "where does he come from, that he's starved like this?"

I shook my head. In a few moments I set the coffee also on the table. He dashed the cream into it, and then drank feverishly. Now, as his hunger was somewhat appeased, he glanced at me and said, deprecatingly:

"It's so hard not to be just an animal."

Then his eyes turned to the door. He made a movement as if to rise, while his flushed face paled.

"I thought I heard some one," he said.

"No," I responded. I could not explain to myself why I should feel somehow drawn to this poor wretch, who showed so plainly that he was once a gentleman and still wished to be one. And why should he expect to see some one here?

The next moment the stranger had risen from the table.

"I can't tell you how I thank you," he said, and he bowed to both of us, infusing into the salutation a lovely deference.

"I beg you will let me wait here a little," he continued, looking at me.

"You'd better have him into the sitting-room, Miss Armstrong."

I noticed that Mrs. Ridge spoke in a milder tone. That bow had had its effect upon her as well as upon me. "You can stay with him," she added.

So I took the stranger into the room, which was littered with sheets of music and music-books. A piano was in one corner; a banjo lay on a chair, a guitar on the table. There were various old-fashioned pictures on the walls, "Washington Crossing the Delaware," "The Surrender of Cornwallis," and the like of them. At the end of the room was a very striking portrait in oil of Miss Runciman. This canvas had been sent here because, as the lady had explained, she had just now no better place for it. It represented her as standing, head uplifted, the pose full of regal life, the eyes dominating you the moment you met them. And yet the face had the winning softness of a coming smile upon it. It was Miss Runciman at her best, and her best was something quite indescribable.

The strange man advanced slowly into the room. As I looked at him I wondered again that I should ever have feared him in the least. His face, now that the fierceness

of hunger was gone from it, was gentle and refined, and
in some way appealing.   But there was something of shame
and deprecation in his bearing which I accounted for by
his poverty and his being obliged to beg.

I saw his eyes go from one thing to another in the room.

"Music—always music!" he muttered.   He turned to me
and asked, quickly, "Do you sing?"

"I am learning," I answered.

"God forbid!" he cried ; then instantly and humbly, "I
beg your pardon ; a beautiful voice is a gift from Heaven!"

With every moment I was becoming more and more
interested and curious.   He walked farther into the
big room, that looked quaint by reason of its low ceiling and large beam running along it.   Now, right before him was the portrait.   He stopped, instantly and
markedly.   I was watching him.   I saw his hands close
tightly, the nails growing white.   His profile was towards me ; his features stiffened, then seemed to relax
and melt, then glow.   I had never in my life seen that
glow, as of some ineffable emotion, upon any human
countenance.   The sight of it sent a thrill through me.   I
had a feeling that I ought to leave the room.   Then I recalled common-sense and prudence, and they told me that
I did not know what this man might be, and I must stay
and watch him, and at last turn him out into the storm.   It
was storming now—I saw the snow drifting past the windows—saw it even while I was watching my companion.

He walked quickly nearer the portrait and stood before
it.   I could not see his face now; I saw only the tall,
emaciated form with its bent shoulders.   I heard him murmur :

"Oh, my God!   My God!"   I sat down quickly by the
table and shaded my eyes with my hand.   I was ashamed

for myself that I had watched him so closely. What did
I know about Miss Runciman's life? Absolutely nothing.
But I did know a little about her charm and power, and I
thought I could guess at the hardness in her. But perhaps
she was not hard; perhaps she was only strong. I find it
difficult to place my impressions of people and incidents
just where they belong, and not confuse them with beliefs
and impressions formed later.

I do not know how long the man stood there gazing at
the portrait, which gazed back at him with what, merely by
contrast, seemed an insolent prosperity and happiness; for
in reality there was no insolence in the pictured face.

At last I heard the stranger move, and I raised my head.
He had turned towards me. Tears were dropping fast
down his face.

"Does she look like that now?" he asked.

"I have never seen her look just like that," I answered.

"It's older, but even more attractive," he said. "I
haven't seen her for ten years—ten horrible years."

He walked across the room and back again. He still
had an air of listening. He stopped in front of me.

"I came to see her," he said, abruptly. "Isn't she
here?"

"No."

"What?" with a sharpness like a cry.

I repeated my one word. The ascetic, worn, and yet
tender face grew whiter. The man uttered some kind of a
despairing cry. Then he plainly tried to pull himself together.

"I made sure—I made sure," he said.

In a moment he thrust a thumb and finger into his waistcoat pocket and pulled out a bit cut from a newspaper.

"The paper is not a week old," he said, "I knew I should

find her here; I never doubted it an instant. I thought God was willing to stop my suffering—after ten years."

He sat down quickly and leaned his head forward, covering his face with both hands. The paragraph read thus: "The celebrated prima donna, Leonora Runciman, is occupying a house near Wallingford that she may be out of the way of disturbance. We learn that she is contemplating even greater treats for music lovers. If she desires solitude, the old Holloway house is—"

Here the paper had been torn away.

"She was here," I said; "this paper is late with its news, that's why you've been misled. Haven't you seen—" I stopped, for I didn't know where he had been.

"I've seen nothing," he answered. "I could not see anything."

He seemed to be unable to recover from the shock of not finding Miss Runciman. "No, I could not see anything, and I would not ask. Whom should I ask? I haven't read the papers. By accident I saw this—and like a fool I built upon it. What a fool I've been all my life!"

He had lifted his head to speak thus. Now he bent it and again covered his face. Looking towards him I saw beyond him the snow driving still more furiously by the window, and the wind had begun to shriek about the chimney.

"It's the beginning of a terrible storm," I exclaimed irrelevantly. I rose and walked to the window, standing there and gazing out, absently watching the whirl of snowflakes and acutely wondering what I should do. How cold it was! Frost figures were already forming on the panes of glass. Several snow buntings were gayly disporting themselves in the yard. I heard a sound in the room, and I turned. The stranger had risen. He made a fumbling movement, as if to button his coat more tightly across his chest, but he found it already buttoned.

"I must be going," he said.

He went towards the door; there he hesitated; then he came back and stood near me. He reached forward, took my hand, and bowed over it.

"You've been so kind," he said, tremulously. "I thank you."

He still hesitated.

"If you will be so good as to add to your kindness," he continued, in his old-fashioned way, "by telling me where Miss Runciman now is."

I answered that she was in the South, that I did not know more definitely than that. She had planned to come to New York and Boston in the middle of spring.

He stood silent for a moment.

"She is successful?" he asked.

"Very."

"She has taught you?"

"For a while she taught me."

"Then you would be likely to catch her mannerisms, her ways. You have been so good. Will you sing one song to me? After that I will go."

I hesitated; then I walked to the piano and sat down. He followed and stood near, not looking at me, but at the portrait on the wall.

"Do you care what I sing?" I asked. "I don't know many things. I can sing something from the *Trovatore*. Miss Runciman has been particular for me to learn that."

"Go on," he said, and there seemed eagerness in his manner. I began and sang:

> "Of love like this, how vainly
> Do words attempt expression."

Half way through the solo I stopped, my hand striking a discord on the keys. I could not go on, for the man had sunk down on his knees by a chair; his face, covered by his hands, was pressed into the cushion, and he was sobbing openly.

I was saying to myself, "What shall I do?" I gazed helplessly down at him. But only for the briefest space. He sprang to his feet with more alertness of action than he had yet shown.

"I was a fool to ask you to sing!" he cried. "You have her trick of voice, but you have something more. Young woman, let me tell you one thing—go back home, if you have a home. Go back to it."

He left the room so suddenly that I was startled to find he had gone. As soon as I could collect my senses a little I ran to the kitchen, where I found Mrs. Ridge gazing from the window. She was looking at the figure of the stranger. He was breasting the wind, staggering, reeling before its violence.

"I'm thankful he's gone," she said. "Have you been singing to him?"

I did not answer her question. I was watching the man and thinking it was an unkind deed to let him go out in such a storm. A yet stronger blast came thundering from the northeast. That ill-clad figure reeled still more—it fell.

"I can't bear that!" I exclaimed. "He'll die out there. I'm going after him."

Mrs. Ridge took hold of my arm.

"Let somebody else take him in now," she said. "We've done our share. He'll get to some place, never you fear." But I shook her off.

"It's a cruel thing not to help him," I said.

I snatched a shawl from a chair, put it over my head, and

hurried from the house. The wind caught my shawl and flung it across my face. But I went blundering on. I reached the man and bent over him, holding out my hand to him. He grasped it strongly and rose to his feet.

"It's my weak ankle that made me fall," he explained. "I'm greatly obliged to you. I shall do very well now, I think."

He took off his hat to me.

"But where are you going?" I asked.

"Where? Well, I've not quite made up my mind. You have my thanks, miss."

He attempted to go on again. The wind sprang at him fiercely. I saw plainly that it was simply impossible for him to walk in this storm, reduced in strength as he was. I made him take my arm and we started back towards the house, the wind now blowing us on so that we must hurry. When we entered the yard Mrs. Ridge flung open the door and waited for us.

"I do wonder," she said, angrily, "how you dare to do such a thing, Miss Armstrong."

I made no answer to this remark. I helped the man to the old lounge that stood in the kitchen. He laid himself down upon it as one whose strength is spent. He closed his eyes and hardly moved.

"Aren't you willing to let him stay there for the rest of the day?" I asked of Mrs. Ridge.

She replied sulkily that it wasn't any affair of hers, and she washed her hands of it. So he did stay. The storm was the very worst of the season thus far. It raged all over the Northern States and strewed wrecks on the coast. It was three days that I did not get out to the post-office, and three days that the stranger remained beneath the shelter I had first given him. During that time he said very little.

He sat quietly by the kitchen stove during daylight hours, and at night lay on the lounge.

Once when I was alone with him he suddenly looked up at me and said, quickly :

"I didn't warn you against singing because singing is wicked, but because that life of praise and excitement unfits you for any other. It takes the sweetness out of calm days."

He seemed to make this explanation as if it had been on his mind to do so as a matter of duty.

On the third day it cleared. The sun came out brilliantly at noon, shining on the deep drifts that lay about the house. By the middle of the afternoon the teams were breaking open a pathway. The mercury in the glass that was fastened by our north door kept going down until in the evening, when I took a lamp and went to examine it, it registered eighteen degrees below zero. My hand on the latch stung as if it were burned.

"He can't go away to-night," I said to Mrs. Ridge, when I returned to the sitting-room.

"I do wonder what Miss Runciman would say," was her response to my words.

She put down her knitting, and, shivering, drew nearer the great coal stove, whose sides were glowing red with heat. There was the sound of sleigh-bells outside in the road.

"I pity any one who has to drive to-night," I said.

As I spoke there came a loud knock at the front door. Immediately the door from the kitchen opened. Our guest appeared on the threshold. His face was colorless, but eager and hopeful.

"Perhaps she has come !" he exclaimed.

XI

"YOU'VE NO IDEA HOW PERSISTENT I AM"

THE knock had excited me. It was nearly ten o'clock, and in this place the hour was late. While Mrs. Ridge was bustling towards the door I recalled that a train from New York stopped at our station at nine every evening. I stood in the middle of the room, listening. The stranger —he had not told us his name—had withdrawn into the kitchen, where Mrs. Ridge had of late insisted that he should stay. I could imagine how intently he was waiting to know who had come. Was not that a man speaking in the hall? Surely. My cheeks grew hot as I stood there. It seemed a long time before the door was opened.

Mrs. Ridge came in first. There was a stumping of blunt sticks on the carpet, as of crutches moving rapidly.

"Ah, ha!" exclaimed a triumphant voice, "I've found you. I was bound to find you."

It was Vane Hildreth, in a long fur coat, a fur cap, with fur gloves on his hands, and crutches under his arms. He paused and pulled off his gloves, flinging them and his cap on the floor. He held out his hands, and I went forward and put mine in them for the space of a second of time. The young man's eyes were sparkling, his voice glowing.

"They told me I was an idiot, and should freeze to death," he said, trying to hold my hand longer. "But I should have been an idiot not to come. Please ask me to take off my things and stop awhile."

Here he laughed joyfully.

"Take off your things and stop awhile," I repeated.

"Thank you; I don't care if I do. In fact, I mean to stay until morning, perhaps longer. You wouldn't turn even a dog out to-night—much less a popular tenor singer."

And he laughed again. He seemed bubbling over with good spirits, and it was impossible not to be cheered by his presence. Even Mrs. Ridge looked enlivened.

"Do present me to this lady," he said; and I performed the introduction.

I drew a large chair up to the fire. Vane threw off his coat and sat down, leaning his crutches against his chair. He glanced at them and then at me.

"It was all because I was after the flowers, you know," he said; and then, in an undertone, "and because the flowers made me think of you, Miss Armstrong."

I ignored this last sentence, and said, briskly, that he seemed quite active, and I hoped that he wouldn't have to use the crutches for long.

"For long! Haven't I been hitching about upon them for a century already? And isn't Maverick singing in my place all this time? And he's a man to sing himself into the good graces of anybody. Has he sung himself into your good graces, Billy?"

He gazed anxiously across the space that separated us as he put this question.

"I've never heard him sing," I answered.

"Ah! That's where I'm in luck, then. I'm going to call you 'Billy,' you know. You are going to let me call you that, aren't you?"

After our life in the house carriage it seemed as if it

would be silly in me to insist upon the Miss Armstrong, so I answered yes. Vane now leaned back in his chair and thrust his feet out towards the stove. Mrs. Ridge was gazing at him with undisguised admiration.

"By spring I'm promised that I may fling away these things"—putting a hand on his crutches.

"Oh, I'm so glad!" I exclaimed.

He turned his shining eyes my way.

"Thank you, thank you." Then he looked at me for an instant without speaking. I turned away and moved a pile of music from a chair to the floor. Were my hands trembling? But it is discomposing to have a person come so unexpectedly.

"Why don't you ask me how I escaped from Rachel Cobb?" he inquired. "Did you think I was going to pass my entire life in Miss Cobb's bedroom that led out of the sitting-room? Did you? Tell me that—and don't prevaricate."

"I thought you would escape as soon as possible," I replied.

This young man's aspect was so radiant that one could not very well help basking more or less in that radiance. I saw that Mrs. Ridge's face looked brighter than I had ever seen it. She now rose from the chair in which she had been sitting and smiling delightedly.

"You must need some coffee and something to eat," she said, "and I will go and get your supper ready."

"Thank you," returned Vane; "this cold does whet up one's appetite."

And he rose to open the door for Mrs. Ridge. He carefully closed it behind her. He did not take his crutches; he limped back quickly and stood in front of me.

"Oh, Billy!" he exclaimed, in a half-whisper.

I did not reply nor look up. I was remembering what I had thus far since his coming forgotten, and that was what Miss Runciman had told me of her nephew's proclivities. But the next moment I said:

"Now is a good time to tell me how you left Miss Cobb."

"No," he answered, decidedly, "I'm not going to talk of Miss Cobb. Wait until Mrs. Ridge comes back for that subject to be taken up."

"But I want to know about her," I insisted.

"Sorry to disappoint you. Miss Cobb will keep any length of time. Billy—"

I rose.

"Mr. Hildreth," I said.

He caught hold of my hand.

"I think you are treating me shamefully," he remarked. "Can't you improve?"

"No—yes, I'm going to try to improve." I stammered.

"What do you mean by improvement?" he asked.

"This," withdrawing my hand, "and this," sitting down a few yards away.

"But, you know, Billy, I'm not going to stand any such conduct on your part. No, really, I'm not going to bear it."

He followed me. I hated to see him limp.

"Don't you remember how I told you, before witnesses," here a smile, "that—"

"Yes, yes," I interrupted, hastily; "I remember. There's no need to repeat—"

"But I want to repeat—I'm going to repeat it this very minute. Billy, I—"

"Oh, I wish you wouldn't!"

I was afraid.

"But I will. Billy, I love you!"

He had followed me to my chair, and he now bent over me.

"I should like to kneel down at your feet," he went on.

"Perhaps it is your custom to kneel on such occasions," I remarked, in rather a loud voice.

"What did you say?"

I repeated my words with much distinctness, not faltering before the grieved and perplexed expression which came to his face. How excellently well he did it!

"Really, you are admirable!" I exclaimed, and I laughed.

He drew back a step. He became quite pale. I continued to smile. He sat down quickly in the nearest chair.

"We are not rehearsing," he said, after a moment.

"Not?"

"No—ten thousand times, no!"

I was silent. I had my hands clasped in my lap. I recall that one of the predominating wishes in my mind at that moment was that I might succeed in preventing my fingers from tightly interlacing; I wished them to lie loosely.

Vane rose again. It did hurt me to see him limp.

"I'm in earnest," he said, "with all my heart and soul in earnest."

I looked up at him; then my eyelids dropped. I would certainly keep my hands loosely clasped.

"I was drawn to you from the very first day when Aunt Nora brought you to the carriage. Oh, I loved you from the first! And when I sang to you that night by the bars—do you remember?"

He waited for my answer, and I replied, "Yes."

"I loved you then, but thought you'd be shocked if I let you know it. So I tried to make a jest of the song. Do you remember?" with a lover's repetition.

"Yes."

I wished that he would not make me answer him in that way.

"My dog knew it—Lotus knew it."

Vane stood silent now and gazed down at me for a moment.   Then suddenly he drew a chair close and sat down in it.   He took my hands.

"Don't be cruel to me!" he murmured.

He kissed my hands ardently and repeatedly.   I sprang up and stepped away.

"We won't go on with this scene any longer," I said, sharply.

Vane sat upright and stared at me.

"Why do you call it a scene?" he asked, authoritatively.

"Because that's what it is," I answered.   "Now, if you want me to stay in the room, you will begin directly to talk of something else."

A curious expression came into the man's eyes, and something peculiar to the curve of his lips.   There was silence for a brief time.   Then Vane said, in a sort of casual way:

"I suppose you are taking singing-lessons?"

"Oh yes," and I went on, with great glibness and unnecessary particularity, to tell all about my practice and my teacher.

Vane had returned to the easy-chair and was now leaning back carelessly in it, easily twirling the charm on his watch-chain, listening to me not very intently, but yet with great politeness.   The change in his manner was so marked that I was angry in thinking how extremely well he had acted.   Or, perhaps, he had not been acting; perhaps he felt what I will call a spasm of interest in me.

I could not be sufficiently thankful that I had behaved

as well as I had. A scorching blush covered my face at thought of the possibility of my having felt a tenderness for Vane Hildreth. I was obliged to own that he was precisely the man who might be successful in winning a girl's fancy. That he should try to make me love him! Looking at him now I almost doubted, from his appearance, that he had tried. That steel shining in his eyes, that cynical, smiling lip, that assured air, strengthened my doubt. He met my glance with a full look, and it was as if a little imp peeped at me from his eyes.

"You've been pegging away so at your singing," he said, "what if you give me a specimen of what you can do? You know I'm a judge of that sort of thing. And when I see my aunt, I'll report."

My first impulse was to refuse; but the tone and air of the speaker irritated me, and were in some way a challenge. Should I let him think I could not sing, merely because he had chosen to make love to me?

"That is so good of you," I responded. "My teacher reports occasionally, but perhaps he would wish to speak well of his pupil."

I went to the piano with an air of promptness. He should have no die-away, love-sick song. But what should I sing? I knew really, as I had told the stranger, so few things, that my choice was limited. I sat a moment with my fingers on the keys. I could not attack anything with much feeling in it. Stimulated and indignant, I dashed into that gay little thing—

"You are just a porcelain trifle,
    Belle Marquise,
Just a thing of puffs and patches,
Made for madrigals and catches,
Not for heart wounds, but for scratches,
    O Marquise!

> "Just a pinky porcelain trifle,
>   Belle Marquise!
> Wrought in rarest Rose Du Barry,
> Quick at verbal pout and parry,
> Clever, doubtless, but to marry,
>   No, Marquise!"

Before I had reached the second line Vane had risen and moved to the end of the piano, and he was leaning there, looking at me as I sang. Though I did not return his look, I yet saw him plainly, and I think the notes never fell more easily from my lips. I had been afraid of failing; I now felt as if I could not fail. When I had finished Vane continued to gaze at me in silence until I began to think that, after all, I had done ill. When he did speak, he asked, coldly:

"Does Aunt Nora know how you sing now?"

"She has not heard me, of course."

I was distressed, and I inquired, in a faint voice:

"Do you think she will be very much disappointed?"

"How can I tell? Try something with some emotion in it."

I hesitated. It is rather curious that emotion, as ordinarily used, is very limited in its interpretation. No, I decided to myself, I was not going to sing emotionally simply because Vane requested me to do so.

"Sing whatever you please for yourself," I answered.

"All right, so I will."

When he had said that I was seized with terror lest he should begin what he had called his little encore,

> "To you, my love, to you."

But I need not have feared. He reached round and touched a note for the key. Then with his eyes unswervingly on me he began:

"A silly shepherd woo'd, but wist not
    How he might his mistress' favor gain;
For on a time they met, but kis't not,
    And ever after that he woo'd in vain.
Never stand on ' Shall I ? shall I ?'
    Nor command an after wit.
He that will not when he may,
    When he will he shall have nay."

I had not known that Vane had such a masterful way with him while singing; but then I had not known much about him. I had barely thought thus when he suddenly left his position. He had taken my face in his hands and was bending over me, the light in his eyes streaming into mine, when the latch clicked. He started back and stood upright. He uttered some expletive which I did not quite catch. I felt sure that I hated him. Did he think it impossible for a woman not to love him? Mrs. Ridge entered.

"I begun to think," she was saying, "that the water never would boil. You see, the fire had gone down 'fore I knew it. But the coffee's ready now. Please walk out, Mr. Hildreth."

Vane followed the housekeeper into the next room. I was not going, but Mrs. Ridge expressly requested me to come; so I went. The man whom we had sheltered was sitting on the lounge there. Perhaps Vane was preoccupied, for he did not at first notice that other occupant of the room.

In a moment the stranger rose, and then I looked at him. He was standing grasping a chair and gazing at Vane absorbedly. I could not in the least interpret the expression on his face, but it was an expression which held my attention immediately.

"If you'll tell me your name, mister," said Mrs. Ridge to

the elder man, " I'll introduce you." As she spoke, Vane
turned on his crutches. I saw his eyes dilate, his jaw drop
in the first instant of his surprise. He stared persistently.
The two knew each other. That was evident enough.
Gradually the unknown man reared himself upright and
met the scrutiny fixed upon him with a more courageous
air. ·

"Well," said Vane at last, "this is a surprise! When did
you get out?" I tried not to start as I heard that phrase.

"Three days ago," was the concise reply. Food and
warmth had given strength to the speaker, for he answered
unflinchingly.

"And you came here?" Vane, in his great surprise,
seemed for the moment to forget that there were others
present. His face showed that he could hardly believe
his eyes.

"Yes; why not?" responded the man.

Vane shrugged his shoulders. " Well, as a matter of
taste, I would not have come," he answered.

"It wasn't a matter of taste," was the answer, "it was a
necessity. I had to come. I heard she was here. What
made her come here? Was it a matter of taste with her?"

"It was rather an accident, I imagine. It's her house,
you know. But you didn't find her."

"No; I didn't find her. She is prosperous. She hasn't
been near me all this time; she has not written. Do you
think I would have treated her so?"

Vane's shoulders went up again. " You can't expect a
woman to thank you for dragging her down—at least, you
can't expect Leonora Runciman to do it."

" Dragging her down! Good God! Hear what he says!"

The man flung up his hand with an uncontrollable gesture. His pallid face grew almost purple. Vane turned

away from him. He remembered that there were others present who were ignorant of what these two were speaking about. He gave himself a slight shake as if trying to throw off an influence.

"Really," he said, "we ought to beg pardon of you ladies. I don't need any introduction to this—this person. His name is Robert Dreer. Though I haven't seen him for ten years or more, I remember him perfectly. I suppose you've been pardoned out, eh?"

I did not like Vane Hildreth as he spoke thus, and I was conscious of a wish to shield the man whom he addressed. I did make an involuntary movement towards him. I checked that movement and stood quiet. Vane was hard.

"Dreer?" now exclaimed Mrs. Ridge. She had the coffee-pot in her hand. She set it down on the stove, and put a hand on each hip as she regarded the man standing in front of the lounge. "Don't I remember something about Robert Dreer? Wasn't it in the papers?"

Mr. Dreer lifted his head still higher, while the purple deepened on his face. He put his hand up to his throat. He did not look in the least like a criminal. How could Vane speak to him as he had done?

"Yes," said Mr. Dreer, huskily, "it was in the papers—the trial—everything; and I was the accused man—forgery, embezzlement, robbery of the man who had been my benefactor. It was all in the papers — my sentence — my behavior in court — ten thousand things for people to gloat over. Perhaps you read it?" looking at Mrs. Ridge, who had gradually moved back until the table was between her and the speaker.

"And we've had you here these three days!" she cried.

"Oh, I'm quite harmless!" he said.

"Accused?" repeated Vane, with inexpressible scorn in

his manner. "You were more than accused—you confessed your guilt."

"So I did—so I did," was the response.

At this Dreer looked squarely in Vane's contemptuous eyes.

"How did you get out?" asked the young man again.

"I told you I was pardoned—for good behavior."

Vane laughed.

"And now I'm going." Having said this the man turned and marched with head up towards the outer door. Half way to that place he staggered and fell forward, face down, his arms spread out. I heard Mrs. Ridge cry, "Oh, what shall we do?" Vane did not at first move. I ran and knelt down by the man. He was quite senseless. The next instant Vane came to my side.

"You have done it!" I said to him fiercely.

"I? You don't know what you're talking about," he retorted.

Somehow, among us all, we got Mr. Dreer on to the lounge.

"I want him carried right away, somewhere," declared Mrs. Ridge; "I can't have him here another minute. Why, he might have killed us in our beds!"

"Absurd!" I said, shortly.

"Why, he's just out of prison! He says so himself. I s'pose he came straight here from Sing Sing. Yes, it's a wonder we were not killed in our beds!" The woman's voice exasperated me. What if he had come from Sing Sing? He was not a wicked man. I said aloud that he was not a wicked man. Vane glanced at me.

"He must be taken right away," reiterated Mrs. Ridge. I thought that she was going to repeat her remark about being killed in our beds, and I felt as if I could not bear to hear it for the third time. I did not stop to think that it might be strange that I should unhesitatingly espouse this convict's cause. I did not care how surprisedly Vane gazed at me.

"Don't you know of anything to do?" I asked, turning upon Mrs. Ridge. "Why do you stand there doing nothing? You see he can't be carried away this cold night. You wouldn't turn a brute out! I won't have it! I say, I won't have it!"

Before my imperiousness Mrs. Ridge bestirred herself. And Vane helped; I will say that for him. After Mr. Dreer had revived and was lying with head averted on the lounge, Vane took my arm and led me into the sitting-room. His lips were compressed and his eyes stern.

"You're like a woman," he said. "You're very unreasonable." I bent my head in silence. I would listen, but nothing he could say should make any difference with me.

"Entirely unreasonable," he went on. "I see you condemn me directly. Why do you do that? Do you dislike me so much?"

I was silent.

"Do you dislike me so much?" more sternly than before.

"I don't dislike you at all. But we needn't talk about that."

"No, that's true, we need not. You thought me cruel to that man. What do you know about him?"

"Nothing; only I mean to help him if I can," a little defiantly.

"Regardless of his past?"

"Certainly. His past is nothing to me."

"Have you written to Aunt Nora that he is here?"

"No."

"You should not do so. What right have you to keep
him in her house?"

At this I hesitated; but in my mind I did not retreat
from my resolution.

"I shall not do anything to harm Miss Runciman," I
answered at last.

"What has he told you about her?"

"Nothing. He came here because he thought he should
find her. He was much affected at sight of her portrait
there." I glanced at the picture on the wall. Vane moved
and looked at the portrait, and I watched his face, which
the lamplight shone upon. He turned his back towards
me.

"We owe a great deal to Miss Runciman," he said.

"I owe her a great deal," I answered, warmly. I thought
he was going on with the subject, but his countenance
suddenly changed, as if a light had flashed through it.

"Can't you love me?" he asked, softly. "Are you sure
you never could love me the least in the world?"

I wanted to answer promptly, but for some reason I could
not do it.

"You're not sure, then?" he went on, with a touching
eagerness in his manner—at least, it would have been a
touching eagerness if I had not understood his tendencies
so well. I raised my eyes.

"Oh yes," I answered, "I'm perfectly sure."

Vane sat down and leaned his crutches against his chair.
I still found it impossible to see those crutches without a
pang. You know I had not had time to become at all
accustomed to them, and Vane had been so gayly, almost
insolently, active.

"Then that is done with," he said, gloomily. "I've
been a poor fool all this time, thinking of you night and

day. Sometimes I hoped, and then I despaired. I suppose that's the way with lovers."

"You ought to know," I retorted before I thought. Then I blushed with keen discomfort.

He looked up quickly. "What do you mean by that?"

I put on a bold face. "Because it's a part you've played so many times," I answered.

"Oh yes," he responded. "Of course, a tenor is continually playing the lover. But I didn't mean that—I'm not acting now. I wish I could think you were."

I saw no reason why this scene should be continued. I walked towards the door. Perhaps Mrs. Ridge would try to turn Mr. Dreer out of the house, and I must be present to protect him.

"Are you going to leave me?" Vane asked. He was leaning forward, with his hands on his knees. I just glanced at him and then turned away.

"Go, then," he exclaimed, passionately, "but you've got to love me—it's your fate! I can't stop loving you, and I wouldn't stop if I could. Remember, every time you think of me, think, 'That man loves me—he's going to love me as long as he lives!'" Here he burst out laughing, with not much merriment. "That sounds something like a curse, doesn't it? But I don't mean that my love shall be a curse to you." He now leaned back in his chair.

"Wait one moment," as I put my hand on the latch. "You needn't avoid me after this, thinking I shall keep harping on my love. I won't annoy you, you'll see. Now, promise me you won't try to keep away from me. I'm going to be here a few days, unless you drive me off, and it'll be very uncomfortable for both of us if you are to regard me as a person who is liable to talk love at every opportunity. You've no idea how well I shall behave."

I was puzzled by Vane now; but I gave the promise he asked for. It would be quite ridiculous to try to keep out of his way in a quiet place like this. But I did not like his remaining. I thought he ought to go immediately, no matter if he froze to death in the awful air outside. That was my idea of how a rejected lover should act. Now I turned the latch and left Vane alone. I hurried into the kitchen, to find Mrs. Ridge sitting dejectedly in a chair by the cookstove, her feet on the stove hearth, and her hands clasped over her knees. Mr. Dreer was lying on the lounge, motionless.

"I've been trying to think, and I can't do it," said Mrs. Ridge.

I did not make any response. I found that I was trembling for some reason. I sat down and tried to hold myself quiet.

"I s'pose," went on the woman, "that this is the selectmen's business, if they have such things as selectmen here. But who's to go and hunt 'em up such a night 's this, I should just like to know! That man's going to be sick "— sinking her voice —"and what's to become of us I can't guess."

"I'll help take care of him," I answered, promptly. I could be prompt on that subject. And I kept my word.

The next two weeks were made up of strange days. I stopped practising and taking lessons. Dust gathered on the piano and the guitar and the banjo. Vane did not go away, to my surprise. He sat and read in the sitting-room, or walked out slowly on the snow. The cold held on wonderfully.

The sick man lay in the chamber over the kitchen. Now that he was relegated to a bed, and could not possibly get up and murder us in our beds, Mrs. Ridge's instincts as a nurse had full play. She dosed her patient with a great many different kinds of herb teas. She called in the doctor, whose opinion was that the man would rally after a while, if fed with nourishing food and allowed to rest. "He has evidently been under a great and prolonged strain," he said. Perhaps the physician had a suspicion that there was no fund from which his fees would be forthcoming, and so he left us with the remark that if anything new set in we might send for him. Nothing new did set in, but for the first week I felt sure that Mr. Dreer would sink away and die just from lack of a motive to live.

He was not wildly delirious, but he continually mistook me for some one else. He called me Leonora in a feeble, pleading voice. It was so pitiable that I was guilty of the deepest sympathy, and sympathy is "ruled out," they tell me, in these days.

At the very first I overheard Vane saying to Mrs. Ridge that she need not write to Miss Runciman anything concerning this new occupant of the house, and the next day he gave me the same advice. He explained that the knowledge might trouble her, and in the height of an opera season she should have all her strength for her work. So I did not write; indeed, I was not in the habit of sending letters to Miss Runciman.

I have no need to dwell further upon this episode of my winter in the old Holloway house. On the third week Mr. Dreer struggled upon his feet. He looked like a ghost. He said he would go now; he tried to tell us how kind we had been to him, but he choked and stopped. I didn't have much money; I had $10 and some change in my purse. I sought a private interview with Mr. Dreer, and I made him take the $10. I thought he would faint when I offered the money to him. It was some moments before he understood that I would not be refused. Then he tried again to speak some thanks, and again could not.

No, I told myself, though he had spent all his life in prison because of a confessed crime, he was not a wicked man. This was one of my convictions, and I began to think that I was one who acted out a conviction—or why should I have a conviction ?

Mrs. Ridge, having done kind acts for this man, began to feel kindly to him. Isn't there a theory that to feel a certain thing one must perform an act in that direction ? For instance : you will not have the emotion of anger until you have struck some one. It's a fine theory, and will bring you out to quite curious conclusions sometimes.

Well, Mrs. Ridge, I suppose, was acting after the manner hinted at in the above paragraph, for she brought forward an old, heavy gray shawl that had been the property of her deceased husband. She made Mr. Dreer wrap himself in this shawl, and she prepared sandwiches for him. Thus equipped, the man said good-bye to us and started forth. At the gate he turned and looked back at me and at the house—he looked longest at the house—a persistent, mournful gaze that haunted me. Vane was not present. It seemed heartless in him to be away just then. In about an hour, however, he returned and came to the sitting-room, where I was at the piano. He held out two $5 notes.

"These are yours," he said. "I saw Mr. Dreer at the station, and he sent the money back to you. He said he knew you had but little."

"But," I began, "he will need—"

"No, he'll get along," interrupted Vane. "You see—"

Here he hesitated, and I filled out the sentence. "You gave him some money."

"Yes—a little."

I was thankful to learn that Vane had not been so hard as I had believed him to be. Perhaps I looked my gratitude, for my companion's face suddenly kindled. "You thought me a hard-hearted wretch!" he exclaimed. He came close to the piano.

"You seemed hard."

"Seemed? When in truth I'm the softest-hearted fellow on the face of the globe—but persistent—ah, Billy, you've no idea how persistent I am."

Here Vane gave me a glance.

XII

"LONG LIVE THE KING!"

IF this were a novel I think I should know just what thread of the plot to take up, but as it is only the record of the life of a girl who once tried to become an opera singer, I sometimes am in doubt as to what incidents I ought to relate. Have you never noticed that in one's own life all incidents seem important? Just as, when we come down to breakfast in the morning, we think it is a matter of interest to tell the people at the table how we slept and what we dreamed. But they don't care in the least whether we slept or dreamed; what they care for is for us to listen to their tale of how they spent the night.

However, it is strictly correct for me to think that the 17th of March of that year was an important date to me. It was on the morning of that day that I received Miss Runciman's telegram. It was written on the train, between Buffalo and New York, and this is what it said:

"To Wilhelmina Armstrong,

    "The Old Holloway House,

        "Lally's Falls, near Wallingford, N. Y.

"Go to New York on the 2.15 train if no one calls for you before that time. Go to the S—— Hotel and wait. Imperative—imperative.

        "LEONORA RUNCIMAN."

Do you imagine that these words set my heart to beating? In ten minutes from the time the message had been

received I had a satchel packed with some of my belong-
ings; ten minutes later I had taken those things from the
bag and put in others; I had not the least idea what I
ought to carry, and this was more than four hours before I
was to start.

Mrs. Ridge, whom I consulted, seemed to think I should
be "safe"—that is her word—if I filled my bag with stockings. She said a girl always felt a kind of self-respect if
she had plenty of stockings within reach of her hand. So
I packed stockings; but a half-hour after thus doing I had
removed them and had substituted handkerchiefs.

Between these occupations I reread the telegram, and I
looked at a New York newspaper of the day before. I had
found in one of the columns an announcement of the coming of the Runciman opera troupe. The praise bestowed
upon these singers was very great; it made me flush and
my temples throb to read it.

Would any one call for me? I hated to go alone. I had
never been to New York in my life. I was afraid of the
city as if it were a great ravening monster. But I would
brave it, nevertheless; I would run the risk of being devoured. Nothing would prevent my getting, some way, to
the S—— Hotel that afternoon. I counted over my money.
I should not dare to try to go by street-cars from the station to the hotel; I might get lost. I would take a carriage. Would $8.73 pay for a carriage?

I put this question to Mrs. Ridge, who hastily shook her
hands from the dish-water as if she could not tell me if she
hadn't her hands free.

"Mercy, child!" she cried, "I sh'll go with you rather
than have you go alone. I ain't much acquainted in Ne'
York, but I sha'n't have you spending your money on hack-
drivers."

I wandered aimlessly about the house. I sang with fitful enthusiasm. My hands were cold, my cheeks hot. I was continually looking at the clock. The hands barely crawled over the face. A train from the city stopped here at 12.03. It would kill a little time if I went to the station. It is always an excitement in a lonely place to see a train come in. It is as if a hand from a live, palpitating, far-away giant reached forth and touched you with the tips of its fingers.

The engine came puffing up, dragging its burden behind it. A March wind whirled about the bit of a station, but it was an April sun that glittered on the building and on the bare fields about it.

I stood staring at the train. I saw two women alight, one of them with a pug dog, who strained and choked at the leash, pulling his mistress incontinently over the platform. I watched them. Everything interested me this morning. To myself I was humming,

> "Lace up my shoe ;
> Put on my basquina ;
> Can you see my black eyes ?
> I am Manuel's duchess."

Just as I had reached for the second time the words "I am Manuel's duchess," the train drew along over the rails and went, faster and faster, out of sight.

The station-master was assorting the mail. The first letter he took in his hand he gave to me. It was from mother. The man glanced up, and then asked, "Did you miss your visitor?"

I said I had no visitor.

"Oh yes, you have. Man got off the train—wanted Miss Wilhelmina Armstrong. I sent him to the Holloway place. He's gone."

I hurried on up the road.   As I hurried I sang inaudibly:

> " Lace up my shoe ;
> Put on my basquina—"

Ah !   There was a figure ahead ; a figure quite different from that of Robert Dreer.   This must be the person who had come to take me to New York—a man in a long coat and a silk hat, who was swinging on rapidly.

Perhaps he heard my footsteps, for he stopped, gazed down the slope, then hastened towards me.   I am far-sighted, and it was not until the stranger was within a few yards that I recognized him.   It was Mr. Maverick.   He came up, hat in hand.

"I begged Miss Runciman to let me come," he said, quickly, after we had shaken hands.   The man's keen eyes were glancing over me.   My impression of those eyes was the same now that it had been in Chilton at the Ottawa House.   They were ruling eyes.   But his manner was deferential and gentle in the extreme.

I held mother's letter with unconscious closeness in my hand.

"I wanted to see you," he went on, "for myself as well as for Miss Runciman."

He looked me up and down.

"I'm glad you're tall," he said.

I laughed with some constraint.   I did not relish being appraised in this way.

"Oh," he continued easily, "you must not be offended. A tall woman is much more effective on the stage.   When we get to the house you'll sing to me."

"Did Miss Runciman wish you to hear me sing?" I asked, quickly.

This man's air of command excited rebellion in my mind.

"She did not tell me so."

"Then you'll have to excuse me," I responded, with decision.

He smiled as if he said: "We'll let this child think she has her own way—since to think so amuses her."

And I did not sing to him. I let him stay in the sitting-room while I hurried to my own chamber. In less than an hour I should be on my way to the city and to Miss Runciman.

But now there was mother's letter. My own home seemed in a "country that was very far off." I unfolded the sheets and gazed blindly for an instant at the illiterate, painstaking hand. But this time the writer had expressed herself fluently, not hesitating for words, as I knew she was usually obliged to do. There were several written pages. At first I could not quite put my mind on the lines, and I seemed to myself to be wicked for that reason. My thoughts would fly away to Miss Runciman, to the man down-stairs, to the future, and I could not help singing, in my mind:

> "Lace up my shoe;
> Put on my basquina,"

though I was not in the least thinking of the song; it was that sort of sub-consciousness which, after all, forms so large a part of our lives.

But in a moment everything else dropped from my thought; I was absorbed in what I was reading: I was sitting again on my little footstool by my mother's chair.

"MY DEAR WILHELMINA,—I did not write to you last week. I tried three times, but when I got my paper on the table and my pen and ink, somebody came to disturb me. To-day your father has taken Lowizy over to Great Medows"—mother was never quite certain about her spelling—"and I am all alone in the house. Even the cat isn't here. The cat is dead. I know you will be very sorry to hear that. We think she must have eat some poison that your father put in the barn cellar for rats. She is buried at the head of the lane, under the wild-apple tree."

My heart swelled as I read this news. The cat had been given to me when she was a four-weeks-old kitten, and I was a child always running about the yard. She was a part of my childhood, and that wild-apple tree at the head of the lane—did I not know every crook in the branches, and just where the robins had built for so many years; and the sharp, puckery quality of the small, blood-red apples? I shut my eyes, and for the moment I was back there, smelling the scents of the river-banks, hearing the frogs, holding the cat in my arms while she purred and narrowed her eyes in the sunlight. A keen pang went through me. Presently I went on with the reading:

"It's just as still here to-day as can be, and somehow I feel as if I could write freely; I can't do that usually; my pen seems like something that stands in the way of my thoughts. I cried about the cat. I thought how you'd feel. Your father laughed at me. He said the cat was real old, and that there were plenty more. He said I was foolish, and I know I was. Seems as if your father had grown old. All to once, you know, folks begin to look old. Maybe something troubles him; he don't speak of anything troubling him.

"How curious 'tis for me to feel just as if my pen wasn't stopping me from saying things to you! I guess it's 'cause there ain't anybody else in the house. I can hear the sound of the falls real plain, though the windows are all shut.

"I wish you felt like writing home more about how you get along with your singing. You don't mention much of anything, somehow. I suppose you don't have time. Your father gets a daily paper sometimes when he goes to the village. Twice I've seen things in praise of Miss Kunciman's singing and acting. I wish I could believe in that woman more. You know, I don't believe in her, though she does make

you feel so pleased with yourself, somehow. But I hope you've got
sound principles to make you straight wherever you are. I don't s'pose
she gambles, or drinks, or any of those things. I think of you all the
time, Billy. I bear you in my heart. I've got so I dreem almost every
night about you. I wish I didn't. Always I'm trying to save you from
something—from fire, from drowning, from some dreadful thing ; and I
struggle after you, and reach my hands to you, and I can't quite get to
you ; and I wake up all covered with cold sweat. Then I pray and
pray for you until I fall asleep again and go all over the same thing.
So I don't get so much good rest as I ought to have. But you needn't
think I'm complaining. Last night my dreams were more real than
ever, but so confused, you know. I was trying so hard to get to you.
You were with a man who had such strong eyes, and he had you in his
arms, and was carrying you off all the time, only he was always just the
same distance away. And I was screaming to him to stop, and he
smiled and wouldn't stop. You had your arms round his neck, and you
looked at me over his shoulder, and you kept crying ' Mother ! mother !
can't you save me ?' And the man changed into that young singer
named Hildreth, and all the time I tried to run after you and I couldn't
run, till I thought I was going to die. Finally I woke up, groaning,
and your father had to get me a few drops of brandy in some water, I
was so prostraited. I can't get over that dreem. It hasn't been out of
my mind a minute all day, and the more I think of it the more that
man who was carrying you off makes me think of the man that came here
and bought a horse of your father last summer, and just as much of the
Mr. Hildreth, too. How odd that is ! It makes me feel sick. He had
a great diamond in a ring on his finger. He was handsome, and I
guess he always has his own way. I don't s'pose you remember him ;
perhaps you'd forgot all about him, and you won't be likely to see him.
Now he'd call it silly, and so 'tis. But, oh, if you felt like coming
home ! I feel as if you wasn't safe where you are. But I know that's
all a notion. I tell myself twenty times a day that it's all a notion. I
wouldn't speak of it to your father, because he'd call it silly, and so
'tis. But, oh, if you felt like giving up trying to sing, and would come
home ! You could sit in the seats Sundays and sing. My dear little
girl, my own Baby that I've prayed over ever since you were born, do
be good—do be good. I'm trying to be good ; every day I try. When
the Lord comes—and He's coming—any day He may come—I want we

should go together to everlasting Blessedness. I feel as if I couldn't be Blessed ; no, I couldn't take Blessedness from the Lord if He didn't give it to you, too, my dear daughter.

"I sha'n't dare to read this over, for fear I sha'n't think I ought to send it. I don't know what your father would say if he should see it. I'm going to sit by the window and watch for the baker when he comes from Great Medows and ask him to mail it for me. I want it to go now. I feel as if I couldn't wait a minute for it to go.

"Laura Lincoln is going to marry John Haskell. You know they were engaged two years ago, and she broke it off 'cause she got bewiched with that book agent. But the agent left her, and now John Haskell has begun going with her again, and they are engaged. The minister called here last week. He asked particular about you. He said he always understood that a singer's life was one of great temptations. I told him I hoped you had good principles, and he said no doubt you had. And you have, haven't you, my dear daughter ? It's most time to begin to look for the baker. I feel as if I could keep on writing for hours. I guess it must be 'cause I'm alone in the house. It does seem as if I heard bells. I must hurry.

"MOTHER."

When I reached the last word I turned back and began again to read, almost as breathlessly as I had read the first time. And now I saw, scribbled across the top of the first page, these words :

"I hope you won't happen to meet that man I dreemed about. He was exactly like the one that bought a horse of your father. I do hope you won't meet him. And like that other young man, too."

Why, he—one of them—was down stairs at this very moment, waiting to escort me to New York. There was no mistaking that one.

A cloud of doubt and fear and homesick longing came over me, and thickened and deepened as I reread mother's letter. Perhaps, as I had thought before, something of the mystical vein in her nature was in me. I was afraid as I read. And the longing to go to my mother grew upon me to such a degree that I suddenly started from my chair with the letter pressed against my bosom.

But no. How could I sacrifice my work in life—my glorious work that I was loving more and more? And it was not wrong to be a public singer. And mother really was fanciful and imaginative. She had taken this fancy about the man down-stairs and about Vane. It was strange that her letter came when he came—the same train brought them. Father approved of my leaving home and learning to sing. No, mother ought not to make so much of a confused dream. Why, everybody had dreams, and what would become of us all if we paid heed to them? As for Mr. Maverick, even if he wanted to work any harm to me, how could he succeed? And there was not the slightest reason for his wishing to harm me.

I hurriedly dressed. I pinned mother's letter inside the waist of my gown; it seemed to me like an amulet that would help to keep evil from me. I had spent so much time in reading that letter that it lacked but a few moments of the hour when we must leave the house for the train, for we were to walk. I was glad there was no need for me to wait. I could not linger a moment now before I was on the way.

Mrs. Ridge had given Mr. Maverick a cup of coffee, and he was now sipping it with as much an air of leisure as if he were going to remain all day. The very sight of him doing this made me impatient. I tried to drink my own coffee, but I could not; and I could not eat, though Mrs. Ridge remonstrated with me, and said it wasn't any way to start on a journey and run the risk of being faint the first thing. Mr. Maverick put down his cup and looked at his watch. I was standing motionless by the window.

I was obliged to hold myself rigidly quiet; I did not wish Mr. Maverick to think I was "nervous."

At last we stepped out of the door into the wind. Mr. Maverick carried my satchel; he said Miss Runciman would send down for my trunk. The sunshine was very bright; though the March winds were blowing, "heaven had put on the blue of May." I was so thankful that the sun shone. It is always a good omen to go out into sunlight.

I remember with gratitude that Mr. Maverick did not talk to me on the brief journey, and he let me sit in my seat alone. There were very few passengers. My companion sat behind me and read. I looked out of the window blindly. I was going to Miss Runciman. She would perhaps make me sing, or she would not have sent for me. I was both frightened and exhilarated. I was not trained —I did not know how to sing or to act.

The landscape flew by the car; before I had begun to think it possible we were near our journey's end; the houses grew more frequent; there were big buildings with verandas all about them, and in front, on arched signs, the words, "Beer Garden." There seemed to me a great many places where one might get lager beer. I wondered idly about this. Then soon there were long rows of brick buildings standing in what seemed to be desolate fields—the city had not grown to them—and tumble-down shanties and goats; and then the train shot into a long, dark tunnel, the lights in the cars burned dimly and shed strange gleams on the faces of the passengers. There were many more people in the cars now, and presently they began to move, to draw their wraps about them, to take down bundles from the racks, and to talk about friends who were to meet them.

Mr. Maverick took my satchel; he helped me put on my jacket; then he drew on his own overcoat. But he would not hurry when the train stopped. I noticed that, among the men and women who crowded by, several looked at my companion, then glanced again, and one said: "It's the singer—it's Maverick. You ought to hear him as Lohengrin—magnificent!"

Mr. Maverick heard the words, too, I was sure, for I saw him smile slightly under his mustache, and a gleam of gratification came to his eyes. Then we also left the car, and my escort made me take his arm as we walked through the long station. He signalled imperatively to one carriage-driver and motioned the others away. In a moment I was on the seat of a close carriage, Mr. Maverick was sitting opposite me, and we were going rapidly, in and out, among a thousand other vehicles; the city was roaring all around us; I was in New York.

"You were never here before?" Mr. Maverick leaned very near me that I might hear what he said; and he smiled right into my eyes, in a curious way, that struck me even then.

"Oh no," I answered. "But, then, I've never been anywhere—only to Mount Holyoke," and I laughed excitedly.

He laughed also, with a kind of good comradeship that was delightful. He talked with me now and then, for the drive lasted more than a quarter of an hour. I thought we must come to the end of New York very soon. Mr. Maverick's manner was not in the least condescending; it had a genial deference and half-veiled admiration which made him charming. I felt that he was not bored by being with an ignorant girl.

At last we turned away from the noise and crowd of Broadway—Mr. Maverick said it was Broadway—into a still wider thoroughfare, where it was almost quiet, and where the brown houses stood tall on each side. Then we stopped at a taller, larger building than the others. The carriage door was banged open. We entered a beautiful room, where there seemed no effect of roof, it was up so high. There were pictures on panels, a half-light, a half-sound of I know not what.

People moving, some of them bowing and smiling to Mr. Maverick and just glancing at me. But we did not linger here. We entered an elevator and stepped out into an upper hall, only less grand than the place we had left. My companion knocked at a door, which was immediately opened by Bathsheba Hildreth, who reached forward, took my hand, and pulled me in quickly, kissing me and saying:

"Howdy, Billy? So you've come, have you?"

Bashy's face was pale and tired; there were dark circles under her eyes, but she seemed alert and bright. She was dressed in a gay, soft wool wrapper, which swept about on the thick carpet. She just nodded to Mr. Maverick, who said he hoped that Miss Runciman had not gone out. Before Bashy could reply Miss Runciman herself came from a connecting room. As she came forward Mr. Maverick bowed and went away. Miss Runciman kissed me, then she stepped back and looked intently at me. She also had dark circles under her eyes, and she was pallid.

"Well?" she said, interrogatively. "Have you worked?"

I could truthfully say I had worked, and I added, "But I don't know whether I do well or not."

"Oh, aunt, Billy's one of the conscientious kind, isn't she?" remarked Bashy. "Why don't you tell her what the Signor says about her?" The Signor was my singing-master.

"He says he is proud of you," said Miss Runciman, promptly.

"Oh, does he?" I exclaimed, feeling my checks flush. "He never praises me — he has told me that my singing was not entirely execrable."

Bashy laughed.

"That's like him. He was afraid you'd relax your efforts."

"When you have rested I'll try your voice," said Miss Runciman.

I sat down in one of the big soft chairs that seemed to embrace me. Bashy sat down near, and clasped her hands over her head, questioning me. I did not know why it was, but I felt a sense of disappointment. But what had I expected? I could hardly bring my mind to listen to the girl who was asking me this and that. I replied so mechanically that she suddenly inquired where I was. Then I roused myself. I felt mother's letter in my gown. A fleeting wish that I had given up all this and gone home came to me. I heard Bashy say that her brother was rubbing up his voice again ; it had become rusty. "But it's better than ever now," she asserted, "and sometimes he walks a bit with only a cane." She did not say where he was, and I did not ask. I wondered if he had told about coming to the Holloway house ; and for fear he had not done so, and that it should be discovered as if it had been a secret, I said :

"It was very kind of Mr. Hildreth to come out to see how I was getting on."

"Mercy!" exclaimed Bashy. "You don't mean that Vane has been to Lally's Falls?"

"Yes," I answered, boldly, "and I thought it was so kind of him." Bashy turned.

"Aunt Nora," she called, "Vane has been to Lally's Falls to see Billy."

"Has he?" in an indifferent tone, but I thought that Miss Runciman gave me a quick glance.

"Yes, and how odd that he didn't mention the fact?"

Here Bashy contemplated me with open curiosity, as I remarked that he probably had not thought of his visit. Bashy giggled. "Not thought of it!" she exclaimed. "Pray how long was he there?"

"Really, I can't remember just now," I replied.

"More than one day?"

"Yes."

"More than two days?"

"Oh yes."

"Mercy! Aunt Nora," turning again, "Billy thinks Vane was at Lally's Falls more than two days."

"Very well," with the same indifference.

"Hasn't he been secret about it, though? Was he there a week?"

"Yes."

Bashy glanced apprehensively at her aunt, who was at some distance in the large room.

"Now, I want to know one thing," she went on in a whisper, "and you might just as well tell me as not. Did Vane make love to you there?"

I was somewhat prepared for the question, so I laughed and answered. "Find out, if you can," and then I felt very flippant, and quite ashamed of myself. I would not have replied in that way if I had supposed there had been real seriousness in Vane's "love-making."

"Certainly I shall find out," she responded, and I thought she was going to say something about her brother's tendencies in the direction of making love to different women. But she did not. She sat gazing seriously before her and kept silent.

14

The next night the Runciman Opera Company began
their season in New York. They began with *La Sonnam-*
bula, and Miss Runciman commanded me to sit in a box
and watch and listen. She said that I must sit in the rear
of the box, and that I must keep behind backs. There
were two older women who occupied the box with me. I
obeyed. I sat behind backs, but I saw and heard everything. It was my first opera. I heard Mr. Maverick, and
Bashy, and Leonora Runciman. On the whole, I have decided not to try to tell what that first evening was to me,
knowing how I should fail in the attempt. I was cold and
prostrated at the end of it. When I was sitting with Bashy
and her aunt in the carriage later I did not wish to speak.
Miss Runciman, when we reached her rooms at the hotel,
drew me towards her. She looked at me keenly.

"I don't want any of your praises," she said, "but what
is your criticism of me? You'll tell the truth, because you
can't help it. Your criticism?" I hesitated. This woman
had carried me to heights I had never dreamed of — she
had made me live within the last few hours. "Your criticism?" she repeated, harshly.

I opened my lips — she was actually pale as she waited.
It was very hard for me to say what I did say.

"Sometimes your voice seemed to be — to have — oh, a
kind of thread in it — your breath trembled across something — oh, you make me tell it!"

"Certainly I make you tell it."

Miss Runciman turned away and sat down. She put a
hand up across her eyes. I followed her and stood close
beside her. I was suffering with her. At first she did not
seem to notice me. I heard her say to herself: "I knew
it! I knew it!"

After a moment I whispered: "Why did you make me

tell you? Oh, I don't want to say it! and you were glorious, magnificent—I can't tell how you affected me. I did not know I could feel so much!"

Miss Runciman tried to smile. She looked up at me. "My little Yankee girl," she said, softly, "you enjoyed, and thrilled, and criticised at the same time. I'll wager you caught every false note, every untrue phrasing there was perpetrated through the whole opera. I knew your ear was marvellously accurate, and your judgment is unvitiated. You are to hear opera in the back of that box every night this week. Every morning the Signor is to drill you in *Trovatore*. Are you brave? Are you going to shrink?"

I said I was brave, and I was not going to shrink. I did not tremble; I was tense. Give up trying to be a singer because mother had fancies? Miss Runciman smiled with indescribable bitterness.

"If I ever relinquish my crown I give it to one whom I have chosen," she said, not to me apparently. "But," turning towards me, "you needn't expect that I can love you. What king ever loves the heir-apparent? I don't mean to hate you, if I can help it, and perhaps you'll fail."

A fire seemed to go through my very bones. I stiffened myself straight. "No," I said, fiercely, "I shall not fail."

Miss Runciman's eyes shot a swift glance of interrogation. "Not fail?" She rose quickly.

"I am the count," she exclaimed, "you are Leonora. You know the scene." She sang:

"My whole desire is for vengeance. Go!"

She made a gesture of command, and drew back as I

dropped on my knees at her feet. I burst out into that
agonized appeal of Leonora's :

> " Witness the tears of agony
> Here, at thy feet, now raining."

How old and time-worn the solo seems to me as I write,
but it still moves me, it always will move me as long as I
have ears to hear it. I sang it now with a very passion of
appeal. I gave myself up to its anguished supplication,
but I was conscious every instant of something in me that
governed every note of my voice, every enunciation. Afterwards I was told that that something was the "artistic
sense." Possibly it was ; I know it was something that I
was obliged to obey as a boat obeys the rudder. While I
gave myself up, I yet controlled myself. I forgot to wonder whether my listener would approve. She had drawn
further away, and was standing with her hands resting on
the back of a chair, gazing down at me.

> " But spare the Troubadour !"

I sang, and I knew that my heart had gone into the words.
I rose to my feet. I pressed my hands on my bosom, and
I felt there my mother's letter. Miss Runciman did not
move ; she stood looking at me over the chair. When she
spoke she used the same words she had used on that early
morning when the gale had blown against the house carriage
on the Massachusetts coast : " The king is dead ; long live
the king !"

After a moment she added, "I am satisfied with you.
You will have some technicalities to overcome—you may
seem fresher to jaded-opera-goers if you never overcome
them. I'm sure you have the essentials. And you are

new, and young — young! Now go. I hope I shall not hate you. It would be wicked in me to hate a girl with a violin face—the very girl I selected. Why don't you go?"

A great wave of pity had come over me. I obeyed the impulse that urged me to go to the woman and put my arms about her neck. "Oh, forgive me!" I whispered.

XIII

" FAREWELL, LEONORA "

THE week passed so quickly that I was bewildered.
Every morning at eleven I went to the Signor, who scolded
and scolded, and drilled and drilled, and always it was
Leonora. He never praised. Rarely he would say, "Not
quite execrable." I felt that I was getting so that I did
not know anything clearly. I have never been certain
that those mornings with the Signor were of benefit to me ;
they gave me such a conviction that I was more of a machine
than anything else. But I used to recall what I had been
told in the last summer: "First be as accurate as a
machine." So I submitted, on the whole, gladly. Every
evening I was in the rear of that box at the theatre listening and watching—ah, how I did listen and watch! I found
that Bathsheba, though an unreliable singer, was frequently
a very telling one, and that she had many admirers. Maverick sang superbly, but there were moments when his voice
showed how much he had used it, and when he did not
quite rise to the occasion. His stage presence, however,
always had the effect of great and magnificent success, and
was confusing to one not versed in the technicalities of
vocal performance.

As for me, you may be sure I was screwed up to a pitch
where everything vibrated across my nerves. But I had
never felt so strong in my life, nor so capable of accom-
plishing whatever I should undertake.

Il Trovatore was announced for the Monday night following this week, and of course Miss Runciman was ad-
vertised as the Leonora. On that afternoon she ordered
a rehearsal of the whole thing, an order that was obeyed
with some grumbling, as the company had been playing the
opera in every city where it had stopped through the winter. Miss Runciman came to me as soon as we had left
the dining-room of the hotel.

"You are to rehearse in my place this afternoon," she
said. I bent my head. It was my duty to obey.

"And now I wish you to listen to what I tell you: You
are not to sing out fully; go through everything so that the
rest of them will not know how you can sing. That's my
whim. Will you do so?"

Again I assented.

"You may be called upon suddenly to take my place. I
may have a cold—a sore throat—a fever—the cholera"—
here the speaker paused to laugh with the bitterness which
was often in her manner of late. · "You are summoned.
You do as well as you can in the emergency. It is also my
whim to have you do this. That is all. No—come back."

I returned.

"Are you afraid?"

"Yes, I am afraid—but I mean to do the best I can, all
the same."

I knew that my voice trembled as I spoke. Miss Runciman's eyes, somewhat hard, were fixed on my face as she
asked, carelessly:

"Have you ever told me what you think of Mr. Maverick?"

I don't know precisely what I replied. Something in the
woman's manner confused and perplexed me. She walked
away and I left the room.

On the Monday evening I was in Miss Runciman's dressing-room at the theatre. She turned me about and examined me. Then she bade Bashy, who was with us, pencil my brows, and "bring out my eyes" more. I submitted, but I was rebellious inwardly. I did refuse to have the carmine put on my lips, but I am not aware of the reason why I drew a line there.

I had passed through the rehearsal—how, I did not know. The members of the troupe had been curious, but had not snubbed me very much. Oddly enough the person who seemed to despise me unspeakably was Leonora's attendant, Inez. All of us rather walked through our parts, so that my very inadequate singing was not peculiar, but we performed the stage business.

And now it was evening. Miss Runciman again drew me to one side. The opera had already begun. Ferrando and the soldiers were on the stage. We could hear them singing, and tramping back and forth. It would require some time for Ferrando to relate the story of the gypsy. Bashy was in the garb of Azucena, her face a dark brown, big rings in her ears, a gay but dingy costume making her picturesque.

In a lull, from where we now stood, I could detect the occasional clatter of seats swung down for late comers. All through the air was that peculiar odor of cigar smoke and perfume and brandy and coffee which pervades behind the scenes. Perhaps it was not brandy, but it smelled like it. Miss Runciman herself frequently drank a cup of scalding hot bouillon when she came from a particularly exhausting scene.

"You are to stay where you'll see and hear me all the time," she said. "I mean to sing my part until Act II. Then, without any announcement, you will fill my place in the cloister of the convent. You are about to take the veil. You know the whole. From that to the end it is you who are Leonora. Now let us see what the public will say. Are you calm? I mean, are you so excited that you are calm?"

She put her finger on my cold wrist. I don't know how the pulse beat there, but she smiled. I obeyed her to the letter. I had never heard her sing so divinely, or seen her act so magnificently. How she sang that first solo!—and the warmth, the ardent sadness of the "Of love like this!" A blackness came over me at thought that I was to go on after her. The audience applauded vigorously—again and again. Bouquets came—she bowed and bowed. I could see her eyes shine with triumph. Perhaps she would change her mind and continue through the opera. But no. She was at my side at the moment. I was strung on steel. The Count had given his "Oh, fatal hour!" The nuns were singing within the convent. I had on the white gown and veil. I was sorry it was Inez who was my companion. The voices of the nuns ceased. Miss Runciman was still with me in what seemed, from the audience, to be the convent.

"Courage!" she whispered. I moved forward, the attendant Inez a pace in the rear. She seemed to be shedding tears. Again I heard Miss Runciman whisper sharply, "Courage!"

Inez and I went down the convent steps on to the stage. I turned towards her and sang, "Why art thou weeping?" There is very little in this question. I had hoped I should not be in the least aware of the audience; I had hoped that the glare of the footlights would make a wall of fire between me and the people beyond. Inez sang her answer. Then I went on. I was conscious of a stir and rustle in the semi-darkness where the crowd sat. But when the Count "enters suddenly," I forgot the people, as I had wished to do.

When Maverick as Manrico led me off the stage and the curtain went down, I became aware that there was a curious and perplexed hesitancy beyond that curtain. Maverick retained my hand and kissed it warmly. But before he could speak there came a thunderous sound beyond. It continued.

"We must go," he whispered. Then he led me outside. The lights were up now—there was one great flame before my eyes, and in that flame I saw what seemed to be thousands, but what were really only a few score opera-glasses levelled at me.

" Bow—bow deeply!" said my companion.

I did so.

"Again—again !"

I obeyed. Bashy had drilled me in that profound courtesy, but I was aware that I did it very awkwardly.

Something came sweeping from one of the boxes at my left. I saw a woman fling it—it was a bunch of red roses that she had been holding. Maverick picked up the flowers and presented them to me deferentially. I felt so wretched all at once that it seemed as if I should never get back behind the curtain without tumbling over my white train. But my companion caught up the trailing folds of the gown in which I had been about to become the bride of the Church.

"I cannot tell you how I congratulate you," he said in an undertone, and he looked at me with a lingering glance. I hurried to Miss Runciman's dressing-room. She sat there alone, with a fur cloak wrapped about her. She was ghastly white, and not by reason of powder, I thought.

"I heard them," she said. I put the bunch of roses on the table among the rouge and paints.

"And I heard and saw you," she went on. "You committed a dozen solecisms, but you sang — oh yes, you sang." I could make no response. I was beginning to feel the reaction.

"Pull off that gown, put on a wrapper, and lie on the couch there, or the next scene will kill you. You know it's Azucena's turn now."

I was glad enough to do as she bid me. I stretched myself out on the couch and lay motionless. After a while I was able to draw a deep breath and to relax somewhat. But I could not really rest—until the work was done. Miss Runciman did not speak again, and I began to go over and over in my mind what I had yet to do.

In recalling that night my memory now goes straight to what happened later. You will remember that Leonora's next appearance is in the tower scene. In a clinging black gown, with a cloak about me, I enter with Ruiz. I must have sung "On rosy wings of love" with more or less of a mechanical effort, for I cannot remember anything about it. I only know that I must have sung it, and that I ought to have made much of it. It has gone out of my mind, perhaps, because of what occurred after.

When Manrico in the tower began to sing, my pulses leaped and then would not go on—at least, I thought that they would not go on. I gasped in that first intent moment of listening. It was not Maverick singing there invisibly. It was that voice which somebody had said was like the odor of the jasmine. When it had finished singing "Farewell, love; farewell, Leonora," there was no acting at all in my wailing forth that "faintness o'erpowers me."

If the singing of the chorus within had not given me a

little time, I could not have gone on with my part; but
somehow I did go on with it, and then came the long-famous
solo of Manrico in the tower. My very heart was drawn
out of me—that is a figure of speech that but poorly hints
at the emotion I felt as I knelt there in my black gown,
alone in the middle of the darkened stage, and listened to
Vane Hildreth—for it was Vane who was singing to me,
calling me his love, and bidding me farewell. I wonder
if that solo has ever been sung with a more solemn and
passionate fervor. I was young and unsophisticated; perhaps now I would not feel as I did then, but my soul was
in my tones as I burst out, "Can I forget?" And then at
the end the audience literally rose at us. We had to do
it all over again. I saw the white handkerchiefs waving, I
heard the applause, and I remember but hazily how I performed my part with the Count. The next thing that stands
out distinctly is my walking uncertainly off the stage after
my compact with Di Luna, and at the wing a man catching
my hands and drawing me to him.

Vane was in his ordinary dress. He stood there waiting
for me. He pulled me back into the dusk, saying as he did
so, sharply and huskily :

"How much do you think I can bear ?"

"I don't know what you mean," I answered, breathlessly.

"Don't know! Did you fancy I could let that cursed
Maverick sing the tower song to you ? Dear Billy ! Dearest ! Don't you love me any ? Not any ? Oh, my darling !
My darling !" He kissed me, and I clung to him. I must
have clung to him, for the next instant I started away with
a sensation of fright at what I had done. His face in the
gloom where we stood was brilliant enough to have illu-
minated the dusk.

"Dearest !" he murmured again.

"Where is Mr. Maverick?" I asked, quickly. "How did you keep him away?" Vane laughed slightly.

"Oh, he was detained; I arranged that, and then I ran up the steps to that grating in the tower; and when I began to sing he couldn't very well help himself. He'll have to finish, though—he'll be singing in the cell with Bashy in a few minutes. I suppose he'll want to cut my throat. But he can't do it. To think that I couldn't sing with you first! Bashy told me that you were going to take Aunt Nora's place, and then I thought I'd play a small trick myself, and Bashy helped me. Bashy's a trump, anyway. Let me put you into the carriage when the thing is done. There, they're at it in the cell. Hear Maverick! Oh, he must be furious! But no matter if he is."

"I must go," I said the next moment. I wanted to get away from him, and from myself. Vane held my hand tightly; two "supes" hurried by us. When they had gone Vane said:

"Yes, I know you must go. You must rest for the last scene. But—dear Billy—you love me?"

"Yes, I love you."

It was said; and now I wondered that I had not said it before. Vane's eyes flashed a soft fire; his whole aspect was so eager, so intense, that I drew away from him, whispering swiftly:

"Some one will come. I must go." I darted down a dim alley, and the next moment I was in Miss Runciman's dressing-room. She was in street costume now, and was sitting back in a large chair.

The sight of her brought to me as in a vivid bar of light the recollection of what she had said about Vane's tendency to fall in love, and now he fancied he was in love with me. I became suddenly cold. I sank down on the lounge, and hoped that she would not speak.   But she did speak.

"How happened Vane to sing, then?"

She put the question abruptly and sternly.   It did not seem quite truthful to say I did not know.

I began: "He said he wanted to sing with—with me."

"It was unwarrantable!" she exclaimed.   "I shall tell him so.   And I'm sorry he is amusing himself with you. He always has such a way of seeming in earnest."   She said no more.

I turned my head aside.   As I sat there in the dressing-room, in the midst of paint and powder and silken and velvet garments, recalling Vane's words and glances, there suddenly unrolled before me, with absolute clearness, the picture of the farm-house at home—the sunlight upon the river path and the orchard, and myself kneeling by mother's side.   I heard her saying: "The Lord will come on pillars of white fire."

I wanted to put my hands over my face and sob.   You will not wonder that I was excited.

"It is time for you to get ready to go on," said Miss Runciman, coldly.   "You must be a ghastly, blue white. Come here and I will make you up."

The next day Bashy spent an hour in looking through the morning papers for criticisms.   She made merry over them. She read me brief extracts.   One critic said I could not sing, but might learn to act; another that I could not act, but might learn to sing; and so on.   In one thing all the papers were unanimous; that I was a novice who must study a long time if I wished to be a real prima donna, and one writer had the kindness to say that "though the public must regret the severe and sudden illness of Miss Runciman, the public was grateful that she had had so promising a *protégée* to put forward last evening." Then followed a tale about my having been found by the prima donna playing a tambourine and singing in a Southern city. I took the paper to Miss Runciman and asked her if she would contradict some things.

"Why should I?" she responded.

"Because they are not true," I answered, hotly. "And you were not ill last night."

"I don't think I'll contradict," she said.

"But they're not true." As I spoke these words again my companion's face, turned towards me, showed an intense dislike. I shrank away a little. Did she really dislike me? Was she tired of her whim?

"No," she went on, "I'll not try to make any change in the story, since it was I who gave it to the reporter."

"You?"

"Certainly. The dear public, for some reason, seem to prefer that an opera singer should first have been a tambourine girl. It is a favorite notion. Now, Billy, do you want to hear a few truths?"

I did not answer. I stood gazing at my companion, who, somehow, seemed to be some one else, and not the woman who had come to my home and taken a fancy that she would have me taught to sing.

"They say," she went on, after a moment, "that truths are always salutary, even if not pleasant; that's why I don't like them. Perhaps you think, because the audience applauded you last night, that you are already a *diva*. Well, you are not. The people were surprised into applause because you are young and new; and you did sing well part of the time. Yes, you have a voice, and dramatic instincts. If you will go abroad and study four or five years, say with Marchesi, you may become a prima donna. But in five years, since you are now almost twenty-four, you will be quite an old lady. I've been thinking over things. I'm not going to give up yet. I shall sing to-night. The chances are that the next time you were heard the audience wouldn't raise a hand in applause. But you may try it, if you choose. We give *Il Trovatore* next week. I'll let you take Leonora if you wish."

As she ceased speaking Miss Runciman reached forward and took up a paper, running her eyes over the columns, as if my decision as regarded Leonora was of no special moment to her. I stood there trying to speak. She was tired of me; she was sorry that she had ever meddled with me. She had told the truth when she had announced herself as a woman of whims. Why is it that you always believe that, though others may be the object of a fickle notice, you may not be? There is something in you that will make interest permanent? I did not know I had felt thus, but I know it now.

At last I gave up the attempt to find any words. I turned away and walked to the door. There I paused. I remembered that Miss Runciman had spent what seemed to my mind a great deal of money upon me. I went back to my former position in front of her. She looked up.

"Well?" she said.

"I think my father will pay you back—" I began abruptly. I was burning with anger now, and I could hardly speak steadily. She made no reply. Her eyes returned to her paper. In the face of this silence I could not say anything more. But I did stammer out something to the effect that perhaps I could earn the money myself in time. Then I left the room. In half an hour more I was stepping into the elevator with my satchel in my hand, my hat and jacket on. Bashy was just stepping out, having come in from the street.   She glanced at me, then turned and resumed her place.

"Have you killed anybody?" she asked in a whisper as we began to slide downward.   I shook my head.

"What, then?"

"I'm going home."

She gazed at me in silence for an instant, then she gripped my hand and exclaimed:

"I knew Aunt Nora could not stand it!"

"Street floor!" announced the boy.

We walked to the entrance.

"Couldn't stand what?" I managed to ask.

"The promise of your being a better singer than she ever was.   Oh, dear!   I'm so sorry!   But it was sure to come. The fact is, the person who depends upon Aunt Nora is— well, is lost.   And she begins so sincerely, and is just love-ly.   Are you going to take a street-car?   I'll go to the sta-tion with you."

In the car Bashy sat by me, and I forgot that I had not at first received a good impression of her, and had thought her sharp teeth looked ready to bite.

"I'm awfully sorry," she said two or three times.   "Do you know," speaking into my ear as the car clanged on, "I couldn't do it myself, but I've been glad to have some one along who wouldn't drink nor smoke a cigarette, and who insisted upon telling the truth, and who "—here a jolt, and I lost her words; the next I heard was: "I guess I've for-gotten that I ever lived in the country and breathed pure air."

At the station I found I should have to wait an hour and a half.   At first Bashy proposed to wait with me, but this soon proved too much for her.   She insisted upon knowing how much money I had.   We found that, after buying my ticket, there would be sixty-five cents left. She turned the contents of her own purse into her lap and discovered that there was enough to purchase the ticket, and she walked off to procure it without heeding my remonstrance.

"You'll want a bit left in your pocket," she said. Then she kissed me, repeated that she was awfully sorry, and left me. In a moment more she had returned and had asked:

"How about Vane?" I tried to meet her eyes and failed. I could not answer.

"Very well," she said, as if I had answered.

This time she did not return. When she was really gone I bethought me that I ought to have made her promise that she would not tell her brother that I was sitting an hour and a half in the Grand Central Station. Having thought that, I fell to watching the people who were continually coming in, wondering if one of them would be Vane Hildreth. I did this in spite of a strenuous resolution not to do so.

I hoped that he would not come—hoped so most earnestly, and yet, when the moments had gone on to the limit of an hour, I was very unhappy. It was useless to reason that he could not have more than time enough to reach the station if he should start the very moment his sister could inform him. It seemed to me a curious thing that, though I would surely have prevented him from meeting me here, I was yet longing for him to come.

The never-ceasing stream of men and women finally seemed like a blurred line before my eyes. I could look at them no longer. And now I might take my place in the train. Shall I confess that I waited until the very last moment, and then I hurried along and sank down upon a seat in the end of a car? I sat there rigidly upright, my satchel upon my knees. I fancied that I felt like an old woman whose dream of life is over. I was going home to live as I had always thought I never could live. Perhaps I should become like Rachel Cobb; perhaps I should learn to visit half my time, and to carry about a much-rubbed leather bag, and wear eye-glasses.

And there was mother; I was going home to her. My heart was so sore that I could not think of mother without tears. I resolutely wiped the drops from my face and tried to sit even more rigidly straight.

I heard a man outside shout:

"'Board!"

Two or three late-comers darted up the steps; the train gave a slight hitch. A man who had been sitting with a woman in front of me kissed her hurriedly, passed through the door, and I saw him let himself down to the platform, lurching forward as he dropped. We had started. I was holding the handle of my bag with a grip that made my hand stiff. Yes, everything was all over. Miss Runciman was tired of me; I could never learn to be a singer now; and Vane had not come. That was very well, indeed; I was so thankful that he had not come. Perhaps his sister had not told him; perhaps there had not been time; perhaps he had not cared to come.

Yes, it was very well, and just the way I would have arranged the matter. I drew a long breath and tried to look out of the window. The car door slammed close to my seat; the brakeman had come in and was walking down the aisle. Then some one bent over me, and Vane said close to my cheek:

"Thank Heaven!"

A sudden wave of delicious happiness went over me, submerged me! I had resolutely hoped, intellectually, as they say, that he would not come; I had done nothing to make him come; but here he was. I looked up at him for one instant, not thinking at all what my face might tell him. I suppose it did tell him something, for his eyes suddenly blazed, his lips quivered as he whispered:

"My darling, you are glad I came, aren't you?"

I could not make any sort of reply. I had never been so happy in my life; but I couldn't tell him that. My eyelids fell, and I said nothing. Vane was leaning one hand on the arm of my seat, the other was resting on his cane. He had given up his crutches.

"If I had been one moment later I should have been too late," he said. "I barely scrambled on to the last car. Bashy told me; she came right to me without losing an instant. Bless Bashy, I say."

To this I made no reply. I still sat there quietly; but now the light shone for me. I could not remember at such a moment the things Miss Runciman had told me about her nephew. I forgot how wretched I had been a moment before. I knew that the wretchedness would come back to me soon enough, but it was gone now. I was not feeling a bit like a Puritan; it was very foolish of Bashy to call me a Puritan. Vane stood up and looked down the car. My seat was the short one at the end; I had dropped into it in my despair when I had entered the train.

In a moment Vane took my satchel and said:

"Come!"

I followed him, and we were soon established, sitting side by side. I leaned up against the window and gazed through it. We were silent for a time. Into my mind, like a serpent, there had now stolen again the remembrance of all Miss Runciman had told me concerning the man who had just joined me. It was Vane who broke the silence.

"Where are you going?" he asked. "Are you really going home, as Bashy said?"

"Yes."

I could not turn towards him. I was trying to arrive at some definite decision as to my course. I was afraid that old simile about standing on the edge of a precipice was in my mind. But, think as I would, and warn myself as I would, I could not put this lovely happiness from me.

Vane sat with his elbow resting on his knee, his face turned my way. Apparently he was not in the least endeavoring to be warned in any manner. His whole face was luminous and satisfied. It was hard for me to meet his gaze, and yet his eyes were seeking mine imperiously. I could not have him talking of love, and he must banish that expression from his face. I made a great exertion.

"Mr. Maverick was furious last night," I said.

"Very likely; but I don't wish to talk of Maverick."

"Oh, very well. Do you think it is likely to rain?"

"Perhaps; but I'm not going to talk of the weather."

"Indeed! Possibly your lordship will suggest a topic."

"Yes, I will. Dearest"—bending nearer—"I love you —I love you."

"But I'm not going to talk of love," lightly.

"Still, you'll listen to me when I talk of it, won't you?"

"Certainly not. Just now I'm going to converse upon the average rate of speed of passenger trains."

I laughed. No, notwithstanding all my reasoning, I could not make my heart heavy. How could I imagine that the sun was hidden when I was in its brightest, loveliest rays? Vane laughed, too. He drew himself up.

"I'll have my revenge some time," he answered. Then,

with a seriousness which rather startled me, he asked:
"Did Aunt Nora send you away?"

I related the particulars of my interview with Miss Runciman. Vane looked more serious still.

"Leonora Runciman is a tiger," he said; "all velvet
and claws. When she is velvet she is entirely charming;
when she is claws she is—not charming. I've made up my
mind, after close observation, that she is perfectly sincere
in both phases. Naturally, people suffer from this com-
bination. She fully believed she could resign herself to
the fact that you would some day be a better singer than
she is. She thought that she would like the *éclat* of bringing you out. But, after all, she couldn't bear it. And
there was Maverick. He admired you too much. Previ-
ously he had admired her. I don't mean she loves him—
I wonder if she loves any one? But she has a sort of softness that makes you think she could love. She is one of
those women who yield to some tender emotion, or to pen-
itence, or that sort of thing, if she happens to feel inclined.
But who cares for the caress of a sheathed claw? And she
has a way of making women like her—I don't know how
she does it. You liked her. And now, in a half-hour she'd
make you like her again. She has a kind of power of be-
witchment. I don't know what it is. And she can seem
so frank. She has moods of frankness and tenderness and
generosity. I've made up my mind that she doesn't feign.
For the time being she is genuine, therefore she is successful—you trust her. If a poor creature ever turns upon her,
what do you think she says? Why, that she had given fair
warning. Hadn't she told you that she was liable to
change her mind? Oh, my aunt Leonora is a person who
does exactly as she pleases. I once heard her say that God
had given us certain natures, and we were obliged to act

accordingly. There's something in that, too. When she is through with the squeezed orange it is dropped. What, Billy, are you taking all this so hard?"—with a tender glance. "But of course it hurts, and the worst of such an experience is that it is likely to make you distrust where you ought to believe."

"Yes." I said, bitterly, "it makes you distrust."

Vane gazed at me intently, a slight frown in his eyes.

"Do you know," he said, "that you make me suspect that you are going to distrust me? Are you?"

"I don't know," I answered, weakly.

It was impossible to meet his serious, impassioned looks. I moved uneasily. I knew, or I thought I knew, that I ought to doubt him. But in the very bottom of my heart I felt the conviction that I believed in him absolutely. This conviction at last made me turn impulsively towards him. I put my hand on his arm.

"Vane," I said, tremulously, "I believe in you. Will you be true to me?"

The shining of a great glory came into his countenance. I had never seen such a look on any face. And I thought it would be a cruel injustice to remember again the things Miss Runciman had said to me about this man. In the emotion of that moment I wished that I could do something to prove how sincerely I repented of the wrong I had done my lover in my thoughts. For I accepted him as my lover; and now I liked to think that I had loved him that first time I had seen him, when he had come up the path from the falls at his aunt's bidding, and I had thought him "foreign-looking."

He did not speak. At first it seemed that he could not. And at the same moment I imagined that we both re-called the fact that this was no place in which to allow a face to express too much. I turned quickly again to the window and gazed blindly out, my pulses throbbing in throat and temples.   I heard my companion's whisper :

"My darling, my darling, I will be true to you—I couldn't help being true !"

XIV

ON THE TRAIN

THERE was a silence after these words. I would not turn from the window. The train was now dashing on at a great speed. It would be the whole day before we should arrive at the town where I must leave the express for the local train that would take me to the station nearest my home; and that nearest was a distance of several miles.

It had not occurred to me that Vane was not going the entire distance; and then I could present him to father and mother. Of course they would like him. Here I stole a furtive glance in his direction. Mother would not approve at first, perhaps; but she would soon do so; and father—

Vane was looking at his watch.

"Only three hours more," he said, "for I can only go to W—— Junction. There I catch an express back to New York. If it were not for this express I don't know as I could have allowed myself to come—now, and yet I might have come. How could I have waited until my return from England?"

"Are you going to England?" To my country-bred thought he might almost as well have said Africa or the Himalayas.

"Yes, and that is one thing I wanted to tell you about. A cable despatch yesterday—great chance for me—the greatest I have ever had.   If I care to do anything in my profession I must go and see Alford.   You've heard of Alford?"

I shook my head.   I was trying to be quite calm, and to behave like a reasonable being.

"He is a famous impresario.   You advise me to go, Billy?" leaning towards me again.

"By all means," I answered.

"I knew you would.   It's the best thing that has ever happened in my work.   But I may have to be gone a year—"

At this I folded my hands; and once more I made the effort to keep them loosely clasped.

"Dear Billy"—this in a sudden, quick whisper and with an apparently uncontrollable movement nearer to me. "Dearest, if you could—if you would only go with me!"

"No—no."

"Don't decide in a moment like that," hurriedly.   "It's dreadful to hear you say 'No' in that manner.   I—"

A tall man in a clerical coat came down the aisle, glanced at us, then stopped and shook hands cordially with Vane. He looked my way.

"I wish you'd present me, Hildreth.   I heard this young lady sing last night.   I was one of those who applauded her."

The gentleman smiled genially as he gazed in my face. Vane named a name I had heard as belonging to a clergyman who was well known as a great lover of music. Bathsheba had said once that we were sure of one listener, anyway, and that was Mr. Moreton.

The gentleman stood and chatted a few moments.   He said he was taking a run to W—— Junction; he went every month to pay a little visit to his mother.   "Very glad, indeed, to have seen you, Miss Armstrong.   Let me urge you to study for the profession that has so plainly called you. Really, I could not bear to think the world was going to lose your voice. I'm in the drawing-room car, back here. Perhaps I'll see you again. This is good luck, indeed." He lifted his hat and sauntered on. Vane sat with his head bent upon his hand. I stole a look at his profile, and saw how set and severe it was. He seemed to be thinking intently. As for me, I had enough to do to bear myself calmly.

At length Vane raised his head. I was half afraid of his eyes, and I did not meet them. He put his arm on the back of the seat, and his hand up to make a sort of shield for his face.

"You said you loved me," he whispered.

"Yes," I answered in the same way.

"And you trust me, and believe in me?"

"Yes."

If he only knew how fully, in the revulsion from doubt, I did trust him!

"Bless you for that! Oh, bless you for that! Now don't be shocked and don't shrink at what I'm going to say. I want you to go with me to Mr. Moreton's car and let him marry us—now, this very hour."

I did shrink, and at first I could not speak. Then I said "No."

Vane drew a deep breath and appeared to be trying to possess his soul in patience.

"I thought you loved and trusted me," he said.

"So I do—so I do," fervently.

"And you're going to marry me some day?"

"I suppose so."

"You are certainly going to be my wife. Now here is Providence—or chance—sending Mr. Moreton right to us. Why do you object? Don't you think I love you enough?"

I did not answer this last question. I was thinking of mother, and that I could not—no, I could not go away from her in such a manner. As soon as I was able to command my voice I told him this; and that it was not because I did not love him. He must wait.

"Wait! If I were only to be near you! But how can I wait thousands of miles away? And I'm jealous of Maverick—I'm jealous of time, and distance—of everything. Billy, please don't tell me to wait. I simply can't do it!"

There was something childish in this outburst that made me able to smile at him, and that also made him seem a great deal dearer and nearer. Did you ever notice that when a person has asked of you a thing you cannot possibly grant, and then gives that thing up, begging for something else which you thought was also impossible—then you say yes to this second request?

This was what happened to me. And now, as I write about this day, it seems to me to be the first time in my life when I acted as if I were some one else. Was it really I? Have not we all asked ourselves this question in regard to some circumstance? Yes, it was I who gave a consent which I regretted the moment I had given it, and which appeared to open up to me afterwards, when I could think, a new phase of my character, and never since then have I thought myself strong. Always now I believe that I also may be borne along by that "wind of destiny" which wafts our bark to fair or stormy seas. And what is that wind of destiny but the attributes with which God endowed us? This is not the way mother thinks; she prays that I may be led to believe otherwise. Perhaps I shall. Sometimes, in an ecstasy of longing, I, too, pray that I may come to believe as my mother believes. No, I am not a strong woman, though youth is almost always certain of that one thing—strength.

Vane sat leaning his head on his hand again. Meantime I felt hard-hearted and cruel. I could not bear to grieve him. Why did he ask me to do such a thing? He turned to me and pulled out his watch for the second time.

"We have only an hour and five minutes left," he said, "and then I must leave you—for a year probably. I can explain all that at some other time. It is like death to go away from you, my darling. You don't know—"

He paused. Ah, didn't I know? I had been thinking of his love ever since that time in the little room at Rachel Cobb's—the memory of his words and voice and look had been underneath all my thoughts and deeds. Why not confess this to myself now? But I could not confess it to him. I shrank from such confession as every woman at first shrinks.

"There's Maverick," he went on.

Here I smiled and exclaimed emphatically:

"That is ridiculous!"

"Oh, you don't know that man as I know him. And there's my aunt; it is not impossible that she may change her mind. She has as many shades of moods as a peacock has colors."

"I am done with Miss Runciman," I said, bitterly.

"No matter; I don't know why I feel so horribly uncertain. It is enough that I do feel so."

Vane was talking fast; a flush had risen to his face. There was something desperate in his manner.

"I give up asking you to go with me, Billy," he said, "but I can't give up my hope that you'll let Mr. Moreton marry us here on the train. Stop! Don't speak yet! You are going to be my wife. Why not marry me now? You have no reason—unless you don't love me enough. Billy, did you mean it when you said you loved me?"

He looked at me with an agony of entreaty in his eyes.

"Did I mean it?" I cried.

"Yes, did you?"

"Oh yes, yes," in a distressed whisper.

"Then marry me now. I tell you it is God himself who has given us this opportunity. Then I shall cross the water with the thought of my wife in my heart."

Why need I repeat all he said, and all my heart responded? I consented. Vane went back to find Mr. Moreton. I sat cold and still, and without a coherent thought in my mind, awaiting his return. In a few moments he came back for me and I followed him. His face was so set and pale, and at the same time resplendent, that I could only give it one swift glance. He took me to a compartment where were Mr. Moreton, two other men, and a woman. "Witnesses," I thought dully, when I saw these latter.

Mr. Moreton grasped my hand in a firm way as he said rapidly that under the circumstances he had consented to do as his friend Mr. Hildreth had asked him to do. Of course it was a little irregular, but in good faith, and would be as binding as if I were in my father's house with bridesmaids about me. Here he smiled slightly.

Ten minutes later the ceremony had been performed. Mr. Moreton congratulated us, and then the unknown two men and the unknown woman congratulated us. The latter, pitying my position, I think, kissed me and whispered that I must "bear up." Vane tried to listen to something that Mr. Moreton told him about the certificate. Vane's face still had a very determined expression upon it. He turned from the clergyman and for the third time looked at his watch.

"We have just fifteen minutes before the train stops at W—— Junction," he said, stiffly.

The woman hurriedly said something to the men, and the group quickly left the compartment. Vane and I were alone. I sat down and he placed himself beside me. He put his arm about me. With his other hand beneath my chin he gently lifted my face until he could look down into my eyes.

"Wilhelmina," he said, solemnly, "remember—remember always that I love you—love you—as I've never loved any human being in this world. God forgive me! Oh, how I love you!"

Then he kissed me with something of the solemnity he had used in speaking. We hardly spoke again. The train was dashing on at a great speed. Vane and I sat close together, he holding me to him. Finally he said:

"I shall come back as soon as I can. And I shall write." Then after a moment, "You will never know how I thank you for doing this—for showing me your love."

The train began to slow. It stopped.

"Tell me you love me," he whispered.

"I love you," I answered. He kissed me again.

Three minutes later Vane was gone, and the train was gathering speed as it left the Junction behind it. I began to be keenly afraid that some one would come and speak to me. I rose and left the car, going forward until I came to the car I had first entered. I found my satchel in the rack where Vane had put it; we had both forgotten it.

An old man was in the seat beneath the satchel; he made room for me to sit beside him. I sat down and put my hands together. At first I was fearing all the time that the old man would speak to me. At last I saw that he was asleep. Then it came over me with a terrible power that I would give everything, my life even, I thought, if I could undo what had just been done. Oh, why had I done it? I longed to start up and scream that question aloud.

I held myself down on my seat and did not open my lips. I had consented to the marriage; and I loved Vane. There was no doubt as to my love for him, surely. Then why should I feel this way about the marriage? It was its suddenness, its clandestine character. And now that I was away from Vane I thought I could see plainly that an engagement would have been far better until his return. Then, all at once, my thoughts took a turn, and I thrilled with happiness because I had not refused, because I was his wife. The memory of his face was like his caress; and his eyes, the beautiful, magnetic eyes, that had made me love him from the very first— I would tell mother everything. She would not approve, but all the same she would comfort and counsel me.

This last resolution gave me a superficial peace for a time. Then presently I went through again the entire round of frenzied regret at what I had done, the ecstatic joy in Vane's love; and I groped after the peace my mother's affection would give me; but that fleeting peace would not come again. I hardly thought of father, and that seemed strange. The day wore on at last. By the time I had reached the town, which was the end of my car ride, I was so worn out with that constant whirl of thought that my mind was mercifully dulled.

I stood on the platform and watched the train glide away. I had a fancy that it took from me the last vestige of the episode in my life which belonged to Miss Runciman. I thought that all my fervid ambition to learn to sing had been destroyed. I had come back humbled and old. Yes, I smile now as I recall how old I felt as I waited in front of the bit of a station. There was no one there at the moment but the agent, who was hauling some freight towards the shed provided for it. The big boxes made a scrunching noise, and the sound grated terribly on my nerves. The station-master had looked at me, and I had said I supposed there was a depot carriage to Worthing: and he answered: "Oh, yes, but sometimes it was a little late."

So I walked back and forth, gazing at the desolate brown landscape with its bare trees. Only some willows by a brook showed in their branches that it was April—their reddened bark betrayed that the sun had come north. Very soon I heard the rattle of wheels. Two brown horses came up to the door of the station, bringing the familiar, long, covered wagon with its trunk-racks at the end.

It was Bidwell Blake who sprang from the seat and strode forward, not seeing me, and calling out to the agent:

"Any plunder for Worthing to-night, Nat?"

"Two barrels and a woman," was the answer from the shed. Then Bidwell turned to find the woman and saw me. He grew red, hesitated, then came forward.

"What, Billy! I declare this jest knocks me!" he cried, and then we shook hands warmly. "Folks ain't expectin' ye, are they?" he asked. The old familiar way of speaking affected me as I had not thought it would do, and at first I could not speak. But the next moment I replied that I had suddenly decided to come home.

"Jest for a little visit, I s'pose," remarked Bidwell as he tucked the carriage blanket about my feet.

"No, for a long time," I answered.

16

He did not respond directly; then he said, cordially:

" That so?   Now that's good.   Won't your folks be set up, though?"

Then I summoned courage to ask, almost in a 'whisper though, as if I feared the answer:

" How are they all at my home?"

" Oh, prime, first-rate.   I've seen your father look better, but he ain't complainin' as I know of."

"And mother?"   I leaned forward towards Bidwell as I spoke.   Somehow I suspected that he was telling that things were better than they were.   As so often happens, now that I was approaching home, I was seized by an uncontrollable anxiety as to the welfare of the people there.

" Oh, she's tollable chirk," was the reply.   " I've seen her look better, too, and I've seen her look worse."

Here Bidwell left me, and presently I heard the thumping of the barrels as they were loaded on to the back of the wagon, and I heard the voices of the two men.

A squirrel came down a tree-trunk across the road, ventured within a few yards of the horses, paused and gazed keenly about, then darted back up the tree.   The sight of the little thing gave a strange, exultant throb to my heart. I liked to think that it was a good omen.   When the barrels were loaded and strapped, Bidwell mounted to his seat, the horses wheeled about and trotted strongly over the soft road. Bidwell turned half round towards me.

" Frost's 'bout out," he said, cheerfully; "didn't know one time but we were goin' to be frost-bound all the spring. But it's got to give when the sun gits along this way.   Yes, it's got to give.   I put in early pease three weeks ago, south of my barn, ye know.   We'll have a mess 'fore the 17th of June, you be sure."

My eyes stung and my throat swelled as I listened.   I

would have said it was ten years since I had heard the
country dialect instead of a few months. A breath of fresh
air, of air clearer and sweeter than any I had known for
ages, swept across my face. My nostrils dilated to inhale
it. It was as if I had breathed only heavy, luscious per-
fumes, but now— I sat up with greater erectness. Something kindled within me. I asked how Bidwell happened
to be driving the depot wagon, and where was Mr. Nute?

"Oh, Nute's be'n laid up with rheumatism, 'n' he wanted
me to take his trips for a spell. But I couldn't stan' his
old hosses, so I put my browns in. Ain't they beauties?"

The speaker turned and looked affectionately at the animals he was driving. I questioned him concerning every
one I had ever heard of in Worthing. I felt a quite unaccountable interest in everybody. He told me with a laugh
that Rachel Cobb had sprained her ankle six weeks ago
when she was going out to feed her hens, and that he, Bidwell, had "tended to the Cobb fowl ever sence. Rachel's
niece, Myra, from Great Medders, was stoppin' with her;
Myra had a constitootional objection to takin' care of hens.
But Rachel was 'bout able to go visitin' again."

So Bidwell talked on in response to my inquiries. But
we fell silent when the chimneys of my home came in sight.
I did not know I cared so much—so much. And I had
been so eager to go away. Grandmother's face was at the
window. I knew that she was sitting in the big rocker
there. And they would all look when they heard the depot
carriage coming. It was almost dusk now, but the April
days were long.

The door opened, the south door under the porch. and
there was mother gazing questioningly at us. I saw the
light come in her face, and grow until the delicate features
shone. Bidwell hurried to help me alight, but I was out of

the carriage before he could reach me. I sprang into mother's arms.

"Why, my dear little girl!" she exclaimed, as she clasped me to her. And how strange, how entirely inexplicable, it was to me that the instant I saw her I felt as if I could not tell her, it would be simply impossible to tell her, of that marriage a few hours ago on the train. As I thought this I clung still more closely to the frail form. I must be the gentlest, the most loving, the most obedient daughter, but I could not tell her of my marriage. I would wait; yes, I would wait.

Bidwell had set my satchel on the stoop, jumped into the carriage, and driven off. My trunk Bashy would send on as soon as she could think to do it. Grandmother came forward walking waveringly, as the old will walk. She gave me a dry little kiss from withered lips, and said she "couldn't b'lieve S'rissy when she said 'twas Wilhelminy."

"'N' how be ye? I s'pose you c'n sing 's well 's Methitable Crossley now, can't ye?" Miss Crossley had sung once in the chorus of *Judas Maccabæus* at Chilton.

They told me that Aunt Lowizy was spending the day with Rachel Cobb. And where was father? I was nervously waiting to see him. I recalled his figure in its high rubber boots, stooping forward in the wind and the rain as he had left me at the shore on that day when he had come on Bidwell Blake's behalf. Having just met Bidwell, I could almost doubt that he had been knowing to that visit.

"Your father's out milkin'," said mother, in response to my unuttered question.

She had been taking off my hat and patting down my rumpled hair. Her eyes kept filling, and the tears would drop on her cheeks. She led me to a chair, and gently pushed me down into it. She stood before me, her eyes fixed on my face. I met her gaze, and my heart sank as I knew again, with still greater emphasis, how impossible it was for me to tell her now. Yes, I would wait. But it seemed as if she must know instantly that I was keeping something of importance from her. I jumped up from my seat and put my arm about her; I walked with her to the open door.

"Oh, how natural everything is!" I cried. "Nothing has changed. I don't think I could have borne it if anything had changed. There are the same loose shingles on the east roof of the cowshed. I'm glad that no new ones have been put there. And there's the turkey-gobbler that used to run at me."

I was conscious of trying to talk, and this consciousness troubled me deeply. The words in my mind were, "I am Vane Hildreth's wife, and I want to tell my mother, but I cannot." She gazed at me wistfully. At last she asked:

"Have you come home for a little visit? You did not write that you were coming."

"No, I did not write. It was all very sudden. I only decided about half an hour before I started. I'll tell you all about it soon. I guess I'll go out and surprise father. Is he well?"

I stepped down on to the broad, flat stone at the door and turned towards mother as I put the question. Her face grew troubled.

"He don't complain none," she answered, "but it seems to me he ain't what he was six months ago."

I hurried across the yard to the barn. At the open door I hesitated an instant. A hen with a brood of white, fluff balls on legs came hastening up to me, expectant of food. I heard steps in the barn. I walked across the big room we called a carriage-house into the place beyond where the

horse and cow stalls were. I stood in the entrance an instant watching father as he raked some hay down from the
mow. He had not stooped like that when I had last seen
him work. I was shocked by his looking like an old man.
I hesitated still longer at the threshold. He lifted his rake
full of the loose hay he had gathered to put into the rack
of the cow near him. As he swung round the rake he saw
me. He hastily flung the hay into its place and came forward.

"Hullo, Billy!" he cried, but I thought not in his old,
boisterous good-humor. He came to me, shook hands, and
kissed me; was it my fancy that there was something mechanical in his manner? And I actually wondered if he
were glad I had come.

"How's the opery business?" he asked.

I answered that it was good, I believed. Then I added
bravely that I thought I was through with it.

"That so? Wall, I ain't supprised at anything you c'n
tell me 'bout primy donnas, 'n' that's a fact. Company
broke up?"

"No; but I've had a — a misunderstanding with Miss
Runciman."

"Oh, that's it, is it? Mebby you could sing too well,
after all." I thought my father was very shrewd to think of
that, but I said nothing.

"Goin' to stay to home now?" he asked.

"Yes," I replied, "if you want to have me, father."

I spoke rather timidly. The thought came to me, for the
first time in my life, that perhaps my father would think me
a burden. This thought turned me cold.

"Stay jest as well 's not," he answered, indifferently;
"mother 'll like to have ye; 'n' so sh'll I, of course."

This was so different from his former rough and exuberant manner that I felt colder still. I recalled that since that time when he had taken the journey to the shore to see me on Bidwell Blake's behalf, he had never sent his love, never a word in mother's letters. Was he "laying up" something against me? Was it my refusal to become engaged to Bidwell?

"Your mother 'll be glad. Have ye told her?"

"No, not yet."

"Ain't ye? Yes, she'll be mighty glad to have a chance to make ye into a Second Adventist."

Now father laughed and winked, something in his old manner, but I thought there was a drop of bitterness in it. I wanted to go back to the house. I was so disappointed and pained that I could hardly keep the tears from my eyes. And how old father did look as he stood there leaning on his rake!

"D'you come over in the deepo wagon?" he asked.

"Yes."

"Then you seen Bidwell, I s'pose?"

"Yes."

Here father shot a keen glance at me; then he put his hand out and took hold of a stanchion with a tight grip. Certainly every moment made it seem more and more impossible to tell of my marriage, and I had to ask myself in bewilderment if that marriage had really taken place. I had not even a ring. Perhaps that was as well, until Vane came back, but I did wish that I had a ring. You will see that I was often very weak and childish.

"Bid's be'n a great comfort to me this last winter, 'n' 'long back," he said.

"Has he?" I asked, faintly.

"Yes; he's be'n a real friend. I'd have be'n in a tight place if it hadn't be'n for him."

I tried to say that I was glad Bid had been kind, but I could not. I was so afraid that father was going to renew the subject he had mentioned at the shore that I had no words.

"Bid's a first-rate feller, 'n' no mistake," he went on, "'n' I guess he's goin' to git a good wife. Bid deserves a good wife."

In my relief I dared not look up, but I knew that father was gazing sharply at me.

"So he does," I answered in a barely audible voice.

I thought my companion chuckled, but I wasn't sure.

"That's so. I expect he's taken with that girl Rachel Cobb's had to her house a month or two back. You know Rachel sprained her ankle 'n' had to give up visitin' for a spell. Folks round are tryin' to be reconciled to her not comin' to see um. She's got her niece from Great Medders stayin' with her—girl with great eyes that seem to ask a feller to guide her 'n' take care of her, ye know. Fellers like to have a girl make um feel that way. Myra Foster's one of them kind. Myra sot out that she didn't want to take care Rachel's fowls, but she'd do everything else. She told Rachel this right 'fore Bidwell, 'n', of course, Bid was glad 'nough to say he'd come over twice a day 'n' see to the fowls. I tell you, when he ain't busy, that twice-a-day business takes up 'bout the whole time. She wa'n't with him when he went to the deepo this afternoon, was she?"

"No."

"Wa'n't? Wall, she goes out real often behind them brown hosses of his. She's kinder takin'. I guess you'll like her first-rate." Then with an abrupt change: "Opery goin' on jest the same?"

I thought that the sooner I explained how I had left the

better.   So I hurriedly related the outline of the case.   But
I found that I could not speak very freely, because my
father did not seem the same.   When I went back to the
house the dusk had deepened.   There was a lamp lighted
on the kitchen table, and mother was stirring up some
"cream-y-tartar" biscuit for supper.   She gave me a joyful
glance when I went up to her and stood for a moment with
my arm about her.   I was continually thinking, what if I
should say, "Mother, I'm married—I married that tenor
singer, Mr. Hildreth."

I hoped that when I had been home a few days I should
cease to have these words in mind.   And when Vane wrote
to me, perhaps the address on the envelope would tell the
story; then I would explain everything.   While we three
were sitting at the supper-table the door opened that led
into the wood-room, and light steps came quickly towards
the kitchen.   Some one who was very much at home was
coming.   The kitchen-door was flung open, and a young girl
entered with a little run that brought her to father's chair.
She paused with her hand on his shoulder.

"Oh, Uncle Lem—" she began : then she seemed to see
me for the first time, and she did not go on with her speech.

She was certainly very pretty, with what I thought a
gaudy, uninteresting prettiness of pink and white.   She had
a way of arching her brows and opening her blue eyes very
wide, with a baby stare that wasn't agreeable at all.   And
why did she call father Uncle Lem?   He was not her uncle.
Who was she, anyway?   Father seemed pleased to have
her come to him in this way.   He put his hand up and
patted her fingers that lay on his shoulder.

"I didn't know you had company," she said.

"Oh, this is only Billy," was the reply.   "She's be'n in
the opery business for a spell."

"Is it Billy? Well, why don't you tell her I'm Myra?"

She walked around the table and held out her hand to me, a bit of a hand that I took, though I did not care to take it.

"How do you do, Miss Foster?" I asked, formally.

"Oh, pray don't call me Miss Foster!" she exclaimed. "I'm just Myra, that's all. I d' know what Bid would say to hear me called Miss Foster"—here she gurgled a laugh —"do you, Uncle Lem? Ain't it funny to be called Miss Foster?"

"Almighty funny, I declare," said father. "Won't ye se' down 'n' have some hot biscuit? My wife knows how to make biscuit."

Though father said this, he was eating very little himself, and he used to be very fond of his food, taking enormous quantities.

"I don't care if I do," said the new-comer. "Don't you get up, Aunt S'rissy"—as mother made a movement to rise—"I'll get my plate 'n' cup."

She tripped into the pantry and came back with the articles she had mentioned.

XV

ANOTHER CHANCE

I PRETENDED to eat my biscuit and drink my tea, and I tried not to be annoyed. Myra sat opposite me. It was so dark now, for our supper was late, that a lighted lamp was standing in the middle of the table, and its rays fell full upon her face as upon mine. When I made an attempt to look at our guest I found that she was looking at me. Her round, doll eyes did not fall as they met mine, as why, indeed, should they? She chattered almost incessantly and laughed.

She had little teeth that were milk-white, and bright red lips; there was a dimple in her left cheek. It was an extremely pretty dimple and cheek. Why was father so pleased with her? He watched her and laughed at her and led her on. I saw that mother only smiled in her gentle way, and that she did not seem so joyful at sight of this girl.

" I've jest eat one supper at Aunt Rachel's," she said : " ain't it funny to eat two suppers close together? But I made the biscuit down to auntie's, 'n' they wa'n't half so good as these. These are jest tip-top, I call um. Why don't you eat more of um, Uncle Lem? D'you know Bid's brown hoss, the nigh one, was a teenty-tonty bit lame the other day? He was jest as worried 's he could be. I told him he hadn't a friend in the world he'd worry 'bout 's he would

'bout one of them brown hosses. Is that honey, Aunt
S'rissy, in that bowl? Oh, ain't it clear 'n' nice? Our
bees never make honey like this."

Having put a honeyed morsel of biscuit into her mouth,
she was of necessity silent a moment. Father gave up
making an attempt to eat. He sat back in his chair with
his hands thrust into his pockets, looking amusedly at the
girl. He did not notice me, and hitherto he had always
been talking to me, or laughing with me.

"They ought to make sweet honey with you 'round," he
said now. Myra bowed deeply; then she giggled and remarked that there couldn't none of the young men pay com-
pliments equal to Uncle Lem. Uncle Lem beat um all. I
tried to smile pleasantly. I was ashamed of myself that it
was such an effort to smile at all. Was I so small natured
as this? I made a great effort. I asked cordially if she
did not find it lonesome staying with Miss Cobb. "Great
Meadows is quite a village, and it's so very quiet here."

"Lonesome!" with a great opening of eyes and uplifting
of brows. "Well, I guess not!" Here father chuckled,
and then Myra began to laugh, showing her teeth, her
whole face having something the appearance of a fine
baby's face.

"There's be'n lots to take up a gal's mind down to
Rachel's," said father. Myra took a small spoonful of
honey, gazing at me meanwhile. When she had swallowed
the honey she asked me if I could sing like that singer in
the Roman Catholic Church in Chilton. She had heard
that woman once and it had been just like heaven.

I could not resist saying that I did not think that my
singing was at all like heaven. Father shoved back his
chair and remarked that he hoped I hadn't come back
with any objections to smoking.

"Of course she hasn't," said mother. There was an anxious expression in mother's eyes.

Myra now declared that she did like the smell of a pipe, and she thought Uncle Lem smoked better tobacco than anybody she knew; she wished Bid would smoke.

She remained a half-hour longer, prattling incessantly. When she had gone father's face lost its smiling look of interest. He sat smoking, with his stockinged feet resting on the hearth of the cook-stove. I washed the dishes while mother mixed the dough for rising overnight. It was warm with the fire in the stove, and I opened the back door. The sound of frogs came in loudly and cheerfully through the mild April air.

"I wish you'd shet that door," cried father, "I hate that continual peepin'."

Mother closed the door in silence. Presently father went to bed. He left the room without saying good-night to us. Mother and I were alone together. I followed her about until the dough was set in a big pan on the broad shelf above the stove. Then we sat down on the sofa in the sitting-room. I put my head on her shoulder and she held me to her in silence.

I had not known how tired I was until now. After a few moments my eyes closed—a moment more and I was asleep. It was not until nearly an hour later that mother wakened me, saying that we should take cold, and that I must go to bed. Then she took me to my old room. She had kept it ready for me; she explained that she liked to have it so, for that made her feel as if I were coming home. She left me, saying that to-morrow, when I was rested, we would talk. I clung to her for an instant, then I let her go. I slept that night as if I had no secret that I had not the courage to tell, and as if there were no trouble in the world.

The next day we did not talk, though mother had said that we should. We went on exactly as if I had not been away, save that I helped about the house more than I had been accustomed to do. I knew now that I should not be questioned, and that I was to be left to tell just what I pleased of my life during the last few months. I related very freely to mother everything that was not connected with Vane. When I mentioned him it was as "Mr. Hildreth," and my tongue refused to touch the one subject that never left my thoughts. I was wondering when Vane would write. I longed for a letter from him, and yet I dreaded its coming. He could send me a word before he sailed; after that it would be a long time before I should hear again.

The next day father did not go to the village. It had been his custom formerly to drive there nearly every day. But I would not speak of this fact; I would wait; I would not even ask a question. The day following he did not go either. This was hard for me. Father sat a good deal in the three-cornered, flag-bottomed chair by the stove. This was so strange that I tried not to remark upon it. I did ask mother "Isn't father well?" and she answered, "He don't complain any."

Myra Foster came over four times in the first three days, flitting in and up to father as if she, and not I, were the daughter of the house. On the afternoon of the third day there was a trampling of hoofs in the yard, a shrill little laugh, and, looking from the window, I saw Myra jump from Bidwell's open buggy before he could leave his seat. He glanced at the house, saw me, and smiled in his cheery way. The smile was so much brighter than anything in our house that it quite did me good. I thought it would be pleasant to see Bidwell sometimes; but evidently he was occupied.

"Where's Billy?"

I heard Myra's voice, pitched high, asking this question, and I went forward. She held a thick letter in her hand. My heart jumped. It surely was from Vane—and how had he addressed it?

"Wilhelmina Armstrong," pronounced Myra, extending the missive to me. I did not know whether the hand I put forth was steady or not, but I did know that all were watching me. I said "Thank you," in an easy way, and stood, holding the letter, while I asked the girl if she were having a pleasant drive.

"Oh yes," laughing and dimpling, "ever so good; 'n' now we're going to get some arbutus; we'll bring you some, Billy."

She flew back to the carriage and alighted on the seat by Bidwell as if she had been a bird. She nodded at me and called out, "We'll be sure to bring you some flowers." Then the brown horses were turned and trotted down the road.

"I wish I was havin' 's good a time 's Bid Blake's havin'." As father spoke his face seemed to grow black. I remained a moment standing there with the letter, which was burning my fingers. No one seemed to notice that I had it; and presently I left the room and went up-stairs to my chamber. Even then I could not at first open the envelope. Now that I was alone I suddenly began to tremble.

Then I hurriedly tore the paper and drew out the folded sheets. I saw the words "My wife!—my love!—my love!"

It was true, then; it was not something I had imagined. I had really been married to Vane Hildreth on the train a few days ago. Before I read any further I bolted the door. Then I sat down, and, shivering with excitement, thrilling to the love written on the sheets before me, I read on and on, the lines telling all the story of my husband's love from the moment he had met me—repeating again and again—but what lover does not repeat?

There is no need to give the letter here. Having read it, I turned back to the first page and devoured it once more. How fond he was—how ardent—how foolish he was about Mr. Maverick! It was really funny that he should speak in that way about Mr. Maverick. On the last page Vane mentioned that he directed his letter to my old name, as he did not know whether I would announce our marriage before his return. If I had not done so, perhaps it might be as well to wait until then; but that should be left with me.

Here I breathed a long sigh of relief. When he came back everything would adjust itself. Then I could tell father and mother. Till then—I rose and stepped softly about the room. I held the letter clasped closely to me. Till then I would stay here and help mother, and all things should be as they had been before I left home. This was what the foolish girl said in her heart. Did she not know that, having tasted another life, things could never be as they had been?

I did not dare to go down-stairs for a long time. I was afraid that my face would reveal something that I would wish unrevealed. At last I dashed water on my burning cheeks and eyes, and then joined my mother. I knew that it would be held very strange if I should not speak of my letter; so I said as soon as I entered the room that Mr. Hildreth had written to me—he was just starting for Liverpool and had sent me a long letter; he had a fine opening in London; he expected to do wonderfully well.

Father sat dozing by the stove. He lifted his head, darted a keen glance at me, and asked:

" That's the feller that got his bones broke, 'n' stopped at Rachel's so long, ain't it?"

" Yes."

" I thought so," and father laughed in a way that made me tingle with anger.

But he said no more; he appeared to go to sleep again.

In the weeks that followed nothing seemed as it used to seem. On the third day from the arrival of that first letter from Vane I received another sent from the outgoing steamer by the pilot, but this one I happened to take from the post-office myself, and I could not make up my mind to mention it. Since father did not go to the village often, I took it upon myself to harness one of the horses, or sometimes I went on horseback. So I carried my letters to Vane, or received his, which came by every steamer which brought a mail from England. But when one was delivered to me by Myra, or Bidwell, I always spoke of it as coming from Mr. Hildreth. No one asked me any questions. I was thankful for that, but it was strange all the same.

Aunt Lowizy had come back, but she did not stay; she went to Ryle to be with grandmother. She would have questioned me, and showed that she watched me; I was glad to have her go. She manifested such unbounded surprise that I was at home that I could hardly restrain my irritation.

I worked harder than I had ever done before. I took the butter-making from mother, and butter-making is the hardest kind of labor.

When the long May days came I began to wander down the river path; and I began to sing. I took up the practice where I had left it. It was as if I couldn't help doing this. There was something stirring within me that Miss Runciman had been the first to waken, and that would not be smothered into inaction. I must sing—I must sing better and better. It was a long time before I could bear to go to the falls, and to the place where the house carriage had been. How long ago it seemed! But it was not yet a year.

The thought of Miss Runciman was a bitter-sweet one— she had been so kind and so cruel; how cruel I did not yet begin to realize. She had taken me up with ardor; she had set me down with cold scorn. In those days I was constantly asking myself if there were not some way in which I could learn to sing. I would not think of Vane. Until the marriage was announced I was still free to do as I would, or rather as I could. All the time this goading desire to sing, to move great multitudes with my voice, grew upon me. I thought of it as I washed dishes and as I "worked over" the butter.

I knew that father would not—perhaps he could not— help me to go abroad and study. Yes, I wanted to go to Marchesi; that was the name Miss Runciman had said. The boldness, the daring, of this wish rather overawed me at first; what was I that I should think of such a project? Sometimes my mind was so filled with this thought that the thought of Vane was below it; still, he was always present with me, a burning thrill of memory, or the more quiet consciousness. Possibly it was the secret I was keeping from mother that was the cause; at any rate, as time went on we had none of those confidential talks which had once been such a comfort to me, and perhaps to her. She was always gentle and patient and loving. Often as I sat with her or worked with her the secret I carried with me uncoiled, as if it were a snake, and bit me. I had the insane idea that I could see its mouth open and its forked tongue dart out. Then I would wish to throw myself at mother's feet and tell her that secret.

I knew that I had physical courage, which is, after all,

but a poor sort of thing compared with the thing I did not have, moral courage. I could not bear to hurt mother, and I could not bear to be blamed. Always, since I can remember, this fear of being blamed has at times been a kind of torture to me. But we are curious beings, we humans, for there were some things in which I would persist, whether I were approved or condemned. I would not drink wine, though my companions had laughed at me and called me a "temperance reformer." I did not think this such a term of reproach as they thought it. And Bathsheba used to smoke cigarettes, and she swore occasionally, rapping out an oath as fierce and pat as if she had been a man. I didn't like such things, and I didn't feel a coward about them; but now, here at home with father and mother and my secret, I couldn't understand myself. It was now for the first time that I had seasons of turning my thoughts inward upon my own character, and of trying to interpret it. But I had no more success than I fancy others have at the same work. We are riddles to our own selves.

One day in the fourth week Bidwell drove into our yard in his farm cart. Tied to one of the stakes was a brindled dog. From the dog's collar depended a small, thin board. I saw it dangle as he stood. I was picking up chips from where father had been making hoop-poles in the winter. My apron was full of the chips as I stood up to see who had come. The dog looked at me and began to wag his whole body violently and to whine. Of course I knew him: it was Lotus.

"I've got something for you," called Bidwell. "Found him over to the deepo this mornin', 'n' they wanted me to bring him along. He's ticketed to you, Wilhelmina Armstrong, Worthing. That's you, I reckon."

He took the rope from the dog's neck and Lotus leaped to the ground and dashed at me. The chips fell from my

apron, and I nearly fell myself before the onslaught. Tears
came to my eyes, but I succeeded in hiding them as I greet-
ed the new-comer. I knew very well that it was Vane who
had had the dog sent to me. Bashy had informed me in
the winter that Lotus was in the country with a friend. I
was so glad to see him that I was afraid Bidwell would see
how glad. But he did not seem to notice. He took off his
hat and handed me a letter from it.

"B'n to the office," he remarked. "Folks all well?"

I nodded. I saw the letter was from Bashy. I hardly
noticed Bidwell as he drove from the yard. I hurried to
the woodshed and sat down on the chopping-block. The
dog hurried with me and threatened to make it difficult for
me to read the letter. But I did read it; it was short
enough, like all of the writer's epistles.

"My Dear Old Billy,—Vane wanted me to have Lotus sent to
you. I ought to have got him started before, but somehow I didn't.
Singing business over for the year. Aunt Nora isn't well. Her voice
almost gave out at the last of it; but she managed to squeak through.
Critics down on her—they are barbarians, anyway. They say I flat
more than I did the first of the season. It's rather tough being with
Aunt Nora when she's like this. One day she said she missed you.
Think of that, by Jove! She's a queer one; but she's done a good
deal for me. Hope you're having a good time; I ain't.

"Your Disconsolate Bashy."

Presently I again filled my apron with chips and went
back to the house, Lotus at my heels. I was willing that
mother should see this letter, but I felt awkward about
showing this when I had not shown the others.

"Whose dorg's that?" asked the father, crossly, as Lotus
bounded in. I hastened to explain that Bathsheba Hildreth had sent him. Father, who was lying on the lounge,
pushed Lotus from him as he exclaimed:

"I call that cheeky enough! What d' she think you wanted of a dorg, I sh'd like to know?"

I made no answer. I put some of the chips into the stove and the rest went into the wood-box. Mother came from the pantry with a pan of skimmed milk, which she gave to Lotus, calling him "poor doggie" in her gentle way. I wonder if mother ever knew how I loved her? Father dropped his head on the lounge cushion and shut his eyes. From that time Lotus was as if he had always belonged with us, and particularly to me; but he never noticed father, and father did not notice him.

When Myra came in that afternoon she made a great show of being afraid of Lotus, gave little cries, and ran to father to be protected. I didn't in the least believe that she was timid, for all her behavior.

It was not long after that day that I came cantering home from the post-office to find mother coming down the road to meet me. It was June now, and she had on her faded blue sunbonnet; but the bonnet didn't hide the pale, anxious face. She came right to the horse's head, and that was something strange for her to do. She caught hold of the bridle, and I saw still more plainly how excited she looked.

"He has come!" she exclaimed, in a low voice.

I started; I must have grown red, then white.

"Vane Hildreth?" I cried.

She gave me a strange look.

"I was sure you loved him," she said. She added immediately: "No, it's not Vane Hildreth. It's the other one."

"The other one?" I repeated, confusedly.

"Yes; it's Mr. Maverick, and he's waiting to see you."

Here she laid hold of my skirt, but did not let go the

bridle. We were in the road just outside of the yard. I remember that I heard the sound of father's hoe in the garden back of the barn.

"Don't go yet," said mother, in a sharp voice.

I was agitated myself, and intensely curious, but I could not see why mother should be so excited. Her large, sensitive eyes were dilated painfully, and her cheeks were red.

"Don't go yet," she repeated in the same voice.

"No, no. Why, mother, why do you feel so?"

I bent down and put my hand on her shoulder. "Mr. Maverick can't harm me," I added, "and I'm sure I don't know why he is here. It's probable that he was travelling near the town, and so thought he would call. What are you afraid of, mother?"

"I'm afraid; oh, I'm afraid of everything!" she exclaimed, still in her half-whisper. "My dream, Billy, my dream!"

I couldn't help shuddering as she spoke. I had forgotten her dream, but I remembered it now distinctly. I threw up my head and laughed.

"I hope we are not so foolish as that," I said.

"And I saw his diamond on his finger," went on mother. "It sparkled so, and shone so, right into my eyes—jest as if it were laughing at me; jest as if it was tellin' me that no matter what I felt, he was going to have his own way."

I laughed again, but I was not merry. There was a wild look in mother's eyes.

"Don't you fear," I said, soothingly.

But mother did not let go of my skirt or of the bridle. It was pitiable to see her fingers clutch.

"I've suffered," she said, "these months back. I've suffered, 'n' I've had to keep it all to myself. Don't go with him, Wilhelmina; don't go with him!"

"Why, mother, of course I sha'n't go with him," I answered in as calm a voice as I could command.

"Promise!" she commanded.

I was becoming more and more alarmed. I did not like to give my word, and this seemed unnecessary. Seeing my hesitation, mother's face grew in excitement.

"You've got to promise," she cried, but always in the half-whisper. "If you do I shall know you won't break it, spite of that man's eyes."

"Well, then, I promise," I answered, "but there isn't the slightest need."

Mother sighed deeply; she loosed her grasp of bridle and skirt. She plainly tried to regain her usual manner, but as plainly could not succeed at first. Her lips trembled as they formed something like a smile.

"I guess you'll think I'm 'most crazy," she said, "but I've been through a lot sence you left home, 'n' I guess I couldn't stan' much more."

I reached down and caught her hand.

"Dear mother," I cried in a whisper, "you needn't bear anything more."

Then I thought of my secret. I am tempted to write that word with a capital, and I wished that I had told her when I first came home. But I had felt that it would shock her so, and grieve her so, and—well, something outside of me seemed holding me back—only I knew really it was only my own cowardice which held me. She looked up pleadingly into my face.

"Are you sure?" she asked.

Then I did not reply. I only exclaimed, "Oh, you know I don't want to do anything to trouble you!"

Mother turned away and I rode into the barn. I slipped down from the saddle and put the hook of the hitch-chain

into the ring of the horse's bit. I stood there an instant.
I pulled off my gloves and pressed my hands to my hot
face.   Then I hurried to the house and into the gloomy
parlor where Mr. Maverick sat waiting.

He rose as the door opened and came forward quickly.
How well fed and well groomed he looked! And somehow
I resented this fact.

He took my hand firmly and looked intently at me as he
said :

" After all, the country's the place, isn't it ?"

I withdrew my hand.

"The country is lovely in June," I responded.

Mr. Maverick drew forward a chair, saw me seated, and
then sat down in front of me.   A ray of sunlight, coming
through a chink in the blind, brought an answering ray
from his diamond that flashed in my eyes.

I had seen many gems while with Miss Runciman, but
for some reason this gem from the first had a peculiar sig-
nificance for me.   That was a fancy, like fancies that had
come to my mother ever since I could remember.

" Beautiful! beautiful!" he replied, enthusiastically.   " I
walked up the river path from the falls. Ah, isn't that Hildreth's dog ?"

The door had not been latched, and it was now pushed
open by Lotus, who walked in and sat down by me, very
close, as if I might need protecting.

" Yes," I answered, " Bathsheba sent it here."

"Good fellow!   Give a paw, sir!"

Mr. Maverick reached forward a hand, but Lotus only
grinned in a very suggestive way.

The gentleman smiled.

"Dogs have their notions," he remarked. He leaned
back in his chair, not at all discomposed.

" I hear Hildreth is doing finely—finely—across the water," he went on. "It was the opening of his lifetime— splendid chance. To be with Alford gives one magnificent prestige. I suppose you hear from him, Miss Armstrong?"

I resented this question, but I sat up straight and an- swered, promptly, "Yes, I hear from him."

Mr. Maverick twirled a little gold book that hung on his watch-chain. He was looking steadily at me, and my color began to rise.

"I really hope, Miss Armstrong," he began, "that your affections haven't become entangled by Hildreth. Capital singer, and destined to be better, but not the man for a woman to love—that is, for a woman like you."

I said nothing; I was so angry that I could not speak; besides, I had nothing to say, and I was indignant with my- self because his words, though I did not believe them, were yet like a poison diffusing itself through my mind.

Mr. Maverick was perfectly at his ease. He smiled as he asked me to pardon him. He said that there were things concerning Hildreth that he might communicate to me, but that he was no melodramatic creature coming to the heroine of a story to tell her a dreadful secret concerning a man who wanted to be her lover.

Here the speaker put his hand up to his mustache and laughed gently. He conveyed the idea that it was utterly absurd and out of the question that I could think of Vane as my lover.

I did not reply to this remark either, and Mr. Maverick changed his position, now sitting sidewise in his chair, with his arm on the back, looking at me.

" But I didn't come here to talk about Hildreth or any one else save yourself, Miss Armstrong—just you, yourself. Are you interested to have me tell you a few things?"

Here he waited for a reply, and I answered yes. I was very uncomfortable and extremely vexed, but I was interested.

"It's about your singing," he said, and here I involuntarily bent forward a little; then I drew myself up again.

"You have superb promise—glorious promise," he went on, his manner growing enthusiastic. "If nothing happens to you, you may command the world."

I felt my eyes dilate and my face redden, but I tried not to be so affected. My pulses were beginning to beat in that suffocating way that is so difficult to control. To sing —to sing and move myself, and the multitudes who heard me—was that an ignoble ambition? How cruel—how diabolically cruel—Miss Runciman had been to awaken this ambition and then to fling me away as she had done! I felt that I hated her. But even at this moment I could not help recalling her moments of exquisite kindness, recalling them with a sudden melting of the heart.

Mr. Maverick rose and began to walk about the room. He filled and pervaded it.

"Yes," he said, with a gesture of the hand, "it is a sin, a crime, if you are to be buried here. I cannot allow it! I will not allow it! You must study—why, with your powers, the beginning you have made, perhaps a year's study with Marchesi would be enough. You have that wonderful electrifying power—you start the blood—you appeal to the heart—your voice goes to the very life of your listener. Are you going to let it waste here? Are you willing to sink down again into a mere New England country girl, when you can sing with the voice of an angel and of a woman? I tell you, Wilhelmina Armstrong, if you contemplate such a thing I won't allow it—no, I won't allow it. I'd take you away forcibly—I declare I'd abduct you and carry you to

Marchesi before you should bury your talent—nay, your
genius—here. Once with Marchesi, once in the singing
atmosphere, and I'll wager nothing could take you away,
nothing. Fancy yourself standing on that mimic stage
where Marchesi's pupils sing—fancy singing to ears that
can appreciate, to a taste and experience that can direct
and instruct, until you are—Miss Armstrong, it is I who tell
you that you can be the equal of any prima donna who has
ever intoxicated the world. You see, after all, that Miss
Runciman couldn't endure to have you sing better than she?
What woman could endure it? You sang with even more
promise than she had expected. She told herself that she
would give you your chance—but she could not keep to her
resolve. It was too much—too much. Could she stand up
and hand you her sceptre—yes, more than that? It was
grand of her to think she could do it; but it was natural to
find that she could not. She has suffered much; I don't
believe deeply in Leonora Runciman, but she has suffered
much, and I'm sorry for her. She is losing her voice. By
Jove! I'm sorry for her. So would you be."

He stopped in front of me. I had risen to my feet. I
could not sit still and hear his words, every one of them like
a torch that left fire behind it.

"Yes, yes," I said, huskily, " I am sorry for her."

But I was not thinking of Miss Runciman, save superficially. I was not really thinking; I was longing to begin
now—now—to study to become what this man said I might
become. He had spoken with impetuous and ardent emphasis; it was impossible to doubt the truth of his conviction as to what I would be able to do, and he was a judge;
he knew of what he spoke. My soul was " up in arms." I
twisted my fingers together tightly—I must make some
bodily movement. In a moment, however, I recalled the

truth ; and the truth was that I could not study to become a singer. I had no money. And Vane—I was married— what would my husband think? He should be consulted. My close-clasped hands unclasped and dropped apart. A chill came to me. "No," I said, "all this is not for me."

"Not for you? Pardon me, for you above all others."

Mr. Maverick's eyes caught mine and held them dominatingly.

"Is it that you have no money?" he asked.

"It is true that I have no money," I replied.

"That objection might be overcome," he replied, quickly.

"No," I said again, "and there are other reasons, strong reasons, why I cannot think of such a project."

I was trying to be reasonable. Who is it that has written that to be reasonable, to use common-sense, is sometimes like lying down upon paving-stones? I felt as if I were making my bed upon paving-stones, and the sooner I became accustomed to such a bed the better for me. Did you ever think how piteous it is for the human being of splendid possibilities and opportunities to turn from the glory of them and take up with hard and arid days? Aye, but that way heroism may lie. And I was not made for heroism, I feared. Why had this man come to talk thus to me? He did not apparently yield at all in his resolution.

"I won't admit the other reasons," he answered, promptly. "Let us attack and demolish them."

"No, no!"

He smiled. "Yes, yes. Now, listen to me. God has given you a voice that you might make the most of it. I'm an instrument in His hands. I'm going to lend you money —only just enough—it will not take so very much, for I know you'll be economy itself. But the lessons are expensive and must be paid tor. This is an investment of mine. I choose to put two or three thousand dollars, as the case may be, into your hands. You give me your note promising to pay with interest, and you can easily pay me the first year you begin to sing. I shall then have saved to the world a voice for which the world will thank me. You perceive that I don't consider your own satisfaction at all. Merely a business transaction. There can be absolutely no objection to this arrangement. Miss Armstrong, you can't bring an objection. I'm going abroad this summer. I'll see Marchesi—I'll attend to every detail. Very early in the fall you will go—you will find even your room engaged, and your chum, some American girl studying like yourself, secured."

As he spoke, Mr. Maverick would take a few steps about the room, then return to my side, his words coming swiftly, warmly, and with that accent of conviction which goes so far towards convincing another. His eyes, with a peculiar, concentrated glitter in them, appeared to seize my gaze and hold it.

No words within my reach can tell how powerfully I was tempted to say yes. I was not afraid to borrow the money; I was positive I could return it ; it was, as he said, only a business transaction ; it involved no emotion, and no gratitude that was unbearable. Oh, to be free to take this chance, to step forward into this life !

I turned away from my companion. I could sing, then ! I was not mistaken—I could sing. I walked to the window. The light there struck blindingly upon my eyes. How could I have given that promise to my mother ? She did not know. The old did not know for the young — they could never know. They had lived their lives. Now they should let the young also live. Oh, I must learn to sing !

Without a word of explanation to Mr. Maverick I ran out of the room. I would find mother. Surely I could make her understand, and she would release me.

XVI

CHANGE

I ENTERED the kitchen first. Father had come in from the garden and was pumping water at the sink. He stopped as I hurried forward. He had the tin dipper in his hand, and was about to drink. I had ceased to expect that he would seem to me as he used to seem. He gazed at me over the edge of the dipper.

"Where's mother ?" I asked, quickly.

"I d' know," he answered.

I was going to pass him, when he put out his hand.

"What ye up to now ?" sharply. "What does that man want ?"

I hesitated. I felt as if I could not tell father what was Mr. Maverick's errand. Father's eyes were full of a hostile curiosity.

"What does he want ?" he repeated. "You'd better send him away. I've had enough of your actions, Wilhelminy— goin' off 'n' pretendin' to learn to sing—'n' turnin' a cold shoulder to Bid—'n' comin' back 'thout amountin' to any- thing. You ain't neither one thing nor another now. 'N' there's Bid's been sensible enough to take up with a gal that 'ain't got no silly notions—cute gal, too, and one that knows she can't run across a feller like Bid every day. You didn't care to do anything to please yer father—you didn't care how yer father got 'long—'n' spent lots of money

on ye. But what's he got for it? Nothin'; jest nothin'.
Git out!" This last, with a kick towards Lotus, who had
just walked in from the other room.

I stood quite still. Father looked at me as if he hated
me. And was there not an odor of whiskey on his breath?
This last suspicion I immediately put from me. I could
not try to explain anything to him. What could I explain?

"Oh, I'm so sorry," I began, weakly; then I stopped before the fury in his face.

"Sorry!" he repeated, with great scorn. "You ain't sorry,
neither. You don't care. If you had cared you'd got engaged to Bidwell 's I wanted ye to. Pooh! Jest 's if you
cared what become of me, anyway! 'N' what you keepin'
up writin' to that singin' feller for? You hear from him
real often. You think I'm blind 'n' don't know nothin'?
Not by a long chalk!"

A quickly moving figure was seen in the yard.

"There's Myra—she knows when she's well off—she does.
I tell you it makes me thunderin' mad to have you turn out
so; and we not knowin' which way to turn."

Father set down the tin dipper with a clash in the iron
sink. Then he hurried out of the house in a way to avoid
Myra, who tripped in with her flat sweet smile on her face,
and asked, with a pretty vivaciousness:

"Where's Uncle Lem? I thought I seen Uncle Lem in
here." She glanced at my face, which I was fiercely trying
to get under control. "Mercy! What's the matter? Has
anything happened?"

"No," I answered, "nothing has happened. If you'll excuse me I'll find mother. I have a visitor in the parlor."

But Myra hastened to the door, saying that she hadn't
meant to stop, and must hurry right along. I said nothing

to detain her. I ran through the sitting-room and pantry trying to find mother. I looked from the window and saw her going through the orchard. In a moment I was at her side. I caught hold of her hand.

"Mother! mother!" I cried, "you must let me go! You must give me back my promise! Oh, I must have the chance to learn to sing!"

I can never forget the face she turned to me. Now I know that it was full of grief and disappointment—disappointment in her daughter. She waited a little before she spoke. Then she said, calmly:

"Yes, I give you back your promise. You must do as you think best. You are a grown woman. You must do as you think best."

I did not stop to thank her. My only feeling just then was that of release—freedom. A moment later I opened the parlor door. Mr. Maverick had been standing by the window. He turned quickly towards me. He looked much moved as he grasped my hands.

"You have changed your mind!" he exclaimed.

I have never been quite able to understand what it was that influenced me then, that came almost like an audible voice commanding me. Perhaps it was because of the look in my companion's eyes—the look from which I shrank. Instead of saying yes, I said "No" in a loud, hard voice; and I snatched my hands away. Mr. Maverick grew pale.

"I have resolved," he responded, in a very low tone.

Then, notwithstanding my wish that my eyes should not meet his glance, they did meet it, and were held just as my hand might be held in an unyielding grasp.

"I have resolved," he repeated.

I made no response. I stood there looking at him. Though I could not remove my gaze, I felt my resolution

18

not to assent to his proposition growing and intensifying, and I was becoming angry. What sort of force was he trying to use upon me? I knew little or nothing of the occult talk of the day. A sort of fright began to mingle with my anger. Every instant that I yielded was making my resisting power less—and I would not yield. In a vague sort of way I was telling myself that this was why this man's eyes had always seemed so peculiar to me.

Then a faint film came over my own vision; my eyelids became heavy, I could not keep them up. But I would not let them fall. I made an effort which appeared to take every particle of moral and physical strength I possessed. I moved; I looked towards the window; I saw the blessed sunlight outside; I heard a robin murmur on the lilac. I put my hand to my forehead. Confusedly I was aware that Mr. Maverick uttered some kind of an ejaculation. His voice sounded fierce. I was not looking in his eyes now. I had escaped, and he knew I had escaped. He moved quickly nearer to me. He tried to take my hands again, but they were clasped behind me.

"Miss Armstrong," he exclaimed, in a half-whisper, "surely—surely, you must know that I love you! You must know that."

I was trembling. I could not tell whether I feared this man more than I hated him. How could I have thought of allowing him to do me a favor? I did not reply. I thought that I could not speak. I turned my eyes again towards the sunlight, which had never been so beautiful.

"And I have a right to love you." I heard these words, and they made me turn towards my companion. It seemed to me a strange thing that not until this instant of the interview had I remembered Vane. But now the memory of him came to me with great sweetness and strength. And I recalled his words, "I am jealous of Maverick."

"Nothing can prevent my loving you," went on Mr. Maverick, authoritatively, "and winning you, too."

He was standing now very erect, head upflung and features set; his eyes shining under their brows. He was very white, and there were drops of moisture on his forehead.

"Yes," I returned, "I shall prevent you. If we should live ten thousand years, I should never love you."

As I spoke I grew more confident. My indignation at the attempt he had made to hypnotize me was so great that it stimulated me. I began to wonder now how I could have been affected in the least. He smiled, and his smile was so exasperating that I felt that I could not stay in the room with him. I turned and put my hand on the latch of the door.

"Oh, you need not go," said he, quickly. "I will be the one to go."

He walked to the table, where he had placed his hat. With his hat in his hand he came towards me again, and now I saw that in that brief time his whole aspect had changed greatly. The assertion in his manner was gone. He stopped in front of me.

"Bear with me for a moment longer," he said, with gentleness. "You must not be angry because I love you."

"No," I answered, "I'm not angry with you for that reason."

"Thank you for so much," he returned, "and you must not let me go away without hope—even the smallest grain of hope I will be content with now—no, not content, but I will endure with courage whatever happens. You'll give me that smallest hope, Miss Armstrong?"

It is true that there was something very winning in his

manner now; or this something would have been winning had it not been for the experience of the few moments previous.

"No," I said again.

Mr. Maverick looked down at his hat; he passed it round and round in his hands, and I watched him mechanically, absorbedly. The diamond on his finger flashed a ray at me. All at once, as in a scene in a theatre, there came before me the parlor of the hotel in Chilton where I had first seen this man when I had gone to meet Miss Runciman. What if I had never gone to meet Miss Runciman? Why are we so foolish and weak as to ask such questions of fate, for fate will not answer?

"You are sure that you can never love me?"

He put this question without raising his eyes.

"I am sure," I answered.

"Ah, well, then, nothing remains for me but to say goodmorning."

He now raised his glance to my face. His eyes were not good to see, and mine instantly fell before them.

"Before I go," he went on, "let me say that you need not attribute what I have said about your voice to anything but the coolest judgment, uninfluenced by my feeling for you. Your voice is your talent. If you do not make use of it you commit a sin against yourself and against the world. And now, good-morning. Sorry to have intruded thus upon you, I'm sure. All good fortune attend you."

He passed through the door, out into the sunshine; with his hat still in his hand, he turned back and said, smilingly:

"I beg, Miss Armstrong, that you will not put too much faith in Vane Hildreth; capital fellow, and fine tenor, still —but, good-morning, good-morning."

He walked down the narrow path that led to the gate between the two rows of dark-green box. At the gate he looked back once more, swung off his hat to me, and then went briskly along the road. I stood in the doorway watching him until he was out of sight. Then I hurried into the house, intent only on finding my mother. Again I could not find her in any of the rooms, and I ran into the orchard. I knew mother's ways—her "Second Advent ways," father used to call them. The low drooping apple-tree branches brushed roughly against my head as I went. Yes, there on the slope to the west, under the sweet russet tree, was my mother on her knees. I saw her arms clasped about the tree-trunk, and her head laid against the bark. Should I never get to her to comfort her? I threw myself down by her side.

"Mother! mother!" I cried, "he has gone! That man has gone!"

She lifted her head and looked at me.

"Don't tell me that," she said, "if you are to go, too."

Before I could make any reply to this, mother, still on her knees, turned about and grasped me by the shoulders.

"I've had a vision," she said, and her voice was shrill, and unlike her voice. "Since I've been here I've seen myself, myself as I was at your age, come back to me—come walking up from the meadow down there. How curious it was! It was like me, and it was like you, too, Wilhelminy."

"Don't, mother, don't!" I cried out.

"Let me go on. You needn't think I'm out of my head, Miny. You jest listen, 'n' don't you be frightened. Yes, I came up from the meadow, and I was just as I was when I married your father, only I had your eyes, my little girl; and havin' your eyes, p'raps, made me able to understand 'bout things, 'n' see them plainly.

"Yes, that girl walked up to me and she put one finger on my shoulder so," touching me, "and she said, 'S'rissy, don't hold her back—don't hold her back.'

"Then I burst out that I must—I must hold you back—I couldn't let you go. And then this girl, that was me and you both, looked at me with your eyes and she said, 'She's gone, S'rissy—she's gone. Now you must let—let her.'

"Oh, how strange it was to see your eyes in my face! I kept staring at her until I almost went blind. Mebby I did go blind, for when I could see again she was gone. I've been tryin' to think how foolish I am. I can't have my girl do jest as I think; I couldn't do jest as my father 'n' mother thought. The young folks grow up different, somehow; 'n' us older ones mustn't think they're wrong 'cause they're different. Jest because I have such a feeling about that man, don't make it that he's wicked. 'N' dreams ain't anything, anyway."

So mother talked, and I stood beside her, for she had risen. Perhaps I had begun to have a little different feeling about mother from what I used to have. I could see now that she was a "dreamer of dreams," that she was full of superstition; that she believed in "signs"; that her wide, sensitive eyes saw things that I could never see. None the less I loved and reverenced her; and I knew that there was something in my own nature that answered to hers, though the practical mingled in me with the visionary.

When mother became silent I began to reassure her. I said that I shrank from Mr. Maverick, and that I did not believe in his integrity. I remember how the robins flew about us as we stood there, and one hung, and fluttered, and scolded without cessation. We were near his nest in the branches above us. Mother stood gazing at me. She was holding my hands closely. When I had finished speaking, she said, slowly :

"But the other one? Miny, you love that other one?"

I opened my lips to say, "I am his wife," but before I spoke we heard a shrill scream from the direction of the river path. I recognized the voice, and I exclaimed, indignantly :

"What is Myra Foster shrieking about now?"

Then Myra herself came running up the acclivity ; she was rushing on towards the house, when she saw us and changed her course.

"Perhaps she has seen a mouse," I was saying to myself.

"Oh, come quick !" she cried, breathlessly; "Uncle Lem --he's got a fit ! Down here—on the path !"

We both started to run, but I reached the place long before mother, who seemed to be held back as if her feet were chained together. There lay father, face down on the ground. His arms were stretched out. I bent over him and tried to lift him. How heavy he was ! Myra wouldn't help ; when I asked her, she said she didn't dare to touch him, for she was afraid he was dead. In a moment I had turned him over so that he lay with his face up towards the sky. A bluebird circled down close to that motionless form.

Myra gave another shriek. I wanted to turn and strike her for making such a sound. Father's face was dark, almost purple, his jaw hanging heavily, his eyes partially open. Mother came staggering up and knelt down on the ground.

"Lemuel !" she said; "Lemuel !"

I turned to Myra. "Will you take the horse and ride for the doctor?" I asked.

"Oh, I can't ! I can't ! I'm so frightened !"

"I'll go, then," I said. I bent over mother. She did not

seem to notice me. I told her that I was going to ride to the village for Dr. Shores. She made no response, and I left her crouching over that senseless form. As for myself, just at that time I seemed to have no feeling, save the feeling of hurry to the village.

But the doctor could do nothing. Father must have been dead when Myra had left him. She said she had met him on the path and he had called out, "Hullo, Myra!" and the next instant had fallen as we had found him. Apoplexy, the doctor called it.

When the funeral was over mother and I began life by ourselves. Aunt Lowizy came and stayed a week with us, but she had to go back to Ryle, for grandmother needed her. So we were alone, Lotus being our only companion. Bidwell was very kind; everybody was kind. It was Bidwell who milked the cows and did all the "chores," for chores must be done, whether people live or die.

In the second week after the funeral I proposed that we hire a boy; I thought I could do a great deal of work myself, and with a boy to help us we might get along until something permanent could be arranged. Instead of replying, mother rose from her chair and went to the old desk that always stood at the end of the long kitchen. She unlocked it, then she stood a moment looking at the key which she had withdrawn from its place.

"It was in his pocket," she said; "he has carried it for 'bout a year, 'n' kept the desk locked. I feel wicked lookin' 'mong his papers that he kep' so close. He never used to keep um so. Wilhelminy," turning tremulously towards me, "I think we're poor—I think we 'ain't got a cent."

I rose and flung open the desk. I sat down before it, determined to know what could be known. Mother drew a chair close to me and watched me as I took out paper after

paper and examined everything. I can tell in a very few
words what I learned. We didn't own anything. The
farm and everything on it belonged to Bidwell Blake.
Father had lost all he had ever owned of money and
horses and land in a stock company he had joined—a
company formed to carry on a large horse-breeding farm
in Kentucky. And, in spite of my resolve not to believe,
I yet had to believe that father had not been honest. I
was sure now that even when he sold horses he had not
been honest, and the neighbors knew it—oh yes, the
neighbors knew it, of course. But I hoped that mother
might be kept ignorant. But even as I hoped I recalled
her face as I had seen it many times since I was old enough
to remember—her face when she had been listening to
father. Yes, she had always known; but she had loved
him; I was quite sure she had loved him; and it is a terrible thing to give affection to a man or woman whom you
cannot respect.

I stole a look at mother now as she sat close to my
chair. Since father's death she had looked like an old
woman. We had both tried to be calm. As for me, I
seemed to be grieving for the father of long ago—the jolly,
kind-hearted man who had seemed to love me. Within the
last few days that man had come very near to me, and I
knew that I should forget his later self.

"What shall we do?"

Mother put this question a long time after I had told
her that we had nothing in the world. I rose; I could not
sit still. I was thinking of Vane. He would take care of
us. He had sent two money drafts since he had gone, but
I could not make up my mind to use them. They lay now
in my little desk, the desk father had given me on my four-
teenth birthday. I shrank from touching Vane's money

until he came back and the marriage was known. It was wrong; I had done a wrong thing when I consented to a marriage, as I had done. Yes, Vane would take care of us; but not until he came back. Meanwhile something must be done.

"I must think," I said. I walked into the yard, Lotus at my heels.

On the bench by the shed door was lying the folded newspaper that I had taken out to read but this morning. It was a New York daily that Bidwell had left. It was four days old now. Without thinking of it or caring to look at it, I yet unfolded it and absently ran my eyes down its columns. It was some moments before my mind responded to my eyes. When it did respond I found myself reading this paragraph:

"Country board wanted for the summer by an invalid lady; a quiet place, with good air; absolutely a quiet place. Address ——."

Sometimes one makes a decision at once. I did this now. I read the advertisement twice. The address was a post-office box in Worcester, Mass. With the paper in my hand I hurried back to the kitchen, where mother still sat by the old desk.

"Here is a chance to earn money through the summer," I said; "and then we can make other plans. We will hire the house of Bidwell for six months. After that, perhaps, I can teach."

I spoke with more hopefulness than I felt. It devolved upon me to take up the burden of care, and I would endeavor to do it cheerfully. Meanwhile I tried not to think of Vane. I wondered if any other girl was ever in just such a position. The more I thought of telling mother, the more I shrank from knowing that she would blame Vane for what he had done, and he was blameworthy, but so was I. Mother fell in with my proposition, but only dully and mechanically. She said there would be many replies to that advertisement, and that it was probable that the lady had already engaged board, there had been so much time. She hoped I wouldn't "build on it."

Nevertheless I did "build on it." I couldn't help doing so. I wrote my note, and then I saddled the horse and galloped off with it. I was in a feverish haste to earn money. And deep in my heart I still hoped some time to be able to repay Miss Runciman every penny that she had spent upon me. I tried not to think of Miss Runciman, for the thought of her galled me so.

I mailed my note, and then I had to wait as patiently as I could, which was not patiently at all. On the third day I took from the office an envelope with a compact superscription upon it.

"'Tain't your usual one," said the postmaster, with a significant smile, which I resented. I would not break the envelope until I had ridden out of the village. Then, sitting in the saddle, I found that the writing within the wrapper was very different from that on the outside, and I knew the dashing characters well—it was Miss Runciman's hand that had drawn them. My heart jumped and my fingers trembled. Here is what she wrote:

"MY DEAR BILLY,—Do you think it is fate, or God, which made you answer my advertisement? Let us call it God, for I suppose there is a God, and if there be one He would be likely to meddle in the affairs of His world sometimes, wouldn't He?

"The moment I saw your envelope I said to myself, 'Could this have come from Billy?' I don't know why, I'm sure, that I should be so glad to think I may go to your home for the summer. For you must let me come—you must. Perhaps you hate me. But you must remember how you are commanded to use those who have wronged you. I'm in wretched health. I talk as if I should get well; but I shall not. I'm going to die soon—soon. And people who are going to die soon want to be forgiven, don't they? Let me come immediately. I will make as little trouble as I may. I shall not be alone; but you must take us both. Don't wait to write; telegraph—telegraph as soon as you can ride over to that little station where the wire stops. Go now and send me these words, 'Come quickly.'

"LEONORA RUNCIMAN."

My hand, with the letter in it, dropped down on the pommel. Can you explain why the bitterness that had been in my heart towards this woman suddenly fell away from me? Surely it was not merely because she was ill. Was it because she was just Leonora Runciman? There was a dimness in my eyes as I looked down at the paper. She was not alone—then Bashy was with her. I was sorry for that. Bathsheba's sharp teeth, and the especial, carnivorous look of biting they had, had made an impression on me which had never been effaced, and yet the girl had been kind in her way, and she was Vane's sister. Somehow she never seemed like Vane's sister.

I thrust the note into my jacket-pocket, I gathered up the bridle rein and cantered on towards the station just as Miss Runciman had bidden me, and I sent the precise words to her that she had dictated—"Come quickly." Then I rode homewards as fast as I could, and my horse's neck and sides were wet when I dismounted in the barn.

I longed to rush into the house to mother, but first I made myself unsaddle and rub down my steed as well as I could. There is often something comforting and soothing in contact with some animals, and when I was ready to meet mother, though I was red and perspiring from my work, I was quite calm. I was prepared for opposition, and resolved to overcome it. Mother looked startled and alarmed when I read the note. She shrank away and put out her hands as if to ward off something; but when I read again those words about the writer's illness mother's face changed to pity.

"Poor thing!" she exclaimed. "Let her come. It's not for us to judge."

Of course it was Bidwell's horse I kept and used. He had tried to make me believe that I should be doing him a favor if I would keep it until the fall, and he was so earnest about it that I consented. Have I set down here how kind and thoughtful Bid was? I think he did not often come to see Myra at Miss Cobb's without walking up the river path to ask if he could do anything for us. It was on one of those visits that I arranged with him concerning the rent; I would go right on paying what father had agreed to pay; only, just now he must wait, I must earn the money; and I would keep the hens, and one cow; these mother and I could care for. Bidwell had the appearance of dealing with me as if I were another young man, and he could never know how I thanked him for that.

After I had sent the telegram mother and I fell to house-cleaning like mad. We cleaned the south front room and the bedroom adjoining. I was sore and lame every time I waked in the night, but I did not care for any physical ills; or I thought I did not.

The next afternoon it was I who seemed calm and mother who was, as she said, "as flustered as she could be." A telegram received in the morning informed us that our boarders would arrive on the 6:30 P.M. train. Could I meet them?

I had just led the horse, harnessed, to the carry-all that had once been father's, and that was now Bidwell's, into the yard. Mother was at the door, and came out to say

good-bye, as if I were going on a journey.   Her eyes looked
more timid and sensitive than usual.

"I do hope we've done right," she said, in an unsteady
voice; "but now the time has really come, I almost wish
we'd said no.   You know, I don't believe in her, Billy."

"It isn't necessary," I answered, briskly.   "I don't believe in her, either."

So I drove off.   At the first corner I met Bidwell with
Myra on the front seat of his carriage, and Rachel Cobb
on the back seat.   Rachel had on her glasses and peered
sharply at me.   Bidwell pulled in his brown horses, and
called out, cheerily:

"So you've got started, eh?   I'm jest takin' Rachel out
a piece.   She's be'n shut up so long I thought 'twould do
her good."

Then he clucked to his horses, Myra "snuggled" yet
closer to him, and I was left to continue my way.

"I suppose that's the kind of girl men like," I said, aloud;
and I added that I wished she was in any measure worthy
of Bid; Bid was such a good fellow!   Having thus expressed myself, I forgot them.   I had plenty of subjects to
think of besides Myra Foster and her admirers.

I reached the station half an hour before train time in my
fear lest I should be late.   I carefully hitched the horse,
and then I walked up and down on the platform.   The
agent occasionally came out and looked at me.   Once he
said he "s'posed" I was Lemuel Armstrong's daughter.
Having informed him that I was, he went back and probably meditated on that fact.   Presently he returned and
again gazed at me intently a moment before he remarked
that he guessed I must be the one that had been studyin'
to be a great singer; was I?

"Yes."

He stepped back as if the better to contemplate such a being.

"Well, be ye a great singer?"

"No, I'm not."

He walked to the utmost edge of the platform and squinted reflectively along the rails. Without removing his eyes from their occupation, he said:

"I guess it didn't pay, did it?"

"No," I answered.

This conversation consumed a few moments of the half-hour, but the time that still remained was heavy. Even the knowledge that the fact that I had studied to be a great singer, and failed, was making me an object of interest, did not allay the excitement with which I waited for the train.

The shadows cast by the hills to the west were long and cool. Above them the summer sun was still brilliantly shining; but here the day seemed nearer an end, and the birds were flying about, making their soft little calls to each other. A great peace appeared to have descended upon the world, but, try as I would, I could not partake of that peace. Sometimes nature is so alien, so unsympathetic. A certain vague, distant sound, or rather vibration, became perceptible. The agent, who had come out again, now pulled his watch from some very deep receptacle, and remarked, as he examined it:

"I guess she's goin' to be right on the tick."

I stood up straight. Why should my pulses beat so because Miss Runciman was coming? There she was, descending the steps—pale, thin, with hair more gray, with no suggestion now of physical power, and yet still a notable woman. I stepped quickly forward. She put a hand on each shoulder, and looked at me.

"This is good of you, Billy," she said earnestly. "Now I can die in peace up here in the country."

She kissed me, and I did not shrink. I thought that I ought to shrink. I was indefinitely aware that there was a figure behind. Where was Bashy? Miss Runciman turned.

"Billy," she said, "here's some one you have seen—and you were kind to him, too; but then you're a kind little girl. Robert—"

I did not hear what else she said, for the man who stepped forward, laden with wraps and satchels, was Mr. Robert Dreer, the man who had come to that house where I studied last winter. He was now remarkably well dressed, and his face was happy, in spite of its expression of anxiety.

"Billy," said Miss Runciman, as if she were presenting an ordinary acquaintance, "this is my husband, Mr. Dreer. Is that your carriage? Do you know, I'm to have the gray colt sent up here? I pretend that I'm going to ride him, but I never shall; no, I never shall."

She walked slowly forward to the carriage. Mr. Dreer hastened after her, piling his wraps as well as he could upon one arm so that he might offer the other arm to his wife. But she turned to me with a smile:

"You help me, Billy." She took my arm, and Mr. Dreer walked on to put his shawls and bags in the carry-all.

XVII

THE WHOLE STORY

I DID not ask a question. I was too bewildered to do so, even if I had thought it courteous. In that first moment I was not even putting inquiries to myself. Mr. Dreer turned towards us as we came forward. Miss Runciman made a movement to signify that she would not be put into the carriage directly. She leaned both hands on the shaft and looked above the horse into the distance. Presently she said, not addressing any one:

"I don't know why God made such a beautiful world just for us to die in."

"But we live in it first," I responded, with some eagerness. She smiled.

"You say that because you are living; but I am dying. Robert"—to Mr. Dreer, who stood close beside her—"help me in. I'm tired."

I watched the man as he obeyed. The tenderness in his worn face was indescribable. I recalled the time when he had gazed at Miss Runciman's portrait in the low-ceiled room at Wallingford. She had been his wife then; I felt sure of that. Let me say here that I am going to call her Miss Runciman to the end of these chronicles, for it was by that name that I always thought of her, by that name I remember her now.

There was hardly a word spoken during the drive home.

19

The two new-comers sat in the back of the carriage, with the woman leaning her head on her companion's shoulder, her eyes closed nearly all the time, Mr. Dreer holding her carefully, as if he would shield her from everything. As mother came out into the yard to meet us the moon was shining over the tops of the poplars that grew at the end of the house; it shone directly upon Miss Runciman's face, and when mother looked at her I knew that there was nothing but pity in her heart.

After a few days the invalid seemed so much better that, instead of sitting or lying almost all the day on the piazza, she would walk about the yard, always on her husband's arm, and she began to say things that reminded me of her old self. This improvement continued until I, for one, began to think she might get well, or at least much better, and she did not cough nearly so much. The terms which she had set for board seemed to me munificent, but she insisted that it was worth even more to have a sick woman like her about the house, and she might die on our hands at any time. At this she smiled, and Mr. Dreer, as he stood behind her couch, tried to repress a shudder.

Later I often watched Mr. Dreer, thinking to myself that he must have loved much to be able to forgive so much, for I felt sure there had been need of forgiveness on his part. Perhaps there was some spaniel-like quality in his nature. He did not notice me, save in a merely civil way. But once he took occasion to thank me earnestly for what he said I had done for him at the Holloway House.

It was at this interview that I proposed to Miss Runciman to allow her board to cancel the debt I must owe her. I had resolved to say this, though it was difficult for me to do so. She raised herself on her elbow that she might the better look at me.

"What debt?" she asked.

"For singing lessons, and—and—" Here I stopped.

"Come here," she said.

I approached the lounge.

"Sit down on this footstool."

I obeyed.

She was silent for a time. She put her hand on my head.

"I told you that when you are going to die soon you want to be forgiven. You owe me nothing but forgiveness. It was a cruel thing to take you and leave you as I did. I suppose I have done many cruel things in my life. But they never troubled me; and I'm not much troubled by them now. That's a curious fact, isn't it? Now, there's Robert—I suppose he loves me—he really loves me. Billy, if you'll close that door leading into the house I'll talk to you a little. I feel like talking about myself. But if Miss Cobb should come over, and should happen to hear me, I should be sorry. Miss Cobb isn't a woman in whom I would confide. I really am strong to-day—quite like myself. Odd, isn't it? Robert thinks I may get well, but he is wrong—wrong. Come back here to the footstool. You see, after all, I couldn't bear to have you sing better than I could sing. I couldn't bear, when the time really came, to have people say 'that girl some day will far outshine Miss Runciman.' They did say that. Then I hated you. And Maverick was taken with you. I don't wonder, of course. There's a singular simplicity in your character and manner which is like a drink from a cold mountain spring on a hot day. Speaking of drinking, I was always afraid you would begin to take wine. It seemed so against your whole self —odd notion, wasn't it?"

Here the speaker paused. She was silent for so long a

time that I glanced up at her. Her eyes were closed, and from beneath the lids two tears had started. Impulsively I leaned forward and kissed those drooped lids. Even as I did so I knew that the reasonable feeling for me to have was the feeling of repulsion towards this woman. But, thank God, we are not always reasonable.

"That's lovely of you," she murmured.

She opened her eyes and added, with animation, "And you don't run any risk in regard to me now, for I shall not get well and do any more unprincipled things. And Robert is safe too. Poor fellow! I'm glad he's safe. He has suffered horribly through me. But having loved me, he couldn't stop loving me. That was strange, too. Billy, will you be bored if I talk about myself? I am in the mood to do that. It is as if I were standing off and contemplating my own individuality. And you are such a sympathetic, intense kind of a listener. Shall I bore you?"

"Oh no, no!" I answered.

"Very well, I'll go on, then. I married Robert when I was nineteen. I thought love was a fine thing. I suppose it is; people seem to believe in it. But I became weary of it. Robert didn't weary, however; he continued to be devoted. He isn't like a man in that respect—nor like a woman, either; perhaps like some dogs, and a very few human beings. I knew that I could sing before I married, but it was not until later that I learned that I might do something with my voice. We were poor; I was a country girl, like you, Billy, and Robert had a good opening in business with Mr. Hollander. I see you remember that name.

"At a concert at which I sang a professional in singing heard me. He sought me out and prophesied a great future if I would study abroad. I was set on fire by his words. I told my husband that I must cultivate my voice; but we were poor then; he wanted me to wait. How could I wait? The Hollanders were very kind to us both. But I'm sure that Mrs. Hollander never liked me. Her husband was too fond of leaning on the piano and staring at me when I sang. And I confess that I used to glance at him occasionally. Why not? And Mrs. Hollander sometimes saw me do it. It was about this time that Robert became his employer's confidential clerk. He knew as much about the business as Mr. Hollander himself knew. I was wild for money then. I was discontented and unhappy. I was constantly telling my husband that he must get money in some way. Now, you must know that Robert isn't a strong man in some respects, and that he is wonderfully strong in other ways. That's the way with us all, I fancy, only in not so marked a degree.

"I'm to blame for it all; I can see that plainly enough. You don't care for the particulars of the affair. Robert, eager to get money for me, when he saw an opportunity, acted. You don't remember reading in the papers about the Hollander frauds. You were too young. Rachel Cobb showed you a few paragraphs. The transaction involved the firm. Robert's spoils were $20,000—not large, as frauds go in these days, but it seemed a great deal to me then. And he put the whole sum into my hands and sent me abroad. Mind you, I knew it was a fraud, and I helped him with my acuter brain.

"We thought, as criminals usually think, that we should not be found out. Everything would be 'squared up' before discovery. It was a 'great deal.' But the crash came, nevertheless, and Hollander was disgraced utterly, as well as made a poor man. What does Robert do then? He comes forward and confesses that it was he who had done this thing, he who was guilty, and that he had used Hollander's name to float the thing. People talked about the affair for a time; it was a little more interesting than the ordinary embezzlement, and, for some reason, it was generally believed that I was really the power that had moved the puppet to make a criminal of himself. My extravagance, this thing and that, were dwelt upon. Mrs. Hollander started all that. Of course, the woman didn't feel too kindly towards me. She and her husband had to move into a poor part of the city and take boarders for a living. They didn't have even $20,000. You may be sure that I arranged so that I needn't lose that. I was smart. I was learning to sing. Robert was sentenced to eleven years' hard labor. They pardoned him at the end of ten years for good behavior.

"Meantime I had become famous. I took my maiden name, but some ferret of a newspaperman published a few facts in the case. I was famous, all the same, and the crowds came to hear me. At first I used to think about Robert, but I grew to think less and less about him. Why should I remember him? It did him no good. It must have been a curious remnant of sentiment that made me go to that old house in Wallingford—that made me take you there last winter. It was there Robert and I spent the first few months after our marriage; and Robert came there from prison. Poor fellow! He kept right on loving me all the time."

Miss Runciman, who had been sitting up on the lounge, now laid herself back on the pillows. I sat perfectly still. I was feeling very far from her. I was wondering if there were many people like her in the world. And did those men and women who had committed crimes have any "realizing sense" of what they had done? Did the capacity to do an evil deed nullify the capacity to repent of it?

Did people repent just from pure sorrow for their actions, or only when those actions brought suffering to them? And what did God—God, who really knows us—think of us? To be God's child is to be loved by Him, and understood by Him—so He understands why we do a bad act.

Mother believes that God looks tenderly upon a wicked child. How does He look upon a woman like Leonora Runciman? I rose from my place on the footstool by the lounge. I walked to the edge of the piazza and leaned against one of the pillars.

There was my father. He had cheated people. I was convinced that it was his practice to cheat whenever he could do so. And I was quite sure that his conscience never troubled him, and that he was only troubled when he did not succeed. But mother—she was upright—she was a person of integrity.

"Billy."

It was Miss Runciman who spoke. I went back to the lounge. The pale, attractive face was towards me, and the eyes were looking earnestly at me.

"I knew you would feel just as you are feeling," she said, "but I had a strong wish to tell you. That's another marked weakness of humanity—the tendency to confess. Now, why should I have told you this? Such telling serves no purpose whatever. I simply wished you to know about me. My inhibitive power ought to have kept me silent. But it did not. I have risked your feeling, thrust away from me by my evil deeds. It's a strange thing that I'm not made unhappy by the thought of them. I ought to be unhappy."

Here she coughed. When she could speak she said: "I wish you would sit down here again." I resumed my place. She put out her hand and clasped mine.

" It's such a strong, young hand," she said. " And now I'm going to talk about your future. You are going to study under Marchesi. Oh yes "—as I started uncontrollably—"you grow pale at the very thought—and no wonder. I have made my will. I have saved some money. If I don't die, you have the money all the same — $5000. That will be enough for the way you will live. I propose that you and your mother go this fall. I have already written to Marchesi concerning you. It is not yet time for a reply. I can see your future resplendent. To sing — to move hearts—to make the blood leap—to play upon the pulses—"

Miss Runciman rose to a sitting position. A bright red came to her face. She began to cough again. After a time she took up her talk once more.

" I am so grateful that you didn't become entangled with my nephew," she said.

I could not help a quick, slight movement. I could not tell whether she noticed this movement. She went on :

" Such an entanglement would most likely be fatal to your future as a singer. Yes, I'm very glad that such a thing did not happen. Billy !"—suddenly.

Miss Runciman seized my arm and pulled me down towards her. She looked alarmed ; I could see that, even in the midst of my own confusion.

" You know I warned you !" she exclaimed.

" Does warning ever do any good ?" I asked. I had, on the moment, made a resolve. I withdrew myself somewhat and tried to look in Miss Runciman's face as I said :

" Vane and I are married."

" What !"

But I did not think of repeating my words ; I could not have spoken again immediately. The look that came into the countenance before me had a very strange effect—it frightened me thoroughly. But why should Miss Runciman's eyes fill with horror? She stared at me an instant in silence. Then she roused herself and looked about her as if in search of some one.

"Where is Robert?" she asked. "Find Robert for me."

Without any response in words, I turned and went along the yard towards the path that led to the river. It was in this direction that Mr. Dreer had gone for a walk. He was never away for more than an hour. I should be likely to meet him. I had no more than reached the bars of the fence when Miss Runciman called me quickly. I hurried back to her. She was standing now, with one arm clasped about a post of the piazza. She looked full of alert, and I might almost say defensive, life, in spite of her pallor.

"Come here—come close," she said, in an eager whisper. "Before you call Robert tell me more. Does your mother know?"

"I have never told any one until this moment," I answered. I also was on the defensive now. Was she going to blame Vane? I could not bear that.

"Did Vane wish the marriage kept secret?"

"He did not say so." I spoke stiffly, and as if I should resent too much questioning. "Under the circumstances, I thought I would remain silent."

"Even to your mother?"

"Yes, even to my mother." Miss Runciman put her hand up to her head a moment. Then she asked, peremptorily:

"What were the circumstances?"

I hesitated, and as I did so my companion said, with still more command in her manner:

"The date? Tell me the date instantly."

I mentioned the day of the month, and, instead of putting another inquiry, she stepped down from the piazza and walked a few yards, exclaiming as she did so:

"I must find Robert!"

There was a touching anxiety and helplessness in her appearance; it was particularly affecting to see a woman like her helpless in any degree: I felt this even in my preoccupation.   I hurried forward.

"I will go," I said, shortly.   She paused, and I went on towards the path.

In my vague alarm there was much indignation, and this latter emotion grew as the moments passed.   Why should Miss Runciman appear like this, even though my marriage had been, in a measure, clandestine?   I began to run along the path.   It was a very irritating thing to meet Myra Foster coming up the slope, swinging her hat in her hand.

"Mercy sake!" she exclaimed.   "There ain't nothin' happened, has there?"

"No—no," trying to pass her.

"I'm so glad.   I was comin' up to ask you to go out to Great Medders with us towards night—Bid 'n' I, you know."

"Thank you — my time is so taken up — excuse me — there's Mr. Dreer," and I dashed on.

It was really strange that I should dislike that girl so much.   And what could Bidwell Blake see in her?   But father also had liked her.   Confusedly I was thinking thus as I hastened towards Mr. Dreer.   As soon as he saw me he came quickly to me, his ever-present anxiety intensified. I hastened to give his wife's message, and to assure him that she was no worse.   Having done this, I lingered.   I did not care to return immediately.   I walked down to the hackmatack-trees, where I had strolled and sat so many times with Bathsheba and her brother. There was the spot where the big carriage had stood.

I went back and leaned on the bar of the fence as I had done when Vane had sung his little encore song to me. My heart was aching. My dry, hot eyes turned vaguely this way and that. I was continually asking myself why Miss Runciman had looked so horrified—and why had she so wished to know the date of my marriage. It was that fact alone which concerned her.

I put my hand in my pocket and drew out Vane's letter. It was my habit to keep one letter with me until another one came. He wrote constantly, and with the ardor and abandon of a lover who loves absorbingly, and without caution. It has not seemed necessary to mention these letters; but I read them unceasingly, it seems to me now as I look back; and I thought of the writer from morning till night, and dreamed of him while I slept. Those letters, and the memory of their writer, filled the summer with a glow and a subtle and delightful excitement that colored everything. No matter of what I was thinking, I was thinking also of Vane. I was enveloped in something which made it impossible for any grief or pleasure, not connected with this one subject, to touch me deeply.

Perhaps this confession reveals a very selfish person; it is the truth, however. But, notwithstanding this truth, I never ceased regretting that marriage. Still my thoughts of the ceremony grew more and more indefinite and shadowy. Now, since Miss Runciman's question, these memories started out into a brightly defined distinctness again, and were not like the remembrance of a dream. And the incomprehensible and contradictory gladness in that I was Vane's wife was stronger than ever. Fortunately for me, I did not try to understand these things. The human heart,

which is desperately wicked, is also quite as mysterious.
What else is capable of two distinctly contrary emotions at
the same time?

When I returned an hour later Miss Runciman was lying
on the lounge on the piazza. She did not open her eyes as
I came softly forward. So I passed on into the house and
to the kitchen, where mother was sitting. When I entered
the room she asked quickly why Mr. Dreer had gone off
in such a hurry, and why he had gone to Chilton. I could
answer neither of these inquiries. She informed me that
Mr. Dreer had saddled the gray colt, which now submitted to be ridden by others besides its mistress, and
that he had galloped off as soon as he could go.

As it was a thirty-mile ride to Chilton, Mr. Dreer could
hardly return until the next day. Of course, I would not
ask any questions. Miss Runciman, the next morning, did
not leave her room until nearly noon. When she did appear she showed plainly that she had not slept; and she
could not eat. She drank a glass of milk and then established herself on the piazza again, asking if I could sit beside her. I was expecting her to refer to the subject which
had been of such interest to her the day before. Finally
she said:

"Poor Billy!"

I resented this exclamation, and showed that I did so.

"Don't be angry," she murmured.

Then she said nothing more. She was uneasy, and when
afternoon came she was constantly going to the end of the
piazza, where she could see the road that led towards
Chilton, and gazing in that direction. It was almost night
when the gray horse appeared, galloping steadily on. I
waited by her side until the rider entered the yard. Then
I went into the house and sat down. I was glad that I was

alone. Mother had gone to Rachel Cobb's. I had not
noticed that the window towards the piazza was open until
I heard Miss Runciman ask, in a loud voice:

"Did you find them?"

"Yes."

"And get an answer?"

Then I hastened into the kitchen, where I could not
hear. But I had not been there ten minutes when the door
was flung open and Mr. Dreer came forward.

"Leonora wishes you to go to her," he said. He went
on out of the house. I rose from my chair immediately,
but I hesitated. What would she say to me? As if for a
protection, I took Vane's letter in my hand. Then I joined
Miss Runciman, who was sitting up now, with a fur cloak
about her shoulders. She was holding this cloak together
at her throat, her thin hand showing strained and white. She
had her head flung back as she watched the door through
which I came. With her free hand she motioned me to
sit beside her on the couch. As I obeyed she seemed to
be looking at me.

"I ought to have told you the truth at the very first,"
she began, abruptly; "but who could imagine that Vane
would do such a thing? And what I did say to you about
him was not true. There is really sometimes something
more than a moral satisfaction in speaking the exact truth.
What information did I give you concerning my nephew?"

I answered directly:

"You said that he was always falling in love, and that
I must not think his manner meant anything."

"Oh yes; I remember now. But that was not so. I
thought, however, it would do as a warning. It seems it
did not serve at all."

I remained perfectly quiet as I listened. Miss Runciman

had evidently decided to resume her usual somewhat cynical manner; she was not going to be dramatic, as she had
been in her surprise of the day before.

"No," I returned, after a moment, "it did not serve."

She turned and scrutinized me. Then she suddenly
dropped her calm appearance, and exclaimed:

"He ought to be shot! I did not dream that he was
such a rascal." Having pronounced these words in a high
tone, she evidently made an effort to appear calm again.

"Robert went to Chilton," she said, "that he might send
a cable message to Bordeaux, in France, and await the answer. Here it is."

She opened the hand which had been holding her cloak
together; from it there fell a crumpled bit of paper, which
I picked up.

"Read it," she commanded; "read it aloud."

"Mrs. Olive Hildreth, now living with her mother at Rue
—— No. 17."

I gazed at the words after I had spoken them. I did
not know what they meant; but they must be charged with
something terrible.

"Olive Hildreth!" I repeated, in a half-whisper. And I
waited, for I was not ready to ask questions.

"I will be as brief as is possible," went on Miss Runciman. "I don't believe much in explanations. And you
need not try to act as if you were not moved, as if you did
not suffer; spare yourself that effort.

"It is nearly five years since my nephew married Olive
Jewett. Dear Billy, don't try to be a stoic, please. No
matter who Olive Jewett was. The marriage was very dis-
pleasing to Vane's friends, and they let him know it. He
was furiously indignant, flounced off to Europe with his
bride, and swore he would never mention her to me—par-

ticularly to me, because I was more angry with him than
any one else. That was a kind of silence that I could very
well bear, and I aided it by declaring that I would not
listen to any information concerning Vane's wife.

"In six months they were tired of each other. I will say
that Olive Jewett was a chorus singer to whom men had
made love, but whom nobody had married. Vane got it
into his head that she was a lovely creature who had been
much traduced, and he thought he was in love. Some of
her relatives in the wine business have a house in Bordeaux,
and Olive took up a residence there with her mother.
They considered that Olive had done very well, for Vane
made his wife an allowance that left him with very little
money, indeed.

"Perhaps he was doing penance for his folly in marrying
her by thus sending her so much. Mind you, no one tells
me anything of the Jewetts—I mean that neither Vane
nor his sister gives me any information. But a friend of
mine, visiting Bordeaux this last spring, wrote to me that
Olive was dangerously ill of a fever. Later, this same
friend, then in Paris, wrote that she had heard that Olive
had died. That is the last I have known, and since neither
Vane nor Bashy spoke of Olive, you may be sure that I did
not; in no way was the girl a pleasant subject. Vane's
marriage was never alluded to in any manner. I thought of
it when I saw that Vane was attracted to you, but I confess
that I gave no serious attention to the fact. I was absorbed in other things. But I did give you a casual warning. To do more than speak casually seemed to me to
emphasize matters too much.

"When you told me yesterday that you and Vane were
married, the first thing I thought of doing was to send
direct to Bordeaux to the address my friend had given me.

This is the answer. You see that girl did not die. Such people don't die—they live. It is others who die. You have followed me, Billy ?"

" Yes."

Miss Runciman turned towards me now. But I withdrew further from her.

So Vane was married. While he was writing me these letters he knew that he had a wife living. He knew it ; and yet he wrote like that. And he knew it when he had pleaded with me on the train. I had old-fashioned ideas. I had been thinking of this man as a man whom I had every right in the world to love.

" Billy," said my companion again.

I did not make any response. It did not seem to me that there was anything for me to say. That was fortunate, for I could not speak. Just then it was simply impossible for me to utter a word. Perhaps Miss Runciman perceived this, for she kept silence for a few moments. At last she spoke again.

" I'm not straitlaced. I'm not particularly strict," she began, " and perhaps I'm not shocked at things that would shock you, Billy ; but I'm not going to try to justify Vane. Only let me say this : He used not to be a bad fellow. He must be very much in love with you."

I trembled as I heard these last words. I wished that I might see clearly. There was a blackness over my vision. I passed my hand across my eyes. But I could not see. There was nothing that I could do just now. I recall that I wished to rise and walk away so that I might be by my-self, but I did not dare to move lest I might fall. Yes, all the time that Vane had been writing those letters he knew that I was not his wife. And he must be aware that there was a chance of my being told of his former marriage. He might say that he would risk that chance. But I could not follow out any train of thought—if I began coherently, my mind immediately became obscured, and like the mind of an insane person.

I longed to get away, but I still dared not rise. What if I should fall down there at Miss Runciman's feet? What strange people there were in the world! My mother had dreamed that I was in danger. Did she guess this? No, she could not by any possibility guess this. This was too dreadful for her to think of. Oh, if I only could get upon my feet and walk away to my own room! I hoped that Miss Runciman would not speak again now. But she did speak, and I tried to listen and to distinguish what she said. The words had no sense—I could make nothing of them. And presently the light seemed to go out of the sky.

When I could see and hear again I was on mother's bed in her room, and Mr. Dreer was putting a cold wet towel on my head. His wife was sitting on the edge of the bed holding my hand. She uttered some kind of an exclamation. At first I thought only of her, and that for some reason she had fainted.

" I suppose you were a little faint," she said, soothingly, " and Robert brought you in here. You'll be all right in a few minutes."

" Then it wasn't you who fainted?" I asked.

I did not yet remember anything; but before she could reply, all that she had been telling me came back with burning distinctness. I tried to sit up, but I fell back again. I despised myself for having swooned; I had never had such a thing happen to me before. I had had a contempt for a girl who could be so weak.

" You may leave us now, Robert," I heard Miss Runciman say, " but be within call."

I turned my head on the pillow. I longed to have this woman go away. I wanted to be alone; I must be alone soon or these rushing, fiery thoughts would unbalance my brain; and presently mother would come, and what should I do then? She would have to be told. How thankful I was that the neighbors did not know—that they could not talk about it. Yes, even then I could be thankful for such a thing as that. And there was Vane's last letter in my pocket. As soon as I could I must destroy that letter and all the others. But no—a dreadful horror came upon me at thought of such a deed. Part with those letters? I tried to sit up; I tried to cry out something incoherent. And then it came to me that I was behaving like a weak, hysterical woman. I succeeded in getting a partial control of myself.

When we were left alone Miss Runciman moved still nearer to me. My suffering seemed to give her a fleeting strength. She put her hand on my forehead for a moment. As she bent over me she looked keenly in my eyes.

"Let us have the whole story now," she said, imperatively, "and if there is anything to be done I may see my way clearly to do it. Tell me all."

So I began, and I did tell her all hurriedly, but without a thought of keeping anything back. When I had finished she drew a long breath.

"I have heard of worse things," she said.

"Worse things!" I cried, "and I love him! I suppose I love him!"

I was surprised at the relief it was to me to be able to say those words aloud to my companion. She smiled; then she kissed my cheek.

"If you were a perfectly well-regulated young person,"

she responded, "your love would have died the moment you learned that Vane had deceived you."

I moaned a little as I heard her speak thus, and I found that it was also a relief to moan. I knew perfectly that I had never been a well-regulated young person. But I was not going to lie there and make my moans. I sat up resolutely. I pushed back the hair from my face.

"Wait one moment," said Miss Runciman, commandingly.

I turned towards her. What more was there to say?

"Give me your word about one thing," she said. "Promise me that you will go to Paris in the early fall and go on with your studies. Don't you see that the hand of Providence, if there is a Providence, in all this is clearing the way for you? You go unhampered. That hurried marriage on the train will soon seem even more unreal than a dream. Come, give me your word."

Her manner, her tone, stirred me even more than her words. After an instant's hesitation I replied:

"On one condition."

"Name it."

"That you let me repay the money I shall use."

"Oh yes, if I live."

"Then I will go."

I spoke firmly. A spark of enthusiasm was in my soul. But the next moment I thought it died. Before my companion could speak again I hurried out of the room. As I went up the stairs to my own chamber I heard footsteps near the outer door and the voice of Myra Foster saying:

"I wonder where they all be?"

Mother had come home, and Myra had come with her.

I fiercely locked my door. It would not be safe for that girl to come near me now. How could Bidwell Blake care for a girl like that? The next instant I had forgotten her. I was gathering up Vane's letters. As my eyes caught his written words they seemed different to me—remote in some strange way. It was as if we had suddenly been pushed apart. I was suffering and bewildered. Where was my Vane? My Vane could not have done this thing!

XVIII

TO LEARN TO SING

THE summer went on just as sweetly after this day as though it were assisting at some gay nuptials.

Mother and I were busy at the housework. I learned to milk, and I sent away the boy whom Bidwell had engaged to do our chores. I was young and strong, and I could do more work than I had been doing. Mother expostulated. But I would not listen to her. I labored from morning until night, and the moment I laid myself on the bed I dropped into a dreamless sleep. But between one and two o'clock, always at the same time, I woke with a start, and then I lay staring at the open window at the foot of my bed. Then I recalled every word that Vane had said to me or written to me, every look, every inflection of voice, until I thought I came near going mad. But, thank Heaven, God has made his creatures able to bear a great deal without going mad. Sometimes I did not go to sleep again; sometimes I slept uneasily for an hour. I knew that Miss Runciman watched me. Once she called me "brave girl," and once she said, " It will pass; everything passes." But I made no reply to either of these remarks. I had nothing to say. Lotus followed me about, looking wistfully at my face.

I had immediately written to Vane. First, I wrote a long

epistle, saying many things. That I promptly destroyed.
Then I wrote this:

> "Miss Runciman has just told me of your marriage to Olive Jewett.
> Please do not write to me again."

This I sent; and I tried to forget the date of my sending
it, so that I might not think of the time when he would
probably receive it. Even then I hated to hurt him. And,
like many other women in similar circumstances, I believed
that he loved me. He had done an evil thing, but he loved
me. He had wronged and deceived me, but he loved me.
You will perceive that I was no more reasonable in regard
to him than the ordinary girl would have been. And, indeed, I was but an ordinary girl, and could not be expected
to act differently from one.

And I hope you do not greatly wonder that, now that it
was all over, and I was not Vane's wife and never should
be, I did not tell my mother that I had once believed I was
his wife. I did tell her that my friendship for Mr. Hildreth
was at an end. And I added that some day she should
know all. She acquiesced, and forbore to question me. I
never knew until long afterwards how she had read me in
the silence she preserved during the summer.

It was not quite a month since I had sent my note to
Vane. Of course, his letters had kept coming—those he
had written before my word had reached him. But I did
not open these; I put them with the others. It was now
fall, the early, hot days of September, when, if it be a "dry
time," as it often is at that season, the earth seems to be
about to break into flames and consume like stubble.

Miss Runciman was still maintaining her more comfortable state. The heat was like a balm to her. At the coming of the earliest frosts she and her husband were going

South. They would follow the sun. She might, by doing that, live a few months longer, she said. It was a foolish thing to make a fight for a few months, but it was human nature. She hurried our preparations for leaving home. Once she caught my skirt as I was passing her couch.

"You will learn to sing?" she exclaimed, with her old imperiousness; "you are in earnest?"

I looked full in her eyes, my heart swelling as I answered:

"I am in earnest."

She sank back on the pillows.

"I see I can trust you," she returned. "Well, after all, the world will owe a great singer to my deed."

I went out of the house. I hurried, for I would try my voice. For the first time in weeks I would sing the scale. My heart began to beat at the mere thought of doing this.

I ran down the river patch, as the nearest way of escaping from interruption. I reached the bars, where I paused to recover my breath. Not since that marriage ceremony on the train had I been so stung with the longing to sing. That longing had lain partially dormant, but ready to be roused, and Miss Runciman had roused it. I began the scale. Half-way through it Lotus, who had come with me, made a dash in among the bushes. As he did so Vane parted the branches and came towards me.

I gave him one look that took in his haggard eyes, his pallor, his wretchedness; then I turned. I think I began to run. My one dominant feeling was that I dared not see him. In a moment my arm was caught. I vaguely saw the dog leaping and fawning upon his master, who did not notice him.

"Are you running away from me?" asked Vane, savagely.

I stood, on the instant, perfectly still.

"Yes," I answered.

He held my arm yet more closely.

"Do you dislike me so much?"

I made no answer. He did not repeat the question. He had dropped my arm and was looking intently at me. This I knew, though my eyes were lowered.

"It was because I loved you so," he said, suddenly.

Now I raised my eyes.

"You deceived me because you loved me so?" I said.

"Yes. I was afraid, if I told you, you would turn from me; and I hoped to arrange about a divorce—and there was Maverick—and it all came upon me in the train that if you could only think you were my wife I should feel secure, and I could arrange everything—everything—and I should not lose you—my darling!"

Vane's voice was pitched low, and it thrilled upon the hot air almost as if it were a part of the beautiful day itself. And I knew that Vane's very soul was in his voice and words. But what had come over me? I was excited, but I was in a way unmoved. There was no answering, unreasoning thrill in my heart. And I was keenly thankful for that—yes, I could have gone on my knees then and there and thanked God that Vane's presence was not to me what I had thought it would be, not what I remembered it, not what his letters had been. Why? Ah, yes, why had the strange glamour gone from my eyes? Not because he had deceived me, surely, for they tell me a woman will love the man who insults, deceives, and abuses her. Love goes as mysteriously as it comes. Nay, but "it was not love that went." A matter of glamour, of the senses, of propinquity, of the subtle power of the singing voice, of the romance of youth and ignorance, of a thousand mysteries, but not of

love—oh, not of love! though love may hold in it many
things as mere inferior attributes.

I stood there agitated, sorrowful, but cold. There was
no ardor, no passion, in my heart; but there were pity and
tenderness. I could not understand. I had expected a
great battle with myself if I should meet Vane. As for
Vane, he was silent for a long time, silent and gazing at
me. At length I lifted my eyes and met his. He burst
into a loud laugh, that sounded horribly in the stillness.

"It never occurred to me that you would tire of me so
soon," he exclaimed.

"I'm not tired of you," I answered.

"Who is it?" he asked, sharply.

"I don't know what you mean."

"Why, who has taken your fancy now?"

I shrank away; his words seemed vulgar to me.

"No one."

A spasm of suffering crossed Vane's face. I suddenly
leaned forward and took his hand.

"Oh, I don't understand it," I cried. "I thought I loved
you, but, now I see you, something is different. I know
you deceived me, and I supposed I must fight against my
love, because I had no right to love you; but now I don't
have to fight. Oh, how hard-hearted and strange you must
think me!"

I could not bear to see the anguish in Vane's face. I had
thought that he was the wretch, and now here I was feeling as if I were the sinning one instead of Vane.

"How strange you must think me!" I repeated, feebly.
"Indeed I don't understand. But, Vane, our love was
hopeless, you see, and you were wrong—so wrong!"

"I tell you I could have arranged everything. I would
have moved the world to be free of that woman," he began,

hurriedly, "but I know I was wrong. However, there is no need of explanations."

He drew his hand from mine, and tried to hold himself erect. He turned and gazed off towards the falls. He was ashen in color, and his eyes looked hot and stained.

"You're sure there is no one else?"

"I'm sure."

He thrust his hands into the pockets of his coat. Then he withdrew one hand and grasped the post of the fence.

"Perhaps, after all, you have the artistic temperament," he said.

I could not bear to hear him try to speak lightly.

"What do you mean?"

"Only that you are fickle, and that kind of thing. Well, I think I'll go back to England again. Miss Armstrong, you can regard our acquaintance as a slight episode in your life. Good-bye."

"Good-bye," just audibly from me.

Vane lifted his hat with a slow movement. He walked away. His brindled dog followed him hesitatingly a few yards, paused, whined under his breath, then came back to me.

I folded my arms on the fence rail, put my head down on them, and began to cry as if my heart were broken.

*   *   *   *   *   *   *

In two weeks from that time Miss Runciman and her husband had gone South; they took Bathsheba with them. Mother and I were on board a Cunard steamer. I was going to learn to sing. At the very last moment I changed my mind about Lotus, and did not leave him with Bidwell, who had kindly offered to care for him. The dog was on board the boat. I wanted him.

Mother was holding my arm closely, and we were looking

at the wharf. The steamer had just started. Bidwell was waving his hat to us. A carriage came dashing over the planks—too late.

We saw Vane Hildreth jump from the carriage.

"Oh, I'm glad he can't get aboard!" whispered mother.

She clasped my arm more tightly. "Wilhelminy," she said, with solemn earnestness. "I do hope, if you should ever see him, that you won't think you are in love with him again."

THE END

www.ingramcontent.com/pod-product-compliance
Lightning Source LLC
Chambersburg PA
CBHW060536030726
47498CB00004B/1210